PRAISE FOR
LONG AFTER WE ARE GONE

"A big, beautiful, devastating, and ultimately hopeful novel about family dysfunction and the true cost of heir property. Terah Shelton Harris brings the four Solomon siblings to vibrant life as they struggle to save their family's ancestral land while battling their own demons."

—Erica Bauermeister, *New York Times*
bestselling author of *No Two Persons*

"In *Long After We Are Gone*, Terah Shelton Harris weaves a powerful narrative that begins with the haunting plea, 'Don't let the white man take the house.' Told through alternating viewpoints, this explosive and emotionally charged novel delves into the power of family bonds and the art of letting go. It unearths the weight of familial expectations, the consequences of miscommunication, and the enduring lessons and legacies we pass on to the next generation. A gripping exploration of the complexities that define us and the resilience that connects us all."

—Etaf Rum, *New York Times* bestselling author
of *A Woman Is No Man* and *Evil Eye*

"Through the story of the four indelible Solomon siblings, Terah Shelton Harris sheds light on the little-known concept of heir property with characters who ring achingly true in their weaknesses, hopes, and love for each other. *Long After We Are*

Gone is a tour de force of history, injustice, and the brutal, beautiful, everlasting ties of family."

—Tara Conklin, *New York Times* bestselling author
of *The House Girl* and *The Last Romantics*

"In this timely novel that is as alluring and sensual as it is unflinching and brave, Terah Shelton Harris delves with compassion and insight into the profound complexities of the four Solomon siblings as they confront their shared familial history—a narrative that is both deeply intimate and inextricably shaped by the South's own painful history of racial injustice. Harris, a mesmerizing new voice in literary fiction, weaves an emotionally resonant saga of love and legacy that both enriches and transcends the boundaries of Southern narrative tradition. Your heart will stay close to Junior, CeCe, Mance, and Tokey long after the last page is turned."

—Adele Griffin, National Book Award
finalist and author of *The Favor*

"Terah Shelton Harris's *Long After We Are Gone* is a master class on writing clean, elegant, accessible prose. The individual struggles of the Solomon family are so beautifully told that getting to know them is both visceral and uncomfortable, as though we are sitting across the table from a friend with a dark confession. Harris's ability to create characters so real and flawed that they serve as mirrors to ourselves and our world is astounding. You know this family as you know yourself, and you want them to succeed so that in their victory they may become better people. A hope that, with another chance, we all can. The four separate but interconnected stories of these siblings weave together a beautiful, strong, satisfying quilt that Harris so deftly wraps the reader in. And we thank her for it."

—Jason Powell, author of *No Man's Ghost*

"Terah Shelton Harris has written a viscerally human novel about what we lose and what we keep when tragedy forces us to confront the sins of the past. *Long After We Are Gone* dismantles the romanticized idea of Southern homecomings and lays all its secrets bare through the eyes of four meticulously drawn characters wrestling with demons that threaten their quest to save their ancestral land. Gripping and haunting, this book is a stunning achievement from one of the bravest voices in contemporary Southern fiction today."

—Regina Black, author of *The Art of Scandal*

"Terah Shelton Harris's *Long After We Are Gone* will break your heart, have you standing and cheering, and leave you yearning for just one more day with its cast of richly developed characters. To say that Shelton Harris can capture the depth and complexity of family would be a profound understatement. The novel ripples with the undercurrents of injustice, redemption, and the hundreds of different ways a person can come home. I was, and will remain, moved by this literary journey."

—Lo Patrick, author of *The Floating Girls*

"Powerful and absorbing, *Long After We Are Gone* explores the effects of generational trauma and the struggle for identity in the midst of expectations. With meticulous pacing, Terah Shelton Harris expertly maneuvers multiple perspectives, immersing the reader in the flawed yet nuanced lives of the four Solomon siblings. A masterful sophomore novel, Harris has created another engrossing story that will leave readers talking."

—Meagan Church, author of *The Last Carolina Girl* and *The Girls We Sent Away*

"Few novelists write such flawed characters with this measure of empathy and grace. The Solomon siblings are a mess, but they're striving for better as best they know how. Believe me when I say you will love them for it. *Long After We Are Gone* is a gorgeous and deeply humane novel about family and second chances."

—C. Matthew Smith, author of *Twentymile*

"Once again, Terah Shelton Harris proves she is a powerhouse of Southern literature whose unmistakably poignant prose, profound themes and vibrant characters are built to stand the test of time. *Long After We Are Gone* is a beautifully woven story of familial bonds, generational trauma and the nature of love. Richly evocative, this book will move your soul."

—Quinn Connor, author of *Cicadas Sing of Summer Graves*

"Deeply moving, highly evocative, and heartbreakingly real, *Long After We Are Gone* is a moving testament to the strength it takes to leave the past behind and dictate your own future. This epic family drama explores love at its best, desperation at its worst, and the twisted ties that bind us to our own histories. An utterly gripping tale of familial strength and honor, this story will keep you guessing with every turn of the page. Readers will not soon forget the Solomon family."

—Brooke Beyfuss, author of *After We Were Stolen* and *Before You Found Me*

ALSO BY TERAH SHELTON HARRIS

One Summer in Savannah

Long After We Are Gone

A NOVEL

Terah Shelton Harris

sourcebooks
landmark

Copyright © 2024 by Terah Shelton Harris
Cover and internal design © 2024 by Sourcebooks
Cover illustration by Sandra Chiu
Internal map © Mackenzie Barber at For The Love Co.
Internal illustration by Ivan Burchak via Getty images

Published by Sourcebooks Landmark, an imprint of Sourcebooks
P.O. Box 4410, Naperville, Illinois 60567-4410
(630) 961-3900
sourcebooks.com

Cataloging-in-Publication Data is on file with the Library of Congress.

Printed and bound in the United States of America.
VP 10 9 8 7 6 5 4 3 2 1

For Jamel
Bangkok has us now.

"Men are haunted by the vastness of eternity. And so we ask ourselves: Will our actions echo across the centuries? Will strangers hear our names long after we are gone and wonder who we were, how bravely we fought, how fiercely we loved?"

—Odysseus (*Troy*)

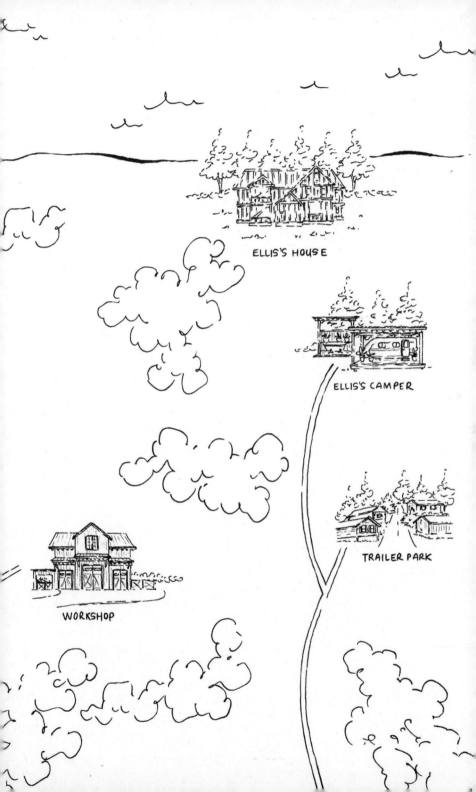

ELLIS'S HOUSE

ELLIS'S CAMPER

TRAILER PARK

WORKSHOP

AUTHOR'S NOTE

Long After We Are Gone tells the story of one family's fight to save their ancestral land, the Kingdom. This story is fictional. Diggs, North Carolina, does not exist. Well…not the one portrayed in *Long After We Are Gone*. There is a real Diggs, North Carolina, but the one you are about to read about is conjured from my imagination, and any coincidences to the real Diggs are accidental. Nor does the Kingdom exist. And yet there are (and have been) many Kingdoms now and throughout time, and the circumstances covered in *Long After We Are Gone* are very real.

After the Reconstruction, Black families began buying land in droves. Around the same time, laws were developed to dispossess Blacks of their land. In the case of the Solomon siblings and so many Black families now and then, the Kingdom was passed down without a will, making it heir property, a form of ownership in which descendants inherit an interest in the land, similar to holding stock in a company. Heir property does not constitute a clear title, which means the land is vulnerable to developers, corporations, and governments to use laws to acquire the land. Other methods, such as partition actions, eminent domain, and property tax sales, are also used to take land from landowners. Heir property is not eligible for federal loans, for private financing, or to be used as collateral. The U.S. Department of Agriculture has recognized heir property as the leading cause of Black involuntary land loss. It is estimated that between 1910 and 1997, Blacks lost about 90 percent of farmland worth billions of dollars.

Even today, the same Reconstruction-era laws and practices continue to dispossess Blacks of their land. In June 2022, the Los Angeles County Board of Supervisors voted to return ownership of prime California beachfront property, known as Bruce Beach, to descendants of Willa and Charles Bruce, who built a resort for African Americans but were stripped of the land in the 1920s. The Bruces suffered racial harassment from white neighbors, and in the 1920s, the Manhattan Beach City Council took the land through eminent domain. In North Carolina, brothers Melvin Davis and Licurtis Reels were jailed for eight years after refusing to leave the land their great-grandfather purchased a century ago. Lastly, at the time of this writing, officials in Gwinnett County, Georgia, have backed away from plans to use eminent domain to acquire the Promised Land, a one-hundred-acre property that has been in the Livsey family since the 1920s, following criticism and community outrage.

If you, your family, or someone you know, are the owners of heir property, I advise you to take the necessary steps to protect your land. This includes planning for the future by writing a will, keeping property taxes current, and talking to a lawyer about your options.

As much as *Long After We Are Gone* is about ancestral land, it's also about family and the secrets we keep, and the things we refuse to let go. All of the Solomon siblings harbor secrets, addictions, and other aspects that may be triggering for some. I feel very strongly about the use of trigger and content warnings and giving readers the option of stepping into the story or not. *Long After We Are Gone* contains instances of overeating, anxiety, the death of a parent(s), homophobia, sexual manipulation, and violence. We each bring a piece of our history into everything we read, and your comfort and mental health matters to me. If you find yourself in this story or identify with any of these topics, please feel free to step away if you need to. I want you to be safe. If you choose to stay, I assure you the handling of each of these topics was approached with the utmost care and consideration for the pain and discomfort they may cause others. At its core, *Long After We Are Gone* is a deep, heartfelt story about the power of family, and I hope that's reflected on the page.

With much love,
Terah Shelton Harris

ONE

———

REALLY, KING SOLOMON DIED before his heart stopped beating. Two knife attacks, one wayward bullet, and a nasty two-story fall collected over his sixty-three years of life failed to do what a whisper could. As his body collapses to the ground, the widow-maker closing the one-two punch, he takes one final look at his beloved house—his father's house, and his grandfather's before—and thinks of his children. He whispers something, a final plea, before slipping away, out of his body, and into a calming dark that wraps him like a prayer.

His children—Junior, Mance, Cecily, and Tokey—don't know yet. Across town from King, Tokey's stomach growls as she approaches the McDonald's drive thru line, the oatmeal and egg white omelet from her first breakfast, the "just for show" breakfast, consumed two hours before at home with her father, not enough. Six hundred miles away from Diggs, North Carolina, in New York City, Cecily agonizes over leaving her toothbrush at home, hoping that today, unlike other days, she won't need it. And back on the family land, near where he will soon find his father's body, Mance practices the sign language for *I love you* with his dry, calloused hands, his pinkie finger refusing to extend in a straight line, not even for his only son.

Five miles away, Junior, the oldest, blinks his eyes open to a new circumstance.

Junior has never seen Simon like this, his face bathed under the morning light streaming through the open window of the loft, his consciousness still caught within the dregs of sleep. He has lain next to him in the seconds after midnight and in the small hours of the morning before the sunlight reveals the truth. Until this morning, Simon belonged to the night.

But this? A delicious first.

"Good morning," Simon says, his voice full of tenderness and sleep, as smooth as velvet, soft and warm. Junior wonders if his voice has always been this gentle, if he noticed it when they first met in his office three years ago or even last night, when Simon asked him back to his loft. Junior whispers his own good morning, himself only slightly above the surface of sleep, and leans into the touch of Simon's hand, the proximity of their bodies, this new reality.

In those words, the start of a new day presents itself in the soft breeze rippling through Simon's thin curtains, the stillness of the morning colliding with the occasional car horn or tire rattling over a manhole cover, the scattered smells of breath, oil, and sunshine.

Simon's up now, his head resting on one hand, the fingers

of his other hand traveling the lean breadth of Junior's back. A subtle but sure touch, giving and patient, practiced at not taking any more or giving any less than desired. Junior loves that connection. He possesses a unique understanding of touch. It's what drew Junior, twelve years ago, to the once most important person in his life. And now, it's driving him toward Simon.

"What were you dreaming about? You were shaking and mumbling something," Simon asks.

"I was?"

Junior never dreams. Dreams are for those who sleep. And he doesn't. Not consistently. He rests his eyes long enough to fuel his life of quiet defeat.

But the day before, she said yes. The day before, Simon said no. Different people, different answers, both leading to this bed, this moment. Because, finally, she knows.

And last night Junior blinked his eyes closed and sleep came for him, and the thoughts did not wake him. Somehow, impossibly, he slept.

"You seem to be battling in your dreams. Who are you fighting?" Simon asks.

A simple question with multiple answers, but only one that matters.

His father.

They share a name but not much else. The differences and distance between them vast, an ocean. Junior presented to the world a strange form of six foot one, all torso and limbs—still three inches shorter than his father, King, and brother,

Mance—with a great mold of a nose and a friendly grin that belied his sober and studious personality, the opposite of his father. More than that, both obligations and beliefs drove them apart. Years of struggle find them at an impasse, and Junior here, on his own and ignorant of his own way. His own purpose.

"I'm a terrible sleeper. Sorry."

Simon moves closer to him, his hand now resting between Junior's shoulder blades. "Don't apologize. I'm sure this old bed didn't help. I could replace this mattress. Get some high-thread-count sheets for you by tonight."

Tonight. The word shocks and thrills him.

Tonight. A moment in the future.

Junior had never considered if he would come back. He knew now that he would come, *could* come back. He had permission. He could wake here another morning and another morning. Plan to meet again, not just a chance opportunity like the others. They could relive last night. Or leave the night unwritten and undefined, at the whim of surprise. They had time.

Usually, Junior doesn't think of yesterdays or tomorrows. Like his students, he lives in the present, what's in front of him, the here and now. But for the first time, the arrangement feels real. The thought of tonight, a type of tomorrow, fills his chest with hope. Opportunities like this do not last days or weeks but fleeting seconds that you can't touch. He wants to live in a future that does not yet exist.

This is what he wants.

And yet.

Junior turns over, feels Simon's hand travel along with him to now rest on his chest, looks at the ceiling and sees too many people there, staring down at him. Last night he felt as if he could power a city with his happiness, but now, slowly, like a shadow, a darkness creeps over him. When he finally drags his face back to Simon, his eyes stripped of brightness and optimism, the outer man, the one Junior folded inside last night, is back.

Simon stares at him, brow furrowed behind his glasses, and Junior retreats with his whole body. Even in this short period, Simon can distinguish the two men inhabiting Junior's body.

"You've put your armor back on," Simon finally says. The same armor Simon so carefully stripped from him last night and other nights before this, when Junior allowed the inner man an audience, when the outer man lowered his sword and shield and surrendered to a force greater than him.

But it isn't armor. Warriors donned armor. Armor could be removed, discarded, forgotten. Plus, Junior can never fully shed what he wears on the inside. He definitely isn't a warrior. That implies the sureness of a fighting spirit, empowerment, courage. His father embodies that. Mance, too. Not him.

Junior softens under the bone-deep sadness pressing down on him like a hand to the chest and strokes a thumb along Simon's cheek, now an arm's length away. "You know how to strip it from me again." He tries to muster a smile to conjure the inner man, once again, and feels himself falling short.

"For a night, yes. Forever, no, I fear."

Junior takes a deep breath and withdraws his hand, trying to imagine a world where forever was possible. "I've told you. I'm a complicated man."

That's the easiest answer he can give. The rest is harder to say. Better in small doses.

"Aren't we all? What are we but what we add and subtract from ourselves? We are not simple creatures," Simon says with a frame of impatience around the words.

"You speak such poetry to me," Junior says. "Even when I don't deserve it."

This is one of the things Junior loves about Simon, his ability to reach below the surface and see the heart of people, the good in them, even him.

But the truth is as simple as it is to swallow.

"I have to go."

Junior moves out of bed and slips on his pants and shirt. He can reconcile later what to do. Just not here. Not now. Simon follows, silent in the seconds it takes for both to dress, to reverse the placement of their clothes from the floor back onto their bodies after having torn them from each other last night.

"I'm sorry," Junior says once he's reached the front door.

"I know," Simon says, not asking what for, but knowing what for, and presses his hand to Junior's sternum. "I know."

Simon could keep him here, with this simple gesture, for another hour. But Junior will not stay, *cannot* stay, that much he knows.

And yet, Junior doesn't move. He stays braced in the warmth of Simon's hand, each waiting for the other to sever the connection, for the end of their magical night.

Junior touches the door handle suddenly, needing to feel something cold and real. Because Simon, last night, all of this, doesn't exist for him, the outer man. Those memories belong to someone else. That inner man treasures his freedom—his life outside of Junior. And Junior long ago set up, and respects, what belongs to the inner man versus what belongs to him.

He's still trying to think of what to do, what to say to prolong the old familiar fear of absence when Simon's hand grips a handful of his shirt and pulls him close, kissing him.

The kiss electrifies and terrifies him for various reasons as images from his world collide in him. It's not enough to make him stay, but enough to make him return.

As they pull back, Junior feels his balance tilt, his vision pitching.

The first drop of blood splatters on the floor between them, followed by more.

Then, a knock on the door.

There's nothing strange about a nosebleed or a knock at the door. But there's something odd about the sequence of events. Junior knows that Simon knows who is there, knows before he opens the door to a woman he's never seen before, knows even without processing what he's opening them all to.

The woman is wearing casual weekend attire: black leggings, a denim shirt knotted at the waist, and a pair of white

7

Converse. Her makeup is subdued, her hair pulled into a high ponytail that accentuates her small forehead with not one strand out of place.

"I need to talk with Junior."

Simon's eyes dart to Junior, hidden from view behind the door, then back at the woman. "Yes," Simon says, stretching the word like a rubber band. "And you are?" he asks, though he doesn't need to.

"Genesis. His wife."

Her expression tells the story of her true feelings; the pain behind her eyes does not. Bright and searching, they sweep the length of Simon, taking in his finely muscled arms, the tuft of chest hair peeking out of his tank top, his bare feet flat on the wood floor, before her mouth opens just a crack.

Her words hang between them. No surprise or anger. From either of them. Simon's expression is devoid of emotion, full of stillness. A kind of vacancy reserved with practice.

Simon opens the door wide to reveal Junior on the other side of it, his chin jutting upward, hand cupped to catch the blood.

"He shouldn't tilt his head back. He gets sick if he swallows too much blood." Genesis opens her oversized purse and retrieves a tiny spray bottle and a handkerchief.

Simon murmurs something incoherent before saying, "I didn't know."

"If I'm going to let him come here, you should at least know how to stop these."

Junior doesn't look at Simon. It will hurt too much, watching his two worlds collide. Instead, he disappears into himself, a coping tactic he learned as a child when King scolded him for not handing him the right tool or during these random nosebleeds or any time when a moment became bigger than him. He allows himself to be led to a nearby chair and closes his eyes, making it all disappear, the scene in front of him, the thoughts, the memories. He allows Genesis to guide his hand to pinch his nose as she presses the handkerchief above his lip. These are practiced moves, a choreographed dance they have been perfecting for almost a decade.

"What can I do?" Simon asks.

"Why is his nose bleeding?" Genesis snaps. "He gets these when he's stressed or when his blood pressure is high. You should know that. What's wrong with him?"

Junior stops pinching his nose and says, "I'm fine."

"Keep pinching. You know you have to hold that for at least ten minutes, or it'll be a true bloodbath in here." She turns her attention back to Simon and crosses her arms, once again appraising him. "I take it that you're Simon."

A question without a question mark.

"I am."

This time Junior allows himself to look at Simon. This moment, he wants to capture, to remember. The moment he lost him. The moment he got close to the heat of happiness and then got scorched by it.

"So he knows, then?"

Simon's forehead knits. "Knows what?"

Genesis falls silent for a moment, then whispers, not to Simon or Junior but to herself, "He doesn't know." She turns to Junior, kneeling. "You don't know."

"Know what?"

She softens as she reaches out and moves Junior's hand from his nose, taking the bloody handkerchief into her hand. Her silence cracks, and the words spill out.

"Your father is dead."

In New York, CeCe, the oldest daughter and third born, has just remembered that she left her toothbrush at home, her first thought as she softly rapped on Mark's door. A strange thought perhaps, hours after breakfast and hours before lunch, but important; she hated a bitter, salty mouth, the taste of old pennies grasping her tongue. Maybe today, unlike others, he wouldn't require it.

Mark, a junior partner at her law firm, waves her in without looking at her, his focus zeroed in on the paperwork in front of him, his shoulders hunched up around his ears. CeCe does a visual sweep of his office, cataloging the familiar space: his large redwood desk, the matching bookcase behind him, which houses volumes of law books, the miniature Eiffel Tower, and framed pictures of his wife and two daughters.

"Ken is asking about the Warren file," CeCe says, leaning over his desk, her long black hair curtaining in front of her, her hands clutching the edge of the redwood. "I trust that you're going to keep your word."

She hates the way her words sound to her, like a question, weak. Of all the faces and personalities she wears, and there are many, Mark likes and reacts to the submissive ones. This coquettishness is for his benefit. And hers.

When he finally looks up at her, it's not to her amber eyes but first to her cleavage, directly at his eyeline. Her intent when she selected his favorite red V-neck sheath dress this morning, which curved her hips and plumped her breasts together, spilling them over the top.

When he finally meets her eyes, his eyebrow raises, and something passes between them, an understanding, before he stands and walks to the door, closing it, the lock clicking a second later.

CeCe knows what will come next, though she doesn't know exactly how. It's what always comes—since Mark discovered her secret three months ago, when she got sloppy. She could almost hear her father now, his thunderous voice, because that was his word throughout her youth: if she learned nothing else from him, learn this, he'd say, *don't get sloppy*. Not in love, not in business. But she did. In both cases. And now there were consequences.

Mark's scent reaches her before his fingers do, before he wraps his arm from behind her across her breasts and the other one around her stomach, before he buries his face in the crook of her neck and his hardness presses against her ass.

He slides his hands up her thighs, between her legs, and slips two fingers inside her. He moans at what he discovers.

"Fuck...you are so wet," he says, his voice ragged.

His breath, his want quicken as he hastily loosens his belt, tugs down his pants, and pushes up CeCe's dress. In one quick motion, he bends her over his desk, yanking her thong down as he plows into her. His penis is small and unimpressive, the smallest she's ever seen; only the tip penetrates.

CeCe loves sex. But this is not sex. Though consensual, this is only a necessary transaction. And sex should never be necessary. It is purposeful, passionate—or so she once remembered. Once upon a time. But now, with Mark, it is necessary.

Mark pumps and bangs against her, a primal groan emanating from his throat in sync with his thrusts. CeCe makes no sound as he smashes her face against the desk, his whole hand pressing down on her head. He doesn't notice, completely content on finishing his end of this transaction, eliciting his own pleasure. And when he does, seconds later, CeCe lifts herself from his desk, brushing away a paper clip embedded in her thigh.

She feels nothing. Definitely no inkling of pleasure between her legs. Nothing mentally either. No sadness. No disappointment. No shame. She doesn't turn and face him yet because, although she feels nothing, she's always been able to feel his pity.

She runs her thumb across the paper clip's imprint, a twisty emblem temporarily branding her skin, grateful that, like this imprint, this entire transaction would soon fade into memory like all of her indiscretions.

"So, you will continue to vouch that we worked together on the Warren file?" she says, clearing her throat, grateful that Mark chose this time to enact his portion of this quid pro quo between her legs and not in her mouth. She has a deposition later and couldn't imagine speaking without brushing her teeth.

"CeCe, look at me," he says, winded by his own effort. His belt buckle jingles, followed by a long zip. His voice fills the room, transforming the space back to a respectable place, where couples finalize their wills and start trust funds for their children.

She can already hear the shame in his voice, the regret. It punches a clock, arriving seconds after the room stops spinning, and the handkerchief he uses to clean himself disappears into his briefcase to be washed, probably by his unsuspecting wife of eight years.

When she finally turns, she sees his forehead scored with beads of sweat and something else. Something she's never seen before. Sympathy.

"How long do you think you can get away with this?"

"With what?" CeCe asks, sliding her black lace thong up and arranging her dress. Her question is technically risky, a dare she can't resist issuing herself, but it won't arouse his suspicion. There have been so many *what*s. Other cases. He only knows about one.

"You know what."

"It's fine. I just need some time to get the money and put it back."

"Let me help you."

Now there's no sympathy in his gaze. Back to pity. And also, sorrow.

The nerve.

Three months since she deposited a client's check into her personal account.

Three months since Mark learned what she did.

Three months since Mark pushed CeCe's head down to his penis for the first time.

Three months since he started sharing her lie and living within the prism of this unspoken deal.

He didn't offer to help three months ago.

It angers her, his weakness. Her father, King, blessed her with the gift of strength, of fight. A lesser emotion or response was cowardly. Mark is a coward.

CeCe wants to unleash her anger, push her frustration out on him, thrash against his chest.

And yet, she still needs him.

"Wouldn't you be liable for covering for me? For lying?" CeCe lightens her tone, careful not to push him away before casting her gaze at the framed picture of his family cheesing in front of Magic Kingdom, a clear reminder, without words, of what he could lose, even if not legally—of the lengths she would go to keep her secret.

Mark follows CeCe's eyes to the picture, and his face pales.

"It doesn't have to come to that," CeCe says, her tone blending into an even softer one than before. "Don't you like this?" She runs her finger down his chest and her hand into his pants down to his cock, still damp and tacky. His pale face blushes as his head tilts toward the ceiling. He likes it, his appetite for her insatiable as he grows, once again, in her hand. CeCe loosens his belt as she sinks to her knees. "Let's just stick to the plan."

She will buy a toothbrush at lunch.

Ten minutes later, CeCe leaves Mark's office, raking her tongue against her teeth, wiping the corners of her mouth, her stomach roiling, when Victoria, the receptionist, waves for her attention.

"You have an urgent call from Junior."

"Tell him I'll call him back," CeCe says, not breaking her stride to the bathroom. She needs to get that taste out of her mouth and settle her stomach.

Victoria repeats CeCe's message into the phone and listens for a few seconds before saying, "He says it's about your father."

CeCe huffs and walks over to Victoria's desk, snatches the phone from her hand in one quick motion, and pretends not to notice Victoria's loud inhalation and crossed arms.

"I told him I would take a look at the papers when I had a chance. That land isn't going anywhere. He didn't need to have you call."

She expects Junior to dutifully resume his role as the eldest, as the defender of King and all that he commands, a role he happily performs, but meets the coldness of silence instead.

"CeCe…King is dead."

The phone slips out of CeCe's hand and hits the desk as she vomits. Sperm, coffee, and regret splash on the floor at her feet.

———

For Tokey, the start of the day is like any other.

"Welcome to McDonald's. May I take your order?"

Tokey twists her lips. She knows what she wants. It's what she always wants. What she always orders. But she doesn't want the perky-sounding cashier to judge her. She didn't drive past the closest McDonald's, where the staff knew her by name and her order by heart, to this one, on the outskirts of town and fifteen minutes from the school, to be judged.

So, she pauses for a menu-scanning beat before saying, "I'll have two sausage McGriddles with an extra sausage patty, five hash browns, and a large Coke with no ice."

Tokey pulls around to the first window to a cashier smiling toothily, her eyes as large and round as the glasses she wears. Tokey matches her smile, practice for the many she would wear today. She wears smiles like clothes, tight and uncomfortable, never fitting. There's always something behind a smile, forced or not. She should know.

"The car ahead of you has already paid for your food," the girl says, her eyes beaming, waiting for a reaction.

Tokey has heard of this before, do-gooders paying for the food of others, but has never been part of such a transaction.

"Well…how much was their food?"

The perky cashier blinks twice and her smile teeters as she processes Tokey's question.

"$4.02."

Probably a normal meal, a sausage egg biscuit with a large coffee. Or perhaps a bacon, egg, and cheese biscuit with a small orange juice. A normal, respectable breakfast with a normal number of calories.

"Would you…like to pay for the car behind you?" the cashier asks, her smile now lopsided.

"What about the car behind the car behind me?"

The laugh lines disappear, and she jabs a finger at the register.

"$4.69."

"How much…"

The cashier sighs, interrupting, her enthusiasm completely diminished like a sneeze in the wind. "Ma'am…you are holding up the line."

"I'm sorry," Tokey says, embarrassed, reaching for her purse on the passenger's seat and rummaging past her makeup bag and journal until she unearths her wallet with an empty M&Ms wrapper stuck to it. "It's just that I feel so bad that someone had to pay so much for my food. I'll pay for two cars behind me." Tokey snatches the wrapper away and crushes it in her hand. "I'm buying breakfast for a coworker. She's running late and asked if I could pick up something for her. The things we do for our coworkers."

The cashier does not smile. Tokey ups the wattage on hers to make up for it.

Tokey doesn't believe the lie any more than she imagines the cashier does. As she pulls her debit card out of its holder, it slips from her fingers, falling between the seats.

"I'm sorry," Tokey says, maneuvering to retrieve it. All she sees is her own leg. There's not enough room. Her car has shrunk over the years. The steering wheel cuts into her thighs. As she unfastens the seat belt and turns, her breasts press against the steering wheel, honking the horn. She slides her fingers between the seat, feeling popcorn from last week's movie, Cheez-its from a quick run to the gas station, gummy bears she ate after work. She turns to the window. "I'm sorry."

And she is. Always. Sorry.

"Ma'am…it's okay." The cashier is exasperated. "Your food is already paid for. You can just pull up."

"No, I want to pay," Tokey says, jamming her fingers once more between the crack until her fingertips graze the edge, and with one final shove, she grabs the card. "Here you go."

The cashier inspects the card before taking it and slides it through the reader once, then again. She hands Tokey two receipts and her card.

"Thanks. You can pull up to the next window."

"I'm sorry."

Just as Tokey reaches the next window, another cashier opens the window and presents the large Coke and then a brown bag of food, the weight of it lacing a sharp pain to Tokey's hand. She looks at it for a wound and notices the reddened skin.

Life is easier with food. She finds comfort in greasy bags

handed out of windows and seeks answers in cakes wrapped in plastic, chasing a high that never lasts long. This meal will be one of six she'll eat that day, and she wants no one to bear witness to her sins. At school, she pulls into her usual spot a good distance from the front door. There, she eats. Chewing her food, gulping her Coke, and swallowing what happened at McDonald's with every bite. She chooses this spot even though she has difficulty walking, knowing that by the time she reaches her classroom, sweat stains will have flowered under her arms, the fabric across her chest will have darkened with the effort. By the time she's finished eating, all those close parking spots will be filled, taken by those who don't have to contemplate their steps, those whose pace is normal, those who are not hungry an hour later.

Tokey wads up her trash and tucks the bag under her seat. She'll dispose of it later.

As she looks back up, she sees Junior hurrying toward her. As the principal of the school where she teaches, he's often in and out of her day. But he's not wearing his usual suit and tie. Her heart thuds when she sees the tears in his eyes.

—

How did the day begin? Before dawn, with Mance thinking it shouldn't be difficult to say, "I love you," to his only child. He looks at the fingers of his right hand and wills his pinkie straight, an impossible task. He has broken it twice and all the other fingers on that hand once. None of them stand erect and never will again. He stretches his left hand; a dislocated index finger and a quarter digit, along with three crooked ones, stare back at him. He doesn't have the fingers for this.

Still early. Still night. And Mance can't sleep.

He kneels in the muted field of green and yellow and pulls up a whisker of bristly weed, watching the way it sways in the breeze when he releases it. He sweeps his eyes over the vast landscape, taking it all in, the house and the land from the edge of the property, including the new secret stretch as well. Mostly, he listens. Listens to the moonlight stretching across the horizon. Listens to the day, close behind, yawning and waking up. Listens to the wind inhaling and exhaling a spring air on the cold side of perfect.

Sound is everything.

Then, he screams.

A guttural sound, a roar, which starts at the back of his throat and reaches both out and down, deep within to places he can't touch. A scream that seizes his entire body. He screams as he grips the dark earth. He screams, trying to reach the place where he won't feel, until he runs out of air, and even then, he continues to push out a sound, tiny but true, until there's nothing left.

Then, silence.

He opens his eyes and the world is still there. And so is the truth. The start of the day continues. He disturbs nothing and no one, receiving no answers to the questions that continue to trouble him. It's a reprieve—the screams, the burning lungs, the nausea from exertion—a self-inflicted consequence. Better he hurt than anyone else. He cannot go back to prison. Not now. He looks up and refocuses on one of the two things that have always tamed the anger inside.

People who don't live here call it the Solomon Plantation after the original owner, John Solomon, who built it in 1782. The locals, including his siblings, call it the Kingdom, in honor of King Solomon, Mance's father, and every firstborn son in the Solomon family. Even for eighteenth-century architecture, the house has a heft and audacity that is striking. A fortress. Too impractical, too big for every iteration of the Solomon family who has lived here.

Mance looks in the direction of the workshop and contemplates his and King's day, set to begin in a few hours. Normally, he doesn't know what King will have him doing. But today, he knows.

The front of the Kingdom is sagging. More specifically, the second-floor porch now droops, the old columns, last replaced a hundred years ago, are no longer able to shoulder the weight of the roof. Thanks to a recent hurricane, the entire facade of the house, not just the second-floor porch, would have collapsed if not for the white columns that circle the house balancing and distributing the weight. Another hurricane or a hit in the right place, and the home his ancestors built will fold in on itself.

They should have been replaced years ago. Mance noticed the wood rot on one of the columns while replacing a few cedar shingles that blew off during several days of spring monsoon weather. King had his own ideas and timeline for renovations, and they always involved Mance's labor but rarely his opinion. Years spent replacing the grand staircase and all the windows, and building and installing all the crown molding, were not in vain. It all needed to be done. The house was in disarray. But the columns—the columns should have been priority.

They are now, which should satisfy Mance, but instead humbles him under the weight of the work King prescribes. King, as always, insists on maintaining architectural accuracy by building his own columns instead of purchasing premade ones, a project that will take a few months to complete and thousands of hours of labor.

"My great-great-granddaddy built this house with his own two hands." King always looks at his ashy, scarred hands, with their own share of half and crooked digits, when he says this. Until today, Mance never looked at his hands. They were well on their way to mirroring King's. Wood has splinters. Tools are sharp. They've dropped a few parts along the way. Such is the life of a carpenter and his carpenter son.

Mance builds things with his hands but never thought they would speak for him. That they could serve as a way of communicating. He presses his fingers against his palm, making a fist, and moves his thumb over his index finger. *A*. Then slowly lifts his fingers and touches his thumb to the base of his pinkie. *B*. He curls his fingers. *C*. He holds the *C* and tries to recall how to form a *D*.

Fuck this, Mance thinks and shakes his hand free of the

inaudible alphabet, lighting a cigarette with it instead. He can do that with ease. The crisp scratch of the flint hitting steel, the sound of burning ash filling his ears. He doesn't need to learn this. Henry is going to be fine. Solomon men stand strong, resilient. They survived slavery, four wars, and Jim Crow. Henry can survive silence.

Mance reminds himself to be where his feet are, the ground beneath him. His land. Ten acres of swampland that no one but him wanted. Not even King when Mance approached him about it.

"We don't need that land."

"It's ten acres. It will give us all of the waterfront. All of the Kingdom should lead to water."

"We have all we need right here."

"If we don't buy it, someone else will. Miss Jessie said she heard some white men in suits asking about it."

"Let it be."

King listened to all of it and heard none of it. Their conversations often went like this, around and around, ending at what King wanted. "*Let it be.*" Mance wasn't meant to oppose him or understand why he reached whatever conclusion. To have a voice at all, really. Normally, he was content to defer to King and keep working. He is his father's son, better and worse, and resembles him, a reclusive solemn giant, in personality and physicality, so completely that he's often mistaken for King, mistaken for the oldest child. But he is right about the ten acres. He knew, and he couldn't sit quietly. And he didn't.

Mance shuffles back across the yard and flicks his cigarette into the bin by the workshop door. They both smoke, but never inside, never around wood; smoke stained and infiltrated and compromised the integrity of it. Lou's excavator sits tucked on the side. They borrowed it one month ago from their neighbor to dig up a busted waterline, bartering its use for a custom fireplace mantle. The work of their hands, not the money in their pockets, paid for the extensive renovations and repairs on the Kingdom. But the job is done, waterline repaired, and mantle installed, and Mance wants the excavator gone, has wanted it off the property for weeks now. There it sits, as Lou's excuses for its removal pile up. Mance curses under his breath as he swings the barn door open.

Inside, Mance runs his hand along one of the finished, unpainted columns, his fingertips searching for cracks, imperfections, rough areas, and finding none, the column as smooth as his hands are rough, the column solid as he is tough. Architecture has always astounded him, how things are made, what holds them together. That a simple wooden column could be all that stands between an uneventful day and disaster. Mance moves to the next column and picks up a sheet of 200 grit sandpaper.

There's an art to sanding a piece of wood by hand—the right amount of pressure to apply, the rhythm of the strokes. *Shh, shh. Shh, shh. Shh, shh.* Back and forth. Side to side. Round and round. It's knowing when to stop sanding or when you've gone too far. He hears this rhythm in the quietude. Heard this rhythm in prison, alone in his cell for eighteen months and

24

again for nine more months. *Shh, shh. Shh, shh. Shh, shh.* Both times it served as the silent melody that protected him and his mind from his surroundings. *Shh, shh. Shh, shh.*

Sound is everything.

And he wants it for his son.

Terrible thing to live in fear, and Mance forgets to be nervous. But when he thinks about Henry navigating the world in silence, his heart quickens—first with anxiety, then with something else. Something he doesn't have the words for yet.

So, he sands. He sands because he can't scream all the time. He sands because the truth won't stop hurting. He sands until the sandpaper tears and the pads of his calloused fingertips go numb, until wood dust floats in the air, until the sun creeps up on the entrance of the workshop.

Mance takes a break and lights another cigarette, leaning against the barn door, watching the way the morning light sets the Kingdom on fire. He loves this land because his father does. It provides a sense of belonging. The Solomons have lived on and farmed the two hundred acres of the Kingdom for the last two hundred and thirty years. He isn't from this land; he is *of* this land. King, Mance, and now Henry.

He flicks out his cigarette and sees the excavator out of the corner of his eye. He will thump Lou's fuckin' skull the next time he sees him if that goddamn excavator isn't removed soon, he thinks, just as he sees King on the ground propped up by the excavator's track frame, his body angled back at the Kingdom, his eyes open wide, nearly without life now.

His hands are on his thighs, open, palms up.

Mance runs toward his father. As he falls down beside him, he hears King say in a shallow breath, his last, "Don't let the white man take the house."

TWO

—

IT WILL TAKE A long time, perhaps a thousand good mornings from now, when it's all over, to understand the impact of King's death. The Solomons will rearrange the pieces they know, question what they will never understand, and reimagine the events in their minds. How it was the best and worst thing for them as a family. How it changed them individually, for the better and for the worse. They will think of King often, what he worked for, instilled in them, believed in. But mostly, positive in the moment, they'll think that they wouldn't change a thing.

But for now? CeCe thinks of only this: the poor people outside her rental car at the Diggs gas station. She has forgotten what it was like to be in the presence of the impoverished, their simple mindsets and attitudes, their willingness to accept their plain lives, their quiet march to surrender. Strange, considering CeCe herself grew up alongside the same less fortunate who are outside of her window and, last night, maxed out her last credit card to book her flight and rental car for King's funeral.

CeCe opens her Chanel purse and counts the remainder of her cash, $282. For a second, she regrets the two hundred dollars she spent on a manicure, pedicure, and perm, the three hundred dollars on a new black dress. But she couldn't come back to Diggs looking like the people she loathes. She vowed that if she ever got out of Diggs, she would never be poor another day of her life. That she would cloak herself in the finest fabrics and wear the finest jewelry. That her hands would never touch dishwater again and she would forget the best oven temperature for baking biscuits. She is stubborn enough to make declarations like this and keep them.

CeCe crinkles her nose as she walks to pay for her gas, her purse hooked in her elbow, her oversized sunglasses covering half of her face. The humid air stinks of minimum wage and food stamps, of fried food and bad decisions. A confirmed observation when she swings open the gas station door. Several racks of fried chicken glow in baskets under golden lights and the two men ahead of her purchase 40s and Black & Milds. She grabs a pack of gum and drops forty dollars on the counter for it and her gas.

"You forgot your change," the clerk calls after her, a hand extended revealing a palm full of change. CeCe has turned almost before the bills hit the counter.

"No, I didn't," she says without turning around.

Here is CeCe's chief complaint about being home: the smallness. Small as quarters in an outstretched palm. She doesn't hate Diggs as much as she feels trapped by it. Diggs never changes. Day after day. Year after year. That's the thing about small towns.

Except, Diggs isn't even a small town. It has never been an actual town at all. Back in the 1700s, two brothers from Virginia, John and Alan Solomon, saw a future among the mosquitoes and humid sun and purchased a hundred acres of swampland and built a home. Soon others joined them. But still, Diggs just exists, everything a compromise, an unincorporated territory, independent of any town or city—operating without a local government, laws, or regulations.

CeCe pauses before opening the driver's-side door, inspecting her Valentino heels for scuff marks, her fingertips delicately balancing her weight against the side of the car.

"Cecily?"

CeCe's palm slaps the car as she loses her balance. Annoyed at the sound of her own name, the fullness of which she hasn't used in a lifetime. She has not been Cecily in a long time and only to one person. She turns and sees an older woman. Not him.

"I thought that was you," the woman says as she studies CeCe, her eyes traveling a straight line down the length of her body before stopping on her shoes for a second. "Wonderin' when you would make it down here. Musta bought a next-day ticket."

CeCe squints as if doing so would conjure this woman from memory. Nothing about this slight woman dressed in a loud yellow dress is something she would *want* to remember. If she had known this person, she erased her, along with everything else about Diggs, when she moved away twelve years ago.

The woman has no problem seeing CeCe, her attention wholly on her. And there's something searching in her gaze—a feeling that she could see inside her, through her—that rattles something loose in CeCe's chest.

"You don't remember me?" the woman asks, stretching the elasticity of each word. The woman presses a hand to her own chest. "Miss Jessie. From down the street."

CeCe hesitates, caught between the truth and a lie, before choosing the latter. "No, ma'am." She grimaces as soon as the word leaves her tongue, at the ease with which her upbringing comes charging back. At the acidic tang it leaves in her mouth. Two hours here and already a *ma'am*.

"Chile…I knew you before you knew yourself. Come here and let me hug your neck," Miss Jessie says, pulling CeCe into a hug. The unexpected and unwanted embrace reminds CeCe of a childhood of forced affection, of come-give-your-cousin-a-hug and give-me-some-sugar. CeCe stiffens her back as Miss Jessie rocks her from side to side, rolling her eyes at the knowledge that with the upcoming funeral, she would be subject to many more of these.

Miss Jessie releases CeCe, but the stench of Blue Magic hair grease and sweat lingers in the air, keeping them bound. "I'm sorry to hear about your daddy's passing. He was a good man." She smiles slightly. This breaks the eye contact, her attention lost in a memory. "Mm-mm. Good as they come."

Guilt rises in CeCe, but she swallows it down with a quick smile and opens the car door. She has already been dealt a full portion of conscience and doesn't owe this old woman evidence of it or of another second of her time, another unwelcome hug, another *ma'am*. Certainly not. "Thank you."

"Let Miss Jessie know if there's anything I can do for you kids, all right?" Miss Jessie scans CeCe's face again as CeCe closes the car door and starts the car.

Years later, CeCe would remember this encounter with Miss Jessie, the gentle way she grasped her own forearms tightly in front of her. She would remember the gray hairs lined in her hair. She would regret her actions and wish she had done it differently. Seeing Miss Jessie, CeCe would listen. She would ask her about King. She would meet her eyes and see.

⊢—

Mance is early. Once again, he didn't sleep. How could he? His father is dead, and his son is deaf.

From his car, he watches Lisha pull into the parking lot, step out of her car, and open the door for Henry. Mance will help her. He'll meet her before she heads to the door. He'll take Henry from her hands. But he needs a few seconds. A beat to breathe, to focus, to forget. He's always liked waiting for her, watching her. She makes him stop thinking.

Mance remembers when he first set eyes upon her years ago. Fifteen years old and still a girl. A friend of Tokey's. Years later, there she stood, within the throes of a party. Twenty-five and suddenly a woman. Her nimble fingers twined in her hair. She wouldn't remember him. Of that he was sure. And yet, a smile. One smile that covered her entire face and expanded the room. One smile and he came undone. But it was her dimple that gave him pause, that stopped his breath. Deep, even from across the room, he saw the dimple beside her puckered lips. A perfect natural imperfection. Like knots in a glowing piece of wood. Nothing stands out more than imperfections in wood.

He sees it now, the dimple, on Henry's face, the same spot, the same circumference, as he takes the carrier from Lisha's hands. Only now, larger on such a tiny face. She marked him. For that, Mance is grateful, pleased that Lisha's soft features smoothed the edges of his sharp ones. Henry has Mance's hands, and by extension, King's hands, a man's hands, with long fingers, steady. That is enough for Mance.

Lisha checks in with the nurse at the desk, who then escorts them to a small room with a wooden bench and exam table. They settle on the bench with Henry in his carrier between them. Unbalanced, the bench shifts with their weight. Mance notices but ignores it, focusing on Henry instead.

He is changing already. His face is a little different today than yesterday, much different than the yesterdays before, his cheeks rounding, his eyes brightening. Three months old, and he's cooing and babbling, holding his head up, grasping everything in his tiny hands. He smiles constantly. Like he is the first to discover whatever holds his fleeting focus, and he likes it and wants to experience it again.

It astounds Mance that this tiny person already means more to him than anyone else does. That one day he existed when the day before he did not. How instantly parental love materializes. A fierce desire to protect him flooded Mance when he first held him in his arms. To fight anything or anyone who causes him harm. Yet he struggles to accept him as he is. He struggles to make sense of such feelings. The two emotions grate against each other and torment him, fracturing his breath and massaging his heart.

Today, Henry is fussy. He needs to sleep during the test, so he has not eaten or napped, and he's ready for both. Lisha unpacks a bottle, and Henry takes to it immediately.

"Here, hold him," Lisha says, lifting Henry from his carrier and holding him in front of Mance. "He'll fall asleep faster."

Mance draws back as if struck. "I…can't."

"Sure, you can," she says to a now calm Henry. "Do you want Daddy to hold you? You want Daddy to hold you, don't you?" She swings Henry in her arms, his attention focused on the emptying bottle.

"I said I can't." Mance's voice is a little stern.

Lisha glances at Mance, her eyes frosting with understanding. She almost always does, including this time. "It's okay. You don't have to."

He doesn't trust his hands to hold him, the memory of holding King, the dead weight of his body still imprinted on him. It's a lot to ask of a son, but this son couldn't, wouldn't leave his father, holding King until King's soul ventured to that next place, until Mance lost feeling in his arms and legs, until the coroner arrived. His heart catches at the memory, the pain of watching a great man draw his last breath too fresh.

Mance rubs his damp palms down his pants, then abruptly stands, and the bench lists again. "When is this doctor coming?"

"He'll be here in a minute," Lisha says, placing a satisfied Henry back into his carrier.

"Fuckin' doctors, man," he says, pacing the small room, his heart racing, the sound of his breath audible. "We had to wait long enough for this appointment. They should be here on time."

Lisha stands, and the bench shifts, the sound of it two tiny knocks in succession.

"Goddamn it," he says, falling to his knees in front of the bench, moving it back and forward until identifying the problem, a warped pad under one of the legs. He lifts it, turns it upside down, and begins shaving the bottom with his knife.

"What are you doing?"

"You don't feel that? It doesn't bother you?"

Lisha walks over to Mance and takes his hand, lifting him. "You don't have to be here. It's just another test."

Only it isn't. Henry referred his newborn hearing screen on the day of his discharge from the hospital. Mance remembers questioning the use of such a fancy term, *referred*, instead of *failed* as if dressing up the word lightened the reality. It's normal for newborns to refer due to fluid in their ears, they were told. At his follow-up visit, he referred again. He should be seen by an audiologist and given an auditory brain stem response evaluation, they were told. Lisha wants to believe in the best, but Mance knows.

Just like he knows a piece of wood is good by its smell, by eye-balling it, his gut doing all the talking. He knows Henry is deaf.

Now, Lisha places her hand on his chest and his on hers, slowing his breathing. This is what she does, how she turns off his mind. Her eyes lock on his. Everything whirs to a stop.

She is too good for him. He knows. Everyone knows. A soft-spoken yet charismatic woman who, as a librarian, dedicates her life to the service of others. Choosing and falling for the dangerous Mance not something anyone expected. She isn't afraid of him, his tough exterior. At five feet five inches, she still stands up to him and matches him in obstinance, hers in pursuit of the greater good, his a natural reflex.

"Your father died yesterday," Lisha says, her voice comforting. "It's okay not to be here. Go be with your family."

"You and Henry are my family."

Lisha softens at this, and he knows his words have reminded her of the proposal still on the table. "You're not okay."

"I…" He hesitates, and he knows she's gotten too close to the truth.

It's the smallness of the room. It's the wobbly bench. It's the late doctor. It's the goddamn test. It's King dying. It's the Kingdom. It's all of these things and none of them. All too heavy.

He closes his eyes, and King's body is there, covered with a white sheet. He opens them to the upside-down, lopsided bench in a doctor's office he shouldn't be in, and his breathing shallows and the room warms, his anger once again crashing to the surface.

His hand drops away from hers, and he pulls away. "I'm good."

He needs fresh air and a field to scream. He needs to fix the rickety bench. He needs his father alive and Henry to hear.

Then, the doctor comes in.

"It's about goddamn time!" Mance says before he even knows he's said it.

The doctor pauses, his eyes wide as Lisha steps forward in front of Mance. The doctor's glance skitters about the room before landing on the upturned bench.

"Dr. Frazier." Lisha extends her hand. "It's nice to meet you. This is Mance, my—Henry's father. He's a woodworker, and was…well, he was trying to remove the wobble from that bench."

Dr. Frazier takes her hand, relaxing back into control with this strange greeting. "Well, this is a first," Dr. Frazier says. "Most anxious parents just pace. I've never had one fix the furniture." He chuckles, easing the tension in the room.

Mance apologizes and turns the bench upright, and they sit. The bench doesn't move again.

Dr. Frazier tells them about the test procedures. Henry will be settled in the crib, and four tiny electrodes connected to a computer will be placed on his head. Earphones will emit sounds at different noise levels as the computer gathers information from the electrodes.

Mance and Lisha watch as Dr. Frazier works and Henry sleeps. An hour later, Dr. Frazier removes the electrodes and earphones from Henry's head.

"He has a profound loss in his left ear," Dr. Frazier says, a wrinkle between his eyes appearing.

Lisha's chest stops moving; her eyes fill with tears, which fall quickly like raindrops on a window. She reaches for Mance's hand, but his reaches her first. He didn't want her to have to be strong for the both of them. She looks at him with wet eyes, and he feels the anger venturing to the surface. How dare his son be deaf, how dare Lisha hurt…

"The good news is that he has some hearing in his right ear."

"Some?" Mance asks. "What does that mean?"

"A moderate to severe loss."

"How's that good news?" Lisha asks, wiping away tears.

Dr. Frazier explains that the degree of hearing loss is based on how loud sounds need to be to hear them. Decibels, or dB, describe loudness. Henry's profound loss registers at ninety decibels; he can't hear a lawnmower or anything quieter. In his right ear, Henry could hear more sounds.

"How is this possible? We don't have a history of hearing loss in either of our families. I don't understand," Lisha says, wrapping the cord of Henry's pacifier around her fingers. Last time, the doctor told them that 50 percent of hearing loss in children is caused by a genetic syndrome. Mance knows this is at least part of why Lisha has held out hope.

"Hearing loss can be genetic with or without loss presenting in the family history. Or maybe Henry's is caused by something else."

"How do we fix this?" Mance asks.

Dr. Frazier frowns. "You can't fix hearing loss. I'm afraid it's permanent."

"You said he had some hearing in his right ear." Lisha asks. "What about cochlear implants? I've been reading up on them. What about them? Will they help?"

Dr. Frazier exhales. "Possibly. But that's if you decide to get them. Not everyone—"

"We want them," Mance says quickly.

"Cochlear implants could provide Henry with the sensation of sound. But I want to be clear. Cochlear implants do not cure hearing loss or restore hearing. Henry will still be deaf."

Lisha swallows and asks, "What's the cost?"

"Between $30,000 and $50,000, depending on insurance."

Mance and Lisha trade looks as Dr. Frazier stands.

"What do we do now?" Mance asks, his voice scratchy.

"We will need to fit Henry for hearing aids. I'll see that we get him scheduled for an appointment."

Dr. Frazier continues talking, but Mance notices that Lisha has drifted off, her mind turning with questions he can't hear. He touches her knee, and she jumps slightly. Later, Mance will remember this moment as the most unsettling part, the realization that their lives will never be the same again.

"I know this may be overwhelming, but Henry can grow up to be a healthy boy," Dr. Frazier says, leaving the room. He tells them to contact him if they have any other questions.

A few minutes later, Lisha tucks a sleeping Henry into his seat in her car, and then she collapses in Mance's arms. "He'll never hear my voice," she says through tears.

Mance presses her close and allows her to cry against him.

He has no idea of the future that awaits Henry, but he will be strong for him, for Lisha, absorb her pain. He can take it.

"He will hear your voice," Mance says, resolute. "We'll get the implants, and he will hear."

Lisha looks up at Mance, her eyes pooled with new, unfallen tears. "They're so expensive."

"You let me worry about that," he says. "I'll fix this."

She has questions, he knows, about what King's death means for them. She won't ask now, but soon. For now, she nods.

"I'll come over later tonight," Mance says, running a finger down her cheek.

Lisha tilts her head, leaning into his love for a moment before stepping back. For all that's wrong in their relationship, their passion has never faltered. "That's not a good idea. Nothing has changed."

"I'm trying."

"You almost took Dr. Frazier's head off," she says. "I need you—Henry needs you—to be better than trying. We need you here, really here with us, especially now. I can't do this by myself."

"You won't. I promise."

"Let me know about the funeral. I want to be there."

He takes her hands and presses them against his chest. "I appreciate that."

"I know all of this with Henry is not coming at the best time."

"You let me worry about that."

"You say that to me all the time, but that's what I'm afraid of. Of you worrying. Getting your blood up. Fighting."

"I'm not. I'm going home. I have something to build."

—

It's been ten years since Junior stepped foot in the workshop. That last time was to announce his marriage to the woman with kind eyes and open face who saved him, whose name symbolized a new beginning. The woman who was a little girl when she accompanied her parents to pick up a custom sideboard King made for them years ago. The same girl who touched him and made the blood stop.

Junior hasn't spoken to King in two days. In a way, they've never spoken or said the words they needed to say.

Now he is back here, and King is not.

His heart quickens as he breaks the threshold; the screeching of an electric saw rings in his ears. The cavernous room is as he last remembered, table legs and chairs, bureaus and shelves, his father's and brother's talents, leaning against the walls and hanging from the rafters. Piles of wood patiently wait their turn to become their next purpose.

Mance turns off the saw when he sees Junior. His gaze, kind and sad, lingers on Junior before he moves toward him. Junior swallows hard and stands up straighter to match his brother, determined not to fray at his edges. They hug instinctively, their embrace lingering longer than it has in years, and tap their foreheads together. As brothers, they remain as close as they can be, considering; the gulf between them forced by circumstances neither can control. They navigate the rough tides well, treading water to stay afloat, too afraid to learn how to swim. But this was different. Their father was dead.

"Genesis here with you?" Mance asks through an exhausted sigh, weighted with things he won't say. Junior has never been privy to Mance's interior thoughts and feelings.

Junior lets out a shaky breath, blinking away tears. "Just me."

Men don't cry. But tears have always come easy to Junior. They've had no place here in the workshop, a lesson he's learned repeatedly. His ability and willingness to cry served as a source of contention between him and his father, whose rough demeanor drove him to tears often. Unlike Mance, stoic and rough-hewn, his father made over.

King built things. And his sons would too. Before and after school, their real education involved chisels and saws, squares and mallets. Junior has always felt like a guest in the workshop. Awkward and heavy-handed, his skills never quite matching his brother's. The wood straight when Mance cut it; slightly crooked when Junior did. King's disapproval evident in his stern eyes and stiff posture. Now, without King, Junior realizes how much of his connective tissue consists of guilt. He waits for the fear and anguish. Without the weight of judgment, what he feels instead is relief.

"I've been in the house," Junior says, diving straight into conversation. There were things to be taken care of. Papers to be signed. Funeral arrangements to be made. Financial responsibilities relegated to the house have always fallen to Junior—those he could do—and once fulfilled, he would finally be free. "They weren't easy to find, but it looks like he had two small life insurance policies. That should be enough to bury him. I'll make all the arrangements."

Mance picks up a planer and runs it along the edge of a piece of wood. "I trust you to do whatever is necessary. He did too."

Junior brightens a little, his brother's words water to a wilted plant. Standing in this very spot in the workshop over twenty years ago, Junior knew he didn't want to inherit King's dreams. How suffocating it would be. To have several chapters of your life already written. But he wanted to please him, then and now. And he tried.

"I can't find anything about the house or the land. None of the deeds. Or a will."

"He never talked about that stuff. You know that. I'm sure they'll turn up."

"When this is all over, we all need to talk about 'that stuff.' The Kingdom and the land."

"We're keeping it," Mance says, without hesitation. His expression does not change, his whole face stiff, eyes locked on the wood in front of him. In Mance's face, Junior sees a flash of King's, confident and defiant.

"Of course, but there's other things we need to discuss."

"Like?"

"Like, how are we going to maintain it? The taxes increase every year, and the house needs lots of repairs."

"We'll manage. We always do."

So comfortable. So certain of himself. Equally certain of Junior. Junior notices that his brother says *we*.

They fall silent to the sound of scraping wood. Curls fall to the floor at Mance's feet. Junior steps closer and runs his hand along the wood grain of the large box. "What's this?"

Mance stops, his face dotted with sweat, his chest heaving with effort, and stares at his creation. "King's casket."

Junior snorts, a hard sound, slightly annoyed that he didn't immediately remember. He's all too familiar with forgetting. Of course Mance would remember, King's wishes second nature to him. "I almost forgot."

In answer, Mance begins his work again.

"Bury me in a pine box; make it right here." King told them when they stood on stools to see the top of the worktable, and again when those stools were no longer necessary. A casket shouldn't contradict the life of the person whose body it holds. A simple box for a simple man. King understood this and Mance remembered.

"I'll leave you to it," Junior says, suddenly feeling small. He reaches the doorway before the workshop quiets once more.

"I could use your help." Mance's voice rises like fog from behind Junior.

Junior turns and studies his younger brother for a long moment, as if trying to decide if this is true. It is. Telling the truth is something Mance does, be it harsh or flattering. He doesn't waste time on lies or regard for someone's feelings. You always know where you stand with him.

This is an olive branch, and Junior's grateful for it, but he shakes his head anyway. "You don't need my help. I'd just slow you down."

"Bullshit."

"I wouldn't remember what to do," Junior protests, shoving his hands into his pockets, his words weighted with old pain. "It's been too long."

"It'll come back to you." Mance extends a clamp to him as Junior returns.

Junior takes the clamp in his hands. Years have passed but he feels closer to the past than to the present. He can't bring King back, but he can grant his wish and help build his casket and, in death, be the son he always wanted and believed he could be. Without being directed, Junior attaches the clamp to the sides of two glued boards and picks up another one and repeats it on the other side as the tears begin to fall.

Tokey swings open the door to King's closet. Her hand meanders over two dress shirts and several pairs of slacks hanging in the dark. In the back, one suit, navy, hangs alone. King's simplistic outlook on life prohibited the ownership of anything more or regular attendance at places such dress required. King loved God but didn't believe in church—the performative rituals.

"*Damn fools,*" he would say about the faithful churchgoers, and by extension, Tokey, who dressed in their best dresses, hats, and suits on Sundays. "*Giving all your time and hard-earned money away to a man who can't walk on water. Damn fools.*" Tokey reaches for the suit, bringing it closer, the hanger screeching along the steel rack. It smells faintly of him despite its irregular use: earthy, of pine and dirt, and its forgotten circumstance, of staleness and stilted air. She would have it dry-cleaned. She wanted people to see him in something besides his dingy denim overalls and white shirt, damn fools or not.

Tokey lays the suit across the bed and tries to picture King in it. His long frame, dark complexion, rubbery skin. She blinks, unable to stop herself from thinking about the last time she saw and spoke to her father. Yesterday morning, at breakfast, his only and her first, before the trip to McDonald's. He looked tired, paler, his skin grayed and ashy. He waved off her question about how he was feeling, a quick downward swipe with one hand as he carried his plate to the sink.

King wasn't easy to love, but she tried; they all did. Because though he was rough, he had a love for each of his children that manifested in different ways. Unexpected things, like changing his diet during their shared mealtimes. When she said that they both needed to eat better, King played along more for her benefit, she knew, than his. In the workshop with Mance, he existed on a diet of pork rinds, RC Cola, and cigarettes. His tall, muscular frame could handle it. Or lunches provided by Miss Jessie. At least once a week, she cooked a meal for him. But that morning, like so many mornings before, with his youngest child, he swallowed the bland egg whites and dry wheat toast without comment. For her, his love visible and invisible, hard and soft.

The Solomon children never really knew their mother. Like most things, King never spoke of her. Tokey, the youngest, vaguely remembers a woman hoisting her in the air, swinging her around and around, up and down. Or maybe that was a dream. And where is their mother now? Still gone, having walked away decades before. Her siblings seem not to miss knowing her, but Tokey does. She grew up feeling wrong and needed someone, a compass to guide her through life when the baby fat never left, when the King height never materialized, when the promise of beauty stalled.

Tokey's legs buckle, and she collapses against the bed. A single tear falls, quick, then another until one cannot be distinguished from the next. Her breathing is short and slight. Silence presses back at her, and she grows aware of the sounds produced by her own body. A slight whistle of air from her nose, the wheezing inhale and exhale of breath, and, as always, a rumble from her stomach. She is always conscious of these noises her body makes, afraid that others will hear them too.

She is hungry. Or so her mind tells her. Always reminds her. Its reminder the loudest when the sadness comes. Tokey reaches for the package of convenience-store strawberry rolls on the dresser. She is never too far from food.

She thinks it; she craves it.

She sees it; she eats it.

Tokey allows her gaze to float upward to the ceiling with yellowed water stains from the leaky roof, as her teeth sink into the soft, sweet roll. She chews and closes her eyes, waiting for the high, for the pain to ease. Her taste buds react first, and her mouth fills with saliva, with the returned comfort of familiarity. She swallows, and all is right with the world. As long as she keeps her eyes closed and keeps chewing, she is comforted.

Loneliness is cruel to the body. People aren't meant to be alone. God said so. *It is not good that man should be alone.* God gave Adam Eve because humans are made to love, to share their lives with others. Tokey dedicated her life to King. It was easier to love someone or something more than she loved herself—to give love without receiving it. It started slowly, almost naturally. With Junior married, CeCe in another state since college, and Mance in and out of prison, there was no one to help run the Kingdom. But by now, she has forgotten the world. Plus, better this than facing the unknown. Until she forgot about life altogether. Without King, Tokey would be alone.

Suddenly there isn't enough air in the room. Tokey stands and opens a window. In the distance, she hears a car's tires crunching through the gravel. She knows it won't be King, and still the disappointment of seeing an unfamiliar silver Mercedes fills her as she chews and swallows the last of the strawberry roll.

As she descends the stairs, Tokey realizes she doesn't remember the last time her siblings were all together under one roof. She certainly doesn't remember the last time they shared a meal. It took the death of their father to bring them together again, and she hates that. They don't need her, their lives moving them further and further away in distance and dependence. But she needs them, especially now, even CeCe, the driver of the silver Mercedes.

By the time Tokey gets outside, CeCe is already parked. Tokey casts a critical eye over her older sister, her brows creasing at her six-inch black heels and red body-con dress, too made-up for Diggs. She's perfect and polished as always. Jealousy, cold and biting, rises within Tokey, encasing her heart in an instant. She loves her sister but doesn't like her very much.

"You too good to wear a seat belt?"

"Hello to you too, Angeline," CeCe says, calling Tokey by her real name. CeCe closes the door and stands in front of it. "It's nice to see you." CeCe studies Tokey, her face, her clothes, her body. It's been seven years since her last visit, and Tokey hoped she wouldn't see it on her, the weight gain. Impossible.

Tokey doesn't step forward for a hug; anyway, one isn't offered. "How long are you staying?" she asks instead, her eyes sweeping across the two large suitcases and makeup case filling the back seat.

"A few days," CeCe says, her eyes behind her dark sunglasses now processing the Kingdom and the land, her arm bent at the elbow to hold her purse. "Is Mance here? Can he help me with my bags?"

Tokey lets out a sudden laugh. "Oh, you're staying here? Not some fancy hotel in Charlotte like you did last time?"

CeCe huffs. "I'm not doing this with you today. Is Junior here?"

"You'll have to carry them yourself."

CeCe looks around, as though willing a brother to materialize. "Tokey...it's hot out here. Where are they?"

Tokey crosses her arms. "Out in the workshop. And no, they cannot help you. They are busy."

"Doing what?"

"Building King's casket." Her words are like cold water on coals.

A shadow crosses CeCe's face, and her posture falters for a second before she recovers. It is a small victory for Tokey, to hurt her, if only for a second.

"Fine. I'll get them myself."

Tokey watches as CeCe unloads both suitcases and carries them to the front door, her makeup misting and perfect hair loosening, her intense perfume filling the afternoon air.

"Is there someplace I can sleep?"

"Your old room," Tokey says, joining her on the porch.

CeCe rolls her eyes and heads up the stairs with one suitcase, leaving the other in the foyer. Tokey watches.

"There's no money here, CeCe," Tokey calls up to her as the steps creak. The words hang between them like smoke.

CeCe stops, her chest heaving. "Is that what you think? I'm only here for money?"

"Well, aren't you?"

"He was my daddy too."

"I know you're not here to bury King or to unburden yourself of being a lousy daughter. You want something."

CeCe ignores her, disappearing around the corner, closing the door to her old room a few seconds later.

THREE

———

JUNIOR STRAIGHTENS HIS TIE and checks the buttons of his black coat as the first of the guests arrive. An hour before the service, and already people want to make sure they get a seat to pay respects to his father, pillar of the community. And Junior will greet them. Today, he will be the best son, the best brother too, his smile on display. He's capable of such theater. As the oldest, this is the part he has to play. To represent the family. To stand and nod. To shake hands with people he only half remembers. And despite his own grieving, to comfort others.

This is it, his last obligation to King. There is nothing left after this but his own freedom. Nothing to live up to. No more expectations to shatter. No more caskets to build. After he performed his duty and spoke the words he was meant to speak, there would be just him—all of him. No longer just an outer man, he would give his inner man life and space.

Junior knows the exact moment he split in two. In the sixth grade when he accidentally walked in on Mr. Shipstead, the gym teacher, in the shower, the first time he saw a grown man naked. That was it for him. A finger in an electrical socket. This confirmed his inkling about himself in both a terrifying and thrilling way, and in that moment, he became two people: an inner boy and an outer boy, operating within the same body but with separate minds and ideals.

He grew into the outer man, who is exactly as he presents himself today: the family man in love with his wife, who also got to be the elementary school principal, the boring brother, the reliable son. The inner man is the container for Junior's secrets, everything Junior hides from the world. He likes men, and before Simon, a couple of times a year, Junior drove them both to Charlotte for anonymous sex. This always satisfied the inner man, tamped down his desire to live independently, and kept him within the confines of Junior's mind. Until recently. Until there was another splitting inside Junior.

"Daddy, Daddy, Daddy!"

Seeing the two little girls running toward him, Junior feels his face rearrange a little, and he realizes, nervous at his slip, that his smile has gone from one of greeter to something more mysterious, more revealing of the images from Charlotte that were just playing through his mind.

The girls wrap their tiny arms around his legs, and Junior squats and folds them into a big hug. "What are you doing here?"

"We came to see you, Daddy," says Erica, the older daughter. "And to say goodbye to Grandpa King."

Julia, the younger, shy one, whispers, "Mommy said that we should surprise you. Are you surprised?" She's proud of herself, flashing two perfect rows of baby teeth.

Genesis moves into view, her black dress swaying from her hips. A high ponytail pulled tight accentuates her button nose and high cheekbones; her bold red lip and nails are obvious against her high-yellow skin.

"Yes, baby," Junior says to Julia but while eyeing Genesis. "I'm definitely surprised."

He hugs them again, tighter, presses his face into their coifs. They smell of home, of vanilla bean, crayons, and sunshine. It's been a week since he saw them. The night he ended up spending with Simon. He flushes with a rush of love followed by the heat of anger.

The girls would not attend the funeral. He and Genesis agreed. Five and three, they are too young to understand the complexities of death, its definition, to see King's body. And yet, here they are, wearing matching black scallop-edged, belted A-line dresses and black Mary Janes, their long inky hair curled in loose ringlets. Genesis often dresses them like twins. For her, it's always about appearance.

"Erica, take your sister and go sit in the front pew on the left. Mommy and Daddy will be there in a minute."

Still squatting, Junior watches Erica take Julia's hand and lead her into the filling church.

Genesis also watches the girls before turning her thickly lined and lashed eyes onto Junior. "I saw you straightening your tie. When you get nervous, you fidget. Straightening your tie, smoothing out your shirt, driving to Charlotte. Be careful. We don't need you to have a nosebleed. Not today."

"What are the girls doing here?" Junior stands and sharply exhales, registering his disapproval.

"They wanted to see their daddy. They missed him."

"We talked about this. The girls not coming. We agreed."

"Well…I considered it again, and I changed my mind." Genesis moves closer to Junior and reaches her lips to his ear. "I've also changed my mind about"—she lowers her voice—"us."

Junior resists the urge to laugh. She would do this here—spring this on him now. The idea of their reconciliation an hour before his father's funeral. In the company of all these people. It is the one lie he tells himself to get out of bed every morning, to keep nurturing the inner man, that he didn't care what others think about his preferences. What his family thinks. What everyone thinks. But he does. And she knows it.

"I thought we agreed on that too. You said I could"—Junior's teeth are gritted, a rictus parting of his lips—"see him."

"Things have changed. You have to take your place as the head of the family. You need your wife and kids, not a boy toy." She's barely five feet, but made taller by self-assurance and grit.

"He's not… I…" Junior doesn't say the words. Not now. To say them again will hurt her too much.

"I let you have your fun, but it's time for you to come home. You're not even…like that. You're just…curious."

He stares at her for a long moment, his grip tightening on

the program he hasn't realized he's rolled into a tight cylinder, then speaks in a quiet measure. "Don't do this."

"Who's going to keep the Kingdom afloat? And don't say Mance. He'll be back in prison sometime soon. CeCe's blowing town as soon as the casket is lowered into the dirt. And Tokey? Well…you know she can't. This is your responsibility now."

This is your responsibility.

This is your responsibility.

This is your responsibility.

"No," he finally says, stopping the echo in his head. One word that stops the world, that ceases the wind in their ears and the sun on their faces. One word that answers two demands.

Genesis smiles through Junior's rebuke. "What do you mean, no?"

"This is not my responsibility, and I'm not coming home. We agreed on one month. That you would let me work through… this. You promised, and I'm holding you to that."

"You can't possibly want to go on with this. Not now."

"I need this, Genesis."

Genesis falters, her attention diving to the ground; then she recovers. As she shakes her head, her smile reappears. "Fine. But don't push me out, not now. Me and the girls are staying. People will expect us to be here. We want to be here. I want to be here. Because—" She stops, swallows, and for a moment Junior thinks she's going to cry. "Because despite everything, I still love you."

Junior doesn't know if he believes that. Or if he wants to.

A week ago, when they finalized the agreement, and he closed the door behind him for a month-long pause, he assumed he had shut the door on his marriage forever. He'd loved her, once. He loved her now. But he didn't know if he wanted to continue to love her.

It isn't the right moment for this, and Junior feels himself slipping into a space between his body and a dark place. He knows how to escape himself, how to fold into his mind and drift off to an existence opposite his reality. He's made a life for himself in that place.

The hearse pulls up then, and the black shine bouncing off it sparks in Junior's eyes, snapping him back. He reaches for his tie, but Genesis's hand reaches it first. She tightens it and lays her hand on his chest and smiles.

"You're okay. You're going to be okay."

Genesis takes his hand in hers and waits. She waits for the refusal that does not come. The truth of her words, the reality, burns brighter than the May sun overhead. He is going to be okay.

Junior squeezes her hand, closing his eyes and submitting to this tiny embrace. He should drop it, expects to, but he doesn't. She's always made him feel strong, all those years ago in the workshop and now. Her grasp safe—familiar.

Genesis reaches into her purse and hands Junior his sunglasses. She knows him. Thinks of everything. Junior finds comfort in that, in not having to know any more on his own.

As Junior's eyes become accustomed to the shade, he sees Simon cloaked in black, the only other color coming from the golden brown of his skin. He watches as Simon approaches the church.

For so long, watching him was Junior's preferred pornography. Simon was a consultant hired to oversee the school's annual accreditation certification. A man who would never be his. And yet, for three years, Junior watched for him, waited for him. At night, he masturbated to memories of him, of the seconds he saw him in the hallway. Three years and nothing. And then Simon touched him, his palm on Junior's back—a blanket drawn across his shoulders—to prevent him from stepping back into him, a touch that awakened the inner man with a fierceness. Junior looked back at Simon, and an awareness passed between them, and Junior understood what he had lost. He thought he had come to terms with his life. Once again, one moment altered the trajectory of everything he knew to be true. Until Simon, he didn't know he needed to be rescued again.

In silence Junior fell for Simon. So quietly he didn't hear it himself. This type of love is quiet. Men don't love each other. Not in the open. Not in rural North Carolina. Not with a father like King.

Now, Junior almost calls to Simon but doesn't. Just a tilt of the head and a sharpened gaze—loving, caring, kind—that speaks a thousand words. Simon sees and knows, but Junior owes Simon those thousand words, and a thousand more, an explanation for Genesis's fingers spread across his forearm.

"Ready?" she says, adjusting the strap of her purse up her arm.

Simon stops and walks back to his car.

Junior extends his spine and rolls his shoulders back. He holds out his hand to an approaching Miss Jessie and says, "Thank you for coming."

━

Tokey takes a deep breath as the doors of the church groan open, and the words spill out, the chorus singing, "Lord, it's in your hands." Sunlight streams through the stained glass windows, the paint muting the bright light. The air smells of fresh-scraped wood, rose-scented incense, and a cacophony of perfumes and colognes.

But also, even though Tokey knows this thought is irrational, of death.

Tokey can't yet see the casket. She can't see much of anything. She's third in the family procession, Junior first, followed by CeCe, and Mance behind Tokey.

They didn't plan to walk in like this. Separately, as individuals. Didn't plan anything together. They haven't come together in the way Tokey hoped they would. They are sleeping under the same roof again, finally, but still operating independently of one another, much as they have for most of their adult lives, never occupying the same place at the same time for too long. They are scattered in their grief. Junior handled the funeral arrangements. Mance spent hours each day in the workshop on King's casket with Junior, and CeCe either stayed locked in her room or scoured the grounds trying to locate a cell signal. Tokey hoped King's death could, horrible as it was, at least be the scar tissue that would link them forever. Now she fears they'll return to their corners of the world and live out their days without so much as another shared breath between them.

Fret about that later, she thinks. For now, she must focus on walking.

Tokey takes a step forward. Because this is how it works to walk, one foot in front of the other. But it's been a long time since Tokey has taken an unwavering step, and her left knee buckles. Mance catches her, his grip on her arm iron. He looks at her, silently asking of her welfare. "I'm okay," she whispers.

Her knee started buckling months ago, always on the first step. Too much pressure, and it gives, threatening to take her down. *Lose some weight*, she can almost hear a doctor say. And she knows she should. But it's more than the most recent fifty pounds. It's the mental weight, too, pressing down on her. It's the figurative step forward that she fears. The forward motion without a plan, a goal. It's moving and not knowing the outcome.

Mance's hand finds Tokey's, and their fingers twine together as they walk. CeCe's hat obscures Tokey's view, an asymmetrical black silk hat adorned with a large bow in the front and black feathers in the back that flop with every step. It angers her. The boldness of it. The confidence to wear such a piece. To command such attention. Tokey feels the people's eyes on her, like mini spotlights, and it shrinks her a few inches. She can't bear their gaze, their sympathy. She doesn't want it. They didn't know him well enough to know he wouldn't have wanted such a display. Tomorrow, this will be over for them, their lives unchanged. King, a memorial carried on in their stories and memories, just as he was in life. But tomorrow she would wake up to a life forever altered.

When CeCe's hat finally swings sharply to the side, the casket is a shock, jarring in its beauty and stature. It looms wide at the foot of the pulpit. A large wooden box, hand-rubbed heart pine showcasing its beautiful grain, spacious enough for two, so perfect for the only man who could fill it on his own. Its decoration is as bold as the design: wood handles attached by wood pegs, custom trim, and the lid adorned with a long cross. A casket befitting a King.

Tokey is winded from effort and sadness by the time they reach King's casket. Mance releases her arm as Junior approaches the casket first, alone. Tokey thinks again that they should all be together. They should have entered hand in hand, pressed their heads together, their family's definition of a hug or kiss, in private prayer, and viewed King's body as one, said goodbye as one. King never wanted this for them, this distance and separation.

They loved King, but Tokey understands that there will be parts of him that they will miss and parts they won't. Both can be true. For King it was impossible to be a good parent all the time for each of them. Not with four children, with their own attitudes and temperaments, aims and aspirations. He could only get it right some of the time. Too much love and you're soft. Not enough and you don't love them enough. Just the right amount and you were the favorite.

Tokey hears Junior inhale. She knows the flood of tears is arriving. He's always cried such enormous tears. He lifts his hand to King's chest as if to lay it there, but stops, hovering it over his heart; finally, he presses it down as he leans in, whispering something. He speaks for only a moment, tears streaming down his face, his lip quivering. Genesis appears then, touches his back, and Junior steps away.

CeCe waits until Junior has moved away from King's casket before she approaches. Two long steps on her six-inch heels, and she's there, her hands gripping it, but not touching King. She, too, says something and quickly walks away.

Mance approaches and releases a long sigh. He places his hands on King's, bundled at his waist, and leans in. He whispers something, short as two words. Even though Tokey is closer now, she doesn't hear what he whispers. It's for King alone. King and Mance shared an unspeakable bond.

A quiet heaviness fills Tokey's chest as she shuffles forward. There's King in the suit she picked. His still face. His tilted chin. Broad shoulders. Strong jaw. In death, his physical presence remains strong. All at once, sadness settles on her like a blanket, and she begins to cry, her body shaking. But King's body is motionless, his eyes closed forever to the world. She places her hand on his; it's not too cold, not too hard. The world deserved a King.

She should say something. But her mind is in another place. She's lost two parents now. One she loved; one she never knew. She is no longer a daughter. The thought enormous, strangling, gutting.

Tokey leans in, hoping to tip words from her tongue. And then, what comes to mind is a question, another weight, she's been waiting to ask since King's death.

"What do I do now?"

She speaks so quietly, she wonders if she said it aloud. Either way, King gives no answer. Even in life, he wouldn't answer that question for her. Tokey turns and doesn't think she can walk from the casket on her own, but she tries, shuffling forward one step, then another.

Then, she falls.

Her knees fold under her, and her arms shoot straight up as she rolls onto the ground. The church gasps, the same uniform sound, a long-pitched inhale. Mance reaches her first. Junior's next. He takes her other arm, and they lift. Pain screams all over her body when she's on her feet.

She looks up at Junior. "But he was fine. He was fine a few days ago."

Tears glass Junior's eyes as he tries to hug her and move her, but she resists, her legs like steel. "He just died? I don't understand. He just died?"

"Come on, Tokey," Mance whispers while also pulling her.

"No," Tokey says, her voice shaking, her fingers clawing at her forearms. "Where's my daddy! I want my daddy!"

CeCe approaches but does not attempt to touch Tokey. She has tears in her eyes that do not fall. "I know. Let's sit down."

A hush falls over the church, movement stills. Suddenly, something clicks in Tokey's mind. "I'm sorry," she says, over and over again to no one, to everyone. Her face is hot, burning, covered in sweat. Her lungs heave, and her heart hammers. To the mourners, she simply fainted, overcome with grief. Tokey has witnessed her share of such hysterics at funerals. But she is not a loved one conjuring empathy and trying to increase the noise in the church. This is not just about her being a daughter crying over the loss of her father.

She knew better than to walk. It's in her nature to stand perfectly still. It was too much to ask her body, herself, to support so much and yet not enough.

She is not even thirty and doesn't know who she is.

King is at his graveside, and he isn't happy. This isn't the first time CeCe has seen him since she returned home. She first saw him on her second day back at the Kingdom, in the field just behind the workshop, and then every day since. Just before he appears, the wind picks up, catching everything in its path, a tiny tornado. Then he's there. It's a younger version of him, hands in his worn overalls, the collar of his dingy white shirt tucked into his chest—the version from her childhood. It's how CeCe best remembers him and how he chooses to reveal himself to her.

He's doing the same thing now that he has done every time: shaking his head to a beat she can't hear. It's directed toward her, she knows. A look of disappointment.

She wronged him, and now she can't apologize. Though she tries. She whispers, "I'm sorry," and hopes the wind carries her message, calms him. She apologizes for not being the daughter he believed in. For spending her life trying to get away from Diggs and, by extension, him. She apologizes for all known and unknown transgressions. His disappointment remains planted across his face.

She would never know for sure what did it, what snapped in her that made her take money the first time. Other than it was easy to take and she deserved it. As a first-year intern, she worked to the bone and barely made enough to live in New York City. This money made up for what she was worth. Besides, she would put it back. She didn't, of course. And the ease with which she took the money only aided her decision to continue doing so. A few hundred for designer dresses to allow her to fit in better than her J. Crew suits, then a few thousand for a Cartier Tank watch and two-carat diamond studs, finally, tens of thousands for a down payment on a loft in the Meatpacking District. A quarter of a million dollars taken to fund a lifestyle she desired.

Junior touches her arm.

The tent flaps and rattles in the wind. The cries of the people snuffed out by the humid heat. The preacher's words lost, too, in the unsettled air.

Her phone rings from deep within her Chanel purse, and she lets it, holding her breath until it stops. It's Mark. Nobody else would call. She has no friends.

Her phone buzzes with a voicemail. CeCe takes her phone out, presses it discreetly to her ear under Junior's quick, sharp look, and listens. The message is short but heavy.

When will you be back?

This makes her step aside from the group. She didn't tell Mark why she left, just that she had to deal with a family issue. She has a right to keep this secret. She never talks about her father, her siblings, her childhood in North Carolina, and she doesn't want to start. Nor does she expect anyone to care. Except, now, for Mark. He tasted something new, a drop of honey on the tongue, and he no longer craved his wife's vanilla. No matter the distance between them, CeCe would be expected to uphold her end of the bargain.

CeCe excels at pretending to be brave, but bravery lasts only a moment each time she calls on it. Her stomach stirs as she closes her phone. How long can she keep this up? It's not a question. Her plan has to work.

"Cecily?" It's a voice she hasn't heard in years from the boy with the beady hair, dusty face, and chipped tooth. She hasn't been Cecily in a long time and only, always, to one person.

Ellis.

Except, he long ago stopped being that boy. In front of her looms a man, a tree casting shade as much with his body as with his easy smile, wide and bright, that covers his entire face and has always flickered something inside her.

"It's been a long time." She recovers, stretching herself upward, suddenly feeling small despite her heels.

"It has."

"You got gray. Looks good."

Ellis smiles again and strokes his beard. "You look…exactly the same."

"Don't be silly. I look much better now."

The Solomons do age well. Everyone says so, and they especially say it about CeCe, even though, maybe in many cases because most people rarely see her, her youthfulness a bright light in their memory. Men have always stared in lust, and still do; young women gawk in envy; older women watch in nosiness. CeCe makes it her business to enhance her good genes. She stays lean and wears heels that elongate her legs and tighten her calves. Her dress, even today at her father's funeral, hugs her curves and pushes out her heavy breasts and thins her tiny waist. Ellis keeps his eyes on her eyes. "You look well" is all he says.

What she doesn't say is how good he looks. Clean, fresh, in a tailored black suit with a crisp white shirt and black tie. His features cut sharp, a strong chin and hard jaw, his smooth deep-brown skin drinking up the light. But with Ellis, it has always been about more than that—an invisible manner that drew her in. Men from Diggs don't look like Ellis. No amount of good genes can erase the weight of circumstance of life, of their surroundings. It's visible, the weight; it ages them, erases youth and vibrancy, dulls the eyes. Not with Ellis. He escaped this fate because he left, moved away before the virus infected him, seeped into the contours of his face and into his dreams, before it swallowed him whole.

He leans in, enveloping her in a hug. "I'm sorry about King."

Guilt bubbles to the surface, almost choking her. She hasn't yet cried for King, but the tears are there, unfallen. She hates crying, the vulnerability of it, the surrender to an uncontrollable force more powerful than will. Shame replaces the tears and quickens her heart. That will have to be enough grief for now.

"Thank you," she manages as Ellis continues holding her, his full embrace tight, comforting. She hugs him back, pretending not to notice the firmness of his chest and the tautness of his shoulders. Long-ago memories surge to the surface, moments that she turns to for comfort, in darker, recent times.

Ellis releases her but stays close, and CeCe forces herself to take a step back. He's always taken up space, in a good way, his energy punching the air and drawing people to him. "He was fine when I saw him a few days ago," he says.

"You were in Diggs a few days ago? Why?"

He laughs at her incredulous tone. "It's home."

"Visiting Ms. Elyse?"

"She died last year."

CeCe watches as grief moves through him, his eyes sobering, and her heart sinks as she remembers a call from Tokey, a message left—the unreturned phone call. "I'm sorry," she pushes out through a tight throat.

"Thank you." He shuffles his feet. "How long are you staying?"

"I don't know. A few more days to settle a few things. You?"

Ellis exhales. "A little longer than that. I live here now."

"I thought you got out of here."

"I did."

When he says nothing else, she nudges him: "And here you are. Living in Diggs again."

"Here I am."

They fall to silence as the air snaps with heat, as the midday sun moves from behind a sheet of clouds.

"Let me walk you to your car," Ellis says, finally, extending his arm.

"I can walk."

"It rained a few days ago. It's pretty muddy in some spots. Let me help you."

"I got it."

"Well…walk this way. There's less mud."

"I know where to walk."

"This way is much smoother."

"I don't want my heel to get stuck."

"At least hold my arm for balance."

"I can walk on my own."

He stops and laughs. "Same ole Cecily."

"Same ole Ellis."

"Still trying to rule the world."

"Still trying to save it."

He doesn't look away. Neither does she. The ease in the air between them vanishes.

That's how it has always been between them, a game in which neither relents. They are the same, their personalities and makeup matching in determination and inflexibility, and a fiery spirit that bleeds into all conversations and interactions since the day, all those years ago, when the boy with the dusty face and freshly dislocated shoulder knocked on their door.

The knock came just after dinner, and King opened the door to a boy with a ripped shirt, heaving gulps of air. CeCe recognized the boy immediately. The boy once in Mance's grade and now in hers. She knew him not only because of his chipped tooth but his scarred face and eyes that focused too hard.

"It's late, son," King said. "You can come back and play with Mance tomorrow."

The boy turned to leave, and the awkward position of his shoulder moved into view.

King pulled the boy inside the house by his good shoulder, looking out in the darkness for anyone else. "You're Fredrick's boy. What happened to you?" King says, closing the door. "Who did this to you? Did he do this?"

Ellis remained silent, his lip curled tight, his breath ragged, fists balled. His pain visible across his face.

"What's wrong with his shoulder, Daddy?" Tokey said. They had all materialized in the foyer, watching.

"It's dislocated," Junior said to Tokey.

King walked over to the boy and kneeled before him. "This is going to hurt, son. But only for a moment. You need to be brave."

The boy clamped his eyes shut, and his chest rose just before King placed his hand in the space between the boy's chest and shoulder while pulling on his arm, rotating it toward the center. It popped into place, and Ellis cried out. The whimper echoed up, down, and across the foyer, and when it stopped the boy's face relaxed.

King stood. "Mance, go get the boy another shirt. CeCe, get him sumthin' to eat. I'll be back."

Ellis never said who dislocated his shoulder, but King knew and left five minutes later, the wood floor groaning with each step of his heavy boots, his sledgehammer by the door gripped in his hand.

King never told anyone what happened. "Let it be" was all he said when he returned. But two things happened after that night: Ellis never darkened their door in the middle of the night again, and he became a permanent fixture at the Kingdom and in CeCe's heart.

Now, Ellis turns. "It was good to see you," he says, over his shoulder. "I'll see you at the Kingdom."

CeCe takes a full step and sinks her entire heel deep into the mud. When she takes another step, she walks out of her shoe. No way is she putting her foot in the mud. Flamingo-legged, she bends down to retrieve the stuck shoe and almost topples over. She looks up and sees only Ellis.

"Ellis," she calls in a whisper.

He keeps walking.

"Ellis!" she calls again, louder.

He turns, hands in his pockets, and smiles at the sight but does not move. "I guess you need my help."

"Ellis," CeCe says, still balancing on one leg.

"Is that a yes?"

Men are simple, predictable, and easily unlocked if you know the right combination. And CeCe knows. She knows how to stretch her eyes, tilt her head, and inject the perfect balance of need and plead into her voice. "Ellis," she says, performing, pressing her hand against her breast, laying her first cards on the table.

But Ellis isn't most men.

Amusement prowls his face. "Men fall for that? You forget...I know you, the real you."

He does know her, the her she refuses to acknowledge, but she smiles back anyway, holding her hand splayed across her chest.

"Do you need my help?"

"Yes!"

He slowly approaches. "I didn't hear you ask."

She huffs and clenches her teeth. "Get over here and help me. Now!"

"Now that wasn't very nice. I think you can do better than that."

"Ellis, help me."

"Ellis, help me, what?"

"Ugh! You are so aggravating!"

He turns his ear toward her, cupping it with his finger.

"Please."

"Much better. For a minute there, you seemed to have lost your Southern manners."

"And you're here to remind me of them?"

"Yes, ma'am," he says, not bothering to dilute his Southern drawl, all grits and cornbread.

Ellis kneels, and CeCe touches his shoulder for balance,

her long fingers pressing ever so lightly. One of his hands cups her calf, the other her foot. They are rough and yet tender, his hands. She feels the scar too, rubbed smooth by time. She remembers his hands on her body once and how they made her feel then and now. That's the thing about touch. You either forget it or remember it forever. And she remembers. Tangled limbs in the dark. Measured breaths in silence not uncomfortable.

She hates how he makes her feel, an exhilaration that hits as a physical sensation, her skin rippling with goose bumps. Ellis somehow forces her to feel every emotion so fully, so completely. Happy, sad, sexy, frustrated, angry, confused. Anger has always been her default emotion to throw at him, the emotion she thinks she understands the best. So, she does that now. Because Ellis will know anyway, see it on her, read it across her face. He's the one person who knows her best.

"You just want an excuse to touch me," she growls.

Ellis frees her shoe and stands. He's close, close enough for his beard to brush against her cheek, for his breath to tickle her ear, for a note of his cedar aftershave to occupy her air. He breathes. And when he speaks again, his voice lowers, a message for her ears only.

"The next time I touch you"—he looks down at her now from underneath thick lashes and studies her face before his gaze lands on her lips—"it will only be because you asked me to."

You see a funeral procession, you stop. It doesn't matter if you don't know the family or if you are on the opposite side of the road, you pull over and stop. You let the procession—the line of slow-moving cars with flashing lights containing the family members, friends, and loved ones of the deceased—trickle past you, no matter how long it takes. You wait. This is how it is in the South, how people pay their respects to the dead, and the living. They stop and clear the way.

They did this for King. They pulled over and stopped. And more. They stepped out of their cars; men pressed their hats across their chests, and women lowered their heads. It was a king's goodbye. Mance had never before witnessed such a sight.

Mance slides his gray 1986 Oldsmobile Cutlass Supreme down the driveway to the Kingdom, and it's lined with some of those same cars, its occupants now inside the house, eating someone else's food, sending up prayers, and sharing stories and speaking words of comfort that they believe will make the grief easier to tolerate. Mance shifts the car into park, and moves to get out, the cracking burgundy interior whining with the fluctuation of his weight.

As he walks, Mance removes his suit coat and slings it onto the ground. He yanks at his tie, loosening it, and pulls it off, not watching where it falls nor caring. He bypasses the house, leaving a trail of clothes behind him.

Enough of that.

In the workshop, there's much to be done, orders to fill. A

house and land to keep up. It's too much to think about all at once, so he doesn't. He focuses on one task—the columns—and starts there, rolling his shirtsleeves to the elbow.

Several hours later, Lisha stands in the door, her shadow at her back, the sun peeking from behind the clouds to take one last look at the day it made. For a second, he cannot comprehend what happened to the afternoon but sees time in his work: one completed column.

"You can't hide out here forever."

For a moment, Mance hopes the voice might be King's. He had a way of sneaking up on him while he worked. But of course it's not, and the knowledge of that burns his heart.

"You've been out here for hours," she says, his coat and tie draped over her arm.

Lisha's beauty cuts like a knife. It slices him open every time. But her beauty isn't enough to make Mance forget about the occasion. Mance sets a finished column next to the others. Three more to go.

"Where's Henry?"

"In the house, sleeping. Tuckered out from everyone fussing over him."

Mance locates the perfect beam for the next column and hoists it up onto his shoulder, then slams it down on the table.

"You have a house full of people who came here to see you and your family," Lisha says, stepping closer, her arms folded across her chest.

"They are here for themselves, not us."

"How can you say that? You know the impact your father had on this community."

Mance measures the beam; the tape snaps back. "He's gone. And now what? What will they expect from us? I'm not my father."

"And you don't have to be."

Mance walks to the door and points to the house. His voice comes out winded with his mood. "Go tell them that."

From the distance, voices and laughter carry across the field.

Lisha joins him. "Mance is not King!" she yells, the words an echoey sound floating across the field. "Mance is not King!"

Mance chuckles but does not surrender to a full laugh.

"How's that?" Lisha asks, with a proud expression of a woman who just conquered a mountain.

She acts like it costs her so little to be strong for him, Mance thinks. He's always been impressed with her ability to know when he needs a little extra love and deliver on it, never being emotionally stingy.

His mood shifts, twists, and turns into something Mance knows but does not have the words for—all he knows is that it does not send worry into his heart. He leans into her, his head lowered, and she runs her fingers across it. His breathing slows to something more purposeful. He looks at her and presses his lips to hers and feels the plushness of her lips. He lifts and sits her on the table.

Lisha's eyes drift open, and she breaks the kiss, frowning. "I know you are hurting, and I'm sorry about that, but I'm not going to have sex with you in this workshop."

"You have before," Mance whispers, his mouth moving to her neck, her shoulder, and his arms, one on each side of the table, trap her inside an intimate cocoon. "Right here, over there, in that chair…"

"That was different."

"It doesn't have to be," he says, finally looking at her.

She leans her head against his shoulder. "We're not doing this, remember?"

Henry's conception was a rare moment of weakness. Hours before, he closed on the ten acres of land. Later, it was just him and Lisha, a blanket, and the deed under a blue-black sky that felt large enough and bold enough to hold their dreams. They stared at it and wished, hoped for a future as bright as the stars. A breeze whipped up from nowhere and pulled a strand of hair across Lisha's face. Mance watched the way she pushed the hair away, the way her dress lifted open, her breasts, low and full, partially exposed, and he could not help himself. When he reached for her, with a kiss that held an illicit promise of more, she welcomed him, relished the press of his body. "Are you sure?" he asked against her throat, his breath electric to her body and thunder between her legs. He saw the future in her eyes, across the land, and above them. He loved her so completely that it often jolted him, their connectedness. In answer, Lisha kissed him back, turning his question into an answer.

There have been no moments of weakness since.

She waited for him while he served his first prison sentence, and then she waited during his second one, Henry's birth barely a week after his release, and now she is refusing to do it again. Mance knows she does not trust that he can control his temper, the reason for both prison stints.

Her love and hand come at a price, and Mance can't afford it.

"We do *this* quite well," Mance says, amusement wrapped in the slow, satisfied curl of his lips, his head still buried in her neck, his hands now finding their way to her zipper.

Lisha hops off the table and dusts wood shavings off her dress. "I need assurances."

"Assurances? I've given them to you. I'm not going back to prison."

"It's not just that. Henry is going to need money. Real money. Not that crazy bartering system you guys use."

"You've never wanted for anything. I provide for you and Henry."

"Yeah…I can buy all the groceries I want and pump all of the gas I need, and somehow no one ever asks me for money. You have an arrangement with my landlord because he was a friend of your father's and because you and Ellis did him a favor. I don't even want to know what that was about. That may work here in Diggs. But in Charlotte, Henry's doctors are not going to take a table or a chair or a 'favor' as a payment. There's no one there who owes you or your father anything."

"Henry will have everything he needs."

"Including those cochlear implants." She blows gently against a pile of shavings. "Hmm, that $50,000 isn't hiding under there…" She hurries to soften her tone. "Henry needs you. I need you. But I can't wait for you again. I won't."

"Then marry me," he says, moving to her. "Live here with me. Let me raise Henry here. I've changed."

"This may be too much for him. There's so much history here."

"No," Mance says, shaking his head, deciding. "He's going to have the same upbringing I had. He's going to learn everything I learned. It doesn't matter if he can't hear."

As the words leave his tongue, his eyes catch on something in the distance, someone, and Mance's vision washes bloody in the rage that suddenly consumes him.

Mance crosses the field in several strides to the group of men laughing and talking. They notice Mance, and their expressions sober out of respect.

"I thought I told you to get that damn excavator off my land," Mance says to Lou, who is standing in the group of men holding mason jars of moonshine.

A flicker of surprise crosses Lou's face as if he has no idea about the excavator.

This enrages Mance further, and he lunges at him, bunching his pressed white shirt with his fists and pulls Lou into him.

Lou doesn't struggle. There's a ripple of tension through the others, but they also lock in place. They know better than to intervene. "I…I'm…sorry. My trailer's broken."

"For weeks?"

"I promise I'll move it in a few days."

Suddenly, Mance is conscious of a face near his, a firm hand on his shoulder. "Let him go, Man," Ellis says. "You're wrinkling his best shirt."

Mance doesn't move or loosen his grip. He just stares at Lou, air streaming in and out of his nostrils. "Fuck his shirt. I told him I wanted that excavator off my property weeks ago."

"And you're sorry about that, right, Lou?" Ellis says, taking Lou's moonshine out of his hand.

"Yeah, I'm sorry."

"And I'm going to get it moved as soon as I can," Ellis prompts.

Lou repeats this too and adds, "I'm sorry, again, Mance— and I'm sorry about King."

"Don't fuckin' say his name," Mance says, releasing him with force. Lou stumbles backward but does not fall. He apologizes once more and staggers away. The other men follow.

"You good?" Ellis asks once they are alone. He smells Lou's moonshine and then takes a drink.

Mance wipes his forehead as the world blends back into focus, the red dissipating. It's only then that he realizes he's made a mistake. Again. That Lisha is gone.

"She just walked back to the house," Ellis says, knowing.

Mance sighs. "Fuck!"

"She'll be fine. Give her some time."

"She's never going to marry me."

"Of course she will. She loves you. You know what you gotta do. You got little Henry now. You can't be this man anymore."

Sometimes, Mance feels as if he were born with a heart of fire, and he isn't sure he can ever extinguish it. He doesn't trust himself enough not to do something bad or terrible that could take Henry away from him. It's a new fear—his only one—that pierces and fills his heart with the odd sensation of something heavy and weighted.

"Because I don't come cheap," Ellis continues, taking another sip, his face contorting at the kick of the moonshine. "I represented you the first time as a favor to King, and the second one was because you're my best friend, but I'm charging your ass next time."

Mance smiles, which transforms into a wince as the cut he didn't know he had on his hand commands attention, the blood red and thick and dripping.

Ellis gestures toward the house. "Come on... You treat an outside wound with rubbing alcohol and an inside wound with drinking alcohol." He holds up the rest of Lou's moonshine. A drop remains. "Let's go get some more of this. It'll work as both."

As they begin to walk, in the distance, CeCe moves across their sight line.

"You finally...?" Mance asks, grimacing and slinging blood.

"Yeah."

"Y'all still...?"

"Yup."

"She needs..."

"I know."

"And?"

Ellis shakes his head and downs the rest of the moonshine. "Oh…that woman," he growls through clenched teeth, his tone laced with pleasure and annoyance.

"I see I'm not the only one with inside wounds to treat."

Before they reach the house, a white man with a gray polo shirt and pressed khakis, a man he's never seen before, approaches them. "Are you Mance Solomon?"

"Who's asking?" Ellis asks before Mance can. They both survey the man from head to toe.

The man doesn't answer, just extends his hand in Mance's direction, revealing a letter. "You've been served."

Mance snatches it as the man hurries away. He rips opens the envelope and unfolds the letter; his eyes scan the single page.

"What is it?" Ellis asks.

Mance hands him the letter, his face clenched into an arrangement Ellis has never seen, and then reads. "'This letter is to inform you that you, King Solomon and all occupants, are no longer allowed on or around the premises of 845 Solomon Drive.'"

FOUR

———

CECE HAD A PLAN. She had a goddamn plan. High school valedictorian. College at Wake Forest. Law school at UNC. Land multiple job offers at some of the most prestigious law firms in New York City. Chief among the items on her list? Get the hell out and stay out of Diggs. And she had.

She called, sent birthday cards, and wrote letters, but those stopped. She was too busy to check in with her family, to attend Tokey's high school and college graduations, to return a few phone calls from Junior and King. But she checked everything from her plan, coming home only once, out of curiosity. That time cost her and she left behind a huge part of herself. She swore she would never do it again.

Then, when King died, a new plan. Attend King's funeral. Convince her siblings to sell the Kingdom and most, if not all, of the land. Take her share of the proceeds and repay the money she stole.

Learning that they had to surrender the house in two weeks? Definitely not part of the new plan.

Being in close proximity to Ellis? This? This was really not part of her plan.

After that fateful night, King took quite the liking to Ellis. Teaching him. Protecting him. Encouraging him. Ellis reminded him of Mance. And King liked that. He was tough, and King fed off strength. Ellis was eager to learn, and King fed off eagerness.

King arranged for a dentist to fix Ellis's tooth, and Ellis ate dinner and did his homework at the Kingdom most nights. Turns out the boy with the dislocated shoulder had more secrets. He was hungry. King began renting out lots of land to owners of mobile homes and Ellis's father, Frederick, helped King in the shop in exchange for his rent. But his wages never made it to the home or refrigerator. It's funny how a plate of fried chicken, mashed potatoes, and collards can open a child up. He suddenly wouldn't stop talking.

He was smart. CeCe learned this one night while helping Tokey with her algebra homework. Ellis hunched over his plate.

"Cecily, it's wrong," Ellis said, shoveling a massive amount of collards into his mouth.

"Why do you call me by my real name?" CeCe snapped.

"I like it." Ellis swallowed a mouthful and took a sip of sweet tea. "It's unique. Like you."

CeCe studied the problem again, unsure how to process

his statement, and didn't see an error. "How do you know? You flunked."

Ellis didn't flinch at CeCe's rude remark. "I know," he said, taking a huge bite of cornbread and then saying, mouth full, "Did you make this?"

"Yeah...so. Why? Do you have something to say about that, too?"

"It's good."

CeCe checked her work and saw her mistake in the multiplication. She didn't admit fault or apologize, but Ellis sensed it.

"Told you," he said. "The other answer is wrong, too." It was the first time he read her, and it wouldn't be the last.

Their teachers eventually learned what CeCe knew. Ellis was not dumb. In fact, quite the opposite. They moved him back to his grade and he graduated from high school with Mance with a full scholarship to Duke University and later to the Duke University School of Law.

"What does this mean?" Junior asks, floating the letter across Ellis's desk. It drifts down onto a stack of papers.

It isn't the right question. It's not the *what* they need answers to. They all read the letter, repeatedly, speculated on the context and phrasing. They know what it means. It's the *how*. How is it possible?

Ellis takes the letter into his hands but doesn't look at it. He's read it too. "This company, Malone & Kincaid, claims they own the Kingdom and five surrounding acres. And as the rightful owners, they claim you are trespassing on their land."

"People have wanted the Kingdom and the land for decades. It's a hoax to convince us to sell," Junior says. "Now that King is dead, the vultures are circling."

"They are not filing a claim. This letter says they own it outright. Legally."

"The fuck they do," Mance says. He's been surprisingly calm and quiet, each hand gripping the seat's armrest. Junior shifts in his position, sitting up straighter, and Tokey sits silently, her hands crossed over her chest. CeCe watches them all from a chair tucked in the corner, her heart tripping and racing in her chest, stealing her breath. She should say something, chime in. She is a lawyer, too, after all. But what?

King called her several times in the months before his death. Could she look at these papers he received from a Charlotte lawyer about the land? As a child, she would sit in his shop and watch him find shapes hidden in wood, reducing it, sliver by sliver, piece by piece, until a chunk of nothing became something, a table leg, a chair, a wooden bracelet. But King couldn't see shapes in letters, and words didn't make sense. She would look at the letter, she said, as soon as she had time. She was busy, a big-time New York City lawyer. For decades, developers wanted the Kingdom, and as development increased around it, interest increased. CeCe knew King would never sell, so it wasn't worth her time. The paperwork was probably another offer that he would never consider. She had time before it became a legitimate issue.

Except she didn't. Now the land is in jeopardy, and her plan unknotting its threads.

CeCe stands and walks closer to Ellis's desk. "What do we know about...Malone & Kincaid? How do we know that they are a legitimate company?" She takes the letter into her hands and looks at it. "A first-year associate could type up something like this."

"I checked them out and they are legit. A $30 million real estate investment company out of Charlotte. They specialize in acquiring resorts and waterfront property."

"Genesis's father, James, has worked with them in the past. They are legit," Junior says.

"Why would they want the Kingdom?" Tokey asks, her voice cracking, tears glistening on her face. "It's falling apart, and they want to turn it into a resort?" Junior places his hand on Tokey's arm.

"Possibly," Ellis says. "I don't know."

"Fuck that!" Mance says, standing suddenly, his anger finally materializing. "I will burn it to the ground before I let them take it from us."

"This can't be possible," Junior says. "There must be some kind of mistake. They can't just claim ownership because they want it. How is this legal?"

"They would not have been able to get a court-ordered notice of trespass without significant evidence proving their rightful claim to the Kingdom," Ellis says.

"What evidence would they need?" Junior asks. "A deed? A bill of sale? They wouldn't have that."

"A bill of sale, yes. A deed, I don't know," Ellis says. "King himself didn't have a deed to the house or the land."

"How's that possible?" CeCe asks. "This land has been in the family for centuries. There has to be a legal deed to the land after all this time."

"King inherited the land from his father via heir property. His father inherited the land the same way. That's the way it's been passed down through all generations."

"What is heir property?" Tokey asks, her voice as small as the room is starting to feel.

"Heir property is land passed down to all living family members by inheritance. It's created when someone dies *intestate*, meaning without a will. King did not have a will."

"Are we sure?" Junior asks, but he knows the answer. They all did, even Ellis. King was from a generation of people who didn't speak of such things. If King had a will, someone, at least Junior or CeCe, would know about it. And they didn't.

"Yes, legally, in this case, a will doesn't matter. You all, as King's heirs, automatically inherit the land, but you may own it with other heirs," Ellis says.

"There are no other heirs to the Kingd—" Junior starts.

"Uncle Shad," Mance says, his back to them.

"Uncle Shad. Uncle Shad," Tokey repeats until it settles within her. "We haven't seen or heard from him in years. He didn't even come to King's funeral."

"They stopped speaking years ago," Mance says.

"If King inherited the Kingdom from his father via heir

property," Ellis says, "he had to split it with Shad, his brother. Heir property is shared equally between children."

"So...Uncle Shad could have sold it to Malone & Kincaid?" CeCe asks.

"Possibly."

"Let's say that Uncle Shad is part owner of the Kingdom and that he did sell it to Malone & Kincaid; wouldn't there have been notice of the sale? How can a house be sold without notifying the other owners? King would have had to sign something," Junior says.

CeCe's heart nearly beats out of her chest, and she hopes no one notices.

"King would never have sold his share," Mance says.

"This is very confusing," Tokey says, touching her temple with her fingertips. "What do we do now? How do we stop the notice of trespass?"

"A law school friend of mine in Charlotte specializes in real estate," Ellis says. "I'm going to talk to him. Junior, I need you to go speak with someone at Malone & Kincaid. Maybe use James as a contact. Try to understand what their motivation is. See what you can find out."

Ellis turns to Mance and stares, blinks once.

"Yeah," Mance says.

"Because..." Ellis says.

"I know," Mance says.

An entire conversation in four words.

Ellis says to Tokey, "I need you to scour the house looking

for any paperwork, titles, deeds, anything that we can use to prove ownership. And…" he stops. "I need you to pack up as much of the house as you can. The notice of trespass ends in two weeks. That may not be enough time to go to court and reverse the decision. Get everything out of the house you may need."

CeCe watches as Junior and Tokey talk to Ellis as they all ready to leave. He gives Junior a reassuring look and Tokey a hug. The Solomons love Ellis as if he is one of them. He is.

Now, Mance looks at Ellis and nods and follows Junior and Tokey, leaving Ellis and CeCe alone.

"What was all that with you and Mance?" CeCe asks.

Ellis smiles, big and bright, and props himself against his desk, folding his arms.

"I'm going to Charlotte with you," CeCe finally says. When he didn't give her a task, she knew he would expect this, but she says it anyway just to assert some authority.

Sure enough: "Of course, you are," Ellis says. "I wouldn't try to stop you. Not that you would listen to me anyway."

"Well…good," CeCe says, reaching for her purse.

"Listen…" he says, stopping her. "King never said anything to you about this Malone & Kincaid? Nothing? It's hard to believe that he didn't reach out to at least one of us about this. Are you sure there's nothing you need to tell me?"

CeCe shakes her head, confident. "No, nothing."

Ellis's eyes burn into hers. He could always see the invisible, even sense her emotions before she grasped them herself. Not only her favorite color or food, but he understood her fully, the *who* behind the *what*. Even now, he knows of the stuff that cuts her up inside, because Ellis has been cut by the same blade. He could always see right through her, see her truth, all of it, as if it were written across her face.

Another memory comes: Ellis and the trailer.

In between his junior and senior year, Ellis shot up four inches. His shoulders rounded, and his lean body rippled and corded. Other girls started noticing his wit and charm and flocked to him. The boy had become a man. It seemed fated that they would be drawn to each other. CeCe liked him, and he liked her, but she didn't know if what she felt was real or the afterburn of proximity and circumstance, so she ignored his flirtations and ignored her own feelings.

Until Lenny.

No boys would come near her for fear of Mance. Except Lenny. They flirted in chemistry class most of the year until one day the flirting stopped, and he barely looked at her anymore. When she asked him about it, he said, "Ask Ellis."

That evening at the Kingdom, she did, running and catching up with him by the workshop as he walked home.

"What did you say to Lenny?"

"Nothing."

"He told me to ask you."

"I told him to leave you alone," he said, walking away.

CeCe ran and stopped in front of him, restricting his path. "It's bad enough that all the boys are afraid of Mance. Now you too? Why would you tell him to leave me alone?"

"Because I heard him tell some guys that he was going to finger you."

"And…" CeCe threw a shoulder. "So?"

"You want him to?"

"Yeah…maybe."

"Have you ever been fingered before?"

"No," CeCe said, sheepishly, embarrassed by her lack of sexual experience. She'd barely kissed a boy, when most of her friends and classmates were already having sex.

Ellis looked relieved before saying, "Good. Keep it that way."

"Good? Why is that good?"

"You're not ready," he said, walking away again.

"I am."

Ellis stopped and walked back to her quickly until her back hit the wall of the workshop. He inched his face closer, studying her, and when he found what he was looking for, he nodded.

"I'll do it."

"Do what?"

"Finger you."

Ellis didn't look away when he said it and CeCe wanted to laugh, but from the intense look on his face, she knew not to. He was serious. Then, she was insulted.

"Don't do me any favors."

He stuttered. "I'm…not. I want to."

"You do?"

"Yeah." The stoniness of his face softened.

"Because you don't want Lenny to or…"

"Because it should be me."

"Why?"

"You know why."

She did and her heart hammered in her chest because of it and of what she was going to say. "Okay."

"Okay?" He raised an eyebrow.

CeCe nodded, nervous but sure. Of him and what she wanted to do.

At this, Ellis nodded too and started walking home again.

"Where are you going?"

"Not here. Not now," he said over his shoulder. "Soon."

Soon came a week later when she found him waiting for her after school. He drove her to his family's trailer on the outskirts of the Kingdom. His father and mother were at work. She didn't know what to expect. He had a rough exterior; he got into fights along with Mance and possessed something of a short temper. But when they arrived at the trailer, he didn't rush. He cooked for her, a grilled cheese sandwich. Nothing special, but food tastes best when you don't have to prepare it. CeCe couldn't recall the last meal she ate that she didn't have to cook.

Afterward, they talked about school and CeCe realized it had never been just the two of them alone and she liked it. She wondered if he had changed his mind, but when he moved closer to her on the bed and laid her down, she knew the before was for her, to relax her. When he ran his finger down her cheek, he seemed like a different person. He had been with other girls, she knew. But she didn't expect his gentleness. She didn't expect him to kiss her, and when his moist lips pressed against hers, a shudder surged through her body. His hand inched down her stomach and then between her legs. Her breathing hitched and her body tensed. "Relax," he said, softly. "It won't hurt." Slowly, gently, the pads of his fingers grazed her folds and applied pressure. CeCe's stomach jerked and she moaned, a new sound to her ears. That would have been enough but when he inserted a finger and moved it in and out, she exploded. And when she opened her eyes, he was watching her, smiling, and enjoying her reaction.

They never discussed their rendezvous becoming a regular thing. But two days later, he picked her up again. And again, a week later. Every time he waited for her, his long body leaning against something, and it was the way he leaned, pumped with confidence and assurance of himself and how he made her feel. Every time she would catch a glint of his dark brown eyes and remember the way her body shivered in pleasure, the pulsing between her legs, and she followed him every time. Until time became a construct, and every time became the same time, and she could not distinguish one time from another.

When she asked him about sex, he rolled over and studied her for a minute just like he did before. "You're not ready" was all he said. And maybe she wasn't. Mostly, she didn't want to get pregnant. So, for once, she didn't challenge him. She was starting to understand that someone else knew her besides herself.

In his arms, on his bed, she experienced an awakening. A light turned on in a dark room.

Not just sexually.

There was no one else for her. For him either. Once they were alone, they belonged to each other, existed only for each other. They talked about their combined dream of becoming lawyers. They shared their secrets, too. Hers that she wanted to leave Diggs and never return. His that his father still hit his mother. At seventeen and eighteen years old, they were too young to mean that much to someone other than themselves. And yet. And yet. And yet.

Now, CeCe shakes away the memory and leaves Ellis's office, confident in a revised postfuneral plan: save the Kingdom, sell it, and as much as she could, stay the hell away from Ellis.

—

The first drop of blood falls before Junior knocks on Simon's door. He thinks of turning on his heels, but his heart won't listen. It never has. It lets in everything, and now it's wide open. It thumps in his chest, the rhythm hard and fast, the kind of pounding when it's no longer yours, when it beats for someone else, belongs to someone else. His hand lifts and knocks on the door.

Simon opens it a crack, enough to see Junior, but not enough to allow him in. "You shouldn't be here."

"You're not going to let me in?" Junior says, his voice muffled by the handkerchief. He forgets to be embarrassed that his nose is bleeding, how he must look to Simon.

"What are you doing here?"

"I wanted to see you," Junior says.

"You don't know what you want, and I'm tired of watching you try to figure it out."

Simon rolls his eyes and stares at Junior. He is poised and unruffled, unmoved by the sight. Junior has always appreciated this about Simon, his ability to stand in the moment and allow his emotions to speak his truth, to be one man with one emotion.

"I'm bleeding all over your front door." Junior looks down at the collection of drops dotting the floor.

Simon pushes the door open wider and heads toward the kitchen. Junior takes a few steps inside.

"Do you have something I can use to clean this up? I don't want it to dry."

"Leave it," Simon says over his shoulder. "I'll clean it up in a minute, after you leave."

Junior shuffles into the kitchen. It smells of cumin and ginger and tomatoes. He smiles.

"You made kingfish stew. It smells good." It was a family recipe, Junior learned over drinks on their first date, when Simon learned of Junior's real name. They laughed at the coincidence. Simon made it for him, here, on their fifth date. The taste touched his tongue, followed by Simon's soon after. Junior's body warms with the memory.

"Leftovers," Simon says, eyeing one empty bowl. "I made it for you a few days ago. I thought it would cheer you up after the funeral."

"Thank you," Junior says, lowering the handkerchief. The

blood is red and bold. He presses the handkerchief back to his nose.

"Why didn't you tell me these were so common for you? You never had one in the year we've been…" He stops. "Now two."

"It's stress induced. I haven't had one since we've been together because I'm at peace with you," Junior says, as if it mattered. He knows it will take more than this to appease Simon.

Simon's eyes soften. "Don't tilt your head back," he says, the edge in his tone blurred. "Isn't that what she said? You're not supposed to tilt your head back?"

Junior lowers his head to meet Simon's eyes, the warmth in them evident but wrapped in a coldness that seems to have increased since they met.

"You'll get sick if you swallow too much blood," Simon says in mock lament. "If you're going to come here, I should at least know how to stop these."

Junior reaches out to Simon. He needs to touch him, remember his warmth, but Simon cringes. He is stronger than Junior, and Junior realizes how much of that strength he draws from. How that strength fortifies him for days, weeks after they've been together, enriches the outer man to forge ahead, and tames the inner man enough to kiss Genesis, to sleep with her, to pretend.

"I'm sorry about that," Junior says, the handkerchief now in his hand. The blood has stopped.

"Are you? Sorry? Really?"

"You know that I am."

"No, I don't, Junior. I thought we had an arrangement. I thought we were going to give this a go. I thought she agreed."

"We do. We are. She did." Junior hears himself and realizes he's not making sense. Junior stops, refocuses. "I saw you at the church. Thank you for coming."

Simon wraps his arms around himself. "I would have stayed, but Genesis had that covered."

"She's my wife."

"Really, Junior? You don't think I know that?"

"She wanted to be there. Her and the girls."

Simon nods. "I wanted to be there for you too."

"There are some things that you don't understand."

Simon crosses his arms, his voice calmer than Junior deserves. "Then, please, enlighten me."

Junior falters. Anger he can handle. The truth is rarely evident in anger; it's hidden, buried beneath the inconsequential. Simon wants answers and Junior doesn't have them yet. "Everyone would be expecting her to be there."

"Of course," Simon says, matter-of-factly.

"We're still on a break." Junior doesn't believe the words himself. It isn't a lie, but it isn't entirely the truth either. There's more, much more, but he doesn't know how to say it.

Simon laughs. "Are you sure? Does she know that? Because it didn't look like it to me."

"She knows. She's playing her part."

"And what role am I playing? How do I fit into all of this? Into your life?"

"We're together."

"I hear you say that, and I don't believe you. Your family doesn't know I exist, and I want to meet them. I would have loved to meet King."

It's Junior's turn to draw back and Simon watches, silently, as the unease rolls through him, the inner man colliding with the outer man.

"There it is. The armor. What am I? Just your little fuck boy?"

Something breaks inside Junior. "That's below the belt."

"Why are you here? What did you want me to do? Bend over for you and make the pain of losing your father go away?"

"That's not it, and you know it. Don't belittle us. It's insulting."

"I'm not the one belittling us."

"You want to push me away? Well…I'm not going away. I thought we were in this together."

Simon draws back as if struck. "You are questioning my commitment? You're married! You have two daughters and a family who need you right now. There's no room for me. I'm in this alone."

"We're in this together. You're not alone."

"For the past year, I've waited for you. I wait for you to call. I wait for you to show up here. I wait for my turn."

"You know that's not true."

"Then tell me something, Junior. Something that will convince me that all of this isn't for nothing."

"You don't think I want to leave all this and be with you?" His voice sounds strange to his ears, too loud. He takes a deep breath to steady his breathing. He inches closer, finally touches Simon, his hand over his. "You are my one bright spot, my one comfort. The one thing that completely belongs to me and me only. With you, I don't have to be on my best behavior. I'm free."

"You can be free. Be the person I know you to be. They deserve to know the real you, all of you."

Junior pulls away at that thought, at all the things Simon doesn't know. "I can't. Not now."

"Why?"

"We're going to lose the house."

He tells Simon the whole story about being served notice of trespass papers and their meeting in Ellis's office. Simon listens, his brows moving up and down with understanding. His frustration has given way to something else—something less hostile. Junior sees it and is grateful for the change because for all the pain and frustration, he knows that Simon still cares.

"I can't believe he didn't have a will or a deed. I'm trapped. His dying was his final act of aggression," Junior says.

"You know that's not true."

"Who do you think is responsible for all of this now? For carrying on the family legacy?"

"It doesn't have to be you."

Junior chokes out a laugh. "*It does!*"

"You can walk away."

"My father lived his entire life for the Kingdom, for that land. I can't be the one who loses it."

"So, don't. Don't lose it. I'm sorry, Junior, I am. But you are not alone in this. You have your brother and sisters. You have an entire community."

"Do I have you?" Junior asks, a quiet heaviness filling his chest.

Simon shrugs. "I don't know."

Junior wraps his arms around Simon's waist and pulls him closer. "I need you," he whispers in his ear, to his neck, to his throat. With every whisper, Junior hears Simon's breath hitching, his body easing and answering the question.

"What are you going to do now?"

Junior sighs. "I have to meet with the lawyer for Malone & Kincaid. He's a friend of Genesis's father. She arranged the meeting."

Simon lets out an audible gasp and jerks away. "You must think I'm stupid."

"What? She's just helping me. This is my family's land. This is important. I would hope you would understand."

"Of course I understand, but I'm no fool. We've been here before. How is this any different?"

"It's different because when this is done, we can be together. I can be the man I want to be," Junior says, his voice calm and assuring.

Simon looks down, his head bowed, his hands in his pockets. He's moved to the other side of the kitchen, far from Junior's touch. A veil of exasperation cloaks his face. Something else drifts in the air between them, a wave of exhaustion, the letting go of something heavy, and it terrifies Junior.

"Please be patient with me a little while longer," Junior says as he retreats to the door. He's said too much. He needs to leave before he causes any more damage. "I'll call you in a few days."

Simon nods but doesn't look at him, doesn't say goodbye, just watches as the door closes between them.

Early in their relationship, goodbyes were hard. Now, as Junior walks away, all he thinks is how good Simon is at living in this repeated moment, every time showing less emotion. How easy he has made it for Simon to watch him leave.

Terrible thing to have family and still be alone. But Tokey won't be lonely tonight. She will have her brothers, her sister, and they will come together. Finally. She will make dinner and they will eat and talk, remember their lives together, remember King. It will be as it once was, better than it was. She wants to know them again and for them to know her. They need to. They have to save the house and the land.

Junior enters the kitchen just as Tokey spoons the last of the collard greens into a bowl. He's been sleeping in his old room since King died. They are trying it apart, he told Tokey, him and Genesis. He didn't tell her why or where he slept on the nights he didn't come home. There are a lot of half-truths regarding Junior. Today, he's been gone most of the day, probably to see Simon. Junior doesn't know that Tokey knows about Simon. But she has eyes and can see, and she can hear too. Once, she over-heard him on the phone and witnessed an interaction between them at school. Tokey never before considered that Junior could be gay, but she doesn't care who he loves. She just wants him to feel comfortable enough to tell her about it.

"Are you hungry? I cooked. I thought we could all eat together. As a family. It's been so long since," Tokey says, pushing all the words out at once. She wants to overwhelm him with words and guilt. Junior's mouth opens a crack. *No* sits on his tongue, the decline in the furrow of his brow, the rigidness of his shoulders. But he won't deny her. Junior has always been everything to everyone, trying to please them.

"Yeah, sure, of course," Junior says, moving to the sink to wash his hands. "What are we having?"

"Pork chops, collard greens, cornbread."

Junior grabs a stack of plates and sets them around the table. He glances at King's chair, his place. He hesitates for a beat and skips it. "You cooked all that? You didn't have to do all that. There's plenty of leftovers." It took two full days for visitors to stop showing up, offloading bags of food. It's what they needed to do. How they relieved themselves of their grief.

The back screen door screeches open and slams once with a whack. Mance enters and stops at the sight.

"What's going on?" Mance asks, a statue in the doorway, his eyes scanning the table.

"Tokey made dinner for us," Junior says.

"Why? There's plenty of leftovers."

"I thought we could all eat together." Tokey places a small salad in the spot where she will eat.

"I'm not hungry," Mance mumbles, wiping his boots against

the mat and taking a step toward the living room. He's covered in sawdust, smells of it; it lies on him light like snow, falls off him as he moves. Since King died, he's practically lived in the workshop, filling orders, finishing the columns. Tokey knows that Mance feels responsible for the Kingdom now, but there's something else: Henry.

"Please, Mance."

Mance glances at Junior who makes an encouraging gesture with his head that falls between a nod and a shake and points at the table.

They haven't said the words, haven't asked what happened at the funeral, but it is clear from the look on both their faces that they want to appease her.

"It better not be any of that healthy shit," Mance says, stepping back into the kitchen.

"It's not," Tokey says. "Now wash your hands."

Mance dries his hands and places one on King's chair. It's pushed all the way in at the table. He pats it twice before sitting in the chair next to it just as CeCe enters the kitchen. Her eyes dart to Mance to Junior and finally to Tokey.

"Y'all weren't going to invite me to dinner?" She's casually dressed in yoga pants and an oversized shirt that hangs off her shoulders, her hair in a low ponytail, makeup at a minimum.

"We all just got here," Junior says, pulling out a chair next to him, where CeCe sat growing up.

CeCe looks skeptical but eases into the chair and sits anyway. "Leftovers?"

"No, I cooked. Junior, would you like to say grace?" Tokey asks when they've all sat.

It's a job that belonged to the head of the family, King, and they all instinctively look at his empty place at the table. Junior swallows hard and blesses the food. A chorus of muffled amens rings out.

They eat in a stillness that unwinds and grows between them. They are there in the heavy air, the words, the discussion they need to share, but no one knows how to start.

A family would be able to say the words that need to be said. Tokey stabs at her salad and looks at her siblings. They look like a family. They share the same blood, but are they a family? Are you only a family because you are bound by blood? Ellis wasn't born into this family and yet they consider him to be an honorary brother. Are you still family if you don't know each other anymore? Are you still family if you don't know the whole story?

"I thought the girls looked so cute at the funeral, Junior," Tokey says. "It's been a while since I've seen them. They are getting so big."

Her voice lifts their heads, and their eyes drift from their plates to each other. Junior nods and takes a long sip of water.

She looks at him searchingly and waits, blinks once, twice.

"Henry is so precious," Tokey says, turning to Mance. "Those fat little cheeks. I can just eat him up."

Mance grunts and pushes his food around before scooping up a bite of collard greens.

"Did you get the test results back?" Tokey asks.

CeCe and Junior look at Mance. "Test results?" CeCe asks.

Mance raises his brows and looks at Tokey, a hurt passing over his face. He looks back at his food before shaking his head, the move nearly imperceptible.

"I'm sorry," Tokey says, and reaches over to lay a hand on Mance's; it feels too much like King's.

"Sorry about what? What test results?" CeCe asks again.

Mance doesn't look up again, doesn't take another bite.

"Henry...he's deaf," Tokey says.

"My nephew is deaf? And no one was going to tell me?"

Junior sighs. "They just found out, CeCe."

"And no one was going to tell me?"

"Don't make this about you, CeCe," Tokey says.

"Don't do that, Tokey," CeCe says. "You don't think I have a right to know what's going on with my nephew?"

"You would know if you came home," Tokey mumbles.

"I'm here now."

"And why is that?" Tokey asks, straightening, her shoulders rolling back.

CeCe drops her fork on her plate, and it rings loud. "Here we go. Don't do that. Don't try to turn this around on me. You've had it out for me since I got here."

"Because you're hiding something, and I want to know what it is."

"I'm hiding something? You think I'm hiding something?"

"Yes."

"Looks to me like we are all hiding something."

"That's enough, CeCe," Junior says.

"No, Junior. She started it," CeCe says.

"She's been through a lot."

"Haven't we all?" CeCe snaps.

"I just want us to talk. Is that so wrong?" Tokey asks. "We don't know each other anymore."

Another silence. It angers her to believe that they could be such strangers.

"No one has anything to say? Our father dies, and we can possibly lose this land, this house, and we have nothing to say to each other?"

They sit for a moment, eyeing each other. A clock ticks on the wall. The refrigerator kicks on.

"CeCe, do you know why Junior is back in his old room and not with his wife and daughters? Mance, do you know why CeCe is still here? Junior, did you know that Mance proposed to Lisha and she won't accept?"

"You don't know what you're talking about," Mance says, his voice a warning.

"What's your point, Tokey?" Junior asks.

"My point is that it's time for us to tell the truth."

"About what?" Junior asks.

"Who we are. The people we've become."

"Let's do that," CeCe says. "You go first. Since you seem to be airing everyone's dirty laundry. What's yours?"

"How about you go first? Tell us why you are really here."

Junior looks at CeCe, and Mance stops eating, the fork in his hand suspended.

"I told you. I'm here to bury King."

"He's buried. Why are you still here? How much money do you need?"

"You don't want me here. I get it. But he was my daddy too. And I have every right to be here."

"And when's the last time you were here? Miss Big City Woman. New York City. Too good to come home. What? Are we not good enough for you?"

Junior's jaw flexes. "Is it true?"

"Is what true?"

"Are you here for money?" Junior asks.

"There is no money, so how can I be here for money?" CeCe says, lacing her fingers. "So was that what this dinner was all about? You trying to out me? I'll play along."

"CeCe…"

"She's not a baby anymore." CeCe laughs. "We can all see that. Don't sit here and act like you haven't noticed the weight gain, the cake wrappers in the trash. Yeah…she's definitely not a baby anymore."

Tokey slumps in her chair. Her whole body quivers with sadness and disappointment. The stinging of tears threatens as she rubs at her forearms in long careful strokes. What is she doing, thinking she can bring them all together? Another long silence stretches again before anyone speaks. When she does, finally, her voice arrives small. "I just wanted us to come together. Put our heads together—remember when we used to do that? We haven't done it once. Not together. It's what King would have wanted."

They know this is true. They know it deep in places they don't talk about.

"We were close once. What happened?"

"We went and lived our own lives," CeCe says.

"And what lives those are," Junior says, his tone barely a whisper.

"Excuse me?" CeCe says.

"He said, 'What lives those are,'" Mance says, his deep voice controlled, even.

There it is, the truth, all of it, open, raw, and exposed. They all feel it, the truth choking them. There's no denying it now.

CeCe's face clouds, and Mance looks to the ground. Tokey stares blankly.

Junior clears his throat and forces his face into a calm arrangement despite the movement of his eyes. "If there's one thing we can all agree on, it's that we are not losing this house. Right?" He holds everyone's stare—Mance's, Tokey's, and CeCe's—but, one by one, they all drop away too quickly. "Let's just stay focused. Everyone do their part, and meet back up when we all have something to report."

⊢—

Mance's fist hovers inches from the door. It's late; he's hesitant to knock and to wake up Henry. Then he remembers. He always remembers when he doesn't expect it, and he wonders how he'll adjust, when he'll remember once and for all that his son is deaf.

He knocks on the door and Lisha opens it a crack, the door splitting her body in half, and stares at him for a second. He takes a tiny step toward her and gently touches a finger to her chin.

"Hey."

"Hey."

This is their ritual. Him never knowing what to say and her finding the words anyway.

"Can I see him?"

Lisha opens the door the rest of the way. "Sure, but he's already asleep."

She's back at her spot on the couch, her legs curled, a book in her lap, by the time he reaches the cozy living room. It's a small place that suits her well enough, but he doesn't fit here; he's too big for the space, his body too hefty, like another piece of furniture, too long for the doorframes. He doesn't mind his discomfort, but he doesn't want her or Henry to get comfortable here. This is not their permanent home.

"You could just use your key," Lisha says.

Mance looks around. "It doesn't feel right. I don't live here."

"You pay all the bills here. This is practically your house too."

Mance would never live in such a house, he thinks, remembering when Earl showed it to him. Ill-conceived. Cheaply constructed. Too many cut corners. "Can I…just look in on him?"

"Of course, but if you wake him," she says, turning a page, "you have to put him back down."

Mance hears Henry before his eyes adjust to the dark. It is the sound of life, his breathing. It's shallow, light, barely audible, but Mance hears it, mimics his son's breaths with his own. His heart expands and contracts when he sees Henry, asleep on his back, his tiny fists at his ears. The sensation fills him with warmth: here is something he made. He didn't know love could feel different, that it isn't the same formula for all. With Henry, it's raw and unwavering; it presses and snakes through him. It makes its own space within his body, creates its own path, and finds a home in his heart.

Mance reaches out, his hand hovering above Henry's stomach, and thinks about a life of protecting him and loving him, creating a world and environment for him to thrive in. He can't help but think of his own father and how he provided for him, cared for him, taught him.

Mance would do the same for Henry. Because that's what fathers do. They protect. They love. And they fight.

I won't.

Those were the two words he whispered to King at his funeral. He won't let them take the Kingdom and Henry's future. "I won't," Mance says aloud to the dark, to a sleeping Henry. The words sound shallow in the nursery, but they stretch their way around. He makes Henry and King the same promise, the heaviness of it rolling in like thunder. Mance slides a finger inside Henry's palm, and he clutches it instinctively, wraps his tiny fingers around it, his grip strong. Mance only sees Lisha in Henry's face, but in this grip, Henry's very much him. A fighter.

In the living room, Lisha stretches across the couch reading. She's always reading, never too far from a book, always lost in a fictional world. Mance glances at the wall of custom bookshelves he surprised her with for her birthday and remembers thinking it would take a lifetime to fill the shelves with books. Now, he smiles at his ignorance and the tiny remaining space there.

"What are you reading?" Mance asks, leaning against one of the flimsy doorframes.

Lisha looks up and back down at her book. "Don't do that. Don't lean."

"I can't lean now?" Mance says with a grin.

"No," she says, her dimples appearing, her cheekbones lifting, without looking up. "Is he still asleep?"

Her mood is playful, considering the last time they saw each other. But Mance ignores it, allows his smile to fall. He knows better than to try to replicate what happened in the workshop or mention the proposal. She's made her position as clear as water. He has work to do. Work he now knows he can't do yet.

"Yeah…" Mance says. The house buzzes with silence, except the ping of drops from the kitchen faucet. Mance angles his ear toward the kitchen and hears it again, drops of water in rapid succession. "How long has it been doing that?"

Lisha closes her book. "Mance, don't fix it. It's fine."

But he is already two steps into the kitchen, already at the empty sink, his face inches from the faucet. A single drop of water forms and splats into the sink. He tries tightening the faucet, but the water continues to drip. He opens the cabinet door and inspects the pipes before wriggling his torso inside.

"Can you hand—" Before he finishes, Lisha extends a monkey wrench in his direction and kneels at his feet. He smiles at her ability to always know and hopes she'll be understanding when he tells her. One more time.

"Earl know about this faucet?" He attaches the wrench to the pipe.

"No, I haven't told him because it's no big deal. I don't even hear…" She stops, realizing. Mance realizes it too, a twinge ripples in his chest.

"You don't have to do this."

"You know I do," he says, his hands moving.

He has to do something. The labor of his hands is all that he has to prove himself to the world. To keep his promises to King and Henry. To provide for her.

"Are you ready to talk about it?" Lisha asks.

"Talk about what?"

"What happened at the doctor's office? With Lou at the funeral?"

"What's there to talk about?"

"There's so much to talk about."

"It's who I am."

"I know. But you've changed, right?"

"No, I haven't changed. I'm the same person I've always been. The same person you fell in love with."

Mance's honest admission surprises Lisha, and her eyebrows lift ever so slightly. "What does that mean? Does it mean that you're not even going to try?"

"It means I can't be that man. Not right now. Not yet."

Lisha stands. "Come out and look at me."

Mance finishes unscrewing the pipe and water bubbles out, splashing on him. He stands, and Lisha hands him a towel from the sink. He dries off before looking inside the pipe. He picks out a bent cylinder of metal with his knife.

"The washer is worn. I'll get Earl to put a new one on, but I gotta turn your water off until it's fixed."

"Forget the washer, Mance. Tell me what's going on."

Mance sighs and leans back against the sink. "They're trying to take the land."

"Who's trying to take the land?"

"Some company out of Charlotte."

"How can they do that?"

"We don't know. We got a letter the day of the funeral telling us that we have less than two weeks to vacate the premises."

Lisha draws back. "What? Just like that?"

Mance opens his mouth, as if he wants to say something, but he's out of words that can convey his anger. He twists and wrings the pipe in his hand.

"What are you guys going to do?"

He tells her of their visit to Ellis's office and their roles. He deliberately omits his.

Lisha notices. "And what do you have to do?"

He looks at his feet and back at her. "I'm going to see Uncle Shad."

Lisha shakes her head. "No, that's not good for you."

"I don't have a choice. They are going to take the Kingdom. Everything that King worked for, everything that I have worked for. My entire life. Gone. My future, our future, gone."

"And what does Uncle Shad have to do with this?"

"We're not sure, but Ellis thinks he could know something about it."

Lisha mumbles something under her breath. "And what are you going to do?"

"I don't know," Mance says, his voice small.

"You know your history with him. You can't go see him."

"I have to. I'm the only one," he says, his eyes on everything but Lisha's.

"Why does it have to be you? Why does it always have to be you?"

"You know why."

"You can be the man who bends, Mance." She's in his space now, on her toes, stretching higher, with her hands on his chest. "You can be that man. There's no harm in it."

He refuses to meet her eyes. She could turn off his mind or start it. She wielded that kind of power. And yet it wasn't enough to break a son's promise to his father, or a father's promise to his son.

Mance steps away, and Lisha crosses her arms. "Nothing

good can come of this," she says to his back. "Your father couldn't talk to him. You think you're going to be able to?"

"I have to try."

"What about Henry?"

Mance doesn't say anything on the way to the door. Lisha follows in silence. From behind, he feels her unease pushing against his back like hands. At the door, he doesn't want to turn to her, to see it all in her eyes.

Instead, he pushes his lips against the top of her head and says, "This is for Henry."

FIVE

———

JUNIOR TURNS HIS KEY and pushes open the front door. He enters the foyer and stands, taking in the sounds and smells of the house. The air pulses heavily, moving as if it were alive. It's quiet and loud, too early for the commotion that accompanies two rambunctious girls, his absence too loud a presence within him.

He's been away for two weeks, and he feels like a stranger in his own home. Two new pairs of shoes sit by the door. A new glass bowl holds mail and keys. A new gold-plated mirror over the foyer table. There's a newness here.

Or maybe the newness lies deep within him. Maybe the shoes, the bowl have always been there, but he was too distracted to notice, or even care.

He thinks not only of his recent absence, but the slowly regressing one: the first gray hair that blooms into a headful, the first raindrop of a summer storm, the one that started just after Julia's birth, weeks after he met Simon. He only noticed it a few years ago, and he wonders if the girls have noticed. Genesis did. And maybe they did, too.

Junior was born with so much love and nowhere to apply it. So, he gave it away. First, to Genesis. Then, to his girls. In turn, he found love and acceptance. He found love in their smiles, their long eyelashes, their imaginary tea parties.

The idea of being anything less than a great father weakens Junior. He's made some mistakes and then some, but raising his girls is the one thing he did right. He's more hands on than most, brushing hair and oiling scalps. He couldn't have made it this long without them. They are his purpose, his reason for living when he didn't know he had one.

He'll make the girls their favorite breakfast: chocolate chip pancakes with whipped cream smiley faces. They will awaken to the smells wafting through the air, and they will know that Daddy is home. They will tumble down the stairs and burst into the kitchen, still wearing their pajamas, sleep still in their eyes. It's the least he can do, act the part of their father, try to be the dad they remember.

Sure enough, thirty minutes later, Junior hears the rumble of feet padding down the stairs.

"Daddy!" they shout in unison when they see him.

He kisses them on their foreheads and cheeks and all over their faces. They giggle and so does he. "Daddy missed you girls so much."

Genesis enters the kitchen, but Junior doesn't look at her. His attention remains on the girls, the next pancake on the griddle to be flipped. Even without looking at her, he can read her thoughts, a gift of a decade of togetherness. She pours herself a cup of coffee, slides into her chair at the kitchen table, and gazes at Junior steadily as the girls climb into their seats.

Junior piles two pancakes on each of their plates, and Julia immediately reaches for the syrup. But Julia doesn't move; she just stares at the steam rising and disappearing into the air.

"What's wrong? Why aren't you eating? Dig in."

She peeks up at him, her lips pursed, her small face clenched, holding a worry she has not yet revealed. She drops her head and shakes it once, twice.

"Come on...you can talk to Daddy," Junior says, kneeling beside her and lifting her chin with his finger. "Tell me, what's wrong?"

Julia looks away, and Junior touches her cheek just as a tear courses down her face and another one chases it. Finally, she begins to speak, the words disjointed, her voice barely a whisper. "Erica says...you and Mommy..." she mutters, "are... getting a divorce."

It's such a big word out of her tiny mouth. It shocks him.

Seconds tick by. Junior looks to Genesis, who takes and processes this news in silence. A veil of emotion, both her disappointment and her satisfaction but not the details of each, cloaks her face. He wonders what his expression is conveying to her.

Junior is here because he has been away from his children too long, but also because Genesis made another demand.

Genesis sprang into action when Junior called and told her

about the eviction notice. Junior was in the middle of a sentence when she hung up. Five minutes later, she called back. She'd called her father. James Reid rules his corner of Diggs from his place as a prominent investor. He's made a name for himself in farming, one of a few Black men to do so, and leveled up to purchasing and investing in real estate, helping Black farmers sell their land for record profits.

Ten minutes later, they had a meeting scheduled with Malone & Kincaid, a meeting she insisted on attending. "I'll handle everything," she said. "Just come home."

The first part was easy.

The second part was not.

This is what Genesis wanted for him, Junior knows—to bear the consequences of his actions. So she says nothing, doesn't intervene. He must be careful not to push her away. Because he needs her today, for this and so much more. She knows this too.

"How do you even know what that means?" Junior finally asks Julia, swallowing back the tears that threaten.

Erica flings her fork back and forth, hand to hand, her eyes watching its movement. Though she looks more like Junior than Julia does, she embodies Genesis's interior life. Hard. Slow to show emotion.

"Sara-Beth's parents are getting a divorce. She told us. Her daddy moved out and never came back." Tears flood Julia's eyes. "Are you not coming back, Daddy? Please come back." The tears fall just as his do, easily and freely.

It's enough to knock a person backward, the tears of a child.

He can take it all, his pain, his hurt, his lie, for himself, on himself, but he can't bear witnessing her pain. Junior pulls her into his lap, his body twisting to absorb her sadness, and relishes the press of her warm body, wiping the tears away. His impulse, always, is to fold into himself. But he can't. He has an audience.

"Daddy's been at the Kingdom with Aunt Tokey and Aunt CeCe and Uncle Mance after King died."

"Are you going to die too, Daddy?" Julia asks. "Like Grandpa King?"

"Oh no, baby. I'm not going to die."

"When are you coming home?" It's Erica's turn for questions, her hard interior cracking around the edges. "You've been gone for twelve whole days."

There it is. The impact of his decision. His failure as a father realized and numbered. He thought he had it all figured out. A pause on his marriage but not on his obligations as a father. He would pick them up from school and take them to dance class, help them with their homework, and tuck them in at night. They have a routine, and he wanted to keep it. He didn't expect this, his daughters crying over pancakes, counting the days of his absence.

Not for the first time, he wishes he were enough. That being here, married to Genesis, father to two girls, was enough.

But he can't be enough.

He doesn't even know what that means.

He reaches for Erica too, pulling her into him, and cuts his eyes to Genesis. She knew this would happen, possibly orchestrated it somehow. His whole body trembles with anger and sadness. It isn't fair for him to face this alone. Maybe she even knows this too. But this is how she will repay him for her hurt. Every second of silence, every tear that falls, is a finger pressed in a raw wound and his punishment for the pause with Simon.

Junior draws the girls closer and touches his forehead to each of theirs and says, "I will come home very, very soon, okay? I promise."

Junior knows better than to make such a promise, especially to kids. Promises are meant to be broken, especially this one. But he has to say something to comfort them, and himself.

An hour later, Junior and Genesis pull out of the driveway and head toward Charlotte. He placated Erica and Julia enough that by the end of breakfast, their smiles returned. Junior appreciates children's ability to bounce off all that hurt them.

"You promised the girls you were coming home very soon," Genesis says, crossing her legs and turning toward him. It has always baffled him that she does this, cross her legs in a car, her inability to relax. "You shouldn't make promises that you are not going to keep."

"What was I supposed to say?"

"I don't know, Junior. How about the truth?" Her tone rises higher and tighter.

"The truth, huh? So...tell them that we agreed that Daddy could see his boyfriend for a month. That truth? That's what you want me to tell them?"

Boyfriend. The word pushes off Junior's tongue with force, and when it reaches Genesis's ears, her body visibly bends as though being crushed.

"He's not your boyfriend."

"He is."

"No, he's not, because you have a wife and two daughters. A married man cannot have a boyfriend."

"You've known this about me. You knew and yet you went along with it."

"I thought you would grow out of it. That it was just a phase."

"It's not a phase. It's who I am. You are going to have to accept that."

Genesis closes her eyes and draws a deep breath. This is how she processes tough information; she draws it in and allows it to settle within her and expand until she must respond.

"If this is who you are, then you must accept the consequences of being you."

"What does that mean?"

"I wonder how the school board would react learning that their principal is…" She doesn't say the word. It's poison on her tongue. "And what about the family? Do they know about your 'boyfriend'?" Junior can almost see the air quotes around the word. "What would they think? I don't think any of that would go over too well."

Junior's chest tightens. This is not her first time threatening any of this, and it doesn't affect him any less than it did the first time. But he can't give her another bullet to load into the gun and fire at him. "I'm prepared for that," Junior exhales, the statement caught between the truth and a lie. They both know well enough that it is a lie that neither are prepared to handle. The truth would expose too much for both of them.

"Daddy called in a favor to get you this meeting." Genesis is pivoting the conversation while still keeping it tethered to how much Junior owes her.

Junior has never liked Mr. James, as the man insists everyone call him, and he suspects Mr. James has never liked him. They carried on with a cordialness that neither poked at. No one is good enough for Genesis, especially not the land-rich, cash-poor Solomons, who bartered and built things for survival.

"Why did you agree to help me? Why do you even want to be with me?"

"I love you, Junior. I always have, through good times and bad times. This too shall pass." The absence of judgment jars him, and he's not sure if she's referring to helping with the land or their marriage.

"What's in it for you?" Junior says, studying her expression, the set of her shoulders and the straight line of her mouth, waiting for more. There's always more.

"My marriage."

So, it really was just that. Genesis's upbringing differed from Junior's. She lived a privileged life compared to his, attending the best private schools in Charlotte, living in a custom-built house on twenty acres in the country, a wardrobe full of clothes purchased in boutique shops in Charlotte instead of the local JCPenney's. The men in her family worked and the women stayed home. Her brother followed in his father's footsteps, graduating from UNC and immediately going to work with his father, acquiring and purchasing real estate. Genesis understood her fate early—her mom made sure of it, raising her to care for others, her role as a mother deeply ingrained in her since infancy. She would be a wife and a mother and nothing else. Just like her mom. Junior often wondered how she accepted her fate so early when he ran from his so quickly.

"Is that why you agreed to the monthlong separation? Because you think these are normal bad times?"

She reaches over and places her hand on his knee. This used to mean something, used to evoke a physical sensation within, but now it's a weight. He has long stopped being sexually attracted to her, except one last time, a few weeks before the pause. That night, Genesis rolled over, slid her hand down his pajama bottoms, and climbed on top of him. Before that, he cannot recall the last time they made love. He wanted to be fair to her. But to her, sex fell squarely within her wifely duties.

"Every marriage has them. It's our turn. We will get through this."

Junior knows she feels the lie as much as he does, but she pretends, just as he does, that the lie connects them, begging them to push back against it, but the moment passes as fast as the scenery outside.

Junior sighs, trying to make sense of it. He's always lived

his life off-balance, and yet recent events have shifted his equilibrium unlike before. Crawling back to Genesis and her father, the painful breakfast with Julia and Erica, the uncertainty of the land and his role in saving it, Simon's silence. Maybe it's all a sign that the future he allowed himself to dream of isn't possible.

Junior has gotten good at losing and at compromising. He lost the role of favorite son. He compromises his one truth and cooperates in a marriage that no longer serves him. But if there's one area where he wins, it's fatherhood.

He's not ready to fail at being a father.

He makes a clumsy effort to hold her hand and keeps his voice casual.

"We will."

—

"It's a beautiful day," Ellis says as he pulls out of the driveway of the Kingdom and onto the highway that will take them to Charlotte. "I love the spring, the rain, the green. The wildflowers should be out by now."

CeCe casts a glance at the sky but doesn't take it in. It's just there as it always is. Soon the wildflowers come into view. She remembers the North Carolina Department of Transportation's plan to beautify the highways by planting beds of wildflowers, back when she still lived at the Kingdom. It keeps happening, memories of King bubbling to the surface, him appearing before her. It has been her habit to shake them away. But this one—this one she keeps and allows to play.

"Waste of money if you ask me," King said. Then he saw the highways in bloom and understood. CeCe loved them immediately, the bold colors, the shapes, the way they moved in the wind, and even convinced King to let her plant a bed on the Kingdom. A fresh bouquet of purple rocket larkspurs, her favorite, sat at the kitchen table from spring to fall.

CeCe stays quiet about her memory. She has resolved that silence and stoicism are best, especially when it comes to Ellis. If she speaks too much, he will truly know everything.

"Don't tell me you haven't missed this sky."

"It's all the same," she says, after a long beat. She watches the scenery change again. "It's the same sky everywhere."

"Nah, not here," he says, angling his neck to look up through the windshield. "I missed this sky every day while in Atlanta. I swore I would never take it for granted again. I swore I would see it."

"How much longer until we get there?" She slides on her oversized sunglasses to block out the colors, the sky, the sun, and hopefully Ellis.

"Two hours."

"Two hours? Did they move Charlotte while I was gone?"

He chuckles. "Tell me about New York." He adjusts his position in his seat, leaning back, settling in for the drive, one arm on the wheel.

"There's nothing to tell." CeCe turns her head even further out the window. She can smell him. Not his cologne or aftershave. The other smell, the scent you know from being up close and personal with someone. With Ellis, it's found at its strongest at the base of his neck. She remembers that spot, where she tucked inside him when they were standing, where she laid her head when they were lying down.

CeCe shakes away the thought. These memories have no place here. "It's a city. Lots of people."

She feels him slide a look at her before turning back to the road. "Lots of people? It's a city? Great description. I can see it clearly now."

"We don't have to do this, you know?"

"Do what?"

"Talk. We can just go to Charlotte and speak to these people and come back. We don't have to talk."

"We could. We could sit here in silence the rest of the way to Charlotte. Or we could catch up because it's been a couple of years since we've seen each other."

"And that implies…"

"It implies that I'd like to know what you've been doing. Do you still bake?" Ellis moans. "Those biscuits and butter you used to make. Your pies."

CeCe cringes at the idea of her hands kneading dough. "Ugh, no." She frowns and checks her phone. "Why would I do that?"

"Because you were good at it."

"I'm good at being a lawyer."

"So what have you been doing?"

"I've been working. That's what I've been doing."

She can feel his eyes on her.

"You know what? You're right. We don't have to talk." He reaches for the radio knob and turns it. Static fills the air. "What would you like to listen to?"

"Whatever. It's your truck."

"That doesn't matter."

"You are the one insisting we listen to the radio."

"And I'm asking what you would like to listen to."

"Just pick."

"Must you always?"

"What?"

"Be so difficult."

"Difficult? I'm being difficult."

"Yes."

"Tell me how I'm being difficult."

"I ask you about New York and you say, 'It's a city. Lots of people.' I ask you what you want to listen to on the radio. You say, 'Whatever.'" He mocks.

"What would you like me to say?"

"The truth."

"That is the truth. I don't care what we listen to, and New York is a city with lots of people."

Ellis huffs and continues turning the radio dial.

She angles her body toward him. "Fine. What do you want to talk about?"

"Never mind. Just keep gawking at your phone."

"I'm not gawking at my phone."

"You've checked that phone ten times since we've left. Are you expecting a call from your boyfriend from the city with lots of people?"

"Maybe. Are you jealous?"

"I could never be jealous of a man from New York City."

"Because men from Diggs are so much better."

"I am."

She knows this to be true.

With Ellis, she saw her future and it frightened her. She closed her eyes and saw her house on the edge of the Kingdom, a small nondescript house, built by her brothers and King. She saw her children, three of them, playing on the grounds of the Kingdom. Her body plumped and full from the pregnancies and a lifestyle that didn't demand anything better. She saw her husband, Ellis, the least regrettable part of the dream, and she would kiss him goodbye as he left for work. She was better than this future, so she left for college, putting her plan in motion and missing out on an opportunity to know how good they could be together.

After their college graduation, the summer before they started law school, her at UNC, Ellis at Duke, they'd both come home for Junior's wedding at the Kingdom. She saw Ellis right away.

It has always been easy to recognize Ellis and Mance in a crowd, their heads poking above everyone else's, their presence like waves, drawing people to them or pushing them away. Ellis looked fresh—white shirt, rolled-up sleeves, and a pair of cargo khakis—a preppy look influenced by Duke, and CeCe liked it on him; it matched her perception of the man she knew he could be. They made eye contact and both instinctively smiled, his a broad one that stopped the world. No, it restarted it for her—the world she walked away from started turning once again. By then, CeCe had kissed her share of men and had given parts of herself to them too, but when Ellis hugged her, a shockwave rocked her body.

It was absurd. She had no reason to believe that feelings could lie dormant and rematerialize with one look, one touch. But hours later, when she couldn't shake the hum of electricity, when her eyes kept finding him in the crowd with glaring accuracy, she realized it was true. Feelings don't die. They wait. They stew and grow and surge back bigger, better, stronger than before. They demand to be felt.

After the wedding, he walked CeCe to her room. Their eyes lingered a bit too long, and in one step, Ellis closed the space between them. But it was CeCe who kissed him, who rose onto her toes and pressed her lips against his. It surprised her, the need to kiss him, and how much she wanted to, how soft his lips were, how much the kiss shredded layers of fight and loosened the knot she had tied between them. It was Ellis who continued the kiss, pulling her into him, who lifted her arms and removed her shirt and bra, who exposed her bare breasts to the air and pushed her skirt down, then her panties. It startled her how well their bodies fit together, like pieces of a puzzle, how easily her lips produced and released soft moans. Of everything she felt, she felt the sense of rightness, the surety of him, and the feelings she had tried to bury.

She opened her eyes, and he was watching her. There was nothing else. No one else, just them. She whispered his name and he hers and the moment became too big for her. It would take her time to make sense of it all and, even now, she still doesn't understand how it's possible to feel this way. There's only one explanation for it, one she was too afraid to admit in that moment. So instead, she closed her eyes and enjoyed the way her body surrendered to his, and to itself, once again.

Afterward, CeCe lay on top of him, her body thrumming, their legs, arms, and fingers intertwined, realizing they had crossed a line in their relationship from which there was no return. And when Ellis reached for her again, when he was inside her again, when the pacing of their movements increased again, she realized one hard and unavoidable fact.

She was absolutely and unmistakably in love with him.

Except.

She couldn't love Ellis, couldn't love a boy from Diggs.

She had a plan. She had a goddamn plan. Ellis was not part of it. So, she left. Again. She didn't call. Neither did he. She was grateful he didn't, preventing any awkwardness and preserving their night as a comma between them.

Now, CeCe clears her throat. "Well…no. A colleague may call, and I don't want to miss it. But there's no boyfriend."

There were men and sex. Probably too much sex. She was searching for something, something she lost and could not find again, a feeling. She found it once; she could find it again. It was only later that she realized it was as much about the person as the act itself. For their own pleasure, the men were all too eager to help her search for it. For her own pleasure, she'd close her eyes and Ellis would be there, just a thought away, and she would hook onto a memory of him. Ellis towering over her. Ellis kissing her. Ellis touching her. When she was alone, she would touch her breasts as he had and reach between her legs and rub as he had and make herself come over and over again as he had. Until her mind emptied of him. Until tomorrow. Always tomorrow.

Ellis nods.

"Since you want to catch up...tell me why you moved back to Diggs."

Ellis shakes his head. "Oh no. I'm not sharing until you do."

"Unbelievable. You are exactly the same. Has nothing changed?"

"I'm the same man you've always known. It's you who's changed."

"I've been here less than a week and you can already tell I've changed?"

"From the moment I saw you at the grave site."

"Oh...and I'm surprised it has taken you this long to call me out on it. Please hold back no more—enlighten me with your wisdom."

"You're hiding something. Like the time we broke that window and tried to hide it from King. Like the time Mama almost caught us..." He stops. Finally, Ellis clears his throat. "You have the same look on your face now that you had those times."

This is exactly the reason why she wanted to remain silent.

But now she remembers that words don't matter. Ellis has glasses to her soul and could always see into it so clearly.

"You used to love these wildflowers. Made me drive damn-near to the mountains so you could get a bouquet of…what's that flower called?"—he snaps his fingers twice, remembering—"Butter and eggs. And now you're acting like you don't see them. What's wrong with you? Whatever it is, you can tell me."

CeCe's face warms. She swallows hard and thinks of a redirect. She can't let on just how accurate his words are. Mark reacted to softness, but Ellis would see right through it. Pieces of the truth would work. "I'm fine. I'm just nervous about what we're going to find out. We can't lose the Kingdom."

Ellis sighs away his frustration in one long breath. "I know. I've been reading up on heir property, and there's so much to it. But we're not going to let these fuckers take the Kingdom. Do you hear me?"

He looks at her and reaches out; his hand hovers just above her knee, then returns to the steering wheel. He wants to touch her, lay a calming hand across hers, but like CeCe, he's stubborn enough to mean what he says: he promised at King's grave not to touch her, in any way, until she asks him to. So instead, he talks about his friend, the lawyer they will meet, and his record and experience with real estate law.

"Everything is going to work out. I promise."

Most would call it confidence, but, more than that, it was that he'd driven on the road to hell, and every other road was heaven.

Ellis turns the radio tuner again. As the static throbs around them, she feels the comma between them hooking her closer to him. But something else too. He could help her. She could just say the words, *I'm in trouble*, and he would help.

He would understand. Ellis has seen the worst in people, experienced it firsthand in his own blood. Nothing could be worse than that. After King's visit, his father never touched him again, but he kept hitting Ellis's mother. It was less frequent, and when Ellis's voice dropped and he could look his father square in the eye, it stopped altogether, except for one last time—one stab wound—after which his father left forever.

"Ellis," CeCe says, her voice soft, lighter than it has been.

He hears it too, the tenderness of his name, and looks at her. "Yeah."

The words sit on the tip of her tongue waiting to jump. But as he smiles at her, the words slip back in. Under his gaze, she blossoms, even if she refuses his light. There is still something between them and she can see it now for them both; she can feel it raging in her heart. Because all those years ago, they were too young to realize that they loved each other. That those feelings meant something bigger than either of them could imagine. Because no one tells you what love feels like, this kind of love, the love that sets you on fire, that burns your insides, a love that's not easily extinguished.

CeCe realizes that Ellis cannot know this, the worst thing about her, and see her differently. She would lose him, and she couldn't lose anything else. No one else.

She turns back to the window, watching the way the wild-flowers bloom under the sunlight, and says, "Nothing."

Mance flexes his right hand once and glances at the hardened scab from the cut he sustained the day of King's funeral. It'll be ripped open again by the end of this visit, he knows, and he wonders if it will ever heal once and for all. If he will allow it to heal. He's going to need his hands, to build things, to hold Lisha. And he knows, as he makes a fist and sees in it the sign for *S*, to speak to Henry.

He's going alone to visit Uncle Shad. His other siblings barely recall the man who dipped in and out of their lives like a ghost. But Mance remembers him. The good and, mostly, the bad. Like the time Uncle Shad pushed him to the ground for accidentally stepping on his shoes. Mance remembers the shock of it, the cruelty of a grown man pushing a child with all his might, the callousness on his face. Fierce and fearless, Mance dusted himself off and charged at him. The meanness on Uncle Shad's face, the downward pull of his features, eclipsed by one of amusement and appreciation as he held Mance by the head an arm's length away.

"King, this other boy of yours has heart," Uncle Shad said through a hearty laugh as Mance squirmed, trying to reach him.

Mance recalls Uncle Shad's wide palm then, with one stiff movement, shoving him once again to the ground.

"Stay down, son," he said, slamming his foot on Mance's chest, pressing the air out of him. "You don't want any of this."

"Let him up, Shad," King warned.

The midday sun disappeared for Mance as Uncle Shad squatted lower to him, his shoes now scuffed even further, and flipped out a knife. The tip of it blurred as it got close to Mance's eye. "Don't ever step on a man's shoes."

Mance hated Uncle Shad. But he didn't hate him for pushing him down that day. He didn't hate him because he was a thief. And he didn't hate Uncle Shad for the eight months Mance served in prison because of him. Thieves are liars, too. And so is he.

Years ago, Uncle Shad turned his back on King and the Kingdom, and now he was something worse than a bully and a thief. He broke a long-standing family promise to never sell the Kingdom. Not a plot of land. Not an acre. Not one inch.

He hated Uncle Shad because he was a traitor.

Mance pulls onto the dirt road to the house he heard Uncle Shad was hiding out in and sees him sitting on the porch alone. Mance needs to recall those memories, regurgitate the hate he feels for him, keep it fresh in his heart. For King. For himself. His breathing, elevated and loud, mocks him.

"You come to kill me, boy?" Uncle Shad says by way of greeting, a cigarette gripped in his tightened lips.

"Should I?" Mance approaches slowly and stops just shy of the porch. "I thought you were dead already."

The sky hangs heavy, and the sun presses hot on the top of Mance's head. Uncle Shad doesn't look at him and continues shaping a piece of wood with his case knife. In the rural South, a man never journeyed too far from his knife. They carried pocket knives to fix things, start a tractor, clean a deer, protect them from evil. And to inflict evil. Dragged sharp, it could cut you just by looking at it. Mance should know. Uncle Shad, too. They wore the scars to prove it.

Mance remembers the first and last times he saw that knife, its pearl handle, the buck edge on the bill; the first time it loomed inches from his eye as he laid on the ground, and the last time, almost two years ago, at his neck.

Uncle Shad takes a drag on his cigarette and blows the smoke above him. "Nah…if you were going to kill me, I'd be dead already."

They could have been twins, Uncle Shad and King, blue-black skin, coarse hair, and deep-set eyes. But Shad was taller and leaner than King, quicker too, like a gazelle. At least, in his younger days. Now, Mance sees the hardship in his eyes, the sagging skin, the weariness in his face.

Cedric, Mance's first cousin, opens the front door but stops when he sees Mance, who turns his body to face evenly between Uncle Shad and his cousin. Cedric doesn't return the greeting equally, just tips his chin at him.

"Ain't you gon' speak to your cousin?" Uncle Shad says. "In my day, you spoke to someone when they entered a room. Goddamn kids ain't got no fuckin' manners."

Cedric clears his throat. He's a diluted version of Uncle Shad without the brutishness and arrogance. Mance senses something fragile about him. More glass than stone. "What's up, Mance?" he says, deepening his voice, moving his hands back and forth before holding them at his crotch, brimming with a nervous energy that almost makes Mance laugh.

"Cedric," Mance says, removing his hands from his pockets.

"Do you see how he turned and made himself small?" Uncle Shad says to Cedric, pointing his knife at Mance, the white pearl in the handle glinting in the sun. "You can't teach that. That's instinct. That's a fighter right there. Just like his daddy. Just like me back in the day."

"I don't do that anymore."

"Bullshit. Once a fighter, always a fighter. What was it?" Uncle Shad takes another drag on his cigarette, the tip sizzling, and talks through the smoke. "One punch. You killed that man with one punch. Shit, I'd never been so proud."

One punch. It's all most people remember about the fight. One punch that took a life. But it wasn't the punch that killed him. As he fell from the blow, the parking sign behind him snapped his neck, and his head broke when it hit the concrete. What Mance remembers about the fight, sees in his dreams, and saw in his dark cell, was the man's open eyes, cold and empty, staring out at nothing. He remembers the unnatural angle of his neck and his long last draw of breath. He didn't learn the man's name until the trial.

Ellis successfully argued self-defense. Enough witnesses saw the altercation and heard the man, but even self-defense wasn't enough for a complete acquittal. Mance had killed a man, one punch or not, and someone had to pay. Eighteen months in prison, voluntary manslaughter, the price for stopping a heartbeat.

Now, Mance shakes off the memory. He may have been provoked into the fight. But he would never be proud of taking a life. "You're proud that I killed a man?"

"That you had it in you," Uncle Shad says quickly, his voice rising. "That Solomon blood. Yo daddy was a fighter. He got soft over the years, especially after you kids were born, everything about the land." Uncle Shad stubs out his cigarette on the side of the chair. "They tried to take it from us when me and him were kids. White man came up and told my daddy he was selling the Kingdom to him and that was that. Do you know what my daddy did? He whipped that white man with the handle of his sledgehammer he kept by the front door."

Cedric laughs and Uncle Shad flicks his eyes at him and his entire face creases into fine lines worn and carved over years of living.

"The fuck you laughing for? They killt my daddy after that. A whole group of 'em came in the middle of the night and drug him out the house, and do you know what his last words were?" He looks at Cedric, who shakes his head, and then to Mance, who says, "*Don't let the white man take the house.*"

Of course Mance knows those words. He feels the weight of them every day just like Uncle Shad did, just like King did.

"Then why did you do it?" Mance asks, his tone infuriated and no longer masking his attempts at civility.

"The fuck you mean why I do it? Do what?" Uncle Shad says, shocked by Mance's sudden change of tone.

"Let the white man take the house."

Uncle Shad takes a huge inhale and waves his hand. "I ain't let the white man take nothin' but a few acres. Y'all still got King's precious house."

Mance feels his blood continue to rise. "We have two weeks to vacate the house!"

Uncle Shad stares at Mance for a long moment and squirms in his chair. "What you talkin' about?"

"You didn't know," Mance says, watching the way his uncle's face shifts with guilt. "You sign papers and don't even know what the fuck you signing?"

"I ain't sold the house. Just some acres down around by the creek."

"You sold the land under the house!"

"Who the fuck do you think you talkin' to?" Uncle Shad says, standing quick. He's never taken kindly to being wrong. Cedric cracks his knuckles and takes two steps down the stairs. "I'm still yo elder, boy."

Mance pivots his weight and balls his fists. "This don't concern you, Cedric. Take your ass back up them steps."

"Or wh—?"

One swift pop to the throat, right and left jab to the ribs, and one powerful punch across his jaw, and Cedric lands hard on the ground before he even knows it, before he finishes his sentence. Mance sees Uncle Shad scrambling toward him, his knife in hand to cut, not to stab, but Mance blocks his motion with his left forearm and presses Uncle Shad by the throat against the wall. The knife tumbles to the ground.

"That's the third time you've pulled that knife on me," Mance says through his teeth, his fist ready to strike. "Next time, I swear to fuckin' God, you better kill me with it."

Cedric struggles to his feet, gasping for air, and stumbles toward Mance.

"Nah…it's okay. Let him," Uncle Shad says to Cedric through labored breath. And then to Mance, "Yeah…there it is. I see it in your eyes." He takes a huge whiff. "I smell it on you. Boy, you ain't changed. Just embrace who you are."

"I will never be like you!"

"Son…you are me. You just don't know it."

Mance releases him with a push and sends a warning look to Cedric. Uncle Shad straightens and smooths his shirt before sitting back in his chair. "Take yo punk ass in the house and let the grown men talk," Uncle Shad says to Cedric. "Matter of fact…brang me that bag."

Uncle Shad fishes in his shirt pocket and retrieves a pack of cigarettes. He flips one out and offers the pack to Mance, who shakes his head. "Huh," Uncle Shad says, throwing the pack at Mance. Droplets of sweat run down his face and mist his cheeks. He wipes it all away with one quick rub of the white towel from the table next to him. "Let's just all settle down now and talk."

"We ain't got nothing to talk about," Mance says, crumpling the pack in his fist and throwing it back at him. He wants a cigarette, needs it, but he doesn't want to take anything from him. "All I want to know is can you stop it? The sale."

"It's done," Uncle Shad says, his tone awash with guilt. "But I ain't mean to sell the house." The air between them becomes stagnant. "They came to me asking about selling some of the land. I told them that King would never sell. They said he didn't have to know. That as an heir I had a right to sell it if I wanted to. They pushed some papers in front of me, and I signed."

Mance paces the porch, torn between stabbing Uncle Shad with his own knife and choking him with his bare hands.

Uncle Shad knows this. Because bad men who do bad things can always feel death around the corner. "You gone kill me now?" He points to his knife on the ground. "Pick it up and do your business."

Like King, Uncle Shad could barely read, so Mance believes he didn't know what he signed. He only understood dollar signs and the numbers that followed, and that was enough for him.

"How much?"

"I took what was mine."

"How much?" Mance repeats through gritted teeth.

"Forty thousand."

Mance's heart sinks. Even the most conservative estimates valued the land at twenty thousand an acre. Uncle Shad has sold the land for half of its worth. The conniving thief and liar was outconned by a bigger, greedier thief.

"We've lost," Mance says, pushing the words out. Not for Uncle Shad's benefit but for his own. He needed to say it out loud, for the reality to start to set in, and when it takes root inside him, it doesn't sit well in his stomach, and he fights to keep the bile from rising. Mance needs to breathe, but the oxygen he requires refuses to reach his lungs. He starts walking to his car.

"What if I could help you?"

"You can't."

"What if you had the money to buy it back?"

Mance doesn't stop walking. "I'm not working for you again."

"Nah…nothing like that. Just some light work. One job."

Mance finally turns. His uncle is standing again. "You just pulled a knife on me. Do you really think I'm going to work for you?"

Uncle Shad holds up his hands. "I'm sorry about that. But I had to see if you still had it."

"The last job I did for you cost me nine months of my life."

"Because you're no snitch," he says, pointing a finger at Mance, "and I respect a man who can keep his mouth shut."

In and out. That's what Uncle Shad had said. They would be in and out in five minutes. Uncle Shad just needed to collect his money. Mance just needed to watch his back. He didn't trust anyone, not for a score large enough that would net Mance the rest of the money he needed for his ten acres of land. Easy work. That's what Uncle Shad had said.

There's nothing easy about dealing with criminals. About the choices you make in a split second. Uncle Shad doesn't play about two things: his time and his money. So when the fence shorted him, Uncle Shad cut him, a quick slash across his face. The fence's bodyguard pulled his gun to shoot Uncle Shad but hit Paul, the son of Earl, Lisha's landlord, instead. Paul shouldn't have been there. He should have been at home, preparing to attend college that fall, but the promise of easy money wins every time. Uncle Shad wanted to leave him, but Mance refused, even when he heard the police sirens grow closer, even while he carried Paul and hid him next door, even when the police arrived and found Mance in a warehouse full of stolen goods and slapped on the handcuffs again, just two months after they had removed them.

Except for Ellis, Mance never told a soul about the events of that day, or the parties involved.

"I owe you," Earl told Mance. Because owing someone meant something in Diggs. Because a favor carries as much weight as a handful of bills. A man's word is his bond.

It would be two months before Mance cashed in that favor. Lisha needed a house and Earl had one. "She pays nothing. Ever. For as long as she wants to live there." Mance didn't hesitate to make such an outrageous request and Earl didn't fight it either. Mance had saved his son's life and then saved him from a life behind bars. Earl shook Mance's hand and signed the agreement Ellis drafted.

"I got a son," Mance says now to Uncle Shad.

"Yeah...I heard about your boy. That's fucked up."

"He's going to be fine."

"Damn right he is. He's a Solomon, and we are always goin' to be all right. The best thang you can do for that boy is to make this money."

"The best thing I can do for him is not go back to prison." Mance starts walking again. At his car, he turns back once more, and just then Cedric returns wearing a new shirt, his hands empty.

"You ain't being smart. You're Mance—the best I've ever seen."

"Smart enough to know when to walk away. To know what's good for me."

Uncle Shad looks at Cedric, who stares blankly. "Where the fuck is it?" Shad says. Cedric blinks. "Damn it, go get it!"

Cedric returns with a black duffel bag. Mance doesn't need to see its contents. He can smell it from where he stands. It smells like renovations on the Kingdom, a diamond ring for Lisha, and cochlear implants for Henry. It smells like freedom from worry and the keeping of a promise.

Cedric unzips the bag and tosses it toward Mance's feet; a bundle of hundred-dollar bills pops out and rolls in the dirt, stopping a few feet from Mance.

"Goddamn! That's what I'm talking about!" Uncle Shad says, slapping his hands together. "That's real money right there."

Mance bends and takes the bundle in his hands, turning it over a few times.

"Why don't you go ahead and take that for yourself."

"Why would you give me this? To ease your guilt?"

"To save you."

"From what?"

"From living yo daddy's life. From maintaining a raggedy-ass house. I didn't want that life of always wondering, working, never getting ahead. I know you don't either."

"What would you have us do? What you did? Betray every Solomon who built and worked for the house and the land?"

"You take what's yours. Just like I did," Uncle Shad says, arrogance once again infusing his words, his voice as thick and sticky as slime. "Now just…just hear me out."

Mance has no reason to stay. He knows whatever Uncle Shad proposes won't be enough to buy back the land. For every reason he thinks of, the obvious one glares back at him: Uncle Shad cannot be trusted.

And yet, he made a promise, two promises, and he never said how he would keep them or the lengths he would go.

And so, he stays, and listens, and considers.

━

Tokey is closing the drawer when she sees it. She found herself back in King's room rummaging through his drawers for anything related to the land, when the corner of a piece of paper wedged between the drawers catches her eye. She shouldn't have seen it. And she will later wonder why she did. She's opened that drawer no fewer than a dozen times since King's death.

Maybe she noticed it because her mind loomed elsewhere.

They couldn't lose the house or the land. Where would she go? Junior would return home to Genesis, CeCe would return to New York, and Mance would live with Lisha. But Tokey had no one, nowhere to go. The Kingdom was home and the only one she's ever known.

She pulls it out and discovers it's an envelope with King's name on it. No postmark. She doesn't recognize the handwriting but, from the loops of the letters, she can tell it belongs to a woman.

It's old, the envelope and the letter inside, both delicate and browned from time. Tokey surveys the envelope before opening it, turning it in her hands a few times.

Then, she knows. She knows who wrote the letter before she's read even one word.

Her mother.

She shouldn't read it, she thinks. It's private, even in death.

Tokey takes the letter and sits on the bed, ignoring the ache of her knees. Silence presses back at her.

She never expected to find this.

But how many times has Tokey dreamed of this? How many times did Tokey ask about their mother? How many times did King not answer? Every time, except one.

"Did Mama not love us?" Tokey asked one day at dinner when they were ages ten, nine, eight, and six years old. The question had been on her heart to ask and, one day, she finally had the courage to do so.

"Yes…" King started, the word soft coming from his mouth.

He cleared his throat. "She loved each of you so very much. And you are not the reason why she's not here, okay?" He looked at each of them for a tick of confirmation. It was the first and only direct question he answered about her.

Now, Tokey unfolds the letter; the paper is soft like it's been read and refolded many times. Her eyes expect a wall of words; instead, five lines stare back at her.

> *My King,*
>   *I did it for us.*
>   *I'm sorry.*
>   *Jessie knows.*
>
>   *Love,*
>   *H*

Miss Jessie opens the door, and her eyes travel the length of Tokey before landing on the letter in Tokey's hand. "I knew this day would come," she says, pushing the door open wider. "Best come on in."

Miss Jessie is unlike anyone else in Diggs. She is single and has traveled the world. It shows in her attitude, demeanor, and dress. Like now—she's a vision of spring wearing a long caftan, colorful and bright, her lips stained this season's brightest red. Her nails and toes, too. Her house is decorated with mementos of a life well lived. Tokey envies her.

"Tea?"

Tokey nods. Miss Jessie disappears into the kitchen and returns a few minutes later with a tray balancing a teapot, two cups, a bowl of sugar cubes, and a small plate of cookies. Tokey eyes the plate of cookies and her mouth waters. She tries to push aside her need. Tokey wants to know about her mother. She has questions and doesn't want to waste time sipping tea and eating cookies. "Miss Jessie...I app—"

"Hush, girl, and have a cup of tea," Miss Jessie says, clutching her caftan with one hand and pouring hot water into both cups with the other.

Miss Jessie hands Tokey a cup, which she immediately places on the table in front of her. Miss Jessie drops one cube of sugar into her tea and slowly stirs before sitting in a wingback chair.

"Now, let me see it."

Tokey hands her the letter and watches as Miss Jessie unfolds and reads it. A sigh when she finishes, and a sympathetic look when she refolds it.

"I remember when she wrote this and when he found it."

Miss Jessie reaches for her tea and takes two quick sips.

"What does it mean?"

"I can't answer that."

"Why did she say you could? How well did you know her? Why does she mention you in this letter?"

"So many questions. Calm down, child."

"Miss Jessie...I just found a letter from my mother, who I never knew, less than a week after my father died. Of course I have questions. Please don't ask me to calm down."

Miss Jessie stands and walks across the room to a bookcase, opens a drawer, and pulls out a folder. "Here," she says, handing the folder to Tokey. "She wanted me to give this to you."

Tokey takes the folder but does not look at it. "What is it?"

"Those are her letters," Miss Jessie says, returning to her chair, crossing her legs.

Now Tokey casts her eyes to the folder, greedily taking it all in—the green with a gold border along the edges, the cover once hard, now soft and worn with age. She runs her hands across it, parts the pages. Her eyes skim over the handwriting, seeing but not reading, her fingertips brushing the indentation of her mother's words. Her mother once held this, she realizes; it belonged to her. An unraveling deep within her floats to the surface. She will give time and space to that feeling but, first, she has more questions.

"How long have you had this?" Tokey says, her voice faltering. She thought, for a second, that she might feel relief that someone alive and willing to talk knew her mother, that she was one step closer to learning about her mother. Instead, she feels more distressed. "You've had this all this time and never thought to give it to us? To King?"

"I promised her that if any of you ever came asking about her, that I would give them to one of you."

"How would we have known to ask you?" Tokey feels her soft tone pinch. "How would we have known that you even knew her?"

Miss Jessie considers this, pursing her lips. "Well…I thought King would—"

"Would have what? Told us something about her? Guess what? He didn't. Not one word. Ever." Tokey is uncharacteristically shouting now, unburdening herself of what she held, of what she didn't know, of what she would discover.

Miss Jessie's face softens under the younger woman's emotion, moved by her spontaneous passion.

"Tokey…honey…I'm so sorry. All this time you didn't know nothing about your mother?"

Tears push at the corners of Tokey's eyes, and one finally falls. Miss Jessie snatches two tissues from a nearby box and waves them at Tokey. She sighs. "I knew King was upset about what happened, but I never thought he would keep her from you kids."

Miss Jessie moves to sit next to Tokey and takes her hand in hers. "You poor girl. You don't know who you are." She squeezes her hand tenderly. "No wonder."

Head bowed and crying, Tokey hears the last of Miss Jessie's words, but she doesn't reply. Maybe because she is tired of the swirling questions and believes now that answers will finally come. Maybe it's because she understands the magnitude of what she didn't know and knows that asking Miss Jessie specifics without context will confuse her further. Or maybe it's because Tokey realizes her shortcomings are now obvious to all, at least to Miss Jessie, no matter how hard she tries to hide them. *You don't know who you are.* So, she doesn't comment.

She continues crying until the knot of tissues in her hand is damp with tears.

Finally, Tokey looks up at Miss Jessie.

"I'll let her talk to you." Miss Jessie points at the folder in Tokey's lap. "Read them, and I'll answer any questions she doesn't."

Tokey gives her a quick, single nod before hesitating a moment. "How about just one question now?"

Miss Jessie raises her eyebrows and tilts her head.

"What was her name?"

SIX

———

CECE'S PHONE RINGS JUST as they open the door to Abrams & Abrams Law Firm. She knows who it is. She's been waiting for his call. It's the reason she has kept her cell phone close, both wishing for a call and wishing one away. She's been gone for a week now, without any communication with anyone at her firm, and she knows that it's been too long. Mark does too.

She gestures to her phone as Ellis checks in at the front desk. In a corner out of earshot, she answers.

"When are you coming back?"

Not even a hello. Definitely no welfare check. Straight to the point.

CeCe feels a chill of the clearest realizations. Mark doesn't care about her or what happened to her. He only cares enough to save himself.

"Ken is asking about the discrepancies in your billing hours again," Mark says before she can answer his question.

"I thought you were going to vouch for me."

"I did, but he's now asking about another client." He sighs. "Jesus…CeCe. There was more than one? What the fuck have you done? What have you gotten me into?"

"What did you say?" CeCe asks, the words aching in her throat.

A pause. Short but long.

"When are you coming back?"

CeCe runs her hand through her hair and turns to see Ellis chatting up the front desk receptionist.

"I don't know. Another week maybe?" She leans into the weakness in her words and hopes Mark hears it.

"My father died. And…" She allows her voice to trail off, adding a hitch at the end. Mark's father died a few years ago.

Mark sighs but doesn't speak.

"His estate is a mess, and…" she says, performing, rushing her words and fracturing the ends of her sentences.

"I'm sorry, CeCe," Mark says finally, breathing out the words. And she hears it. A thin line of pain slicing through his words. It's working. Her chest loosens at this.

"I just…" If she could, she would cry. If ever there was a moment for tears, it's now, but she can't summon them. They were reserved for King. Mark doesn't deserve them anyway. Instead, she whimpers softly.

"I'll hold him off."

"Thank you," she says quickly, dropping the whimper just as fast. "I'm working on clearing up the estate, and when I get back, I'll have the money." She's whispering, aware of Ellis behind her.

"Until then…" It is his turn to let his sentence and volume drift, but in his is a different kind of desperation.

CeCe closes her eyes.

"I'm holding up my end of the deal. You have to hold up yours." The words rake across her, dry. All business.

CeCe's face warms. She tries to picture his mouth saying these words, and can't, even though she's heard him say versions of them before. Separated from him by hundreds of miles, she can really see how he's changed. She understands now that she doesn't know this Mark. The Mark she met five years ago loved the law because he could help people with it, represented most of the firm's pro bono cases, and adored his wife and two daughters, inserting them into conversations to the point of annoyance. This is a new Mark, of her own creation. She falters at this realization.

If Mark was a better man, he would have refused to help her. If he was a better man, she would be in jail. At the time, CeCe thanked the heavens for bad men, men with faulty moral compasses, men who fractured a law or two, men who loved sex but were married to women who didn't.

"Yeah…sure…of course. As soon as I get back."

"No." It's just one word, but the air ripples with the force of it.

"No?"

"Sooner."

"I…I can't fly back right now. But I promise, as soon as I get back, I'm all yours." CeCe adjusts her tone higher and rhythmic, almost singing. "I'll do that thing you like."

Mark moans, deep and long. "Oh…you're going to do that, but I'm afraid that may not be enough anymore." There's space between his words, deliberate. "But I think we can work something out."

"What do you mean?" CeCe asks, swallowing.

"Keep your phone close. I'll be in touch."

The call ends, and CeCe clutches her phone so tight her fingers ache. The world rocks, then steadies. The spacious, quiet lobby suddenly becomes too small, too loud, too suffocating.

"Cecily."

She feels him, that familiar hook of gravity, a magnetic pull, before she hears him; still, her name startles her.

She drops her phone; it skitters across the shiny tiled floor.

"I didn't mean to scare you," Ellis says, moving to retrieve her phone.

A rush of emotion floods CeCe, and her face shifts, into a smile or a cry, she doesn't know. What she does know is that she can't look at Ellis right now, not with Mark's voice still ringing in her ears. She needs a minute to compose herself, to rearrange her face into a neutral one.

She looks past Ellis to the bathroom and points. "I…need to go to…" She doesn't finish, just scrambles away.

In the bathroom, CeCe stumbles to the sink and grips the lip of the granite, pulling at it until her fingers and arms scream. The countertop neither moves nor absorbs all that she's feeling. She collapses against it, her feet slipping from under her.

Her heart knocks so hard inside her chest, she can see her shirt vibrating with movement, hear it in her ears.

I'll be in touch. The statement rifles through her. Over and over and over again.

And she knows that he will. Because now, Mark's in this as much as she is. Except she's no longer in control. She knows that now but doesn't understand how it all went wrong. Before, she could tuck away her guilt. Lie to herself while brushing her teeth or cleaning herself, hidden in a bathroom stall at work, that the guilt doesn't matter, that all of this was a means to an end. Now she's not so sure anymore. He holds all the cards.

Now, she's afraid.

Afraid of what Mark meant by *sooner*.

Afraid that today will go wrong.

Afraid of how much further she has to fall.

CeCe grabs the countertop once again. She ambles to her feet and catches her reflection in the mirror. A stranger looms front and center. She hates this woman. She was raised to be strong, to overcome her circumstances, to fit in anywhere she doesn't belong, and to push forward always. There's nothing strong about the dark circles under her eyes or the dullness of her skin. She is tired and thirsty. She blinks and forces a smile. There. The worst is once again hidden.

CeCe takes a deep breath and brings herself back into the present. To focus on the air in her lungs, her thumping pulse. To focus on the meeting. To feel lighter despite the storm brewing.

And so, for the first time since she left Diggs, CeCe prays.

She washes her hands and prays that this meeting goes well, prays for a solution that will fix everything, prays for strength to hold herself together while she waits for her other prayers to be answered. It is a selfish prayer, and yet, she powders her face and reapplies her lipstick against her doubt. She can do this. She can do anything.

Then, outside the bathroom, she sees Ellis.

It's like missing a step. He's waiting for her just as he had outside of the school all those years ago. Ellis knows how to wait. Now, he's perched against a chair, his long legs stretched out before him, holding her phone and a bottle of water, his head turned away from her. In this stance, she can appreciate the full extent of him. He's a work of art, his dark skin a canvas for his light-blue shirt and navy blazer. He is human and real and kind, and she is still in love with him. This realization washes over her like an unexpected wave. His eyes find hers, and he cracks a slight smile, and it's like the sun peeking out from behind a dark cloud. She feels her body ache with want, the simple act of his comfort, to fall into him, the safety of his embrace.

She doesn't need this to hit her right now. But it does, and the unfairness sweeps across her like a gust of wind. She felt the stirring when she saw him at King's graveside, in his office, and on the ride here, but didn't expect to feel its effects so fully so soon. Another emotion in a flood of emotions in such a short period of time since returning to Diggs.

Well, why not?

"Everything okay?" he asks, extending her phone to her.

What a foolish question. It's a question she can't answer, because she doesn't know where to apply it, doesn't know what it means to be okay anymore, to live free from the ache of worry or of loving him. But for now, she has to be okay, even if it's not true. There is nothing to do but go on.

So she takes the phone and drops it in her purse. "Yeah."

He pushes the water toward her. "I figured you might be thirsty."

Her heart aches at his understanding of her. Her face burns in shame, under the flame of his tenderness. She doesn't deserve his kindness. It'll be short-lived anyway. She wants him to stop being nice to her, to stop reminding her of his goodness, of what she missed out on, of what she will lose. Anger rises in her chest. Because that's the one thing CeCe has plenty of. Because she cannot bring herself to fold into him again.

"I didn't ask you to get me a water." Her voice is clearer, stronger now, bolstered by her anger. Being angry is easy. Loving someone is not. Distance works wonders at quelling emotions. Proximity does not. He is here, breathing, being, knowing, holding a bottle of water she craves.

She regrets her words as soon as she says them, especially as they reach his ears harsher than when they left her tongue, especially when his smile falters under the potency of such unnecessary venom.

She waits for him to push back, or if not, to get angry, to judge her for being so unnecessarily curt in the face of his thoughtfulness. It's not fair for her to treat him this way, she knows. But Ellis's annoyance smooths. He shakes his head, twists the cap, and upturns the water into a plant nearby, a smirk on his face. He throws the empty bottle into the trash and walks toward the elevator without a word.

In the elevator, silence surrounds them until Ellis steps toward her, closing the space between them, a head and shoulder taller. "I don't know what that phone call was about or what's going on with you"—CeCe's lips part, but Ellis talks over her ghostly retort—"but Ethan is a friend and he's doing me a huge favor by taking this case." Ellis leans in closer. Heat climbs up her neck and his voice sends ripples across her arms. "Get your shit together before you walk in there because he doesn't deserve any attitude from you."

CeCe nods, her expression sobered by Ellis's tone, his body's immediacy, his radiating scent.

His eyebrows lift. "Do you understand?"

She nods again.

"Say it," he says, his head bowed over hers.

Ellis has never tolerated her attitude, giving it back to her in the fistfuls she delivered, never shying away from calling her out on her shit. And now she understands. It's in the calm and earnest way he says it that does it. He will eventually break her. She knows it in her bones and all the way to her heart. He will split her wide open, and everything, her secrets and her feelings for him, will tumble out. It is inevitable. He exerts that power over her. But she isn't ready. Not yet. She has to hold on as long as she can.

"I understand." She takes a deep breath to steady her nerves.

Ellis squints and his forehead rucks like a pleat. He expected a rebuttal, and when he hears the resolve in her voice, he studies her face, sees the dimness in her eyes. Questions glint in his, and he wants the truth, but the elevator doors open to Ethan waiting on the other side.

———

Mance knew the house when he saw it.

In its day, the Prescott House stood proud as a fine example of Colonial Revival. But it's changed since the first time he saw it. Time can be a villain to old homes, especially when neglected, robbing them of their youthful facade, dulling them of their character. Now it cowers as if it's afraid of its own shadow. The dormer windows, with tall scrolled pediments, are dingy and dirty, and the once-glossy green-tiled roof is now ugly and mossy.

He was here years ago with King. Often, while delivering furniture, King would take him on tours showing him the best constructed houses in Charlotte. They weren't always the biggest or the most expensive. "It's the little things that make the difference," he said. King appreciated craftsmanship, attention to detail, and most of all character. "They don't build them like this anymore and never will again," he would say, navigating the streets with ease, pointing out details in the houses they passed. He had been in most of them or made furniture for their owners, including this one.

Mance knows about rundown houses and doesn't judge them for it. But this, this isn't a house. That's what King said when they pulled up long ago. "This is a home," he said.

"Like the Kingdom?" Mance asked.

King sighed and turned back to the house. "It was...once."

"This? This is the house?" Now, Cedric regards the house skeptically. He laughs. "Looks worse than the Kingdom."

Mance ignores him, throwing a shirt and a hat at him before closing the truck door. "Put this on."

"Why?"

"Do you think they are going to open the door for two random Black men? We have to look like we really work for the moving company."

Mance slips off his shirt and pulls on the one with a Queen City Moving Company patch stitched to the front. He tugs a hat low, to just above his eyeline. Cedric does the same, all the while watching Mance.

"What are you waiting for?" Mance slams a clipboard into his chest. "Go knock on the door."

"You aren't coming with me?"

"I'll be right there. I'm grabbing my toolbox."

Cedric blinks once and does not move. "Why did you bring a toolbox? We not actually moving anything."

Mance's head throbs at the idiocy of this man, and that true Solomon blood runs in his veins. "I'm here to evaluate the furniture. I'm going to need a few tools to do that," he says slowly, moving back to the truck and rolling up the back door. The screeching noise echoes around them. A rustic wooden toolbox sits in the middle of the empty truck.

Finally understanding, Cedric nods big. "I see. I see. That's all you had to say."

Cedric heads up the stairs to the front door. Mance follows.

At the entrance of the portico, Mance stops and casts his eyes up, up, up at the four fluted Ionic columns that rise to the full height of the house. He almost smiles at the sight of the columns, which support the portico and the entire facade, just like the Kingdom's, and wonders how long it would have taken to recreate them if King had commanded it. He wonders if they are as weak as the Kingdom's. *Shh, shh. Shh, shh. Shh, shh.* Without trying, he hears the rhythm of sanding. *Shh, shh. Shh, shh. Shh, Shh.* Back and forth. Side to side. Round and round. He runs a hand across one. Solid and sturdy.

A calico cat runs in front of his feet and jumps onto the porch railing, bringing Mance back to the portico, to both front doors open but no one there, and to the clatter and bang of pots and pans in the background. Cedric looks at Mance, confused.

"Hello?" Mance says, pushing the doorbell. The ding echoes across the house, but the kitchen noises don't stop.

They wait.

Mance calls out and rings the doorbell again, this time also knocking hard a few times.

"Let's just go in," Cedric says.

Mance shoots him a look right as a figure emerges, an old woman no more than five feet tall, eighty pounds soaking wet.

She's wearing a tortoiseshell ball gown, her white hair the color of virgin snow, a knotted mess on the top of her head, her makeup heavy and smeared. Lying on her chest is a diamond necklace, and diamond chandelier earrings dangle from her ears.

"Well...hello," the woman says. "I didn't know anyone was here. Have you been waiting long?"

Mance waits for Cedric to speak first. When he doesn't, Mance says, "No ma'am. We just got here."

The woman does not speak nor move. She just stares out past them. She is in two places at once. More there than here.

Then, she's back.

"May I help you?" The woman's eyes dart from Cedric to Mance before settling on Cedric, whose eyes do not meet the woman's, but instead stare at the ground beneath him.

Mance clears his throat and looks to Cedric, who shuffles his feet before dropping the clipboard on the ground.

"We are with Queen City Moving Company," Mance says, stepping forward. "We're going to be packing up and moving you next week. We're here to assess the house to see how many men we're going to need."

The woman furrows her brow, regarding them for a moment, and in that moment, Mance's heart stops. "There must be some kind of mistake," she says. "I'm not moving."

Cedric looks to Mance, who starts to say something, but the woman steps out onto the porch and past them.

"There you are," the woman says, padding barefoot across

the porch to the cat. She takes it into her arms. "I've been look-ing all over for you. Where have you been? Where have you been, huh? I've been so worried."

The woman turns to them, cat in her arms. "My son thinks that I'm moving but I'm staying right here." She lifts the cat high in the air. "Isn't that right, Patches? We are staying right here."

Mance begins to breathe again—the inhalation of air, sweet and welcome. "Yes, ma'am. But we spoke to a George Prescott, who asked us to come by and assess the house."

"Yes, that's my son," she says, not to Mance but to Patches, still hoisted in the air.

"Should we call him?"

The woman considers this, pouting, and finally lowers the cat to the porch and looks at them. "He was always my least favorite child. So much like his daddy, Rhett. I married him for his money." She sighs. "I was supposed to marry Wint, but he died in the war." She steps back to the front door. "Come on in. But you have to make it quick. I'm hosting a ball tonight and I must get ready. The governor is comin'."

The woman enters the house while Cedric gawks until Mance pushes him inside.

Mance doesn't know which detail stuns him more: the two-story grand foyer illuminated by a classic antique crystal chan-delier, the fat crown molding wrapped thick around fifteen-foot ceilings, or the wide-plank hardwood floors. Today, such fea-tures, the labor alone, would make the construction of such a house unaffordable.

No wonder Uncle Shad wanted to burgle it.

"The house is full of antique furniture and jewelry. It's an easy score." That's what Uncle Shad's fence said.

Businessman George Prescott, of the legendary Prescotts, was selling their family's mansion and casting everything in it, including his mother, out. While she was shuttled off to a nursing home, Uncle Shad and his crew would be helping some of the state's finest antique furniture and jewelry fall off the moving truck.

"I'm not robbing an old woman," Mance said. "Not even like that."

Uncle Shad blew cigarette smoke above them. "You don't have to. All I need you to do is go in a few days before and assess the furniture."

"Assess? Why? You don't trust your man?"

A large smile grew on Uncle Shad's face. "Trust nobody but yo momma and then cut the deck."

They smoked in silence until cigarette butts dotted the ground.

"Your part is totally legit," Uncle Shad said, finally, handing Mance another roll of Benjamin Franklins. "Think of this and that other roll as payment for your appraisal services."

Mance looked at the roll in his hand and felt the heat from the one in his pocket.

So what if his role is legal? Mance still feels as if he's walking a fine line between right and wrong, the difference between being off by an inch or a mile. Balance matters. In measuring a piece of wood and in skirting the law. Mance hates the idea of being motivated by money. And the need to keep Uncle Shad close.

Now, Mance shuffles a step forward, then another. "Excuse our manners," he says. "We've been talking to you, and I don't even know your name."

The woman brightens. "Mrs. Annie Talbott Prescott," she says, her Southern drawl now thicker and exaggerated. She extends a pale, blue-spiderwebbed hand and Mance takes it, giving it a gentle shake. It's thin and soft as ash.

"It is a pleasure to meet you, Miss Annie. I'm Tim." He touches his chest. "And this is Tom. This shouldn't take too long. Where would you like us to start?"

She looks around and throws her hands up in the air before releasing them. "Wherever you'd like. If you will excuse me, I must get ready. Guests will be arriving in an hour."

Mance and Cedric watch her leave, and when she disappears around the corner, Cedric turns to Mance, eyes wide.

"What the fuck?" Cedric whispers. "We got to get out of here. People will be showing up."

Mance peeks in the living room just off the foyer. With most of the furniture covered in white sheets and the floor-to-ceiling drapes pulled shut tight, the space appears gloomy. He curses. To accurately perform his role, he needs to see the furniture. Even without him touching anything, dust particles float in the filtered light. Lifting the sheets would mean disturbing more dust and leaving a trail of their movements throughout the house, an unexpected complication in an increasingly complicated situation.

"There's no one coming," Mance finally says.

"How do you know?" A mist of sweat dots Cedric's brow.

"Do you really think she's throwing a ball? Here?" Inexplicably, two inflated beach balls bob on an otherwise unfelt air current in the corner of the foyer. "I'll start in there," Mance says, pointing to the living room. "You go upstairs. The jewelry will probably be up there somewhere. Look, but don't touch anything."

Cedric nods and heads up the stairs, taking two steps at a time.

Mance noticed it as soon as he entered the house. The eighteenth-century French provincial grandfather clock. Mance slips on his gloves and runs his hands down the sides, grateful that, unlike most of the other furniture, it's not covered. It stretches taller than the length of his body with fruitwood inlay and fluted sides. Time stopped at 1:15—what date, Mance wonders. These grandfather clocks were rare and could fetch tens of thousands of dollars on the antique market. He opens the door to inspect the inside when the woman returns carrying a bucket. His gaze falls to the toilet brush, shoe, and bouquet of fake flowers inside. A pang of sympathy wells in his chest.

"That clock belonged to my husband's grandfather, Wallace Prescott. He had it shipped over here from Paris."

"It's beautiful. When did it stop working?"

"Harvest moon 1955, the day after George was born. That should have been a sign he would turn out to be worthless. We wanted to get someone to fix it, but Wallace refused."

"Well…at least he had taste."

"He was stingy. A mean son of a bitch too. But he built this house. I guess I have him to thank for that."

"Yes, ma'am," Mance says, laughing. He takes a visual sweep of the space. "What happened to the original crown molding in this room?"

Annie's papery eyelids flutter up, and then her black-eyeliner-and-blue-eyeshadow-smeared eyes narrow at him. "How did you know that?"

Mance freezes, forgetting his place, his role as a mover, not an expert on antique furniture or construction. "We move houses like this all the time and I noticed that the molding is different, the exaggerated kind." He makes a loop and twirls his finger a few times to indicate he was already at the edge of his knowledge. "This molding is flat."

Mance knows that this home would have been built with Victorian crown molding, popular during the Industrial Revolution. Not this Craftsman molding, which would have come decades later.

"There was a fire in this room about twenty years after it was built. Oh, Rhett," she says. "Fell asleep with a cigar in his ha—"

Cedric returns just as Annie stops speaking, her eyes glassing over, her lips still moving. She's there but she's not, lost in her own mind. Then, she shakes her head. "Look at me forgetting my manners. Would you gentlemen like something to drink?" she asks, looking at Cedric.

"Nah."

Annie frowns, her red lipsticked lips turning downward. There are some things in life that you are born with and cannot be taught. Common sense hovers at the top. Somehow, Cedric crashed into this world without an ounce of it.

"We would love something to drink," Mance says. He should have scouted half of the house by now. Mance wants to refuse, but knows he can't deny her kindness. "Mighty kind of you to offer."

Annie beams joyfully, plucking the toilet brush out of the bucket, and leaves.

"What the fuck are you doing?" Mance asks as soon as they are alone.

"That lady is as crazy as a run-over cat. This house is a mess. I ain't drinking nothing from her."

Mance moves closer to Cedric and speaks through his teeth. "If the old white lady whose house you're going to rob offers you something to drink, you fuckin' take it."

Annie returns, attempting to balance a tray holding a bottle of milk, a bowl of sugar, and a pile of saltine crackers. The dishes rattle from the movement of her shaking hands.

Cedric catches Mance's eyes, looks to the tray, and shakes his head.

"Let me get that for you," Mance says. Reaching forward without taking a step, he lifts the tray from her, and sets it on a nearby table.

Annie sits and Mance follows. Cedric remains standing. Mance clenches and unclenches his jaw. He will kill him when this is over. Mance shoots him a look and points with his eyes to the seat next to their host. Cedric eases into it.

"Now…where were we?" she asks, pouring a cup of milk and handing it to Mance. She picks up a napkin and a saltine cracker and takes a dainty bite along the corner.

"You were going to take me on a tour of the house," Mance says, pretending to take a sip of the milk. A pungent smell reaches his nose before the cup touches his lips. He manages to quickly twist his grimace into a grin.

Annie pulls her tiny lips to one side and stands; her napkin and cracker tumble to the floor. "We should start in the kitchen. Rhett was always proud of the kitchen."

She continues talking, pointing at various things, while leaving the room.

"What are you doing?" Cedric asks, yanking his attention from the room Annie disappeared into. "We don't have time for a tour. I saw most of upstairs. Let's go."

"This is the only way I'm going to be able to scout the house. I can look at the furniture as we go. Take yo scared ass back to the truck. I'll handle it."

Annie appears back in the room, her hands on her hips. "Well don't just stand there gawking. That's not what I'm paying you for. We have a ball to get ready for."

—

Hazel.

It drops in, like a leaf fallen from a tree, when Tokey's not thinking about it. Her mother's name. It lingers and repeats itself. She hears the name whispered in her mind as if someone else speaks it.

Tokey loses the light as she finishes packing the last box in King's room, and a snap and crackle fill the air. It will rain. It always does this time of year. April showers. She glances out the window and feels that familiar sizzle of electricity before the first crack of lightning and boom of thunder. Tokey doesn't recall a time when it didn't storm in the afternoon. It's the after-storm Tokey likes. The freshness the rain provides. But this storm feels different.

Tokey sits on King's bed, winded, tired, and hungry. How do you pack two hundred years into a box? A box of strawberry rolls and Hazel's letters taunt her an arm's length away on the dresser.

It would help, she thinks, to picture her face as she's reading her words. But she can't. She clamps her eyes shut hoping something will come. Nothing. Decades of nothing, and now letters, a look into her mother's life, and King's too. Sometimes she forgets that King lived an entire life before her. Because now that she thinks about it, she doesn't know much about him—only as much as a child knows about their parents, based mostly on what they shared, and King never shared. He's as much a mystery as Hazel is, maybe even more.

Relief is not the correct word for what Tokey feels at the possibility of answers. She is settling for hope.

And yet, she cannot make herself read the letters. Not yet.

Now? A strawberry roll. Or two. To ease the pain, to quiet the thoughts, for the courage to read the letters.

This is how a person overeats. It's a fleeting thought. One

liberty. One more strawberry roll. A few chips become an entire bag. A handful of Oreos becomes an entire sleeve.

She rips open the packaging and sinks her teeth into the soft cake, the bittersweet taste of manufactured strawberries oozes onto her tongue. Two quick bites and it's vanished out of her hand. She chews and swallows and waits and waits.

It doesn't come.

Another strawberry roll. Another ripped package. Another one chewed and swallowed.

The high ascends in her, thin and smooth.

But as she chews, her hope cracks. What if her mother's words leave her with more questions than when she started?

She can't take another heartbreak. Not with the Kingdom's future unknown.

She repeats the process for the third time. She should stop but there's no going back now. She feels the call to it. This time, the plastic wrapper shakes in her hand as she pushes the cake into her mouth.

Next time, it'll be four or five strawberry rolls, possibly an entire box of six. Maybe more.

For now, the high lasts long enough to power Tokey's bravery. She reaches for the first letter and begins to read.

Dear Jessie,
Junior King caught me starin at him again. I sat in the choir
stand with my hands in my lap waitin for Pastor Jenkins in
the pulpit to quit all his whoopin and hollerin and carryin on.

You know how he do. I cleared my throat to keep it ready to sang and my eyes wandered over the pew with the Solomon boys and their mother. He held his head down to his lap and then suddenly looked up at me. Our eyes met and I felt heat from a flame all over my body.

It ain't the first time he's caught me starin. They started comin to church after his father was killed. Nosy Miss Dolores say that their mother felt like them and their land was cursed. I thank Miss Dolores believed it to, says the devil had gotten ahold of them and maybe the Lord could help.

Made me no nevermind why he was in church. I liked lookin at him. All the other girls like Shad. Remember how slick and smooth he is. Whatcha used to say? He could charm a gnat. He still can. But Junior King is quiet. Like he carried the weight of the world on em hefty shoulders. He was different than all of the boys in church and at school. He quit goin to school to look after the land when his father died. He is even taller now, his body stretchin more than double the pew and his skin still just as dark as oil. But those eyes are the same. Amber like the color of honey. And I likes me some honey.

Pastor Jenkins finally stopped and it was the choir's turn to sang. I stood and Junior King's eyes followed me. He watched me sang and after church he waited for me outside. "Hi." I said. "Maam." He said and tipped his head down and looked at the ground for a second before lookin' up at me. "I...likes to hear you sang." I smiled. "I like to sang." He told me that my sanging sounds mighty nice and makes it worth the walk.

He shuffled his feet, and my eyes followed. His black boots and the hem of his overalls are coated with dust and looked almost brown. The Kingdom was at least three miles from the church.

"I thank you for comin and for what you said about my sangin."

More people come out the church. But neither of us look at them. We kept lookin at each other. Now I knew it was better to stare when he wasn't watchin but standing across from him, I couldn't help it either. Finally, I hear Mama callin my name. I turned to him and said, "I betta go. Nice talkin to you." He nodded and said, "Yes, maam," before walkin' away. But I wasn't ready to see him go yet. "Junior King," I called to him. He turned, his chin up. "It's just King now." I nodded. "You gone be in church next Sunday? I'm gone sang again." I throw a shoulder. "If you wanna come. I'll make it worth the walk." He smiled and I think the sun gets brighter. "I believes I will." Then Mama comes over and pulls me away by my elbow. "Chile…you heard me callin you. I don't want you talkin to that boy again. He ain't nothin but trouble." I look at him one more time and said, "He nice." But Mama wasnt having any of that. "He po'. Comin to church in overalls and boots. Aint got no decent clothes or respect for the Lawd."

Everybody is po in Diggs. But the Solomons have land over 200 acres and that is the same as money, according to Mr. Jimmy. They richer than all us, he say. But not to mama.

She believes Miss Dolores and thinks they are cursed too. All that land and aint nothin to show for it but a raggedy house.

"You shoulda been talkin to that Webb boy. Now he finna be sumthin."

I like James alright. He a farmer like his Daddy, but he finished school. Everybody know that James wont be a farmer for long. He has dreams that are bigger than all of Diggs. Talk about it all the time. I never give my life much thought. I suspect Is get married and have kids just like everybody else. Like Mama. Neva saw the need to dream. I guess Mama want me to have sumthin' better than her. I guess you know a little sumthin bout that too.

I gotta go. Mr. Curtis yellin again and I don't want him to catch me writin.

I miss you,
Hazel

Dear Jessie,
I enjoyed your letter. I keep starin at the postmark. I still cant believe somebody from Diggs made it all the way to New York City. Country come to town.

I'm sorry to hear about Malcolm. You seemed pretty sweet on him. Betta you know now how things are than later, I reckon. But if Is know you, you gone got somebody else now. I cant wait for your next letter so you can tell me who.

Your letters used to be the only thing I had to look forward to. The days are hot and long. Mr. Curtis always hollerin and barkin orders. I hate him so much. I know I shouldn't say that but I do. He aint my daddy but he likes to act like he is and Mama lets him. She said he her only hope and that I must mind him and do whatever he say or we be out on the street. But I say the streets are better than livin with him. Cant wait until I get married and get out of here.

But now I have King to look forward to. We started meetin after church. I tell Mama that I wanted to walk and I would meet up with King down the road by the creek. We walk and talk. Well...Is mostly talk. He listened. He never did talk much. But I think it gave him pleasure to just listen to me spout off about whatever ran through my head at the time. That he didn't have to think. He was sad. I can almost feel it, him carrying the loss of his Daddy and the entire 200 acres of the Kingdom on his shoulders. His Mamas sadness, too.

Sometimes I meet him after school at this secret place on the edge of the Kingdom down from the cemetery just off the creek. Sometimes I pack an extra sandwich and we have a picnic. I brang some of my schoolbooks or my poetry for us to read. King cant read very well so I read to him. I sang sometimes too. He liked when I sung. He stared into my eyes as I sung and it sent a tickle between my legs. I know this is wrong, but I kissed him. He was a perfect gentleman. He never touched me or even tried to kiss me but I cant wait anymore. I ache for him in all the bad places, and I want it to stop. Why no one ever say that being with a man feels *so good? Did you know? I knows you know. Why didnt you tell me?*

It didn't feel that way with James. He came by the house and asked Mr. Curtis and Mama if he could take me to the dance. They said yes. I think Mr. Curtis thinks James is his ticket to getting rid of me and gettin a job workin for James daddy. But no one wants to hire a drunk. I wanted to go to the dance with King but I knows the trouble that would cause. James treated me all right at first. But as the night went on out came the shine and another side of James. On the last dance of the night, he tried to kiss me and when I turned my head, he grabbed me by the throat and said everyone knew that we were gone get married so we might as well start now. I slapped him and told him to take me home. He said that I would regret it.

When James dropped me off, I pretended to go inside and got on my bike and rode to the Kingdom. I wanted to tell King about James but when he opened the door, I just rushed into his arms. King and I did it for the first time that night. Mama said doing this before marriage is a sin. If this is what sin feels like then Is a happy sinner. He so strong. But so tender and soft. You don't expect it from a man that strong.

Now, we cant get enough of each other. I cant make myself stop thankin about him, wonderin what he's doin, if he thankin about me as much as Im thankin about him. Then I see him and his face lights up and I knows he been thankin about me too. We can hardly wait until we are alone before we tear into each other. I think I like his eyes the best. Not just the color but how soft they can get when he sees me. Its how I knows how he really feels. That he loves me as much as I love him.

King asked me to marry him and I said yes. One day by the creek, he asked and gave me a beautiful wooden ring he made. We gone get married just as soon as I finish school. I just gotta figure out a way to tell Mama and Mr. Curtis. I wish you could be there.

Are you ever coming home?

Hazel

Dear Jessie,

Im sorry I haven't written in awhile. So much has happened since I wrote you last. Mr. Curtis got your last letter and read it. He knows all about King and me and it was not too pretty. He waited for me at the kitchen table after school. The entire house smelled like the cheap beer he drank. That damn girl of yours is flirting wit em boys, he said to Mama, your letter smashed in his hand. Mama looked at me and asked, "You being fast?" "We love each other," I said. I figured I was caught and should tell the truth. Mama took the letter out of his hand and read a little. I walked closer to Mama. "Not that boy. Not him." I told her that I loved him and that we were getting married. He slammed his fist on the table and said that I wasnt marryin no one without his say so. I started *to speak and he clapped me across both my cheeks before the words came out. Mama didn't move or say anything. He said he aint standing no backtalk in my own house! And I aint raising no bastard children when she winds up pregnant. I wanted Mama to say somethin to help me. She didnt.*

I ran out of the house and straight to the Kingdom. I banged on the door and King answered and pulled me inside. I tried to hide the bruise, but King saw it. King grabbed the sledgehammer by the door and asked me who did it. I didnt have to tell him. He knew. I told him about Mr. Curtis and how he treated me and Mama. He promised if he ever laid a hand on me that it would be the last thang he did. King told me to stay at the Kingdom. I called out to King not to hurt him, and King said, "I ain't goin to hurt him. I goin to kill him." Shad walked into the living room eating a drumstick. He noticed the missing sledgehammer and ran to King in the car.

I can tell you this much—nobody crossed the Solomon boys. People called them boys but they aint been boys in some time. They had a reputation of fightin and didnt take no mess off anybody, especially Shad. Everybody knew how their Daddy died but stories about the Solomons go way back down the line. Mr. Jimmy and Ray-Ray were always telling stories about the Kings in the Solomon family.

When they got back, King sat the sledgehammer back in its spot, his knuckles covered in blood. He held his side and fell to the floor. A few minutes later, Shad stormed in with the midwife Minnie. I knew why she was here. She delivered babies but also helped patch people up. After a quick exam, Minnie said that it was a through and through wound. She said he was lucky it didn't hit any organs. Mr. Curtis had shot King.

I held King's head but watched Shad talk to Minnie Merl after she stitched him up. I didnt hear everything but did hear Shad say, "Motherfucka cant take an ass whipping so he starts shooting. But I got his ass." "Is he alive?" I heard Minnie Merl ask. "I dont know and dont care," Shad say. "Go stitch him up if he aint dead. I cant catch a case right now." He left again with Minnie but they didnt get there in time. Shad had cut his throat and he bled out on the street. When Shad returned, he was tired and covered in dirt. The next day, Mama reported Mr. Curtis missin' but the police barely looked for him. He was a drunk and probably got what was coming to him or left town is what they said. Mama didnt know what happened and I knows she suspected but she never said. I think she finally felt free and she finally let me go.

Thou shalt not kill. Thats what the Bible say. I knows its wrong to kill. At church, I pray for God to forgive us but I thinks the worlds better without him. Better him than King or Shad or Mama. A few days later, I hear King and Shad talkin. Somethin about the cemetery next to the creek where King and I would meet and Shad leaving town for awhile until this all blows over. They argued about it and finally Shad agreed. He left in the middle of the night.

I neva went home after that. King and I got married a few days later when his wound healed enough to walk to the county. We didnt have money for a big fancy wedding. I wore a simple white dress and picked a bouquet of wildflowers off the side of the road. King wore one of his father's suits. He looked nervous when we said our vows and if I didnt know any betta I could swear I saw a tear in King's eyes. I promised to love him for the rest of my life through sickness and in health until death do us part and I meant it.

He carried me all the way home to the Kingdom, my new home, and into his bed. I write this letter to you now as a baby grows inside me. He says its a boy. Mama and Minnie thank so too. He wants a big family and I want one, too. King seems happy now even though I knows he misses Shad. Im happy too.

Love,
Hazel

Junior should have seen it coming. Should have known when they were able to secure this meeting on such short notice. Should have known when he rushed to open the door to Malone & Kincaid and were greeted by two men in custom business suits, shoes buffed to a high mirror shine, and slicked back hair that didn't move. Should have known when he noticed Mr. James, himself decked out in a navy suit, white button-down shirt, and yellow tie, standing next to the men with a flat smile on his face. Mr. James never smiles, and these are not the type of men who wait, not for a cup of coffee, not for a table at a fine restaurant, and most certainly not in the lobby of a building with their names on it.

Junior knows the complexities and the dualism of his life, of splitting in two and loving two people, of being completely happy and miserable at the same time. With Junior, nothing is easy, and this was too easy.

"Junior," the man in the gray suit says, stepping forward, a hand extended. Junior immediately feels underdressed and regrets his simple light-blue shirt and khakis. He makes up for it with a firm handshake and intense eye contact. "I'm Davis Malone, and this is Walker Kincaid." He gestures toward the man on his left who also extends his hand.

Mr. James steps forward and not only shakes Junior's hand but pats him on the back while he does it. "Junior," he says. "Good to see you." To Genesis, he opens his arms and walks her into a hug. "Hey, baby girl."

"Just us?" Davis asks, looking to the door behind him. He exchanges looks with Walker, and Junior swears he sees a coy grin curl over Walker's lips. "No one else?"

A minute into the meeting and Junior is already unnerved, doubting and questioning that it is he who is here. They expected someone else, a lawyer, possibly all his siblings. Now that he thinks of it, there should be someone else. At least Ellis. Mance and CeCe, perhaps, and Junior's heart pounds at this miscalculation.

"Why don't we move upstairs?" Davis says, angling his body toward the elevator. "We have a conference room all set up."

As they move toward the elevator, Mr. James turns in front of Genesis.

"Why don't you wait here?" he asks, softly. It's a command delivered as a question.

"I'd like her to come," Junior says, and though he doesn't know why, he does. Or maybe he knows. He has needed her since the day he met her, draws strength from her.

Mr. James smiles and doesn't move, doesn't look toward Junior. "Honey," he says to Genesis. His tone is firmer now. "Wait here. As a matter of fact, your mother's favorite bakery is just around the corner. How about you go get her some of those pastries she likes?" He reaches into his pocket, retrieves his money clip, and flips out two twenty-dollar bills. "Get the girls some too."

Confusion covers Genesis's face, but she doesn't challenge him. Instead, she nods and takes the money, slips it into her purse. "Of course, Daddy."

Mr. James moves to join the men as Genesis steps closer to Junior, who looks to the elevator. "Stay calm," she says, snapping her fingers once and touching her nose twice when he drags his attention back to her. "You'll be fine. Listen to whatever Daddy says."

The truth of her words curls around him. This is an information-seeking meeting only. Mr. James is there. Despite their mutual disdain for one another, Mr. James grew up in

Diggs. He knows the history of the Kingdom. He knew King. He would surely keep the meeting on track.

But as Junior watches her walk away, he feels a chill all over his body. Mr. James never says no to Genesis, always giving in to her, happily and playfully spoiling her. And in the face of that surprising denial just now, expectations seemed to shatter too easily. She is hiding something too, yet another something unsaid. Junior of course first thinks it must be about this meeting, and it is little comfort when he decides, as he forces himself to turn toward the elevator, that it must be something else. Mr. James never involved his wife or Genesis in his business dealings. Women had a place, and it was not in a conference room.

His mind flips again when he reaches the three men holding the elevator. Mr. James smiling, actually smiling, Davis and Walker waiting, Genesis accommodating. It reminds Junior of the opposites game Julia and Erica often play. Up is down, left is right, yes is no.

It can be unnerving, sensing a secret everyone but you can see, feeling you're in over your head but not even knowing in what. But Junior knows something about secrets, how to smile through them while keeping a straight face, and how to swallow one and pretend you didn't. They are doing an awful job at hiding their truths. He's lived too long conscripted to secrets, one after another after another. The truth is bitter, but secrets taste sweet, delicious, welcome on the tongue, and smooth down the back of the throat.

"How was the drive?" Davis asks, pushing an elevator button.

"It was all right," Junior says.

"It's a nice drive. Lots of sky and open fields. It's beautiful. I was telling my wife that we need to get out of the city more often."

"My wife is not going anywhere without cell phone service. The reception out there is awful. How on earth do y'all manage that?"

Junior flicks his eyes over to Mr. James, who watches the elevator progression of floor numbers light up as they travel. Nothing upsets Mr. James more than being perceived as country. Junior has even heard him push back outwardly against such statements. But Mr. James's eyes do not stray from the light display.

Lowering his head, Junior reads his own message in this. He smiles to himself. This is how these people view Diggs, him, and his siblings. Diggs as another poor hick town and them a bunch of poor Black folks who have no idea what they're doing. He smiles again, visibly now, finding strength in this, at being underestimated, and a little anger. If they are playing the opposites game, so will he.

"You know we country folk know how to make do," he says, his accent a topography of dropped letters and slurred syllables.

The men chuckle lightly, unamused. "I hope we didn't offend you."

Junior laughs, voracious and obnoxious. "I'm kidding," he says. He slaps Walker on the back, hard. "Don't tell me you guys can't take a joke up here in the big city."

The men join him in laughter. Mr. James eyes Junior warily as they enter the conference room, a spacious rectangle with a twelve-foot-long wooden table in the center. A wall of windows reveals the Charlotte skyline while a sheet of glass forming the opposite wall reflects it back.

Davis and Walker take seats with their backs to the window. They are not handsome men, but Rolexes on their wrists and hundred-dollar haircuts make them appealing enough. Junior knows he's expected to sit across from them, but first, he drops to his knees.

"Junior?" Davis asks, puzzled.

"My father built tables," Junior says from underneath the table. "This is something of the kind of scale he would have built except"—Junior pauses, rising to his feet; he looks at the two men—"it's not real wood. He only built with real wood. Do you know why?" He looks at each of the men again. "It's not easily broken."

"Junior," Mr. James says. "Why don't you have a seat, so we can get started?"

"Yes, of course," Junior says, finally sitting, noticing that Mr. James has chosen a seat next to Walker. Mr. James won't meet his eyes. He just unbuttons his jacket and adjusts his position in his chair.

"Before we get started," Davis says, obviously the leader. "Would you like something to drink? Coffee? Soda? Water?"

Junior's mouth twitches, but he holds up his hand at the offer. "No thank you."

Davis clears his throat and clasps his hands together. "Junior...I think we know why you wanted to meet with us. But why don't you tell us, in your own words, how we can help you?"

Already, Junior feels the temperature in the room rise. "I understand that you may have purchased five acres of my family's land."

Davis and Walker both open silver folders in front of them. "According to this, your family's two hundred acres, on the Solomon Planta—"

Junior interrupts. "The Kingdom."

"Excuse me?" Davis says.

"You called it the Solomon Plantation. We don't call it that. It's the Kingdom."

The two men trade baffled expressions, so Junior continues. "It was called the Solomon Plantation after the white man who bought the land. But it was my ancestors who built the Kingdom and later bought the land from their enslavers."

Walker once again looks to the folder in front of him. "It says here—"

Junior interrupts again, unnerved now. "No matter what that piece of paper says, I'm sure you can imagine how problematic it is to refer to it as a plantation. My ancestors worked that land, and it's been in our family for over two hundred years. We are proud of that. It's long since stopped being a plantation, and I'd rather you not refer to it as such in my presence."

Davis stutters through his words. "We...we...meant no disrespect."

"Tell me," Junior says, folding his arms cross his chest. "What did you mean? To remind me that it was a plantation at one time? You don't think I'm aware of that? We are reminded of it every day, especially when rich white men like you come and try to steal it away from us."

Mr. James clears his throat, and his cronies appear grateful to give him the room's attention. "I think we have gotten off on the wrong foot."

"I believe we have," Davis says. "I apologize for referring to the land as...not the Kingdom. My apologies." He touches his chest when he says this. But Junior doesn't believe his contrition. There's nothing remorseful about these men in their lobby or their conference room or about their Rolexes on their wrists. Junior sits up straighter.

"How did you come to acquire five acres of my family's land?"

"We acquired it from a"—he pauses to look at the folder again—"Shadrick Solomon."

Junior shakes his head. "And how can you legally purchase land if all of the heirs have not agreed?"

The question seems to amuse Davis; he brightens. "Well... there are legal ways to these things."

"To what? Stealing land?"

Davis's teeth are shark white. "I don't know what you've been told, but I assure you that this is all legal."

He slides a folder across the table to Junior, who opens it and immediately begins flipping through it.

"In there you will see that Malone & Kincaid acquired those five acres from Shadrick Solomon. I believe he's your uncle?"

Junior continues reading as Davis says, "Take all the time you need. We understand that this may be hard for you."

Junior closes the folder and pushes it back across the table. "Don't pretend to know or care about me or my family's feelings. Because if you did, you wouldn't be doing this."

Davis leans back in his chair and flicks his pen back and forth between two fingers. "We're not the ones doing this. We didn't start this. We didn't seek out the land. An opportunity dropped in our laps, and we took it. We're businessmen, and we know a good deal when we see one."

"What does that mean?"

Davis looks to Walker and Mr. James, who says, "How can we help you today, Junior?"

Junior is momentarily stunned by his father-in-law's use of the word *we*.

Walker takes advantage of the beat to slide the folder back across the table. "You are welcome to take this to your lawyer. I assume you have one?"

"Of course," Junior says, quickly.

Walker nods. "Mr. James tells us that your father recently passed. We are so sorry for your loss."

Junior laughs, flashing only the edge of a smile. "I'm sorry he's not here. Better me than him. He would not take too kindly to people stealing his land from underneath him. You know... my grandfather killed a man who tried to do the exact same thing." Junior turns to Mr. James. "You know that story, right? Tell them."

"I don't think that's appropriate."

"Maybe not. I wouldn't want you to think that I was threatening you." Junior laughs again. "It's a really good story, though. It involves a sledgehammer. For as long as I can remember, there's been a sledgehammer by our front door. It's been passed down from generation to generation. From my great-grandfather to my grandfather to my father." Junior stops. "And there it sits by the door. I've seen my father grab it a few times, but I've never seen what he's done with it. Makes me wonder…" Junior sighs. "If you guys are ever in Diggs again, I invite you to come to the house. I'll show it to you."

Davis sits up, his face reddening. "I'm afraid, in a week or so, you and your family won't have a house, and you all will be trespassing."

"Yeah…that's right. The notice of trespass. We will be fighting that. My lawyer is filing an appeal as we speak. But even with my limited real estate experience, I know that you can't legally take a house."

"That would be correct," Davis says, shaking his head. "You're right. But it's on land that we own. If you lose, do you have plans on moving the house?"

Junior's confidence seeps out like a stain, but he forces himself to breathe through it. He cannot let on. "I think we're done here," Junior says, standing. "This was a mistake. I should never have come." Junior snatches the folder and shakes it at them. "I'll have my lawyer look this over, and I'll see you in court."

Mr. James stands as well. "Junior…there's more to discuss."

"I appreciate you setting up this meeting but with all due respect, I don't have anything further to say."

"We'd like to hear your family's plans for the rest of the land," Davis says.

Junior doesn't like the question. It implies that they've already considered the land gone. "That's none of your business."

"Junior," Mr. James says, "you need to listen to what they have to say."

Mr. James nods at Davis, who opens his folder once again and pulls out an envelope. He hands it to Junior and slides his hands into his pockets.

"What is this?" Junior asks, just as he peels the opening back to see a check made out to him.

SEVEN

———

"YOU'RE BEING HUSTLED," MANCE says to Uncle Shad when they arrive back at the warehouse garage where they keep the truck. This brings him much pleasure to say, at least as much as he expected it to. Mance knows Uncle Shad won't take well to this realization, being conned by his fence and losing out on what he deemed a huge score, but it relieves Mance. He didn't like the idea of robbing a sick old woman, but he also didn't want Uncle Shad to prosper. Win-win. "There are only a few quality pieces in that house. The rest is knockoff junk."

"What do you mean?" Uncle Shad asks, pulling a pack of cigarettes out of his pocket, patting one out, and lighting it. He takes a long drag and watches the smoke float out of his nostrils. Another man, who Mance knows as Tony, shakes his head. "The fuck you mean I'm being hustled?"

"The house is a mixed-up jumble of both good-quality and cheap furniture. That doesn't happen by accident. People have conned her too."

Mance saw it before with King on the occasion they were called in to evaluate furniture before a sale. As the elders age, family members begin selling off the most valuable pieces, often replacing them to hide their offenses.

Silence stretches until Shad stands abruptly from his chair, his cigarette forgotten, the smoke billowing on. His eyes dart around the room, failing to land on anything. "There must be something in there. Other pieces you didn't see. Did you go through the entire house?"

Mance slides his eyes to Cedric, lurking in the corner, then back to Uncle Shad. He resists the urge to tell him that his son is a fucking coward afraid of his own shadow and that he had to navigate Miss Annie and improvise the tour all on his own, but he doesn't. "The old lady took me on a tour of the house. I went in all of the rooms." He flicks his eyes at Cedric again who lowers his.

"How much do you think it's all worth?"

Mance calculates. He thinks of lying but doesn't. It's not something he's ever been able to do. While Miss Annie randomly spouted off about her family and the house, Mance took every opportunity to kick the tires. "I wouldn't pay more than twenty grand for all of it: there's a grandfather clock that's half of that on its own. If your fence can move it. It's extremely rare, and a piece like that will draw attention."

"What about the jewelry?" Uncle Shad asks, with a slight panic in his voice.

"I wasn't looking for jewelry. I was there for the furniture."

Uncle Shad turns to Cedric, who steps out of the corner. He's been buzzing with restless energy, waiting his turn, jacked up on testosterone like a sixteen-year-old boy.

"Pop…I saw a big chest thing with all these drawers and boxes of jewelry. There were earrings in there, watches, bracelets, and necklaces." He counts off on his fingers. "And drawers of"—he reaches in his pocket and pulls out a diamond ring, clasping it between his forefinger and thumb—"this."

The room falls silent. Cedric stands proud of himself, chin tilted upward, a crooked smirk planted on his face.

"What the fuck did you do?" Mance starts to cross the room, but Tony and Uncle Shad both extend their arms, blocking him. "You stole that?"

Cedric looks baffled. "What? There were drawers of these. She ain't going to miss it."

"She saw our faces, you fuckin' idiot!" Mance yells.

"That woman was crazy. She ain't going to remember us."

"Fuck!" Mance yells and steps toward Cedric. Tony, once again, places his hand on Mance's chest to prohibit his movement. "Take your muthfuckin' hands off me." Tony complies but does not move from in front of Mance.

"Pop…" Cedric starts to say.

"Don't say a fuckin' word." Uncle Shad extends his palm and Cedric drops the ring into it. Shad holds the ring up to the light and inspects it. He smells it in a long sniff and touches his tongue to it.

"It's real. It's about a carat. Maybe more. I'm not sure about the quality." He turns to Cedric, inching closer. "There was more like this?"

Cedric beams. "Lots more. I'm telling—"

Uncle Shad backhands him across the face and grabs him by his scruff, his paw big enough to clamp around the front of his son's neck. He pulls his ear close to his mouth. "You risked the entire operation for this bullshit ring?"

Cedric squirms, struggles in Shad's grasp. "I thought—"

"You thought? You thought?" Uncle Shad says in a quiet menacing voice. "Who told you to think anything? What did I tell you?"

Cedric mumbles an incoherent sentence. His voice doesn't seem to be working.

Shad tightens his grip on Cedric's neck, and he drops to his knees. "Say it again. Louder."

"You told me to listen to Mance."

"That's right. I told you to listen to Mance. And what did you do? You fuck up and jeopardize everything." He tightens his grip again, the veins in his dark hand bulge, and Cedric whines in pain. "Now…apologize to Mance."

"I'm sorry, Mance," Cedric spurts between gasps of air.

"Say it again," Uncle Shad says, his hardened anger cooling.

"I'm sorry, Mance."

Shad releases him, and he collapses to the ground, coughing as air rushes back to his lungs. Tony helps Cedric to his feet.

Uncle Shad returns to his chair, pulling his handkerchief from his pocket and dabbing his forehead with it. He looks at the ring again and throws it at Cedric. The ring bounces off Cedric's chest before hitting the floor with a ping and rolling to Mance's feet. Mance picks it up and holds it between his thumb and forefinger. Mance doesn't know anything about jewelry or diamonds or rings. But looking at this one, he doesn't understand Uncle Shad's frustration. A chip of a diamond in a star-shaped setting with smaller diamonds lining the dull metal band.

Without trying, Lisha's small, delicate hand appears in front of him with the ring on it. The idea of such a ring on Lisha's finger makes his heart trip and race in his chest. Mance doesn't believe in perfection. Nothing is ever perfect. No piece of wood. No single cut. Instead, Mance believes in flawless execution. In choosing and putting all the pieces together. The ring is as close to perfect as it gets, exactly what she'd want, exactly what Mance would pick out for her.

Mance lifts his head from the ring and back to the scene in front of him. Back to the anger that festered inside of him. Back to the idiocy of Cedric. The silence in the room lasts too long, and Mance doesn't like it. He knows what's found in the dregs of silence, how the mind works, creates, imagines. No good comes from too much silence.

Mance walks toward the door, pocketing the ring. The room stirs back to life. Uncle Shad looks up, and Cedric and Tony shuffle their feet.

"Where are you going?" Uncle Shad asks.

"I'm out." Mance stops. "My job is done."

"What? You can't be out. We had a deal."

"I said I would evaluate the furniture. I did that. I never said I would help you steal from an old woman."

Laughter moves through Shad. "You feel sorry for the rich old woman? Maybe you are getting soft."

"Yeah," Mance admits and scoffs at the way Uncle Shad's manipulation rolls off the tongue so easily. "Maybe."

"What about the money?"

"Unless there's a safe full of cash and jewelry, there's not a hundred grand in that house. It's not worth it."

Cedric, still stumbling, still angling for air, says, "Pop... I'm telling you. That jewelry is good. That house is full of old shit. It's a gold mine. Mance doesn't know what he's talking about."

Mance smiles to himself. "You know what? I don't know what I'm talking about. Listen to your son, I'm out." He starts toward the door again, but stops, adding, "I wouldn't take the furniture, it's all marked. Easily traceable."

Uncle Shad considers this as Cedric says, "Give me back that ring."

"It's mine now."

"I stole it! And I want it back."

Mance tilts his head and rights it again. "Come get it."

Uncle Shad cuts his eyes at Cedric, who lowers his before turning back to Mance. "What about the Kingdom, your family, Henry?" Uncle Shad asks.

"I'll figure something else out."

"You forget that land is as much mine as it is yours." Shad

leans back in his chair, clasping his hands in his lap. "What's stopping me from selling more?"

Mance turns to him. "You wouldn't. Not even you would stoop that low."

"Nah...I wouldn't." Shad laughs. "Trust me."

Mance works his jaw.

"I wouldn't need to sell any more land. I wouldn't need the money if you help me with this job. Last one, I promise." He presses his hands together in prayer.

Mance continues moving to the door when Cedric and Tony step in front of it, their stances weak.

Mance squares up, unblinking. "One way or the other, I'm walking out this door. If I have to put both of you through it first, I will."

"Let him go. He'll come back," Uncle Shad says, his voice rising from behind them. He stands and walks to Mance. "They always do."

Mance faces him and exhales, a mixture of anger and frustration.

"Yeah...King came back too," he says, a smile in his voice and mischief bright in his eyes. "Y'all always come back."

"What if he tells someone about the job?" Cedric asks.

"Nah...Mance ain't no snitch." Shad inches closer. "But he's a coward. He's gotten soft. Just like King. Whatever rot that's in our bloodline has been passed to you. And Henry. There's no running from it."

Mance clenches his fists, the rattlesnake in him slithering to the surface. *You can be the one that bends.* He hears Lisha's voice as if she whispered it standing next to him now and the fight seeps out of him. "Fuck that. That ain't us."

Uncle Shad studies Mance for a long moment, then waves his hand. Cedric and Tony slide aside. "Let him go." Then, to someone else, maybe Mance. "It'll never be enough."

Mance turns to Shad once again. "What?"

"Everything you do." He steps closer to Mance and whispers. "King knew it, and you will too." He leans in. "That's if you don't already know."

Mance knows. Of course, he knows. King chose the land. Mance chose the land every time, too. And still, it was never enough.

So, Mance also knows: Uncle Shad is right. Mance will be back. He is certain of this fact and has no idea why, except there's truth in Uncle Shad's words that Mance can't ignore, and that angers Mance. When he leaves, he slams the door behind him and hopes, by some miracle, he is wrong.

⊢──

"Ellis, my man," Ethan says. He shakes Ellis's extended hand before pulling him into a hug. They are opposites. Ethan's shortness to Ellis's height, Ethan's stockiness to Ellis's slenderness. "It's been too long. I was glad to get your call. How have you been?"

Ellis smiles. "Pretty good, considering what we're here for." He turns to CeCe. "Ethan, this is Cecily, one of the heirs of the land I was telling you about and my childhood friend."

He smiles and extends a hand to shake. "Nice to *finally* meet you."

CeCe hears the emphasis as she takes his hand. From his long stare, she feels as if he knows more about her, a lot more, than she knows about him, but she ignores it. "I appreciate you taking the time to meet with us on such short notice."

"It's no problem," Ethan says, gesturing to a chair. "I owe this man my career. I wouldn't be sitting here if it wasn't for him."

Ellis waves a hand and sits in the seat next to CeCe.

"He's being modest, Cecily," Ethan says, taking a seat behind his desk. "My father died in the middle of our first year. I couldn't focus, skipped a bunch of classes. I would have probably quit law school but this man"—he points a finger at Ellis—"wouldn't let me. He wrote my papers *and* his for the rest of the semester."

It's absolutely something Ellis would do and the last thing she needs to hear, considering the love for him churning freely in her heart. She looks at Ellis, a flutter in her belly, the room warming around her. "I'm not surprised. He's amazing in ways you expect and in ways that you don't."

Ellis's grin back at her is also different; the intensity in his stare tells her so. Her words reach deep within and soften his eyes. She's seen this look once before, in the glorious moments when he hovered over her before his mouth opened and he kissed her, softly, slowly, like he had all the time in the world. Thinking of it now, after all this time, sends aftershocks through her.

CeCe knows Ellis feels it and knows it, too, but just as the moment promises to change again, he clears his throat and turns back to Ethan. "Tell me some good news."

Ethan leans forward on his desk, clasping his fingers. "I'm afraid I don't have any. Heir property is a complicated issue."

"How complicated?"

"Well…" Ethan breathes in, holds it, and releases it. "The Department of Agriculture has recognized heir property as the leading cause of Black voluntary land loss. Heir property is estimated—and this is only an estimation because I truly believe it could be higher—to make up more than a third of Southern Black-owned land, roughly 3.5 million acres worth over twenty-eight billion dollars."

"That sounds good… How's the land loss come in?" CeCe asks.

"The law." Ethan huffs. "There are so many loopholes that almost beg investors and developers to worm their way in."

"How?"

"Heir property is a form of ownership in which descendants inherit an interest in the land, similar to holding stock in a company," Ethan explains. "The practice began during the Reconstruction when many Blacks did not have access to the legal system, and it continued throughout the Jim Crow era."

Ethan continues. "After the Reconstruction, Blacks started buying up land, often in less desirable places with arid soil or swampy plots. I don't need to tell you how valuable that land is now. Everyone wants a beach house, and developers want golf

courses and waterfront hotels, so they began using legal loopholes or mechanisms to target landowners without clear titles."
He stops. "Ellis tells me that your father didn't have a will."

"No, he didn't. Is that going to be a problem?" CeCe asks.

"Unfortunately, yes. But I'm not surprised that he didn't
have a will. Your father was born in a time and place when
Blacks really didn't trust Southern courts made up of white
racist judges. That's why they skipped making a will and instead
passed their land down via heir property. Today, in the country
as a whole, the number of Black Americans without a will is
more than double that of white Americans."

"How does not having a will play into this?" Ellis asks.

"Without a will, there's no clear ownership in the eyes of
the law. Sadly, most heirs are unaware of the tenuous nature of
ownership. Clearing a title is a complex process that involves
tracking down every living heir. There are very few lawyers like
me who specialize in this type of real estate law. My law firm has
cleared hundreds of titles and mapped out hundreds of thousands of acres in heir property in the last decade, almost all of
them for Black families," Ethan explains. "Heir property owners
without clear titles do not qualify for certain Department of
Agriculture loans or federal disaster relief, and they cannot use
the land as collateral for private financing or loans."

"Me and my siblings are not the only heirs," CeCe says.
"My father has a brother."

"I know." He looks down at the papers in front of him and
back up again. "Shadrick Solomon."

"How did you know that?" CeCe asks.

"After Ellis called, I did some digging on the Kingdom and the letter of trespass, and discovered that the five acres were acquired by Malone & Kincaid."

"How did that happen?"

"Your Uncle Shad used a legal doctrine called *adverse possession*, which required him to occupy the land for at least twenty years, or seven years with color of title, meaning that he has reason to believe he has a right to possess the property. Unfortunately, as an heir, he does."

Ellis and CeCe trade looks while Ethan continues. "Your uncle made his argument using an obscure law called the Torrens Act. Under Torrens, he didn't have to abide by the formal rules of a court. He just had to prove adverse possession to a lawyer he paid."

"And that's it," Ellis says. "He was awarded the land. Just like that? And this is all legal?"

Ethan runs his hands through his short-cropped hair and massages the back of his neck. "The Torrens Act was initially supposed to help clear titles. But it has been used as a scheme by the rich to seize the land of the poor. It now has a bad reputation for being a legal way to steal land. And it's happening more often. Most of the time, heirs aren't aware that they've lost their land until someone tells them they don't own it anymore."

"Or serves them a letter of trespass," Ellis says.

"There's no way Uncle Shad was capable of filing the necessary paperwork, of understanding all the legal ramifications of all this. Both he and King could barely read," CeCe says.

"I'm afraid that's what could have made all this possible. He wouldn't need to understand. They promised him money and pushed some papers in front of him and told him where to sign. This is all too common."

"I'm still trying to process how this could have happened without King knowing, without any notice," Ellis says.

CeCe knows what happened before Ethan speaks. A tremor ripples through her, and every muscle in her body tenses. King had, in fact, received notices of the Torrens hearings. At least five notices. Those were the letters he sent her, asked her to read, the letters tucked away in her suitcase at the Kingdom. Letters she was too busy to review.

"It can't," Ethan is saying to Ellis before turning to CeCe. "Your father should have received notice of the hearing."

She swallows hard against his words. "He was always getting letters. People have wanted the Kingdom for decades."

Her defense is as weak as old tea. A lump forms in her throat. The fault lies at her feet. You make time for the ones you love, the ones who love you in return. She hasn't made time because she hasn't wanted to. If she took just five minutes to read the letter, none of this would be happening and now they are on the verge of losing everything.

"There was a hearing," Ethan continues. "According to the court documents, King did not appear or file a motion, so the judge granted your uncle the five acres."

"Can we appeal the decision?"

"That's where I would like to start. I'd like to start a series of appeals and filings asking for the decree to be set aside." Ethan inhales and exhales hard. "You should know that there's a one-year window to appeal a Torrens decision. We just missed the deadline. A judge may not hear our case."

"Where does Malone & Kincaid come into all of this?"

"My research uncovered that Shad sold his five acres to Malone & Kincaid after the decision. Malone & Kincaid is notorious for tracking down heirs and making them a low-ball offer on their land. They know these Torrens titles are uncontestable."

"What about the house? How can they legally take possession?"

For the first time, Ethan smiles. "They can't. They may own the land, but you and your siblings still legally own the house."

"But the house sits on the land that we will be legally tres-passing on in a few days."

"This gives us leverage. We can possibly make them buy the house."

CeCe perks up at the lifeline and a fizz of hope bubbles through her. "Buy us out?"

"Absolutely not," Ellis says. "Mance will not go for that."

"Let's hear him out," CeCe says to Ellis, and then to Ethan, "Would they agree to do that?"

"Legally, they must give you the right of way to your prop-erty. They, of course, will fight this and so will we. Purchasing the house saves them time and gives them what they want."

"You think they want the house?" CeCe asks.

"Yes and no. The Kingdom consists of two hundred acres and the five acres they got Shad to claim are the five acres on which the house sits. This is not a coincidence. I believe it was a strategic move to get to what they really want. The entire Kingdom and all two hundred acres."

Ethan stands and walks over to a table. "Come take a look at this."

CeCe and Ellis join him at the table and see a parcel map stretched out.

"This is the Kingdom," Ethan says, pointing and running his finger along the outline. "And here's the house. I'm sure you are aware, but the Kingdom and the land are very valuable. Look at all this waterfront." He runs his hand over the map again. "They could clear this and build homes or hotels."

"What's this long block of land?" CeCe asks, pointing to another plot along the water. "Is that part of the Kingdom?"

Ethan looks at Ellis and back at CeCe. "No, someone recently purchased those ten acres."

"How much do you think it's worth?" CeCe asks, hoping the curiosity in her tone isn't evident.

"I sent a real estate agent out there to assess, and he says all two hundred acres could command a few million dollars."

CeCe sags with relief. A few million dollars. Enough to erase her debts and then some. She twists her lips. She pauses, thinking about this for a moment. Or at least pretending to. It is an act. It's always an act. She doesn't know how to respond, how to ask questions without raising suspicion, so she waits for him to continue, to possibly open the door for further discussion.

It's Ellis who speaks first. "This land has been in their family for hundreds of years. There's a long-standing family promise to never sell the Kingdom. Not a plot of land. Not an acre. Not one inch."

"Well…" CeCe starts, forcing herself to breathe slowly against the rapid thrum of her excited heart. Ellis watches her for a long moment and a thin line of anxiety rises within her. "I think…we will need…you know…to discuss this with everyone." She trips over her words.

Could it really be this easy? No way, she thinks. There's nothing easy about selling ancestral land. Or maybe it could be. The idea makes her head spin. The certainty of it. Sure, convincing her siblings to sell will not be easy. Hopefully, they will see that selling nets the best outcome. Sell it all and gain something versus losing the house and netting nothing.

But she can't present it as her idea. They would see right through her. But not Ethan. It was Ethan's idea to consider the possibility of selling the land. Not hers. She would merely report back exactly what Ethan proposed and let them decide. The irony of it all leached through her veins.

Ethan nods. "I understand. I just want you guys to be aware of what we're up against and what they may throw at us." He looks at Ellis and CeCe. "I'll be honest with you. This is going to be tough. We missed the appeal window, and we're up against a notice of trespass. But you have my word that I'm going to do all that I can."

CeCe and Ellis thank Ethan for his time. First thing Monday morning, they will file an appeal to the Torrens decision.

CeCe couldn't have asked for a better outcome, she thinks, as Ellis continues talking to Ethan while she waits at the door. She didn't like not being in control, the conversation with Mark earlier, her feelings for Ellis materializing. She is the master of her own fate, dammit. And here's where she takes back control, puts an end to it all. Right here, right now. She has no other choice but to keep going, to lie. She's stitched together by lies. So, she'll tell one more. One last time.

Because deniability, in this case, is easier than the truth.

Because the alternative is worse than the truth.

And yet, CeCe feels more disappointment than triumph, more sadness than relief, the idea grating at her core. Her skin feels gritty, her entire body dirty as if covered with sand. It will take a lifetime to rid herself of her guilt, of feeling like a monster, a traitor to her own family. Her eyes well. She doesn't know if it's from the relief, betrayal, or guilt. It's enough pressure for tears, and she thinks she may finally cry.

The tears fail to fall, but a thought does. She will make it up to them, to Junior, Tokey, and Mance. Ellis too. No matter how hard it will be. She makes this vow. And believes it. She's made promises before and kept some. This is one she'll keep.

The thoughts whirling in CeCe's head are too many, her mind too crowded, and she closes her eyes to beat back the unease. She tells herself everything will be okay and that all of this could be a blessing in disguise. Bittersweetness tastes better on the tongue than anything sour. She keeps her eyes closed and wills her mind to go blank.

———

Junior sighs.

And sighs.

The confidence Junior exhibited earlier is a distant memory as his eyes travel the length of the number on the check, past every zero, past every comma. Two million dollars. He blinks. He is not his father. He shouldn't be here, at this conference table, dealing with this. Why did he think he could? He didn't have it. Whatever *it* was that silenced people when King walked into a room. Whatever *it* was that commanded the respect King garnered. Every firstborn King had it. He didn't even know what it was. Just that he didn't have it.

He sighs again.

The sighs are meant to center himself, to keep himself focused. But his thoughts flow anyway, seeping away like water along dry soil, the measured breaths not enough to stop him from folding into himself. Junior feels his gaze drifting out the window to the clouds in the distance, as a memory to curl into surfaces. He should stop himself, he thinks, just before he fades. This isn't the right moment for this…

"What do you think, Junior?" Davis asks, grinning widely, pleased with himself. Two million dollars—change in his pocket.

Junior is elsewhere. Two places at once, his body at the

conference table, and his mind widening out to the dinner with Simon when he told him about the "pause" with Genesis.

By then, Junior had been with other men to satisfy the inner man. Those men were food to keep his body alive, fuel to pretend. But Simon. Simon was air. Necessary. So very necessary. You can live days without food but only minutes without air.

At the restaurant, Junior pressed his hand on top of Simon's, and Simon's eyes darted to it. Junior never made a public display of their relationship. To all who observed them, they were not lovers. They were two friends having dinner, partaking in a movie, buying ice cream. But on this night, everything changed. Genesis said yes.

"Do you mind this arrangement?"

Simon was quiet, sitting with the question, his wineglass elevated in the air.

"What do you think?" Junior asked.

"No."

Junior drew back, his breath held in his chest. "No?"

"No," Simon said again, but this time a corner of his mouth twisted up. "No, silly. As in *I don't mind*."

A feeling that Junior could only describe as joy flooded him. A year of sneaking around, romps in the backs of cars, all ended here. He could be with Simon free and clear, without guilt. Finally, he could belong to Simon.

As Junior studied Simon, the bump on his nose, the curve of his full lips, his sharp eyes behind his glasses, details long ago memorized, he expected to see joy. Instead, that face fell into one of hesitation. "What's wrong? This is great." Junior looked at the table to his right, then left, and lowered his voice. "We can finally be together."

Simon's eyes also danced around the crowded restaurant. There was a spark in them, but it flickered. "Can we? Can we really be together?"

Simon tried to move his hand, but Junior tightened his grip. He must be clearer. Simon had heard this before; he knew the words by heart. "Yes," he said, raising their clasped hands and kissing Simon's. He didn't look around the restaurant again, his attention locked on Simon, his other hand stroking his cheek. "Yes."

Junior and Simon fell into each other as soon as they crossed Simon's threshold. Through the tug and pull, Junior felt himself breathe in, then out, in, out. He finally had his air. For the first time in a long time, he could breathe.

"JUNIOR!" Mr. James says, a muffled sound.

Junior hears his name from a great distance, and he pulls his mind back to his body.

"I'm...sorry...I," he starts, still tangled in his thoughts. He blinks and sees the hardened face of his father-in-law. How long have they been calling him?

Davis clears his throat and eyes both Walker and Mr. James before speaking again. "I was saying...asking...what you thought. Do we have a deal?"

The sudden shift from his mind back to reality disorientates

Junior and he leans forward, elbows on the table, to pull himself back to the present. A chill of embarrassment crawls through him.

Mr. James's expression hardens further. "We need you to focus here."

"I think...I think..." Junior picks up the check. "This is a very generous offer."

Davis cocks his head, revealing a cleft in his chin Junior hasn't noticed before. "We thought so." He produces another piece of paper, and his fingertips slide it across the table to Junior. "If you just sign right here, that will be all yours. Well... part yours." He laughs.

Walker pulls a pen from his breast pocket. "Why don't you use my pen?"

The pen trembles in Junior's hand. It is all happening too fast. Surely they do not expect him to make this decision right now. "I'm afraid I cannot sign this." Junior places the pen next to the check and slides them both across the table to Davis.

"We evaluated your land, and that"—he points to the check—"is more than generous. We think this is the best solution to our little"—he pauses, searching for the right word—"predicament. Let's leave the lawyers out of this and settle this thing for ourselves."

Mr. James leans on the table and knits his hands together. "Now...Junior," he says, expanding his voice into a boom that vibrates around the room. "This is a good deal. I think you should take it. Think about what you can do with this money. What this kind of money could mean for your family."

Junior holds the check in his hand. Of course, he knows what this money means. It means his freedom.

Mr. James sits back and studies Junior when the silence expands. "Your father had an opportunity like this once," Mr. James says, crossing his arms. "Don't be your father. Don't be stupid."

Even after the revelations of this meeting, Mr. James's tone surprises him. They are not enemies. Not friendly but not this. "What does that mean? Are you calling King stupid because he didn't want to sell our family's land?"

The fake grin again. "I knew your father. I know you, and I know you can see a good thing right in front of you. Can't you, Junior? Can't you see what this is?"

Junior doesn't know how to respond to this. "Of course, but—"

"There are bigger issues at play here, Junior," Mr. James breaks in. "More than you could possibly comprehend."

Suddenly, Junior becomes aware of the moment, of the magnitude of the meeting, of everything. He had an inkling in the lobby with those leering gazes. It's always the weakling that the pack attacks. That's why they smiled and asked about Mance and why Mr. James kept Genesis out of the room. Divide and conquer. He'd ruin it, if given the chance, they figured. They just had to press hard enough and in the right way, attack him full force.

Davis interrupts, speaking over Mr. James. "Why don't we give Junior some time to think about it?" He stands and Walker follows. Mr. James pushes the chair out from underneath him and buttons his coat. His jaw flexes, the tight muscle jumping, his posture rigid and stiff.

Junior doesn't know what to do, and his heart races at this, at not knowing. He reaches down, willing the courage he exhibited earlier to resurface but it's gone. Now all that remains is what's always come easily to Junior, the only thing that hasn't failed him, the first thing he always does, the role he has to play again. He was foolish to think his obligation to King ended after his funeral. And he wonders if it will ever end. If he's being foolish about that too.

For now, back to pacifying. Back to swallowing. Back to smiling through it.

For Junior, this is the hardest part of dwindling himself down, the safe place to step.

So, he does.

Junior smiles.

He smiles wider.

He smiles until the corners of his mouth stretch across his face, until his cheekbones shake under the weight of such a forced smile.

The place before the lightheadedness starts. He normally feels it coming on, and sometimes, he can stop it. But this one arrives with little warning.

He needs to leave.

The key to running away is knowing when you've been somewhere long enough. "I think that's a good idea," he says, abruptly standing. He clumsily scoops up the papers and the folder in front of him into a hazardous pile. "I'm going to take this to our attorney and discuss it with my brother and sisters."

"Okay," Davis concedes, his hands up, palms up. "You do that."

At the edge of Junior's vision, he sees a dot of red on the conference room table. By the time Junior's hand darts to his nose to pinch it, two more dots splat on the table, and a steady stream oozes around his fingers.

"Jesus," Walker says, almost laughing. "Are you all right?"

"Do we need to call for a doctor?" Davis asks, his eyes widening. "There's blood everywhere."

Junior's nosebleed amuses them and annoys Mr. James. Junior pinches his nose and holds his head back. Mr. James grunts and reaches into his pocket, retrieving a handkerchief, irritation radiating from him in waves. "This happens from time to time."

"I'll be fine," Junior says. There's frustration in his voice but sadness rattles there as well. "They never last long."

"Have we upset you, Junior? Is this too much for you to handle?" Davis says. "Maybe we shouldn't have sprung all this on you. That kind of money is a lot to process."

The condescending tone in his voice angers Junior. They knew to expect this, pushed for it, applied the right amount of pressure. The thought is a knife to his stomach.

"And what happens if we don't accept your offer?" Junior asks through his fingers and the handkerchief. It's all Junior can think to say in the midst of his warring emotions.

Through his downward glance, Junior sees Davis lower his

chin to his chest and smile to himself, like Junior said something funny. Maybe he did; the idea of anyone turning down such an offer sounds preposterous, even to him. "Well…let's hope it doesn't come to that. No one turns down that kind of money." Davis walks over to Junior and opens his coat, tucking the check into the inside pocket. He smiles and pats Junior's shoulder. "Clean yourself up and take that to your family. Call us tomorrow when they accept."

Junior can do nothing but stand there and bleed, his face burning. Shame hits him in a cold embarrassing wave. He says nothing out loud. He can only feel a pang of sorrow that this meeting has spiraled into disaster. That he has failed yet again.

Tokey jerks awake with a rumble in her belly. She listens. The house whistles with moving gusts of air, the swelling of wood, the taps and pecks of water dripping, the whirling of ceiling fans, and the groan of pipes. She sees nothing. The dark of night cloaked the outside and inside the house. The reddish glow of dawn breaks against the horizon. It is not yet morning.

As she has before, Tokey dreamed of her mother. It's always the same dream. Hazel lifting and twirling her, laughter and joy pouring out of her, the sunlight brightening all around them. She can never make out the details of her face. She can't distinguish the curve of her nose or the fullness of her lips, her features. Only this time, in last night's dream, the vision incorporated everything new she learned about her. Then and now, in her mind, she sees a woman with her complexion and wide brown eyes and light-brown hair and a bright smile. She thinks she sees a vision of herself. She tries to push past the haze to see more, but she can't; the same vision plays on repeat.

Tokey shifts upright on the bed. Her stomach rumbles again, a reminder of the four additional strawberry jelly rolls she pushed into her mouth. As her eyes adjust to the dark, she sees the empty box and wrappers strewn on the ground.

She didn't plan on eating so much. She never does. It's always one. Just one. Before one becomes two and two becomes four. But the contents of Hazel's letters demanded it. After each one, she waited until her body tingled and the high settled within her. It's where she needed to be—dull enough to read each letter. She fell asleep last night reading Hazel's letters, her words wobbling before her eyes lost focus and she drifted off.

It seems strange to Tokey that she feels a little more complete than she did yesterday. In three letters, she learned more about King than she had when he was alive. Hazel too, of course. King became a different person in her eyes while Hazel finally became a person. The letters flesh them out and make them whole. They tell her that King's dedication to the Kingdom stretches further than she realized, that the death of his father placed responsibility on his shoulders, and that he carried that responsibility for over fifty years. The letters tell her what she assumed: that Hazel and King were in love. And not because of obligation or circumstance. A real, true, honest love that happens once in a lifetime. Why else would King not speak of her?

Tokey wants to wrap herself in their love, to believe that even though she didn't see it, she could be an innocent observer of their love story. She almost has passages of the letters committed to memory. The declarations of love are the ones she likes best and rereads over and over and over again, staring at the way Hazel looped her letters and crossed her *ts*. *Those eyes are the same. Amber like the color of honey. And I likes me some honey... I ache for him in all the bad places, and I want it to stop... I cant make myself stop thankin about him, wonderin what he's doin, if he thankin about me as much as Im thankin about him. Then I see him and his face lights up and I knows he been thankin about me too.*

The letters also tell her what she didn't know: they killed a man.

Her head swims at this. There's no ignoring it. Tokey never expected to learn that their love came at the cost of a life. And she waits to see if she cares. She should care about this more than she does.

Tokey closes her eyes to keep the tears in. It doesn't work. Tokey knows it's foolish to expect this to have a happy ending.

So she reads on, three letters left, with tears in her eyes and a flutter in her heart.

Dear Jessie,
Thanks for your letter. Its been so long. I been writin but the letters kept comin back return to sender. Are you really in Paris now? May Lou smiled big when she handed me your letter. Said she aint neva seen a letter with a mark from Paris.

My life is so different now. Junior King was born seven months to the day of the weddin and Mance a year after that. My Junior King is quiet. He dont like too many noises and sounds so he dont like being in the workshop too much. But not Mance. He wild, fearless, trailin behind King. King said Mance reminded him of Shad and his job as Mance's father was to make sure he dont kill himself.

Speaking of Shad, he comin back home. He gotten into some trouble in New Orleans and he needs to lay low. I know this will make King even happier. I knows he missed his brother and I think he feels like he owes Shad for what he did. You asked me how I felt about what happened, if I feel guilty and I believes I do. I pray and ask God to forgive me. But I also dont want to lie and say that Im not happy he aint here. Mama is much happier now.

King works from sunup to sundown. Its a lot to keep up with the house and the land. I knows its hard on him day after day. Folks around here losing their land. The Wilsons lost their farm. James say they didnt pay the taxes. Such a shame. It upset King, made him work harder. Hes tired but always makes time to play with the boys. James knows some people who want to buy some of the Kingdom but King refuses. Told him to get off his land in his fancy car and expensive suit. James winked at me and says to call him if Is ever need anything. I asked King about James visit and he says he would neva sell, especially to the people James worked for in Charlotte. Theys crooks, he said.

I spend my days with the boys trying to teach them they letters and numbers. I believes another baby grows inside me. Its a girl. I knows it. I can feel it and she feisty and ready to take on the world. I hope to have many more.

I aint sure where to send this if you will even receive it. I look at the envelope with Paris stamped on it and can't believe you are all the way over there. Is it fancy?

Love,
Hazel

EIGHT

———

"I'M GLAD YOU CAME," Junior says to Simon as he settles into the front seat, Simon's usual scent of musk and pine descending along with him. He didn't expect Simon's call. Junior figured it should be him who reaches out first. Simon made his position about the state of their relationship as clear as water. Something needed to change. Simon wanted more, deserved more, and would settle for nothing less. So what did this call mean?

Nervous about the answer to that question, still Junior basks in Simon's proximity. The inner man stirs at his fresh haircut, his shoulders in a button-down, his thick thighs in jeans. Was everyone around him stronger than him? More determined? Simon has the mental fortitude to live his life—his real life—in the open, out loud. The thought sends a wave of appreciation flooding through Junior. There's room there now, anxiety over King's death having finally dissipated.

When Simon called, Junior was poised not to think, but to say yes. Thinking was his problem. All he ever did was think, his mind constantly churning like a hummingbird's wings. Thinking was the last thing Junior wanted to do after the disastrous meeting at Malone & Kincaid, so when Simon called and offered to meet him in Diggs, Junior didn't think—he went.

It is a risk, seeing Simon out in the open. But that risk is just a flicker he dismisses. He needs Simon, his warmth and his love. Junior has grown cold without it. It felt like more of a risk to let Simon have his say over the phone.

Junior will make Simon say his piece to his face. He will sit here in the pale half-light and watch as the dark night covers them in shadow while Simon forms the sentences. He won't let him off the hook easily. Won't let him end their three years and his first love for a man in a single long-distance phone call. If this is the end, Junior wants to be present for it. Junior owes Simon so much, but Simon owes him at least that.

"I could have come to the Kingdom," Simon says, shifting his body to look at Junior. His gaze has penetrating power that drives deep into Junior's heart. He feels disconnected from him but with one look, he comes alive again. "I would have liked to see it."

Junior blanches at the suggestion, inhaling and exhaling heavily, thumbing the steering wheel, staring straight ahead. He would have liked that as well. Maybe seeing what Junior faced would have eased the tension between them. Helped Simon see the grand scale of all that sits on Junior's shoulders. But that can't happen. Not now.

"You're not sleeping. I can tell."

Junior knows what Simon sees: dull eyes that hide none of his exhaustion. Yesterday, Junior slept a few hours. The day before, an hour. Junior turns to the window. The sun hovers at the edge of the horizon. The day keeps pressing, as do Junior's thoughts.

Tomorrow, he'll have to face his siblings and tell them he failed. The sun will rise and shine a bright light on another day when he could not live up to his responsibility. He won't tell them of his blackout or the expressions of the three men when he emerged from it. He won't tell them about Mr. James or his possible role in their family's downfall. That is for Junior to handle. He will tell them he tried and about the two-million-dollar check folded in his pocket. And that he thinks they have no choice but to take it.

"What are you battling in your dreams that's keeping you awake?"

Junior sighs and adjusts his position. "I see him—King—and he's there, holding out a tape measure. I'm nervous because I know if I measure wrong, he'll be disappointed. But I take it and measure. It's wrong, of course."

"What does he say?"

"Nothing. And that's the worst of it. He never says anything."

"So…how do you know he's disappointed?"

"My father doesn't have to say anything for you to know that he's disappointed. You just know."

Simon's face darkens for a second, like a dimmer switch.

There is only one thing left to say, the true reason for his visit. Junior swallows, feasting on the way Simon's lips plump after he pulls them in and releases them. It awakens an eager desire to feel them again on his skin, the pleasant jolt when they touch.

They have been just like this, Junior in the driver's seat, Simon in the passenger's seat, many times before. This is how and where they often met, in the back school parking lot, behind the football stadium, where no one parked except coaches, and not even them at night on a weekend. It's where Junior, before he built up the nerve to go to Simon's loft in Charlotte, first acted on the sexual tension between them after a long day of prolonged staring, watching him move, the ache in him building, his hardness pressing and stretching against his slacks, anticipation coursing through his veins. Once Simon entered the car, Junior didn't speak. He didn't think either. He pounced.

Now Junior just wants to feel good.

He pounces, just like that first time, grabbing Simon's neck tight, each of his fingers taking possession of him, inch by inch. The pad of his thumb massages Simon's neck and feels his thick pulse jump, increasing under the duration and intensity of Junior's stare.

"What are you doing?" Simon whispers, shocked.

"Looking at you."

"We shouldn't be here," Simon says, his eyes scanning the parking lot. He moves out of Junior's reach.

But Junior keeps his eyes on him and grabs his neck again, pulling Simon to him harder. The touch vibrates from his fingers throughout his entire body. It passes over the hollow parts of Junior, filling him and snuffing out his pain. "I know," Junior says, inching closer until his cheek grazes Simon's, until he kisses the crook of Simon's neck, the plushness of his lips devouring the smooth skin there.

He needs Simon to remember their nights right here, in this parking lot, before he says whatever he came to say. He needs to hold him long enough to remember a time when words didn't need to be said and had no place outside of their thoughts. He just has to hold on long enough for Simon to remember it all.

"You shouldn't be doing that." Weakness lines Simon's tone, a softness that only encourages Junior. He knows Simon won't deny him, knows how much his nearness and forcefulness arouses him.

He ignores Simon's unwillingness and tugs at his shirt. "I know."

Junior's alive again. Air flows in and out of his nose, and his heart hammers in his chest. He can't stand tall in a conference room. Can't stop himself from fleeing to the outer recesses of his mind. He can't stop today from ending and tomorrow from coming. But this? This he knows how to do. He can touch. Feel and be, release the ache, the good ache, and fall. Simon makes him feel whole when all others split him in two. Simon gives him peace and comfort and Junior welcomes it, always, because it pushes out all other feelings. Tomorrow is another day, and today is now.

"Are you going to tell me what happened?" Simon asks, breathless.

"Later."

"Junior…" Simon pauses, concentrating on what words come next. "We need to talk."

"No," Junior says, muffled, his mouth once again at Simon's neck and now his hand on Simon's hardness. Junior groans, his heartbeat heavy and fast.

"I—"

Junior makes no apology for the kiss that crashes his lips against Simon's, swallowing his words without tasting them. Simon attempts to escape him, fisting Junior's shirt and pulling, but he can't flee his own attraction, and his resolve cracks. It's one of the beliefs they have in common. That love can be gentle and comforting, but it can also be primitive and sordid. Simon's fight dissolves under Junior's honesty and the softness of his face. Simon matches his kiss with his own.

It's all the assurance Junior needs.

Junior pushes away all obstacles to Simon's skin, gripping folds of his clothes until he is grasping flesh. He touches and pulls at him as if he can't stop himself. He cannot. The car quiets of words and echoes with the sound of the rustling clothes, zippers yelling, buttons popping, and heavy panting. Junior rips open Simon's shirt and reaches for his belt, loosening it with a tug. Sliding his hands inside Simon's pants, he brings Simon's hardness to the air. It jerks to attention in his hand.

"What now?"

Junior looks at him, his eyes aflame with desire, his breath labored. His mouth twitches. "Cum in my mouth."

———

The kitchen is quieter than it should be, Tokey thinks as she lays strips of bacon on a baking sheet. Nine in the morning the day after all the siblings returned home from their respective assignments. They are to debrief and discuss what each of the others discovered. And yet, she stands in the kitchen alone.

She knows at least one of her siblings is awake. That morning Tokey woke to a scream, Mance's morning scream, in the early hours, just before sunrise. She could set a watch to it, every morning the same. She would never tell him that she knew he did this. That she knew it started after Henry's birth. He would view it as a sign of weakness for her to know, when it was anything but.

This morning, he screamed twice. A new one for a new worry: the Kingdom.

He was sad. I can almost feel it, him carrying the loss of his father and the entire 200 acres of the Kingdom on his shoulders.

There in the predawn glow, Hazel's words intrude Tokey's thoughts, and she remembers the pressure King felt concerning the land outlined in her letters. And now Mance feels the same pressure as King.

Ellis arrives as Tokey places the baking sheet in the oven. He greets her with a good morning and plants a kiss on her forehead. It's a scene that has played out so many times over the years.

Briefly, she thought that maybe something could blossom between them. With CeCe in New York and Mance in and out of prison, it had been just the two of them. She held his hand at Elyse's funeral, and he helped King in the workshop when Junior refused and Mance was serving his time. Hadn't proximity brought him and CeCe together? Maybe it would be the same with him and Tokey.

But there has always been only one woman for him. Years passed as Tokey watched him try to get over her sister, watched him date and bring other women to the Kingdom. He got close with one and Tokey thought he'd finally settle down, but none were CeCe. Tokey often wondered if CeCe thought about him as much as he thought about her.

I cant make myself stop thankin about him, wonderin what he's doin, if he thankin about me as much as Im thankin about him.

"Everyone here?" he asks, turning around a chair and sitting backward in it. "Tokey?" Ellis asks. "You okay?"

Tokey shakes her head, clearing it of thought. "Yeah…" she says. "What did you say?"

"I asked if everyone is here."

"I haven't seen them…"

Just then, CeCe walks into the kitchen and stops when she sees Ellis.

"Good morning," he says.

"Good morning."

Ellis and CeCe share a long look before CeCe breaks it. Light pours into the kitchen but Tokey swears it's not just from the sun. Again, it reminds Tokey of something in Hazel's letter and her words echo in her head.

I see him and his face lights up and I knows he been thankin about me too.

"Can I help?" CeCe asks.

Tokey almost laughs. She can't remember the last time CeCe helped, especially in the kitchen. CeCe doesn't wait for an answer. She washes her hands and moves to the counter and starts kneading the dough. Ellis stands and pours himself a cup of coffee before returning to his chair.

Tokey watches as CeCe admires him longingly, and when she turns away, Ellis does the same. She saw them kiss once before they went to college and remembers the tenderness of it. How he cupped her face, and she stared up at him. It was after the incident with his father. He seemed to forget the pain for a second. They never formally announced their courtship, but everyone at school knew. They tried to hide it, but there are some things that cannot be hidden—a smile across the hall—no matter how hard you try. But they were never together at the Kingdom, not out in the open. Here, he belonged to King and Mance. Later, Tokey discovered that they had been meeting in his trailer.

Sometimes I meet him after school at this secret place on the edge of the Kingdom down from the cemetery just off the creek.

CeCe moves a strand of hair from her face with the back of her hand. Ellis walks over to her, and she lifts her eyes to meet his. "You have flour on your cheek," he says but doesn't wipe it away. His hand twitches, folding into a fist and out again. Tokey can almost feel his desire to touch CeCe's face. There's so much yearning; the yearning itself feels physical, like something she can touch.

Our eyes met and I felt heat from a flame all over my body.

CeCe brushes her own cheek and returns to kneading the dough.

She turns the dough with precision, the red of her nails covered in flour. Tokey imagines that CeCe has not baked in years, but there are some things you can't forget, no matter how hard you try.

Tokey never mastered CeCe's cooking and baking abilities, though she tried. Growing up, they all had roles to play to keep the Kingdom going. CeCe's role relegated her to the kitchen to cook all the meals. Tokey, years younger than her siblings and, therefore, too young to be tasked with a major responsibility, wanted to learn and stood next to CeCe observing, itching to cover her hands with flour or learn how to cut up a whole chicken, but CeCe never made time to teach her. She didn't want to be there, hated that such a responsibility fell to her.

Tokey hates remembering such memories and hates the usual bitterness toward CeCe that ebbs in when she does. "Thanks, but I didn't ask for your help," Tokey snaps.

"I just…"

"Now you want to help me? I remember coming to you about these biscuits and you never had time to teach me."

"I was studying."

"And when you were making them, I would ask to help, and you would push me out of the way."

"I didn't have time to show you. I had to make everything and study. Do you know how hard that was?"

"Well…it paid off, didn't it?"

"Here we go," CeCe says, throwing her hands up. Specks of flour fill the air.

Ellis clears his throat and stands. "I'm going to…um…" He moves his head from side to side, looking for an escape. "Not be here."

"What is the matter with you? I'm just trying to help," CeCe says.

Ellis leaves the kitchen, and after he does, Tokey turns to CeCe. "Don't hurt him again."

"What are you talking about?"

"Ellis. He still loves you. He never stopped, and I can see it starting back up all over again."

"That is none of your business."

"You make it my business when you leave, and I have to pick up the pieces. It took him a long time to get over you."

"You don't know what you're talking about."

"I don't? You all have never been as sly as you think you are."

"Why are you so worried about me and what I'm doing? When's the last time you got fucked? Maybe that's the problem."

"Don't you dare turn this around on me. I don't want to see him hurt again."

Tokey refills her lungs in preparation for whatever CeCe will say next. CeCe releases a shuddering breath and stands still. She looks down at her hands covered in flour, inspecting both sides.

"I'm not going to hurt him," she says, finally, her tone lower, softer. "That's the last thing I want."

Tokey's shoulders droop against CeCe's admission. An apology sits on the tip of Tokey's tongue, but she doesn't say it. "Men like Ellis...like King...they love and they love hard."

"King?" CeCe says, eyeing her.

"He loved her, and he never got over it."

"He loved who?"

"Mama."

Tokey doesn't know why she shares that with CeCe now. She doesn't know how their story ends. She still has two more letters to read. And yet, a strong sense of familiarity about whatever their ending is grips her.

"How do you know that?"

Tokey looks up to CeCe with wet eyes and opens her mouth, but Junior walks in, and the words stay inside.

"Hey," he says. "Are we doing this?"

Tokey straightens and wipes her cheeks. CeCe widens her eyes at Tokey who shakes her head with a promise. Later. "Mance is in the workshop, and Ellis was just in here."

"We are both here," Ellis says, entering the kitchen with Mance.

They make their plates of food and sit at the assigned seats of their youth. King's chair sits empty, and more than once Tokey notices one of them looking at it.

He's still here, she thinks. In us. In our lives. She doesn't know how to tell them. Make them understand what she suddenly knows about him and his life before them.

"Our meeting with Ethan went pretty well," Ellis says, looking at CeCe. "He's filing a motion to vacate the trespass notice."

"Does he think we'll get it?" Mance asks.

CeCe answers. "Probably not."

"Why?" Mance asks.

"Because of the length of time," Ellis says.

"So, we have to leave?" Tokey asks.

"We need to be prepared for the possibility," Ellis says.

The table turns to Tokey. "I packed up as much as I could, but it's hard to pack a life in a day."

"We can help," Junior says. "Everyone, just grab anything of importance. We can get the rest later."

"What if we lose the trespass, then what?" Tokey asks.

"Depends." Ellis looks at Mance. "What did you find out about Uncle Shad? Did he—"

"Yeah. He admitted that he sold five acres."

The admission doesn't surprise Junior, who asks, "Why would he do that?"

"Because he could," is all Mance says. "Says he didn't know the land was the Kingdom."

"How could he sell without King's permission?" Tokey asks.

Ellis explains the Torrens Act just as Ethan explained it to him and CeCe. Junior, Mance, and Tokey all look on with wide expressions.

"Wait a minute. If he sold the land, how does that include the house?" Mance asks.

"It doesn't," Junior says. "We still own the house."

"How can we own the house but not the land?" Tokey asks.

"The house is not part of the land but since it sits on it," Junior says, "they are claiming it. Unless we move it."

Mance laughs. "Move a house? That's bullshit."

"And they know it," Junior says. "It's what they wanted all along. They want the Kingdom. All of it. They know we can't move the house."

"So they get it by association?" CeCe asks.

"Afraid so," Junior says.

"Ethan checked, and the workshop is not included," Ellis says to Mance.

The room quiets enough for Tokey to hear Hazel's words again. *Nosy Miss Dolores say that their mother felt like them and their land was cursed.*

"We're not in any better position than we were a few days ago," Tokey says.

"We are. Now we know what we're up against. Who we're up against. We will file the motion to vacate the trespass and if we lose, we file an appeal to overturn the Torrens ruling," Ellis says.

"And if we lose both?" Tokey asks.

"We won't," Mance and Ellis both say.

"But what if we do?" Tokey asks.

"We burn it to the ground," Mance says.

"Or…" Junior pushes his plate away and pauses for a second before saying, "We sell it all."

CeCe's head lifts. "What are you talking about?"

Mance doesn't wait for an answer. "We're not selling."

"Of course not, but let's hear him out," CeCe says. It doesn't surprise Tokey that CeCe would say this. CeCe would latch onto any idea that involved money.

"Malone & Kincaid made me an offer." Junior looks at each of them, his expression pained. "Two million dollars for all of it." He reaches into his pocket and pulls out the envelope.

"All of it?" CeCe asks, taking the envelope and pulling out the check. Tokey thinks she sees relief in her eyes.

"All two hundred acres and the house," Junior says.

"And what did you say?" CeCe presses. She passes the check to Mance, who doesn't look at it.

"I didn't say no."

"You should have," Mance says, coasting the check back to Junior. "You should have told them to go fuck themselves."

"Why?" CeCe asks.

"Is it always about the money with you?" Tokey snaps.

"This is not my idea, and I'm just asking questions. Ethan broached the idea of us selling during our meeting." She cuts a glance at Ellis who nods slowly.

Mance's head jerks up. "What?"

"We should at least consider it. What if we lose? At least we can get something out of it."

"And lose our family legacy in the process," Mance says. "Everything King has worked for."

"Better than to just give it away," Junior says.

"Is this what you want?" Mance asks. "You never wanted to be responsible. This frees you, right? From the land, from him."

"You know that's not true."

"Is your father-in-law pressuring you?" Mance asks. "He's wanted this land since we were kids."

"How do you know that?" CeCe asks Mance, who keeps his eyes locked on Junior. Junior has a troubled look on his face. His habit when Mr. James comes up. Tokey knows they don't have the best relationship, and that Junior contorts himself into who he believes he needs to be for Mr. James, but this was more than that.

Junior shuffles in his chair and his forehead creases before he says, "I told them that I would discuss it with you guys."

"We can't discuss this without Uncle Shad. We're not the only heirs." Mance hits the table with a thud. "We can't sell all of it without him."

"And if we don't sell all of it and we lose both appeals, what's stopping him from selling more?" CeCe asks.

Mance stands in a huff and paces the kitchen before kicking a kitchen cabinet until the door splits in two. He storms outside. A profanity laced scream erupts later.

Ellis scoots his chair back and stands. "Let's not decide

anything right now. We have options. There's still a chance we could win in court."

"And if we don't?" Junior asks.

It is the briefest of pauses, of inhaled breath, motionless movement, but one they all take together.

Junior's question hangs in the air. In that space, Tokey realizes the presence of something bigger than her, than all of them. Unspoken truths and a series of coincidences. The realization hits her that this, all of this, is no accident.

Tokey doesn't have any idea what it means. She needs to finish reading the letters.

———

"You're taking me somewhere in the Kingdom? I thought you were taking me somewhere I've never seen. I've seen every inch of this place."

"Not this you haven't."

After the breakfast at the Kingdom, and after calming Mance down, Ellis suggested working on the case at his office in town before tomorrow's first hearing. But first, a stop somewhere CeCe has never seen.

CeCe knows Ellis wants to get her alone. She remembers his face just as the elevator doors opened to Ethan. She remembers the moment they shared at breakfast. She is so certain of this fact she almost declined his invitation. But she couldn't.

Now, they ride in silence as Ellis turns and veers down the road to the trailer where he grew up. CeCe remembers this road, where it ends, its route worn and traced into her memories. The road curves, and the trees open to what Ellis called home for most of his childhood. But there's nothing there but an empty space.

"What happened to the trailer?"

Ellis slides the truck into park and stares out at the empty lot. He rests his head on the headrest and sighs. "I bulldozed it after Mama died. But I could have ripped it apart with my bare hands." A shadow crosses his face, and his body winds tighter. "I hated that trailer, but she loved it. I offered to buy her a new one, move her into a house, or build her one, but she refused."

CeCe feels the pain in every word, remembers it as if it were a moment ago. Because it was to her and to Ellis. Scabs bleed when you pick at them. She never lost the feeling of that day, the sting in her throat as she watched Ellis sink to the floor. She blinks and she's back in the rundown trailer with patchwork metal for siding, broken windows, and patched holes in the floor. Then to another scene: the living room in disarray, blood splattered everywhere, a bloody Ellis holding a knife and his father on the ground.

The day Ellis's father stabbed him was the day CeCe realized she loved him. It was a white cardigan sweater with a tiny hole in the shoulder that did it. Her brain reminds her of this, the memory as clear and keen as glass. The happiest day of her life was also the worst day of Ellis's.

CeCe didn't know where he had gotten the sweater. She didn't care. The heat in his truck stopped working, and he figured she might get cold on the drive. Adolescent love wasn't supposed to last. It's like a flame. It burns, it brightens, but it eventually burns out. This thing between them lasted through spring drives to see the blooming of the wildflowers, the lazy summer storms peppering the tin roof while they kissed, and the falling of the leaves as they talked. And by winter, it still burned as if just lit. She slipped the sweater onto her shoulders and knew it wasn't just a sweater. It was more, because they were more. The sweater, his love, actualized. And she knew he would always be that comfort—today, tomorrow, and all future days. That realization frayed something inside her and opened her whole heart to him.

They didn't talk once they got into the truck. He tucked her into the crook of his arm and held her close to his body, running his hand across her shoulders for warmth. She didn't feel the cold that close to his body, not while wearing the sweater with the hole in the seam, especially in the knowledge that she loved him.

They didn't talk once they got into his room. What started with his fingers had progressed to his mouth over time. Which was always a surprise to her. But on this day, he pulled her up to straddle him and held her tight against him. He looked at her, studying her face, his thumb skimming her bottom lip before kissing her—a kiss both familiar and entirely new. She wrapped her arms around his neck while his hands found the button of her jeans and then the band of her panties. CeCe gasped and arched back as his fingers found their way inside of her. They had never been like this, face-to-face, and the proximity magnified the intimacy. Ellis tilted her head back and buried his face in her neck, kissing it, as he rubbed her wetness and she ground into his fingers.

It wasn't the first time his fingers left her wanting. But this time her body demanded more. More pleasure. More of him. All of him.

He felt it, too. CeCe could feel his hardness pressing underneath her and reached for his belt to free him. She loved him, and she wanted to give all of herself to him. "Please," she whispered. He searched her eyes, and whatever he saw shattered months of restraint like glass. With heavy eyes, he laid her down and pulled down her jeans and panties.

Then, a truck door slammed followed by the front door and loud voices, arguing. They sprang to their feet and rearranged their clothes back onto their bodies. Ellis opened a book, and CeCe found her backpack and retrieved her notebook. They both tried to steady their breathing against the lust still coursing through them.

Fredrick and Elyse, Ellis's parents, argued often and Ellis and CeCe usually ignored it. But this time proved different. The arguing increased, words said as clearly as if they were next to them, and then a slam against the wall that shook the entire trailer. Ellis told CeCe to stay in the room and left, but when a louder slam erupted, CeCe stood. Out of the window, the Kingdom's roof peered over the ridge. She contemplated jumping out the window to get King and Mance, but she didn't want to leave Ellis. Later, she would be grateful she didn't.

The sound of shattered glass, shifting furniture, and grunts intensified, and CeCe could no longer stay in the room. In the living room, Elyse's body lay still on the floor, and Fredrick wielded a knife before jabbing it toward Ellis's rib cage. Ellis caught it with his hand and blood immediately oozed, but Fredrick pushed the knife further into Ellis.

CeCe screamed, and Fredrick turned his head toward her just as Ellis pulled the knife out and punched Fredrick. When he hit the ground, Ellis was already on top of him, knife at his throat.

Elyse squirmed on the floor and mumbled something. Dark red blood streamed from her nose. "Don't," she managed.

But Ellis didn't hear her. He wasn't there. Blind rage consumed him. His breath streamed violently, in and out of his nostrils. Blood stained his shirt and pooled over his jeans.

Ellis would kill him, CeCe knew. He was that angry, that enraged. Years of arguments and abuse of his mother, his own days being hungry and the dislocated shoulder, had brought him here. It could all end with one quick motion.

"Ellis…don't, please," CeCe said, touching his arm. Ellis didn't move, the knife still pressed against Fredrick's neck. A thin line of blood spilled onto the knife.

"Look at me," CeCe said, moving her face close to his. When he did, his eyes cleared, and he collapsed.

Now, as they look at the empty space where the trailer once sat, CeCe reaches over and takes his hands into hers. "It's gone now," she says. The gesture is an apology. An apology for missing his mother's funeral, for what happened, for every-thing. His grip tightens around her. "He's gone now."

Ellis rolls his head to face her, his eyes soft, and the truck warms. "You were the only good thing about that trailer."

CeCe's heart flutters in her chest, and she feels the long scar on the inside of his hand, stretching from his middle finger down to his wrist, calloused and rough like leather. She remem-bers his hands the most, the pain they held and the softness they administered. Long, sturdy, and strong. Nimble fingers. It's always been her favorite part of him. Before and after the stabbing.

"At night, I'd lie where you did and stare up at the ceiling, listening to them argue. I could still smell your soap and that perfume you used to wear on my pillow." He breathes, and mischief glints in his eyes. "I would close my eyes and see your naked body and hear your moans. Until all of a sudden, I didn't hear them anymore."

CeCe smiles. It's all she can do under the weight of his stare. It's how she protects herself, a shield and a seal against the rush of emotion bubbling to the surface, against the tingle between her legs and the patter of her heart.

"You never told me that before."

"There are a lot of things we haven't said to each other."

"Why start now?"

"Why not now?" And there's something in his eyes that makes her open up.

CeCe closes her eyes, and for a moment, she's in his

bedroom, on his bed. She feels the slick touch of his tongue against hers and the curl of his lip on her breasts. She holds fast to the memory for a beat too long, afraid to open her eyes, and when she does, she finds Ellis watching her with an intensity that doesn't break.

"I got my sexual education and awakening in that trailer." Her voice breaks. "And only one other experience has topped it since." She doesn't feel shame or embarrassment in saying this, but relief.

"It should have been the start of something."

"Of what?"

Ellis doesn't hesitate, the words coming quickly and firm. "Our life together."

"We were too young," she says just as quickly. But she doesn't know if she believes that now.

"Maybe," he says, his eyes glazing with memory. Whatever it is, he keeps it to himself, and the silence stretches.

"There's no going back," CeCe finally says. Those words she believes, without question. Because the truth is always easy. There's no undoing of what happened between them. No way to reverse the course of events.

"And now?" Ellis says. "Are we too young now?"

It's a rhetorical question that CeCe answers anyway. "No," she says, releasing a shuddering breath. "But things are complicated now. My life is complicated."

Ellis nods, squeezing her hand. It's then that she realizes she is holding it, that *she* is touching *him*. Her skin tingles with a heightened sense of awareness. "Do you want to tell me about it? It can be just like it was in the trailer, on my bed." A slow grin tugs at the corners of his mouth. "Except with clothes on."

CeCe smiles as he looks at her, his expression full of everything unsaid between them. He would listen. Just like before when she fed him her dreams, and he swallowed them whole, never telling a soul, never pushing back when he knew what those dreams meant for them. Ellis is good, when there's no reason for his goodness. Most people would understand if he wasn't. But he chose good.

And that's the problem.

CeCe is not good. Good people don't steal, lie, and give their bodies to bad men in exchange for keeping secrets. The world is ugly and so is she. She has become the villain in her own story. She doesn't want to become one in his, too. Honesty is such a heavy thing, and it would be easy to throw herself out of the way of the truth. CeCe could lie to him, but she doesn't *want* to lie to him. Because she now knows that whatever they shared is not over. That it has become its own thing that breathes and has grown into something bigger than them. Despite time, distance, and circumstance, it has not died but thrived.

So, CeCe clears her throat…and changes the subject. "You didn't bring me out here to discuss my problems." She turns her attention away from him to the empty lot. "Wait. What's that?" She points at a camper sitting at the edge of the woods.

Ellis follows her eyes and slips his hand free of hers.

Instantly, she feels the coldness of separation. He opens the door and slides out of the truck.

"Home."

"You live there?" she asks as he opens the door for her.

He laughs. "Where did you think I lived?"

"Not there. Am I the first girl you've brought here?" she asks as they walk. She doesn't know why she asks. Or maybe she does.

Ellis smiles a devilish grin as they approach the camper. "Of course not. This is not a romance novel. I'm a man with needs."

CeCe's chest tightens. She didn't realize how much it hurt to think about him with other women. That other women have had him. She hates the thought, shudders at it, but that doesn't stop the jealousy from rising in her chest.

CeCe crosses her arms. "Well…invite me in. I don't want to be the only woman in Diggs who hasn't seen it," she says as they reach the front door.

Ellis opens the door and steps into a somewhat spacious area despite the outside appearance. CeCe follows him onto the pale wood floors and immediately sees a bed to her right and a dinette table in front of her. To her left, a small kitchen sits complete with a refrigerator and sink and white marble countertop. Her eyes dart around the space, taking it in.

"You wanna snoop," he says, walking to the back. "You can snoop. I'll be back."

It doesn't surprise CeCe that Ellis would live here, like this, in such a minimalist space. He's never needed much, asked for less, and desired nothing.

A few minutes later, CeCe's eye catches on a shirtless Ellis. He opens a drawer and pulls out a clean shirt, slipping it over his head slowly. CeCe expects to see the fat scar on the right side of his stomach. Instead, she sees a tattoo of a long knife, the hilt tucked into the scar, the sheath, and the pointed edge of the blade.

Ellis notices her staring and follows her gaze. "This is a better reminder."

"You want to remember?"

"It's impossible to forget." He slips his shirt on. "Plus, fuck him."

The urge to touch him pains her with a need that verges on agony. It steals all the air.

There are different ways to process the bad that happens to you. You can shut down and shut out everyone. You can cry until your tear ducts rip. You can be angry and punch the walls until your knuckles bleed. Ellis chose none of those things.

How did Ellis process his pain? In the days and weeks that followed, he sat with it and in it. He lived it. Until it was done with him. Until he was done with it. Until he survived it. He made a life on the other side of that knife. He chose to live a life worthy of the second chance he received. To live opposite to his upbringing and to always, always protect women.

And suddenly she can breathe again. Because she knows he is okay. Despite everything. She wonders if one day she'll be okay, too. If she'll ever be able to sit in her guilt just as he did.

"What do you think?" Ellis asks, opening the refrigerator and grabbing a bottle of water. He opens it and gulps it down.

CeCe sits on the bed, for lack of anywhere else to sit, she tells herself. "It's small."

"The space or the bed?"

"Both."

"It's just me," Ellis says, leaning against the wall, arms folded.

"How do you fit all these women you bring out here?"

Ellis smiles, showing a row of white teeth. "Very carefully. Involves a lot of contorting and some flexibility."

"A prerequisite?"

"Absolutely." He flashes a brilliant grin, and it's maddening, and CeCe feels the wattage in her chest.

"Two people can't fit on here." CeCe casts her eyes over the bed.

"Two people can't," Ellis says, his voice dipping lower. "But one body can."

"That's what I'm saying."

"But that's not what I'm saying."

"That doesn't make sense."

"It does if you think about it."

CeCe has already moved on. "Do you plan on living here forever?"

"Here, yes." He gestures. "In here, no."

"What do you mean?"

"Come on...I'll show you."

CeCe doesn't move. For so long, she dreamed of this, of being with him again. Now, he's inches away from her, their love and feelings on display, the ache of loving him, wanting him, too much to bear.

Without thinking, she bounces a few times before patting a spot next to her. Ellis considers it, an eyebrow rising. "Are you asking?"

She pats again, twice, and bites her lip. Ellis reaches up with both hands and stretches against the ceiling. All of her senses attune to him, the bulge of his rippled triceps, the alluring scent of his skin, the touch of his tongue when he licks his lips. His smile falls into something more seductive as he shakes his head to the left and to the right.

"I never had to ask before."

"That was different."

"How?"

"I knew you wanted to be there. That you wanted to be with me."

"You don't think I want you?"

"Not until you tell me. Not until you ask." It's the same voice he used as he planted tiny kisses down her body and how he coaxed her open when he reached his destination.

"Fine," CeCe says, standing quickly, frustrated, instantly feeling foolish for even considering it. *Don't hurt him again*, she hears Tokey say.

Ellis drops his arms, trapping her between the edge of the bed and his body. They stand close, staring, breathing, but not touching. "Cecily," he whispers. She loves her name on his lips, the way he holds it, breathes it, and lets it go. Each syllable vibrates the entire length of her and back up again, setting her aflame. She's forgotten how good it was to exist in his space. It awakens her after years of numbness.

"Ask me to touch you, and I'll do whatever you want."

She knows what he wants her to do, and it's more than asking him to touch her. More than she can do. She could ask and within seconds he would, his touch no longer a phantom hand, no longer in a remembered dream. And within minutes they'd be tangled into each other again. That's not what he wants. It's not that simple. Not anymore. She loves him. She's *in* love with him. She's always loved him. And he wants her to admit it. But she can't do it, give life to those feelings again, even if it meant the end of this torture and the beginning of his pleasure.

She knows his power, and it excites and scares the hell out of her to be the beneficiary. But one thing scares her more. She is not free; her love comes with Mark, a missing half million dollars, and extortion sex.

"No," she breathes. But it's weak to her ears. And Ellis's. Impossibly, there's enough space for him to move closer and lean in, his lips inches from her ear.

"Tell me you don't want me to touch you." His breath brushes her skin, and her shoulders react. "Because I know you do."

"How do you know?" She swallows hard.

CeCe hears his smile, the sound breezy and light, even though she can't see it. "Because I know how your face relaxes when you want to be kissed, the way your lips curl. How your breath hitches when you're turned on."

The air boils around her. He cannot know how much she wants him, missed him, ached to her core for him. The frequency with which she would touch herself and call his name. Or now, how her entire body prickles with both remembrance and want. Her nipples harden; her breath quickens. He will never know. She can hide these signs, make them subtle, invisible to him.

Until he whispers, "Cecily."

A soft groan betrays her. It seeps out, slow and long.

Ellis moans. "Ah, that's what I thought."

They haven't been this close since that night together. Inches separate their faces, and the space ripples with his energy. They share air, each breathing the other's in. She doesn't move, doesn't open her eyes, just tips her lips to him and waits for his to touch hers.

When it doesn't come, she opens her eyes, and he's there, not as much watching as reading her, his eyes traveling over her face. She anticipates the kiss so much that the absence of it lists her forward a tiny step, her feet planted back on the ground even though they never left. She catches herself before she crashes into him.

"Why didn't you kiss me?"

"Do you want me to kiss you?"

"Only if you want to kiss me."

Ellis shakes his head.

"You don't want to kiss me?"

"You're not ready," he says.

"For?"

"What comes after."

Those words bit when he first said them, and they bite harder now. Anger flares in her, and she pouts with lust. She wants him, the ache almost more than she can bear. "And what comes after?"

A huge smile grows on his face, and a muscle pulses in his jaw, but no words leave his lips as he turns away.

"I really hate you sometimes," CeCe blurts out, bitter at the slice of rejection.

Ellis looks back over his shoulder. "You don't hate me."

"Yes, I do. I hate you, Ellis."

"Say it again," Ellis says, turning back to her and collapsing the space between them in two large strides. She retreats until her back presses against the wall. His arms bracket her head, his body closing around her like a blanket. His head bows over hers. "Tell me you hate me."

"It's better that way," she says, breathless.

"I want to hear you say it."

"I…I…" The words die on the tip of her tongue as if she's forgotten how to speak. She doesn't trust her voice.

Ellis's mouth hovers over hers and CeCe fights to hold her ground, biting her lip to keep from kissing him. He will not deny her if she does, if she asks him too, but she can't give in. She can't let him break her. She needs more time.

"That's the thing," he whispers, his voice all gravel and smoke that cuts through her like a blade. "I could strip you naked and fuck you right now." His dark eyes scan the entire length of her body and then her face. "You don't hate me. You wish you hated me. But you don't."

CeCe flutters her eyes up at him. She could never hate him. Not with all the love for him coursing through her veins. This, they both know, and she sees the certainty in his eyes. He knows. He always knows.

"I don't hate you."

He lowers his arms and walks out the door. "Come on... let's go."

Seconds before Lisha appears in the doorway of the workshop, Mance, for the first time in a long time, thinks of his mother. The thought intrusive and unwelcome, dropping in like a wrecking ball. He knows better than to ask about her and he's not sure he really cares to know. She isn't here, hasn't been here. That fact outweighs all the others. As a father now, Mance occasionally thinks of her. He knows nothing could keep him from Henry. If she were alive, he chooses to believe she would feel the same way. If she stayed away, it was for a reason.

He did ask King about her once when they were alone with Ellis in the workshop. Ellis's father had just packed up and left for good after the incident and after another visit from King with his sledgehammer.

"Come here, son," King said, placing both his hands on Ellis's shoulders. "You are always welcome here, you and your Mama. You hear me?"

Ellis nodded.

"You run those doctor bills to me, you understand?"

"Yes, sir."

"And don't you worry. He's gone. He won't be coming back."

"Like Mama?" Mance couldn't help but ask and it surprised him that he did.

"No, son. Not like your Mama," King said. Mance, shocked at the answer, an answer concerning a topic he had long avoided and knew not to press. Instead, he sat with the knowledge until King's voice rose again. "She tried to make it work, tried to make a life here. She's not here so that we can be."

Now, Lisha stands in the doorway, a sleeping Henry in his carrier on her arm. His entire world.

"You've been fighting," Lisha says. It's not a question.

Mance instinctively flexes his hand against the tightly wrapped bandage and winces at the cut Miss Annie accidentally opened when she grabbed his hand and tugged on it hard as she moved him from room to room. Mance takes the carrier from Lisha's hands and places it on the table. He reaches out and touches his son—his cheek, his tiny hand. He pushes against the idea of lifting him and holding him. He's still not ready.

"So, you're ignoring me now?"

Mance moves to the other side of the table, studying the wood inches from his face. "I haven't been fighting."

Lisha moves forward. "Why is your hand wrapped?"

"I cut it."

"How?"

"The same way I've cut my hands a million times."

"You've never wrapped it before."

"Is that why you're here?"

Lisha shifts her weight. "What happened with Shad?"

"Nothing."

"Nothing? What did you find out? Did he sell some land?"

Mance nods.

Lisha curses under her breath. "I'm sorry, Mance." She takes a step closer, almost an arm's length away, but doesn't touch him. "So he just admitted it?"

"Uh huh," Mance grunts. He tells her the full story of how Uncle Shad sold the land. He tells her of Junior's meeting with Malone & Kincaid and the two-million-dollar check they presented to him. He tells her about Tokey packing up the Kingdom and about CeCe and Ellis's meeting with Ethan and the appeals they will file.

"Henry's appointment is next week," Lisha says, after Mance finishes explaining and she's finished asking questions. "They got us in pretty fast. I was surprised."

"I'll be there," Mance says.

Lisha shifts. "My insurance will cover 80 percent but we're responsible for the other 20 percent."

Mance walks over to a metal box and opens it. "Here." He drops a roll of bills in her hand. "That should cover it. Let me know if it doesn't."

Lisha stares at the roll of hundreds in her hand before she speaks. "Where did you get this?"

"Working." It wasn't a lie. It wasn't the truth. Either, Mance knew, would pacify Lisha.

"Working," she repeats.

"Yeah."

Lisha pauses for a moment, the money still propped in the center of her palm. "Did he give this to you?"

Mance doesn't answer.

"Are you working for him again?"

"No." It's all Mance says but the denial feels like a lie. To him and to Lisha. Mance has no desire to see Shad again, but his gut knows better than he does. He knows it's not over with Shad.

"Then why would he give this to you? Give you..." Lisha unwraps the rubber band and fans out the bills, silently counting. Twenty-two hundred dollars. Lisha doesn't say the amount and Mance doesn't watch as she slings the bills onto the workshop table. He hears it, though, a whooshing sound as soft and delicate as feathers falling from the sky.

"What are you doing?"

Lisha crosses her arms. "I'm not taking that. I know what it means for you even if you don't admit it. He's buying you as a way back in, and you're letting him."

"I know what I'm doing."

"What happened to bending? Have you even tried?"

"It's not what you think. Please trust me."

"Like I trusted you about the ten acres? Look what happened. You told me to trust you that it was easy work. You almost missed the birth of your son. You could have been killed."

Mance finally approaches her, slow and cautious. How could he get her to understand? He couldn't, he knows. Their priorities are different, his in service of many, hers in service of one. Henry.

He had to try because the rolling in his stomach wouldn't stop. Something was coming. He couldn't see it yet, but he knew. And he couldn't tell her. He's never been able to lie to her and decides not to start now. In this case, the simple truth, stripped down to its barest form, will have to work.

Mance gathers the strewn bills from the table and folds them into Lisha's hand. "I'm not working for him again. I did him a favor and he paid me for it."

Lisha raises her eyebrows and their eyes meet. Mance feels the question and answers it before she asks. "Legal. Completely legal."

This relaxes Lisha's face but not completely. "What kind of favor is worth $2,200?"

"The kind that involves furniture." He leaves it at that and is grateful when Lisha breaks her stare. The truth works for now, but Mance knows that it won't always. Mance feels the unknown bubbling up inside him, but he pushes through anyway, swallows it back hard and fast.

Lisha stares back, searching his eyes for a trace of something, an inkling of whatever truth he doesn't speak. Mance knows better than to let on, even if what he says isn't the full truth. It's not a lie if it's an omission, he thinks. He had to believe that for her to believe it too. Lies are best told when believed. And Mance wants to believe this one, even though it is the truth.

Lisha walks into his arms and the act surprises him. "Are you okay?" She touches his face and his eyes instinctively close. His heart wrenches with the love he holds for her. It weakens him because he knows whatever comes next, he'll do anything to protect her and Henry. That he must hold on to the two promises he made even if it means crossing the line again.

"I'm fine," he says.

"Have I told you how much I love you?" Lisha asks.

Lisha's sudden shift is disorienting; the change quick as a blink. She presses her body against his and slides her arms across his waist. Lisha inhales and exhales against him, her breasts lifting.

"I'll never tire of hearing it," Mance says, allowing himself to hold her, his chin brushing the top of her head. He inhales her scent, vanilla and baby powder, as familiar to him as his own.

"I love you." She angles her face to look at him when she says this.

"Even if I have nothing?"

"Even then."

"Do you really mean that?"

"I do." She takes his hand into hers and kisses it. "Ask me again and I'll say yes. Me and Henry will come live here with you. We can be a family."

Mance knows what she is doing, and for a second it almost works. She wants him to remember that he has more to lose than just the Kingdom. This has the opposite effect on Mance. He knows now that there's something he must do. He has to help Uncle Shad rob Miss Annie. The sureness of it hitting him at breakfast this morning and rooting in him after seeing Lisha linger in the doorway. He has no other choice.

He kisses her and holds her with all the love in his body and presses his body against hers. He whispers that he loves her too and that he's happy, so happy. For all the half-truths spoken, there's nothing false about her warmth or the soft sounds she releases when they kiss. Or how truly happy he is that she finally said yes. Nothing.

Henry coos, interrupting the moment, and it's the greatest sound in the world. Henry's eyes dart around, then up. From his carrier, he points at a table leg dangling above him.

Lisha signs and it shocks Mance.

"You're signing?"

"Yeah...Dr. Frazier said it's not too early to start. Just expressions and *Mama* and *Daddy*."

She extends her fingers and spreads them out before tapping her forehead twice with her thumb. "This is *Daddy*." She repeats it.

Mance looks at his hands and remembers his attempts to

learn sign language and to contort his stiff fingers into letters. But this sign he can do.

Henry looks and smiles, his dimple deepening. Mance doesn't know if he's seen a more beautiful creation. Mance signs again and Henry giggles. Right then, Mance decides that this is the sound he'll keep in his ears. The sound he'll turn to over and over again for comfort, for peace. The sight, too, of his son laughing and smiling. And the feeling of Lisha's body against his and the smell of her. He brightens and weakens at the sounds, sight, smells, and feelings of a moment of peace he wishes he could live inside of.

He smiles at Lisha's unapologetic presence, her love for him, and he wonders what on earth he ever did right to deserve such a fierce woman and a strong son. It makes him afraid. *There, I admit it*, he thinks. He's afraid for the first time in his life. It's what's been festering inside of him since Henry's birth. He's been unreceptive to it, bucking and denying it. Fear hurts. It's pain unlike any other he's felt in his life. Mance doesn't know what to do or how to process it or what it even means. Instead, he watches and learns the sign for *Mama* as the workshop fills with Henry's laughter.

NINE

———

TOKEY DOESN'T BELIEVE IN coincidences. But the feeling of déjà vu at breakfast could not be ignored. Was it a coincidence that Ellis and CeCe reminded her of King and Hazel? Or that Mance shared King's worries about the land? Junior, too? These are questions she would not have asked a week ago, but that are now made possible by what she knows from Hazel's letters. History seems to be repeating itself.

Tokey doesn't understand fully why she's remembering Hazel's words, but she does understand how her brain chooses to drop them. It's something she doesn't realize at the moment but later, when she thinks back, she wonders how she didn't immediately see it. Now all she knows is what she doesn't know.

She has to finish reading the letters.

She waits until the house empties, until CeCe and Ellis leave, Junior drives to James's office, and Mance disappears into the workshop. They have a right to know about the letters and she wants to tell them, but she doesn't know how to bring them up. They have the important tasks, and hers seems like an errand. Will they even care about what she discovered? They have memories of Hazel that she doesn't have. They seem to understand and accept her absence in their life. She considered mentioning the letters after breakfast, but the debriefing took an unexpected turn. They could lose the Kingdom. Not just the five acres but all of it. The discovery of these letters that meant something to her meant nothing within seconds. She couldn't tell them now, anyway—not until she's read the last two. Not until she understands everything.

Maybe *understands* is not quite the right word. Maybe it's: until she believes in something.

When she's alone, she retreats to King's room and closes the door. Reading the letters in the room her parents shared makes her feel closer to them both.

A tear plops onto the letter. Tokey reaches up and touches her face, her heart beating too fast for someone not moving.

She wants to finish the letters and for them to go on forever. She wants to stop reading and pretend their lives continue this way, happy and content. But Tokey's no fool.

There are no happy endings.

Dear Jessie,
I write these letters more for me than for you. I have no one to talk to about what's going on.

King fell off the roof a few days ago. A storm blew off some shingles and he was up there replacing them. Not sure how he lost his balance. He's been up there a million times. Alls I know is I hear Junior King screaming and I run outside to see the boys standing over King. He tried to get up but his leg was broken so I told him to stay down. He didn't want to go to the doctor so I had Junior King and Mance run and go get Minnie. Besides his broken leg, she say he also had a dislocated back and he needed to rest. King didn't take too well to the news and tried to get up but he fell again. Slipped right through our fangers. I tell him he don't work for two months.

I thought we was lucky when Shad came home. Shad came back with a long scar on his arm. He neva say how he got the scar, but some folks says that it was his own knife that did it. Payback for a job gone wrong but they says Shad killed the man that did it. King hoped Shad could help him with the house and the land just like he had before. He did for a spell. He got a good idea to rent lots of land on the edge of the Kingdom. That helped but it wasn't enough to pay all the taxes and fix up the house let alone provide food and clothes for the kids. CeCe was just born and I couldn't pump no mo so King bartered formula for a sideboard. He stayed up for two whole days to finish.

Shad has become all about the mighty dollar. He don't understand why King started barterin. He said he had better way for King to make some money. Shad had gotten mixed up with some bad men in New Orleans. Started robbin and stealin. He sent some money back home once and at first King didn't want to spend it. But Mance is growing like a weed and outgrow his pants and shoes and he didn't have no choice.

But after while, Shad don't want to help no mo. He say he don't understand why King workin so hard for nothin. He say that he wanted what was his, half of the Kingdom. He told King that James say all this land worth a lot of money and if they sold it they won't have to worry about money no mo. King tells him no and that he knows the family promise not to sell one acre, not one inch. Shad say you can keep yours but let me take what's mine. King said no and Shad didn't like that. They started yellin and King told Shad to leave. He said King couldn't kick him off his land. But King grabbed the sledgehammer and told him that he loved him but he would kill him dead before he let him sell the land. Shad say you gonna pull out that sledgehammer on your own brother? Many of men have seen the end of that sledgehammer. I never thought it would be my turn. Shad say that King owed him for killing Mr. Curtis. King say he do and thinks about it and say that Shad can have five acres down by the creek but he neva want to see Shad again. Shad leave but befo he do he say to King that he will be back and he closed the door.

I try not to think about what happen. I know it hurt King that Shad is gone again and I feel its my fault.

Hazel

Dear Jessie,
I was happy to finally get your letter and to hear that you finally coming home. I sure could use a friendly face. Life

aint been too good. I suppose it's our punishment for what happened. Pastor say what done in the dark come to light.

With Shad gone, the bills pile up again. The lot rent helps but the tax bill come due and its more than eva. It my fault that Shad is gone again and I tell myself that I have to fix it. I didn't know what to do and then I know. I remember years ago James telling me that if I eva needed something to call him. I sees his Mama at church and she says he's doing good. Got married and had a daughter named Genesis. She is a couple of years younger than Junior King. I really hope he can help. I hate seeing King so sad. It reminds me of when we first meet all those years ago after his father died.

I tell King I'm gonna take Mama to her doctor's appointment when I really go to Charlotte to see James. I don't mean to cry but as soon as I sit down the tears come. I tell him everythang and he sat next to me and listened. When I finished I ask him what we could do. Asked maybe if the people he work for in Charlotte could help him like they did the Jacksons. He touched my shoulder and kept it there. He said he could help but what was in it for him. That's when I knew what he wanted. He say King didn't have to know and that it could be our little secret that he always loved me and that I deserve betta. At first, I refused. I tell him I love King but he say if I don't he gone tell the police King killed Mr. Curtis. He says he know what happen cause he came back to say he sorry for what he done. He says he saw the whole thang. He closed and locked the door. I look at the picture of his family the whole time. When he finished his business, he gave me the money and tells me there's mo if I need it. I throws up on the floor just outside his office.

I'm not proud of what I done but I do what I did for my family. I didn't want King or Shad to go to prison and we needed the money. When I go to pay the tax bill they say it already paid, that King had paid a few hours before. I wonder where he get the money and when I ask he just say Shad but I look at his hands and his knuckles got blood on them and he look at my hands and see the money and we both know we done somethang bad. King ask me how I get the money but he don't wait for me to say. He know. He grab the sledgehammer and try to leave but I say he should use it on me, that it my fault. He drop it and cry on the floor. King say that we gone forget it eva happen. And we do until months later my breast get tender the way they do when I'm with child. And I cry and cry and cry. See...King can't have no mo kids after his fall, Minnie say, and I knows this baby not his. I don't knows how to tell him. We say we neva goin talk about it again like wit Mr. Curtis. Is do wonda if this is payback from Mr. Curtis and this curse will keep goin' long afta we gone like all the other Solomons.

Anyway I happy you comin home and can't believe I get to say this but I see you soon.

Hazel

Tokey releases the letter and it fans to the ground as her entire body locks with shock, her mind racing toward a conclusion she can't yet understand.

Outside, CeCe follows Ellis down the worn path to a clearing with a frame for a house.

"You're building this? This is your house?"

"Yeah, we…"

"We?" CeCe interrupts.

"Me and Mance. We've been working on it ourselves, contracting out the electrical and water but everything is us." He laughs. "Mostly Mance. We would be further along if he weren't such a perfectionist."

"When does he have the time?"

"He doesn't. But he makes time."

CeCe steps up onto the foundation. "King knew you were building a house here?"

"Of course, but this wasn't the Kingdom."

"It's not?"

"It's my land," he says, tilting his chin a little higher. "My own Kingdom."

"How?" she asks, moving through the frames.

"The land came up for sale and me and Mance bought it."

"Mance bought land?"

"To expand the Kingdom. It didn't make sense not to." Ellis follows her. "Remember the map Ethan showed us? These ten acres should have always been a part of the Kingdom, and I guess we will never know why they weren't."

CeCe continues walking through the studs taking in the house. Without trying, she could see it, his vision. Ellis will live in peace here, CeCe knows. She can feel it just as sure as the warmth of the sun on her skin. He will live the rest of his life without seeking power, money, or influence, things that must be claimed, and seek everything that didn't: family and love.

If she stayed, this would have been her life. Married to Ellis, living on the Kingdom, kids. She remembers the vision she had all those years ago, how crippling it felt. But now, that life doesn't seem so bad.

"What do you think?"

"The kitchen should face the east," she says, moving to an empty spot. "Right here. That way the morning light can stream in through the windows."

Ellis watches her before asking, "What else?"

"Put the kitchen island right here." She stops and opens her arms. "The living room should go there, with a large wood-burning fireplace."

"Keep going," Ellis says softly.

CeCe's on a roll now. A seal cracked open. "And large windows. For natural light. Lots and lots of windows."

Ellis leans against a stud and sighs. "This is the house I wanted for her."

"Your Mama would have loved it."

"When she died, the world changed for me. It stopped

being this complicated place. It became so simple, and I wanted to live my life like that."

"Why Diggs? We were going to leave. Be one of the few who made it out."

"We did everything we said we wanted to do. It just wasn't permanent." He walks. "I was all set to leave after the funeral, but I just couldn't go. I didn't have that drive to stay away. I wanted to be here. Then Mance got arrested, and I realized Diggs is where I needed to be."

"You don't owe these people anything."

"It's not about owing anyone. Mama died. King's gone. These pillars of the community are dying. Outsiders are trying to buy up all the land. Someone has to keep Diggs going. Help protect it."

"And that's you?"

He laughs. "I'm one man, but I can help."

CeCe shakes her head. "I can't come back here."

"You can come home again, Cecily. It doesn't mean you've failed."

CeCe wishes he was right and that it was that easy.

He seems to read her silence. "It's as easy or difficult as you make it. Your family needs you. Even more now that King is gone. There's a lot going on with them right now."

"They don't need me. They barely want me here."

"Tokey's…not good. She could use your help."

"Help with—"

The buzzing of CeCe's cell phone echoes. Her heart quickens.

"I...I..." She scrambles for distance from Ellis. "I'll be right back."

When she's out of earshot, CeCe answers.

"I'll be in Charlotte tonight, staying at the Hilton," Mark says, and his voice chills her.

CeCe stumbles for words. "I...I don't know if I can get away."

"I'll see you tonight," he says. "And CeCe...I definitely want you to do that thing I like."

The call ends. Every part of her wants to run, and yet CeCe doesn't move.

"Are you okay?" a voice asks from behind her. Only it's more than Ellis's voice. It's a breeze through her. And it's enough to blow her down.

"No," CeCe says this with her back to him. She's lost her urge to move. Her voice whimpers under the force of her admission, but she cannot face him yet. She knows from his tone that he's really asking—not just about the call but about her welfare. He still loves her. Just as fully and completely as he did all those years ago. Suddenly her body feels heavy, so very, very heavy.

"I know." Before those two syllables fully leave his lips, a sound comes from her. Ellis hasn't known her to cry, and he's at her side in a second. But he doesn't touch her. He doesn't have to. She feels his spark of energy against her skin anyway, the current electrifying and jolting. He waits. He breathes. "You don't have to be."

CeCe flinches at the words. She was not prepared for them

and the gentle way he says them. Nor the honesty they carry. It makes no sense. She knew he would break her. But not like this, with a calm tongue, patient as a breath waiting its turn, as simple as a few words scattered. The truth, stirred in softly.

She doesn't have to be okay. She doesn't have to be alone. She doesn't have to carry this burden or continue to keep this secret anymore.

"I know you. I've known something was wrong the moment I saw you at King's funeral," he says, and though he is so serious, his tone is as light as air, telling her it's okay to speak. "What's wrong?"

Though she doesn't know the last time she was asked this question—really asked it—CeCe knows exactly what she should say: "I'm fine," or "It's just work." But the words die on her tongue. She can't lie to him like she would to anyone else. She won't. Still, CeCe does not turn her face to him.

He steps in front of her. "What's wrong?"

She looks up at him with tears flooding her eyes and says, "Everything."

This first admission rises from her shoulders like a balloon, its buoyancy encouraging her to go on. To keep pulling everything she's kept trapped to the surface, and to let it be.

So, CeCe starts at the beginning. The words tumble out with shocking ease. She tells him about the forged billing hours, every dollar she took, about Mark and her interactions with him over the last three months. Ellis listens, his face flattening and smoothing, bunching and raging with a rainbow of emotions. He takes it all in silently, absorbing it. He questions nothing.

CeCe breathes, and it feels good. Better. The first breath of air after nearly drowning.

Ellis speaks, his head bowed, his gaze on the ground. "And that was him on the phone? The one who's been on the phone these last few days?"

She nods and tells him about this conversation too.

Nothing more is required of her than to brace herself and wait. Birds take flight against an innocent blue sky. But Ellis remains quiet for a long moment. Too long.

"Say something," she says.

Is it too much to hope that Ellis understands?

Maybe this is it, then, CeCe thinks when Ellis's silence stretches on, how she finally loses him forever. Too much truth. Too much reality. In too short a time.

Then, in a burst, Ellis moves, pacing the space between them. "What the fuck? What the fuck? What the fuck, Cecily?" Each time, the words escalate in tone and understanding.

She remains quiet, absorbing his anger.

"What were you thinking?"

"I don't know."

"You don't know? What do you mean you don't know? And Mark, that fuckin' Mark..." he growls. "You've been sleeping with him?"

"It's just sex."

"It's extortion!"

"It's consensual. He didn't force me to do anything I didn't want to do."

He whips his head back to look at her. "You wanted to have sex with him?"

"Don't yell at me," CeCe says, turning away at the intensity of his stare.

"Yell at you? I want to kill you! How could you do this?"

CeCe's eyes well. "I don't know."

"You hate it here that much. Hate yourself that much. That this is what you do?"

"Yes, no, I don't know," she says all at once.

"Jesus. Cecily." He paces again, his steps moving him toward the edge of the woods and away from her. Ellis increases the distance between them so much that she can barely make out his body among the trees. A stream of profanity and growls erupts a second later.

When Ellis returns a few minutes later, CeCe braces for another wave of his disappointment and displeasure. When he speaks, his earlier anger has dissolved. "Where's your purse?"

"In the truck."

"Go get it."

"Why?"

He cuts his eyes at her, a warning. "Cecily, go get it."

And when she does, Ellis says, "Give me a dollar."

CeCe opens her wallet and remembers. "I don't have a dollar. I don't have any money."

Ellis frowns. "You don't have a dollar? After everything you just told me, you don't have at least a dollar?"

"Why do you want it?" Her confusion gives way to frustration.

Instead of answering, Ellis retrieves his wallet, pulls out a dollar, and presses it in CeCe's palm. He snatches the dollar back, crumpling it in his hand. "So now I'm your lawyer, and everything you just told me is privileged information. So I won't be required to testify against you, goddamn it!"

"This is my problem to fix. I don't want to involve you in this."

"It's too late for that now. How do you think you're going to fix this?"

"I need money."

She holds his gaze, silently adding the question.

"I don't have *that* kind of money and even if I did, it's not like you can just put it back. That's your plan? To just put it back?" Ellis says, his irritation full-blown again. Then, something clicks within him. "This is why you asked all those questions about the house and selling it. You don't want to save it at all. You want to sell it. You want the money."

"If we sell the Kingdom, I can take my portion and put it back in those clients' accounts."

"You would betray King just to save yourself?"

"What other choice do I have?"

"Turn yourself in. I know a great criminal attorney in Charlotte. He went to law school with me and Ethan. He owes me a favor. You can cut a deal. Maybe even avoid jail time."

CeCe almost laughs at the fanciful notion. "I can't do that."

"Cecily, there's no other way."

"There is." CeCe swallows. "I'm going to see Mark tonight."

Ellis's brow raises. "And what are you planning on doing? Continuing with this bullshit arrangement?"

"Ellis...this is not Mark's fault."

"Bullshit!"

"What would you have him do? Turn me in? Have me go to prison?"

"Yes!" Frustration pulls every muscle in his body tight. "Uphold the law. Because that's what we do. As lawyers, we uphold the law."

"As lawyers, we also skirt the law."

"I don't."

"Not everyone can be as good as you, Ellis."

"Don't give me that shit, Cecily. This is not about being good. It's about you. It's always been about you."

"What's that supposed to mean?"

Ellis doesn't answer. Something in his face shifts, a tension that she can't read.

"Why do you do that?" she asks. "Why do you hold back? Even when we were kids, you've kept things from me. Why?"

"Because there are things that you are not ready to hear yet."

"And when will I be ready? Who decides that? You?"

"No, it's not for me to decide. That's for you. It's always been up to you. But I can't let you go to Charlotte."

"Well, it's a good thing that it's always up to me, then. I know what I'm doing."

"Do you? Do you really?"

She nods, but even she can tell how ridiculous she looks. She makes her tone certain. "I have to do this."

"No, you don't."

"I do," she says, barely audible. "I don't have any other choice."

"You always have a choice. Let me help you."

"Ellis, I don't need you to rescue me. I'm not one of your charity cases. I can handle this on my own."

"Is that all you think you are to me?" Concern pitches his brow. "A charity case?"

Nothing in his eyes tells her this. It tells her the opposite. And that's what hurts. What burns her inside. Because it should be past tense. She was more than that to him. They were more than that to each other. There was a time and place for them to be good to each other, and they missed it. All those years ago, before the tragedy of life stained them both.

"Take me home."

Junior arrives at Mr. James's office at noon precisely. The clock on the wall chimes just as he enters, its two hands joined together, as if in prayer for him.

"I'm here to see Mr. James," Junior says needlessly to Gladys, Mr. James's longtime secretary. Gladys seems to be stuck in the seventies with her white beehive and cat-eye glasses. She locks him into a stare over those dark rims now as she points him to a chair against the wall behind him.

Junior and Mr. James avoid each other as much as possible, keeping their passivity within the understood but never discussed boundaries of Easter, Christmas, and the girls' birthdays. Mr. James has crossed this line only a handful of times over the years by summoning Junior to his office to talk about the Kingdom.

"How's King?" Mr. James would ask. "How's he handling the property tax increase? Is he ready to sell yet?"

Each time, Junior would respond with "You know King." And that would be enough, as James did know King, very well, their ages just a year apart.

With the Kingdom in jeopardy now, Junior knows Mr. James will not be pacified with a one-liner.

Gladys's phone rings. The hands on the clock have separated. Junior adjusts his position and looks at the closed door to Mr. James's office.

Gladys's phone rings again.

Junior knows his father-in-law all too well. The summons today cannot hide behind any pleasant pretense, considering the meeting at Malone & Kincaid. It feels like Mr. James is extending pity, maybe even malice, wanting to discuss the Kingdom, father-in-law to son-in-law, away from Malone & Kincaid.

Twelve thirty-five. Junior stands and approaches Gladys's desk, and as he does, she holds up a long finger without looking at him, her attention on the notepad she scribbles on. Junior looks again at James's door and considers just going in.

"He's not available yet. It shouldn't be much longer. Please take a seat. I'll call you when he's ready."

Junior thinks he should come back another time, but he dismisses the thought. Even still, he doesn't want to be rude. James did him a favor by setting up the meeting with Malone & Kincaid, even if it wasn't a pretty favor.

Finally, an hour past the time James asked to meet, Gladys's phone buzzes, and after she listens to the person on the other end, she says to Junior. "Mr. James will see you now."

James opens the door as Junior approaches. "Junior," he says, opening the door wider, gesturing to a chair. Junior hears the door click shut behind him. "Take a seat."

Junior wants to say that he would rather stand after an hour of sitting. But he sucks the words back in and takes the seat.

The chair is shorter than it looks. His knees are almost equal to his chest. James sits across from him and seems to tower over Junior. He does not apologize for making Junior wait.

"Junior...you would say that I've been good to you, right?"

Junior attempts to elongate his torso. "Yes, sir."

"I paid for your college education. Two degrees."

"Yes, sir."

"Would you say I've been like a father to you?"

This time Junior's quick agreement stalls, and with a modicum of decency he has not yet shown in this meeting, James redirects. "Taking nothing away from King, of course." He smiles, the gap between his teeth visible. He means this nicely. Or does he? Junior doesn't know. He thought James did accept him, but something in the way he asks this now, after everything, seems different. Junior doesn't need to be reminded of his turbulent relationship with King. He lived it every day.

The smile snaps shut as quickly as it opens. James pins Junior with his hard stare. "Though I did all those things for you, I've never liked you, Junior. I thought I would grow to at least respect you, but I never did. Genesis respected you. She loved you. Why, I do not know. Women in Diggs have horrible taste in men."

Junior shifts in his seat.

"Your mother, for example," he says, sweeping his tongue across his lips, subtle, but noticeable, "was quite a woman." His eyes glass over with memories as he stares at the wall just past Junior's shoulders, memories Junior is left scrambling to guess at. "Your father didn't deserve her."

Junior's mouth splits open, but the words clog his throat. Before Junior can give them air—before he himself can breathe again—James silences him. "I didn't give you permission to speak. And that wasn't a question. It's a fact." The word pops off his bottom lip, his brow creased in a different kind of anger than Junior is used to seeing from him. "He never knew what he had. In her. In all that land. How a man like that can be so rich in so many things and yet so stupid."

There's sadness and jealousy laced through this anger.

As Junior's mind races to understand, James shudders, and a more familiar expression settles over him. It is just as dark as the other but held alight by a facade of compassion.

"Let's talk about you," James says, pressing the tips of his fingers together, elbows on the desk. "You're smarter than your father. Aren't you, Junior? I think you are. You seem to have a good head on your shoulders. And if the time came for you to do the right thing, you would do it, wouldn't you, son?"

"And what's that?"

James smiles. "Convince your brother and sisters to sell."

He tosses the words off so easily. One plus one equals two. As if selling the family's land is as simple as elementary arithmetic.

"I don't think I can."

"Ahh…Junior. Sure you can," he says, each word a complete sentence. "I think you can convince anyone of anything." He taps a folder lying thick on his desk that Junior didn't notice. "You managed to convince me, your family, the school board, everyone."

The logical side of Junior tells him to be confused—what in the world could James know?—but another part is jumping around in the background, getting louder with the obvious. It flushes him with embarrassment. Renders Junior still and ties his tongue. He doesn't move. He doesn't blink. Forgets to breathe. It's as if, somehow, he's stopped time. If only.

James isn't affected by the spell. He flips opens the folder to a stack of photos. Junior doesn't need to see the images. He turns his head away and forces himself to breathe.

"Are they hard to look at?" He hears James sigh in mock lament. "Is it hard for you to see yourself with a dick in your mouth?" Junior feels something hit him and turns to look. There's a photo in his lap. James is flipping them one by one, like Frisbees, at Junior. "Look at them!" They land in his lap and feet until the floor is littered with a frame-by-frame account of the night Simon met Junior in the school parking lot. Junior and Simon sitting in the front seat. Junior's head low in Simon's lap, Simon's expression changing as Junior's head moves up and down, but all out of order. All mixed up and wrong.

There is no other sound except the buzzing in Junior's ears.

"Do you love your family?"

It's not exactly the question Junior expects. He manages: "Of course."

"Well…I love mine too, and I don't take too kindly to my baby girl coming to me crying about her husband asking to 'take a break'"—James sounds almost as disgusted by that phrase as by his son-in-law's actions—"from their marriage. When she told me why, I didn't believe it. I said, *Junior's not gay. He can't be. He's married. He has two daughters.* What kind of man leaves his family for another man? So, I rang up my private investigator and had him follow you."

The buzzing has stopped. "What do you want?"

James slows his breathing with one deep inhalation. "You know what I want, but since you are no man, I will tell you. Slowly." He comes around the desk and, stepping on the photos, sits in the chair next to Junior. He doesn't touch him, doesn't even lean toward him. He leans back, crossing one leg over the other knee. "You're going to get your siblings to sign the papers, you're going to go home to Genesis and my beautiful granddaughters, and you will stop putting dicks in your mouth in parking lots. You do that, and these photos never see the outside of this office. No one will ever know."

Junior shakes with rage yet feels powerless within the emotion's grasp, and that makes him all the angrier for it. Breath streams in and out of his nose, the sound ragged.

"Are you upset with me, Junior? Is your nose going to bleed?" He asks that snidely, a schoolyard bully taunting his caught prey. James stands abruptly with a huff. "What kind of man walks into a meeting and shows his weakness? You are so fuckin' pathetic. If you were my son…"

"I'm not your son." Junior feels a bit of power saying it, but James is on him again, stripping him bare.

"Damn straight, you're not my son," he snarls. "No son of mine would be fucking another man. No son of mine would be such a pussy."

"Fuck you."

"Fuck me? Normally I wouldn't take offense to such an insult, but I realize that you very well might fuck me." He leans against his desk. "I don't get it. There's nothing better than pussy, especially the desperate kind. They give it up better. You can get them to do just about anything, anywhere." He slides his fingers around his desk. A hint of a smile pushes against the corners of his mouth before disappearing. "Like I said, your father didn't deserve her."

The words that wanted to come out earlier finally do. "What did you do to my mother?"

"Nothing she didn't want. Nothing your father didn't force her to do due to his stupidity. He practically pushed her at me."

Junior shakes his head. "You're lying. King would have killed you."

James nods, his expression saying that Junior finally said something correct. "I thought I would see the end of that sledgehammer your family is so known for. Every day I waited for it, but he never came. And I figured out why. Because he realized his mistake. He knew passing up that deal was stupid, and losing Hazel was his penance."

"Hazel?" Junior hears himself ask. Her name sounds strange on someone else's lips.

The skin between James's eyes wrinkles. "You didn't know her name."

"Where is she?"

"You should have asked King that. But if I had to guess...I imagine she saw the end of that sledgehammer like so many men before."

Junior's hand flew to his nose. No blood yet, but he felt like throwing up. "Why are you telling me this?"

"Because you need to know so you won't repeat the mistakes of your father."

"What's in it for you? Besides hurting me."

James grins. "A nice commission, of course, and a stake in the boutique luxury hotel the house will become."

"Hotel? I thought they didn't want the house?"

"So gullible. Of course, we"—James emphasizes the word—"want the house. Tourists love authenticity. '*Sleep in a former plantation.*'" He punctuates each word with his hand as though the ad copy floats in the space between them. "The men in your family haven't been the brightest, but they've maintained the house's integrity. They were master carpenters. In fact, we want to hire Mance as the lead contractor."

"He would never work for you."

"I wouldn't be so quick to say that. Every man has his weakness, including Mance. I've learned that once you find it, you just have to press it hard. And we've found it. Just like I found yours."

"What?"

"I think you should concern yourself with your own affairs, Junior."

"So, this is about money?"

"It's always about money, but I—" James pauses, considers. "I don't like losing. And I've been playing this game a very long time. To be successful in business, as I am, you must be patient. When you asked for Genesis's hand, I knew this day would come. I knew I would finally get that land. It's come wrapped up in a different bow than I expected, but here it is, just the same. Here you are, like Hazel, like your Uncle Shad in this office."

"It was you? You got Uncle Shad to sell—"

"Shad knows a good thing when he sees it, and when he came to me, I was all too happy to help him."

"You grew up in Diggs. These are your people. How can you do this? Change the Kingdom that much that fast? You know that anyone with more than an acre of land will never be able to afford the increase in taxes. You will push them out, and then where will they go?"

"Fuck Diggs and fuck them! All men are not created equal. God blesses us one way or the other. God blessed Diggs families with this land. He wanted us to make something of it. And what have we done? We're leasing lots for trailers. I have very little patience for the complacent people of Diggs. Generation after generation of people living as the ones before them, living on the same land, the same way. Every day the same. They are poor by choice. They don't have to be. They are sitting on millions. Do you know how much new land is being manufactured?" James's tone is that of an evil schoolteacher asking a rhetorical question. "None. What's here is all we will ever have, and the ones who want it will pay anything for it. It's foolish not to use that as leverage to improve your circumstances."

"What about family legacy? The generations before us that died so we could have this land. So your granddaughters can have this land."

"You are so fuckin' naive. What has legacy ever done for your family? The Kingdom is cursed. Every Solomon man has died in service of that land. When does it end?"

"It ends now."

"*Now* you want to take ownership of the land? You've never

wanted anything to do with that land. You couldn't marry Genesis and leave that place fast enough."

"You're wrong," Junior says. It comes out small and unbelievable.

"You are meek, Junior. The Bible says blessed are the meek for they shall inherit the Earth. We all know that's bullshit. It's the strong. It's people like Mance who would have never waited an hour outside my door."

He stands and buttons his coat. "You have until tomorrow to bring me the signed papers, or these photos will be anonymously delivered to the chairman of the school board. Harold, right?" He tugs gently at his cuffs and adjusts the cuff links twinkling there. "Yeah…we're playing golf together this Saturday."

"If we sign, what's stopping you from sharing the photos anyway?"

He walks over to the mirror and straightens his tie. "I have no desire to tarnish my daughter's reputation if I get what I want."

James grabs his briefcase and opens the door. "Everyone wins, Junior. Everyone." He starts to leave but stops. "Pick up those photos and leave them on my desk before you leave."

—

"I was wrong," Shad says to Mance, entering the workshop with Cedric in tow. He blows out a cloud of smoke. "I said you would be back, yet here I am coming to you."

Mance stops sanding and removes his goggles. "There's no smoking in here."

Shad laughs and shakes his head, flicking out his cigarette. Gray ash tumbles to the ground. "The apple ain't fall far from the tree."

Shad approaches the table and inspects Mance's work. He squats, runs his hand over the top of the column, and nods. "He taught you well. But you are much better than him."

"What do you want?"

"Let me guess… He had you make these? Authenticity, right?"

"How dare you step foot here."

"Boy…half of this is mine." Shad raises his arms and spins in a circle. "And I'm still yo blood. This is still my home."

"You walked away from the Kingdom and from your family."

Shad narrows his eyes. "Is that what he told you?"

"That's what I know."

"Then you don't know shit."

"Why are you here?"

Shad walks around, looking, touching. "I wasn't always a criminal. I had ideas." He touches his temple. "Good ideas but King never listened to me. It was always his way. The renting of the land was my idea, and it was a good one. I do anything for him and what I get in return? He showed me the end of the sledgehammer after I took a life for him, for your mother. First body on me and it wasn't even for me. It was for him, for Hazel."

Mance flicks his eyes to Shad. "Hazel…"

King believed that less is more, in using materials and especially with words. Never trust a man who talks too much and too fast, he often said. When you work in proximity to someone, you are bound to share thoughts and opinions. But King never shared. Nothing about Shad or his mother. He's heard that name before, once, twice, under King's breath while he worked and once while he napped in the workshop.

"He ain't never want to talk about her after she gone." Shad shakes his head and sucks his teeth. "Yeah…her step-father. Mean bastard. We buried him on the back side of the Kingdom next to the cemetery down by the creek. We marked the tree with an *X*, so you free to go look for yourself, but don't go lookin' too hard. There may be some other things you don't want to find."

"*The Solomon men have done all sorts of things in service of this land*," King said. "*There's pride in owning something, and you never let anyone take that away from you.*" Mance flushes now, realizing he never imagined to what lengths King might have gone.

"Why are you telling me all of this?" Mance shuffles to avoid tipping Shad to his discomfort.

"King knew what he had to do and he did it. Just like you did. Just like you're going to do."

"You think you know me?"

"Damn right I do. Because you are smart. You know now what you didn't earlier. You know ain't shit y'all can do without me. Like I said…half of this is mine."

Mance looks away.

"You need me. Ain't no shame in needin' a little help. Let me let you in on a li'l secret. Yo Daddy came to me asking for help to pay the taxes. Y'all kids were young, and he was just getting back on his feet after falling off that roof." Shad looks up as if at that very roof. "He did a little work for me. Just like you."

Mance holds his stare.

"What? You surprised? I ain't never seen him look so desperate." Shad walks closer. "He looked just like you look right now." He laughs. "What gets me about you, about King, is that you pretend to be good. That people like me are bad. But you are just as bad. You could do anything but you spend your life living for someone else's dream."

"You preachin'?"

"Nah... God walked away from me a long time ago. I've accepted that." He leans in closer. "Every person I've robbed. Every man I've cut." He studies his blade. "I own my shit. You killed that man? Own that shit. Own it."

"No repentance? Straight to hell?"

"There's no heaven for people like me. There's no hell either. I have enough to answer for. Too much for heaven and not enough for hell."

"So you are preachin'."

"I loved my brother but he didn't see what I saw. There's more to this world than this dirt." He kicks the dirt. "Had he listened to me, we all be rich right now. And I wouldn't be runnin' around still doing this shit."

"It's his fault the way you are?"

Shad laughs. "There's an angel and a devil in every family and you don't get to decide which one you are. It chooses you."

"I do this, and we are done. You sign over all your rights to the Kingdom forever."

"Are we negotiating?"

"Call it whatever you want."

Uncle Shad nods. "I like that. Smart. But you love that land that much?"

"You should."

"Wrong birth order. You should know. Second sons in the Solomon family aren't kings. We don't rule anything. Our opinions don't matter. We are the minions. We do all the work for no reward."

"There is no greater reward."

"Than what? Living on land where our ancestors were slaves? Living in a plantation?"

Mance grimaces.

"That's what it is. A plantation. Slavery is over. But you are still a slave to that land, to that house. It still owns you."

"It's our land. It's our ancestors' land. What they fought and died for. It's worth saving."

"You sound like King. He treated you like the firstborn. I could see it all those years ago. But you're not different than me. You don't realize it now, but you will, and you will come to resent it. I want no part of this land."

"Then we have a deal. I help you, and you sign over all of your rights."

Uncle Shad smiles wide. "Of course. Of course."

"And his." Mance points to Cedric without looking at him.

"Fuck you. I ain't signing over shit."

Mance looks at Shad, who shrugs. "Those are my terms. You'll have to work something out with him."

Cedric smirks, and Mance allows it. Cedric is nothing without Uncle Shad, and they all know it. He'll fold like a piece of paper. He is the least of Mance's worries.

"Are we understanding each other?"

Mance doesn't speak, just nods.

"Good."

"We are going to do this, but I never want to see you or him again." It's Mance's turn to step forward. "Because if I do, let me tell *you* a li'l secret: I'll kill you."

Shad laughs. "I don't doubt that you will. Now you know where to bury me."

TEN

———

THE FOUR CAKES GO down as easy and as fast as breathing. Inhale, exhale, inhale, exhale. Thoughtless seconds. Tokey's stomach rumbles, crying for help, but she ignores it. She doesn't care. She reaches for another package, her hands shaking slightly, and her fingers, slicked with icing, can barely grip the wrapper, so she rips it open with her teeth. The cake pops out and lands on the floor. Out of reach, it mocks her, a ship just off the shore.

Tokey stands and her knee bends before it buckles, propelling her forward. She tumbles and crashes into the dresser, her forearms skidding across it. The attached mirror wobbles. In it, Tokey glimpses the stranger she's always been. And doesn't know why she didn't see it before. The light-brown eyes and arched eyebrows unlike her siblings'. Her curved nose and rounded cheeks that hid the semblance of cheekbones. Her vision blurs, her eyes flood with tears, and she can only make out the fuzzy blob. She rips open the box, the wrapper, and jams the cake into her mouth. And another. And another.

Four is not enough. Neither is twenty.

The high floats in the same as always, a cloud drifting across the sky. But there's something else inside of it. An ache, a hole that refuses to fill. A place the high bypasses on its way to filling in all the other spaces. Tokey pushes back against its resistance and seeks to fill it with the last Swiss roll, which she jams into her mouth, chews, and swallows. The clamor in her head lessens, a knob turned down. The world opens and she feels light as air, and a peaceful nothingness fills her ears. She closes her eyes and succumbs to the high. And it's enough. Finally, enough to not feel. It took two boxes of strawberry and Swiss rolls to reach this place.

And where is this place? It's where she doesn't feel anything. It's where she can walk, sit, and stand without effort. It's where her mother and father were happy and live together like in those early letters. It's where she didn't know that terrible thing her mother did, and that King wasn't her father.

Tokey looks up at the person in the mirror, the letters that slipped from her hand only moments before staining the floor behind her reflection. It is her, only it's not. Chocolate and white icing coat her lips and cheeks. She didn't dream of leaving Diggs like CeCe or having a family like Junior. Her place card in life had *teacher, sister, daughter,* and *aunt* written on it. Nothing else, and she could live with that. The only thing more that she wanted was to know her family. But they are not her family. It all makes sense now, the whys to the questions no one could answer. Why she felt different. Why she didn't favor King.

Her high tells her she doesn't care, that nothing matters, and that she needs more. She pushes off the dresser and turns to look at the other thing still in the middle of the floor. One more cake.

She takes one step, then another, and falls to the floor with a thud. Tokey knows she should feel the pain, but she doesn't. She feels nothing and wants to stay locked in her nothingness. She rolls once, over the wrappers and letters, finally reaching the cake. She stuffs it into her mouth, licking the icing off her fingers, just as CeCe opens the door.

She has been conquered by strawberry rolls and six letters.

"Tokey," CeCe shrieks, and she's beside her in a second.

Tokey can only imagine what CeCe sees but she laughs. "Of course, it would be you." She rolls on her side away from CeCe, still laughing.

"Let me help you up." CeCe touches Tokey's shoulder, but she jerks away.

"Stop trying to help me. First at breakfast and now. You don't care about me."

"That's not true."

Tokey's breath catches as a wave of dizziness and nausea threatens to overtake her. "I think I'm going to be sick."

Ellis appears at the door.

"Help me get her to the bathroom," CeCe says.

Ellis lifts one arm and CeCe the other. Tokey flushes with

embarrassment and nausea, both more certain now. They make it into the bathroom and kneel her in front of the toilet just before the contents of Tokey's stomach storm back up. She lurches, her stomach spasming and contracting. CeCe's behind her, holding her hair back. When there's nothing left, Tokey slides away on her butt, propped up by the bathtub.

CeCe gives Ellis a look, and he slips out just as his cell phone rings downstairs. "I'll get that in another room," he says.

Tokey wipes her mouth with the damp cloth CeCe offers. "It must be nice," she says.

CeCe's brow furrows. "What?"

"Being you. To know who you are and make no apologies for it. To have a man who loves you the way he does."

"Stop it, Tokey. This is not about me."

"You're taking pleasure in this. I know you are. There's the fat sis—" Tokey stops abruptly. "Well…I'm not…I'm not…I'm not…"

"Not what? What are you talking about?"

Tokey waves her hand and tries to stand. "Never mind. I forgot. You're leaving after all of this."

"I care, Tokey." CeCe reaches for her and guides her to the bed, then goes and wets another towel and softly wipes Tokey's face.

"He loved her, and she loved him," Tokey mumbles.

"Who?"

"King and Hazel."

"Tokey…what are you talking about?"

CeCe follows Tokey's finger to the letters strewn across

the floor and picks one up, scanning but not reading it. "Mama wrote this?"

Tokey nods, but CeCe doesn't see it. She's reading and when she finishes, she smiles. "I never knew how they met," she says, reaching for another letter. "Where did you get these?"

Of course CeCe would select, at random, the best one. Tokey huffs. "Miss Jessie."

CeCe scoops them all up. "She's had these letters all this time? Why didn't she give them…?" She stops. She's asking too many questions. Then, she seems to understand something. She turns to Tokey. "What's in these letters?"

Ellis returns and asks a silent question that CeCe answers with a quick nod. He shuffles. "I gotta go," he says. "There's… I gotta go."

There's more he's not saying, his face a rictus of tension. Tokey can see it in the way he flexes and unflexes his fists. But CeCe doesn't ask.

"We'll be fine," CeCe says now sitting on the bed next to Tokey.

Ellis stirs in the doorway, running his hand over his head, caught between staying and going, and lowers his voice a measure. "You'll be here when I get back?"

CeCe meets his eyes and holds them, but is noncommittal when she shakes her head.

Ellis leaves, and Tokey says, "The Kingdom is cursed. We are cursed. We should let them take it. It's happening all over again."

Tokey knows she's not making any sense, and so she doesn't try to explain. She's thinking clearer now, and it's not the place she wants to be. Her high is thinning, her peace evaporating, as exhaustion overwhelms her. "I just want us to be a family again."

CeCe pulls the covers over Tokey. "We are a family."

"Remember when we used to press our foreheads together?"

"Yeah…" CeCe smiles. "When did we start that? Do you remember?"

"Junior," Tokey says, sleep pulling her downward. "He said it was better than a hug. I miss that."

CeCe leans down and taps her forehead to Tokey's, but leaves it there until Tokey drifts off to sleep, and whispers, "I miss it too."

<hr/>

Tokey needs her. And for once, CeCe will be there. Later, when Tokey blinks her eyes open, CeCe will still be with her, waiting, and she will listen, allow Tokey to speak her truth about what ails her, and she will take it because she deserves it. She has not been the sister she needs. CeCe will hold Tokey tight and tell her that everything will be okay. And they will start over, reset to zero, and begin again.

None of this happens.

It's not yet dark when CeCe pulls her overdue rental car off the Kingdom dirt road and onto the highway. Mark has called twice. Ellis is still gone, so she has to go now.

No matter what happens tonight, this will be it, she tells

herself, and she believes it. She should have stayed and read the letters that upset Tokey. But tomorrow she can be a better sister. She will be a better everything after this. She just has to get through tonight.

A few hours later, CeCe is straightening her dress in front of Mark's hotel room door. She knocks. He opens it almost immediately, in a rush, and the smell of alcohol hits her first followed by the sight of Mark's reddened face and bloodshot eyes.

"CeCe!" he says, reaching for her wrist. "Welcome."

He pulls her into the room and slams the door. There isn't much for CeCe to take stock of, but what there is says a lot; the table full of bottles and a man she's never seen before sitting in one of the chairs. Her blood runs cold as she feels her face flush.

"CeCe, this is Will, a potential client I'm wooing." Mark's words slur in a silly singsong.

Will lifts his glass at CeCe. "Another one, please."

CeCe forces a smile and takes the glass from his hand. She's often been the only woman in the room, more often the only Black woman. She's used to this. If Mark wants her to play hostess first, fine. "Sure…what are you drinking?"

"Surprise me," he says, grabbing CeCe's wrist tight. "Mark said you were beautiful. He should have said you were a goddess."

CeCe yanks her wrist free but holds her smile. "Well…that was awfully kind of him."

"Will's being pretty stubborn about signing with us so I thought I could get you to help me."

CeCe pours a shot of bourbon and splashes a bit of water in Will's glass before handing it back to him. The men are in the room's only two chairs. She considers remaining standing but feels ridiculous—like a servant waiting to be excused. She perches on the bed, smooths her dress over her crossed legs, and turns to Will.

"I think you will find that our firm is the best…"

Mark laughs, approaching her and placing both of his hands on her shoulders. "Oh, no. Not that."

Suddenly, she feels his meaning, the intent that's been there all along—in the stiffness of his grip and in Will's eager eyes. CeCe bristles, heat rising on her cheeks. "What are you talking about?" CeCe rolls her shoulders back.

Mark leans in and whispers in her ear. "Oh, you know what I'm talking about."

The room warms, and awareness creeps in. Panic sets into her chest. "This was not part of our agreement."

He grabs her by her cheeks and pulls her close to him. "You will do whatever I ask to whomever I tell you. Do you understand me?"

CeCe shoves him away and touches her cheek. She knows Mark is capable of many things, but not this.

Mark pours himself another drink and swallows it. "'Not part of our agreement,'" he mocks. "Well…our agreement changed when you had me lie about a second and third account. I need Will's business to get me squared with Ken again. And you're going to help me convince him."

"And I'm here to honor that." CeCe approaches him, slowly. "Let's just…" CeCe reaches for him, but her face meets the palm of his hand. The sting shocks her and then increases into full pain.

"I'm calling the shots here. Not you," Mark says.

Will laughs. "Damn, Mark. You're going to spoil the goods."

"CeCe likes it rough, don't you?"

CeCe turns, still holding her face. "I'm leaving."

"If you leave, it's over. Get someone else to lie for you."

She takes one step toward the door, and Mark grabs her hair and yanks. Her head jerks back. He then grabs her by the throat, his thumb blocking her air, and slams her against the wall. Her skull… Pain lances down her spine as she falls to her knees.

"Yeah…" Mark whispers. "That's a good place to start." He looks at Will. "If you don't mind, I'll go first." He turns back to CeCe, tugging at his belt with one hand. With the other, he yanks her head back further. "You know what to do. And then you're going to let Will fuck your sweet ass over that chair."

Will laughs, and Mark turns his head to laugh with him. When he does, CeCe punches him in the crotch.

With Mark on the floor, CeCe lunges from her knees toward the door. She manages to get it open, but Will's hand slams it shut.

"Where are you going?"

CeCe is on her feet by now, and acting on instinct, she grabs the phone that rests on the nearby desk and slams it into Will's jaw. He slides to the floor motionless.

"You walk out that door and it's over!" Mark says, more squeak than growl. "It's over! You hear me?"

CeCe opens the door and leaves.

In the hallway, her heartbeat accelerates and lurches. She allows two deep breaths to try to still it, and then she runs. She knows who will be on the other side of the lobby doors before she even opens them. And when she does, CeCe still cannot understand what she sees. It is Ellis. As predictable as her reflection. How is he always here? A circle of light from a streetlight casts a spotlight on him pacing in front of his truck. He is waiting. In a sense, he has always been waiting for her. And CeCe knows now that he always will.

She steps out of the hotel, her arms holding herself. And Ellis is on her in a second.

"Cecily," he says, his face pulled tight, every feature strained. He's looking at her, checking her body for wounds, but most of the damage lies internally.

Her last ounce of fight roars to the surface because anger is still much easier to hold on to. "Ugh!" CeCe vents her frustration. Only it isn't anger. It never has been with Ellis. It is love. It has always been love, seeping out any way it can. "How did you find me?"

Ellis reaches for her. "Come on. I'll take you home."

CeCe moves away from him. "Why are you here? Why are you always here?"

"Where else am I supposed to be?"

"I didn't want you to come. I didn't want you to see me like this."

"What was I supposed to do?"

"You can't save me. Please don't try."

"I can save you, but you have to let me." He couldn't save his mom no matter how hard he tried, but he damn sure would save everyone else, including, and especially, CeCe.

"I can't be who you want me to be. Stop trying to see something in me that isn't there."

"I still see you. The real Cecily. She's still there."

"Maybe not," CeCe says, walking away.

"You have to stop running from me," Ellis yells to her back and she stops walking. Immediately, CeCe understands that he isn't just talking about this time but all the times before.

"I'm not running from you! I'm saving you!"

"You may have all those big city folks fooled, but I know who you are, and you are scared. You are such a coward."

CeCe turns back to him. "I'm a coward? If you know everything, tell me what I'm afraid of."

"You. Of being you. The person who you really are."

"And who's that?"

"A poor girl from Diggs. It can be enough if you let it. There's no shame in it."

"How can you say that? We both wanted to leave."

"I'm always going to be a country boy from Diggs, and I'm okay with that."

CeCe turns to face him. "I blew it! I blew everything. Is that what you want me to say? That I should have called you after our night together? That I should have stayed?"

"Only if that's the truth," Ellis says, coming toward her. He tilts his head. He's staring at her neck. "Did he do that? Did he hurt you?"

"CeCe!" a voice calls from behind. It's Mark, staggering drunk. "Where are you going? Come back here, damnit!" He slams a beer bottle down on the ground. "The party has just begun."

CeCe blinks, and Ellis is gone from her side, tackling Mark at the waist and lifting him. Mark's legs fly in the air, and he lands hard on his back. Ellis punches Mark across his face several times and his head whips back and forth. Then, Ellis stands and kicks Mark hard, repeatedly.

"Ellis, stop!" CeCe yells. "Please."

But Ellis doesn't stop. It's only when CeCe touches his arm that he does.

"Look at me," she says, reaching up with both hands and touching his face, centering it on hers. "It's okay. It's okay."

Against their will, they are back in the trailer all those years ago. They've come full circle and they both know it. And they are going to keep circling back here, back to each other. The moment grips them both, and there's nothing to do but wait, and sit in it.

Pressure is needed to break something. The pressure CeCe feels is enormous and familiar. And this is enough to crack the last ounce of fight she had, and it fills her with a sense of urgency she's never felt before. Ellis loves hard and true; he will not be denied no matter how hard she tries.

"I love you," she says, the words falling out of her mouth like the first raindrop in the middle of a drought, with audacity and purpose. And it doesn't hurt. It's what she should have said all those years ago. Because she loved him then. She loves him now. Always will. Nothing can stop that. Not time or distance. All this time she was caught between who she was and who she believed herself to be. And now she knows who she is.

Ellis looks at her, and she watches the way the words move through him. CeCe presses her damp forehead against his and they breathe together. CeCe doesn't know how long they stare at each other. Seconds? Minutes? Her three words hang between them.

Mark stirs on the ground. "This is over," he mutters. "I'm reporting you. Do you hear me, CeCe?"

Ellis turns his attention to Mark, but CeCe guides his face back to her. "Let's just go."

"I'm fine," he says. "Let me handle this."

Ellis takes two steps toward Mark, who folds into a defensive fetal position. Ellis flips him on his back with his foot and kneels, slamming a knee on his chest. "My father was a violent man, so I don't particularly like violence. That said, I can be a very violent man, as you can see. I am, after all, my father's son." Ellis leans in closer. "Please believe me when I say that if you come near her again, touch her again, threaten her, or call the police, I will fuckin' kill you. Do you hear me?" Ellis presses his knee in harder. Mark whimpers. "Look at me and tell me you hear me. Do we have an understanding?" Mark groans again. "Now…Mark, I think you can do better than that."

Ellis stands and pulls Mark to his feet. "Let me help you up. Up, up, up." Mark staggers and groans, clutching his side, but Ellis steadies him, holding him by his collar. "There we go. Now, nod to show that you heard me because I'm really not in the mood to hide a dead body. But I will. I know of a spot where your wife and two daughters will never find you." Mark's eyes widen, wild with pain and disbelief. "Of course I know about your wife, Maggie. She's the one who told me which hotel you were staying in. She had just tucked Jodi and Stacey into bed. Don't be a hero, Mark. Go home. Go home to Maggie and your kids."

Mark grunts a confirmation.

"That's all you had to say." Ellis straightens Mark's shirt and brushes off a few pebbles. "You're going to be fine. It's just a few broken ribs. But let me check." Ellis punches him again, and Mark doubles over, screaming in agony. "Yeah…they are definitely broken. They hurt like hell, don't they? But they'll heal. Now get the fuck out of here."

Ellis watches Mark reel a few steps and limp back into the hotel, before walking over to the passenger side of his truck, and opening the door. He doesn't look at CeCe. "Get in."

⊢

Junior storms into his house, listening for Genesis. He hears the first-floor bathroom sink running and meets her in the adjoining living room. Midmorning, and Genesis is not dressed, wearing only a pair of sweatpants and a baggy T-shirt. Her hair is pulled into a messy top bun, and her face, free of makeup, is pale and misty. Her house shoes swish across the floor with each step as she shuffles into the living room.

"You told your father about Simon? About the pause?"

She lowers herself onto the couch and pulls a pillow into her lap.

"How could you do that?"

Genesis narrows her eyes at him. "How could I do that? How could *you* leave your family for another man? I was hurt, Junior. I needed support. I needed someone on my side."

"He 'summoned' me to his office." Junior paces the living room. "He wants me to sell all of the land to Malone & Kincaid."

"He thinks that is what's best for the family. He doesn't want to see me get hurt or for you to lose the land without anything to show for it. Without anything for your children to show for it."

"Bullshit! He doesn't care about me. He wants our land. He always has."

"He does not," Genesis inserts. "He's just trying to hel—"

Junior continues, speaking over her. "He's blackmailing me!"

Genesis's face collapses into a frown. "What?"

"Yeah…he's blackmailing me." Junior flings the folder he's been holding at Genesis. James told him to leave it on his desk, but Junior took it anyway. It lands at her feet with a splat, and several pictures scatter across the floor. She averts her eyes.

"Look at them."

Genesis shakes her head and crosses her arms.

"I said, look at them," Junior says, talking through his teeth and taking a step toward her.

"No," she says, standing and walking out of the living room and into the kitchen.

Junior scoops up the pile and follows her.

Genesis is at the sink now, filling a glass of water, her back to Junior.

"I want you to look at them. This is who you married. This is who I am." Junior shoves a picture in her face. Genesis turns her head in every direction to avoid the pictures.

"Junior, stop, please." The water in her glass splashes all over the floor.

"I want you to see what your father is doing."

Genesis stares at him for a long moment before snatching the pictures and throwing them on the counter, and when she speaks again, her voice arrives quick and menacing. "My father is not doing anything. It's you."

"Me?"

"You are unbelievable. Never taking responsibility for anything. Running from everything," she says, anger roaring to the surface. "All of it. The land being sold from underneath your father. My father blackmailing you. This is all your fault."

Junior quiets for a second as he absorbs the sting of the

words, as the mental fog rises. Enough of this. Who was she to say such things? He didn't have to listen to this.

Genesis snaps her fingers. "There you go again. Go ahead. Do what you always do. Disappear into yourself. Is Simon in there? Does he make everything okay? Does he make it okay to leave your family and abandon your father and brother and sisters?"

"How is this my fault? How is any of this my fault?"

"You should have been there for your father, but you ran from him just like you are running from your responsibilities as a father and a husband."

"I was miserable! I didn't want to live his life. What was I supposed to do?"

"Be a man."

"I am a man!"

"Then act like it!"

Junior lifts his arms in the air and drops them. "Oh…here you go. You sound just like King. I've heard it all before."

"It's in you. You can step up and be a man. The man I know you can be. Forget about Simon. Come back home. Consider Malone & Kincaid's offer."

Junior slides into a kitchen chair and clasps his hands together in prayer. "I can't do that."

"Do what?" Genesis says, sitting in a chair next to him. "Come home or take the offer?"

Junior looks at her. "Both."

"You don't love me anymore? Is that it?"

"Of course I love you. You are the mother of my children."

"Is that all I am to you? A mother?"

Junior looks away, avoiding the heaviness in her eyes. "Genesis, please."

Tears fill her eyes and fall. "When did you get to be so cruel?"

"I'm not being cruel. I'm not trying to hurt you. I'm being honest."

"Well…honesty hurts too."

He places his hand over hers. You can't save what you don't love. "It's too late. We can't go back now."

Genesis wipes her eyes, brightening a little. "We can. We can get through this."

Despite everything, Junior wants to laugh. The idea of reconciliation, once again, at a time like this. "Even if I weren't who I am…" Junior blanches but pushes on. "Your father is blackmailing me into selling my family's land. If not, he's going to spread these pictures all over town. And you think we can just go on after that?"

"He won't. I'll talk to him. Because you're going to convince everyone to sell. You have to."

"Are you kidding me? Are you not listening to me?"

"We need this. We need this for us, for our family."

"I can't keep living this way. Living this lie. And I can't sell my family land. It's all we have. It's all King ever wanted for us. I can't be the one who loses it."

"Am I not enough?" She stops, regretting saying the words that she knows the answer to. "Are the girls not enough? Is being a responsible father not enough?"

Genesis starts to cry again before a deep belch erupts out of her mouth. She has just a few seconds before she hurls all over the floor.

Junior stares in shock. He cannot remember the last time Genesis threw up. Then he knows. He knows before she even says it.

"I'm pregnant."

———

Minutes before the moving trucks arrive in front of the Prescott home, Mance pulls his Oldsmobile Cutlass Supreme onto a neighboring street and pops the gear into park. He settles into his seat. Guilt twists in his gut. Mance doesn't want to be here. On the passenger's seat sits a pair of gloves, zip ties, garbage bags, tape, his knife, and a hat, supplies you expect of a bona fide mover. Everything but the knife.

Mance knows he can't trust Shad. A betrayal looms. But he can't begin to see how. Last night Mance tried to think of all the ways Shad could double-cross him or scenarios that could go wrong. And he tried to prepare for them. He wouldn't get into any of the trucks with the merchandise. He wouldn't step foot into the warehouse where they planned to stash the goods. He would drive his own car to the Prescott House. He would wear gloves and a hat. As long as all he did was move furniture from the house to the truck, it wouldn't be considered theft. They were, after all, actually moving the Prescotts. He has convinced himself that this was a legitimate move, and as long as he wasn't caught with any of the merchandise after the expected delivery, he wasn't committing any crimes.

Except for one thing.

The ring.

He still had it.

Mance pulls the ring from his jeans and holds it between his forefinger and thumb. The diamonds twinkle, catching the light with every turn. He can see it on Lisha's finger. He will get Lisha a ring like this one day. He will stay up late building whatever he needs to build or calling in every favor to afford such a ring. He contemplated keeping it. The Prescotts wouldn't miss it and would assume it originally was stolen with all of the rest of the missing jewelry. But Mance has already added and subtracted too many titles from his life. A carpenter. A convicted felon. A father. A murderer. Mance is done with that kind of math. He wants to focus on being just one. A good person. He will put the ring back.

The first truck pulls into the driveway followed by the second. Just as they planned. Tony driving one and Cedric the other. Shad will serve as their boss while they load the trucks. They disembark and nod in acknowledgment, more of the plan than of each other. Mance takes a deep breath as he approaches the front door. He slips on his gloves and tugs the hat down on his head.

There's no one to greet them, and the door pushes open before Shad can ring the bell. The look and the feel of the house is different from Mance's first visit. It's a hollowed-out kind of quiet. No running water or cats. It's clean. The clutter that blanketed the foyer and the adjoining rooms has been removed; nothing remains except the large pieces of furniture.

They trade looks, having a silent conversation, until a tall man carrying a clipboard emerges from the back of the house.

"Good," he says. "Right on time. You can start in here." He walks past them and into the formal living room. "Mr. Prescott would like for you to be finished by four o'clock."

Shad steps forward. "Looks like somebody else has been here," he says and adds a lighthearted chuckle at the end to mask his nervousness.

"Mr. Prescott hired two moving companies. One to move the smaller, more valuable items and you"—he surveys them up and down—"for the heavier items."

Mance's forehead beads with sweat. All of the jewelry is surely gone. Without the jewelry, the job is a bust. But, also, he wouldn't be able to put the ring back.

"My work order don't say nuthin' about a second moving company," Shad says, pulling out a piece of paper from his pocket and unfolding it.

The man disregards the paper and moves away from them. "Change of plans," he says. "When you are finished in here, move on to the dining room before heading upstairs."

Like statues, they stand frozen until the man clears his throat and widens his eyes. Mance moves first and Tony second. They approach a wooden sideboard and lift it, carrying it out of the house.

When Tony and Mance return from loading the sideboard

into the truck, the man is gone, along with Uncle Shad and Cedric. Upstairs, they find Shad and Cedric in the master bedroom speaking in loud whispers.

"I swear, Pop," Mance hears Cedric say. "This is where it all was." Cedric gestures to the wooden jewelry cabinet that stands open and empty.

"Are you sure?" Uncle Shad asks, his eyes wild with disbelief.

Mance steps forward. "He's right. I saw it when she gave me the tour." Mance remembers seeing necklaces hanging and rows of brooches and rings, now all gone.

"We ain't got nothing without that jewelry," Cedric says, shakily. There's panic laced in his voice.

Shad considers this and looks to Mance.

"I say we walk away," Cedric says. "It ain't worth it."

But Shad continues staring at Mance, silently asking the question. Mance doesn't break his stare nor confirm that, surprisingly, he agrees with Cedric. He won't be the one to tell him to abandon the job. He can't. He needs to uphold his end of the bargain or Shad will back out of his end.

Mischief dances in Shad's eyes and Mance stirs under it. "We finish the job," he says, finally.

"Pop—" Cedric starts.

"How much for this?" Shad asks Mance.

It's a game. He's been here before; he knows all of the moves and secret codes. He's lost and won at this game so many times. It isn't chess or checkers but a game only they know.

So, he plays.

Mance answers, "About a grand."

It's a slight overestimation, one that Mance says only to please Shad, but he doesn't care. He wants to finish the job and leave.

Several hours later, Mance loads the last of the nightstands onto Tony's truck. He watches Cedric and Shad's truck turn the corner and disappear. He sighs, and refreshing relief washes over him. It's Tony's turn to pull out, but as he does, a police cruiser turns into the driveway, blocking his path. Mance looks at Tony, whose eyebrows lift into his forehead. Mance shakes his head, almost willing him to remain calm. There's no reason to worry, he wishes he could say. They are just movers finishing the first leg of their job. Tony has a copy of George Prescott's paid receipt in the glove compartment. Mance made sure of it.

The police cruiser pulls in front of the truck and stops. Two police officers step out when they don't move.

"We were just..." Mance starts to say, taking a few steps to meet the closer officer.

"That's far enough," the cop says.

Mance stops on a dime and raises his hands in a low don't-shoot pose.

"What are you doing at this house?"

"We're movers. We just finished loading up."

Mance slides his eyes at the truck. Tony's hands hang out of the window. He's speaking to the other officer, but Mance can't hear what he's saying. Mance sees a little of Tony's face. He doesn't know him enough to know his expressions, but he knows what panic looks like, and it's painted all over him.

"You got any paperwork?" the officer asks, turning his attention back to Mance.

"Yes, sir," Mance says, pointing to the truck.

By now, Tony is handing the receipt to the other officer, who inspects it. The officer in front of Mance watches.

"Is there a problem, Officer?" Mance asks, his speech slow and unassuming.

The officer jerks his attention back to Mance. "Nobody asked you to speak. You got some ID?"

Mance's breath hitches, and his heart bangs an irregular rhythm. "Yes, sir," he says. He stops. "I'm going to reach into my pocket and pull out my wallet. Okay?"

"Slowly."

Mance keeps one hand in the air and his eyes locked on the officer. It's an eternity before his hand reaches his front pocket and pulls out his wallet. When it reaches the light, he feels something else, too late. He hears it ping on the asphalt.

The ring bounces again and again before settling in the space between Mance and the officer. Their eyes both travel to the ring and back to each other just as the other officer joins them.

"Is that your ring?" The officer picks it up and inspects it.

"Yes...I mean, no, sir."

"Well...what are you doing with it? Did you get that out of this house?"

"Yes, sir."

The officers look at each other. "So, you admit you stole it?"

"No, it's not—" Mance drops his hands and takes a sudden step toward the officers, and they reach for their guns. "Stop right there!"

Mance raises his hands again, higher in the air. "I was saying that it's not my ring. I found it while we were moving."

"Yeah, right," the officer says. "This looks pretty expensive." He hands the ring to the other officer. "Tell that to them downtown."

Mance knows what to do. He raises his hands and places them on top of his head and waits for the cuffs.

ELEVEN

———

WHEN ELLIS IS NOT gripping the steering wheel tight, his fingers drum against it, quaking with anger and frustration. His breathing, even after an hour, is ragged as a bull's.

"Do you need—" He stops. "Do I need to take you to the hospital?"

"No" is all she says. She can't look at him, see the disappointment in his eyes. But when he turns down the road to his camper, she finally slides her gaze to him.

"You can get cleaned up here and then I'll take you home."

Ellis leads her to the back of the camper to an open-air bathroom and turns the water on, where it falls into a free-standing, claw-foot tub set on wide-plank wooden floors. Above is a half ceiling with Edison bulbs that Ellis begins to click on. The aged tub, now filling with water, is flanked by a paneled half wall and a long wooden vanity with a deep bowl sink. CeCe marvels at the sight and wonders how she didn't notice the cozy bathroom earlier. She watches as Ellis moves to light a series of citronella candles spread out around the bathroom.

"Take your clothes off and get in and don't fuckin' argue with me," he growls, turning off the water.

She didn't have any strength left to fight. So, she doesn't, and when she starts peeling down her dress, Ellis leaves.

CeCe dips a foot into the water and then settles the rest of herself inside. Immediately, the warm water and the calming atmosphere comfort her sore body and tired mind. She stares out into the dark and up to a sky full of stars. She doesn't see stars in New York and didn't know how much she missed them until now. And the sounds of the night, the rhythmic tick and whine of the cicadas, that provided a nightly soundtrack throughout her childhood. And the feel of the humid air, just the perfect temperature, against her face. She pulls her knees in against her chest and holds them. She stares and listens and, for the first time in too long, feels.

She should feel guilty about Mark, tonight, and everything she faced. And she will. The guilt lies there, dormant, and she will give time and place to it later. But right now, all she feels is grateful.

A knock against the half wall casts her mind back to the present.

"I brought you towels and some clothes." Ellis appears from around the corner. He doesn't look at her as he steps up into the space and places the items on a nearby stool before turning to leave.

"Stay," CeCe says. Ellis stops but does not turn around. "Please."

Ellis sits on the step across from the tub, his arms on his knees, his gaze drilling into the floor. He's still angry, the frustration crashing off him in waves, the sound not heard but felt.

"I didn't…umm…you know."

Ellis's entire body collapses. "What happened?"

CeCe hugs her knees tighter. "I didn't go with the intention of doing that again. I thought I could talk to him. But he was drunk and there was someone else in the room."

"Did he touch you, too?" The muscle in Ellis's jaw flexes.

"No." CeCe instinctively presses her hand to the side of her cheek. It's tender to the touch and stings.

They sit side by side as a deep quiet settles over them. Silence is never their way. They fuss. They argue. They laugh. They were never silent. They always had something to talk about. She doesn't know what she expects or wants him to say. But she knows him better when he challenges her. His silence frightens her.

And it's not just the silence she fears.

CeCe knows her life will be different in the morning, the day after, and months from now. She stands to lose it all, her law license, her job, and her freedom. It's what the bottom looks like. She deserves it. And she can withstand the loss. She will open her hand, the same hand she kept clenched so tight, and allow the life she thought she wanted to float away. But, she realizes suddenly, as the water cools her, Ellis is the only thing she can't bear to lose.

"Say something," she says, trying to make the words light despite the anxiety beating in her chest.

"What do you want me to say?"

"I don't know. Tell me I'm stupid. Ask me how I could do such a thing."

"I'm not going to say any of those things."

CeCe sighs, her face burning with shame. "I'm sorry."

Ellis huffs. "Do you even know what you are sorry about?"

"For the way I am. For what I did," CeCe says, resting her chin on her forearms. "Do you know what's funny? It seemed like a good idea. To try to be someone else. Live someone else's life. And for what?"

Ellis lets out a shuddering breath and finally looks at her. "We are all broken in some way. Pieced back together anyway we can."

"How did you do it? Piece yourself back together."

Ellis's mouth quirks into a crooked grin. "I met this hard-headed girl with a family who took me in and loved me as one of their own. I wouldn't be the man I am today without them. A father figure who became a father. A man who became my brother and best friend. And a girl who…" He stops, sighs. "I love you all."

"Why? Why are you so good to us? To me?"

"Like I said…King opened the door."

"That was a long time ago."

"Not for me it isn't."

"You don't owe me or my family anything."

Ellis grunts, more surprise than frustration. "Is that what you think? I'm doing this because I owe you?" He stands abruptly. "You're unbelievable."

"Then what is it?"

"I want you and no one else. It's always been you. Then and now," Ellis says, his voice even and sure as if he has been waiting a lifetime to say those words.

His words stretch inside her and root there. She's always known how he felt but hearing the words, out loud, sprouts things. "Why? Why did you wait for me?" she asks, knowing the answer because it's hers too. Feelings don't die. They wait. They stew and grow and surge back bigger, better, stronger than before. They demand to be felt.

"Because we weren't done," he says, the tenor in his words elevated.

CeCe flinches against the force of his honesty and she cannot look at him afterward. "And now? After all of this?" she asks, face toward the stars.

"We're still not done," Ellis says, quickly. "But we can be. If that's what you want. Do you know why I never had sex with you when we were kids? It's because I knew you didn't want to be here any longer than you had to. I figured I would leave, but I always knew I would come back. Like it or not, Diggs is my home. I knew you didn't feel that way. I didn't want to be the person who stopped you from pursuing your dreams. So I let you go. I did it before, and I can do it again. I can let you go, Cecily. If that's what you want. Forever. Just tell me now."

CeCe finally looks at him.

"You told me you loved me. Did you mean that?"

Ellis stands before her, hands in his pockets, body limp with frustration but his jaw grim, a man done. A man who has poured all of himself into something and has nothing left to give and nothing left to prove. He has done enough. Is enough.

It hurts too much, watching him suffer, and her heart flutters at the thought of him walking away. Then she realizes there's no need to panic. She knows what to do.

CeCe stands, her body beaded with water, watching the way Ellis's eyes follow her upward movement. CeCe makes no move to cover herself and Ellis doesn't avert his eyes. Here, for the first time, she feels her soul expand and relax. She likes it, and how it feels. It baffles her that a person has such power over her. Such positive power. And for the first time, the thought of love doesn't scare her or make her think of a means to an end. Instead, she thinks of the future, a long period of being happy and at peace. Finally.

She starts where she owes him. "I do love you. And I have loved you every day of my life since you gave me that sweater and maybe even before then. I know I'm a little late in telling you that. And you're right—I was afraid of being just a poor girl from Diggs. Afraid of what that meant. But more than that, I was afraid of letting you love me. So, I ran. But I have never felt more myself than when I'm with you. And I'm not afraid anymore. I'm not afraid to love you."

He approaches her, looking at her, into her. CeCe has never

known what he searches for when he stares deep into her soul like this, but whatever it is, when he finds it, it pushes a tiny smile to the corners of his lips. He breathes just one word: "Finally."

"Touch me, please," CeCe whispers, her voice full of want and need. "I'm asking you."

And he does, first running a finger down her cheek, then laying the palm of his whole hand on it, and she feels a pleasant flush of warmth as she leans into it. The kiss of the sun against the face after a cloudy day traveling straight to her toes and back again.

And then there's his voice and his truth.

"I love you, too," he says.

A new silence surrounds them and it's not uncomfortable. So much about them, their love refuses to be captured in words. So they don't try.

They crash together, two bodies separated for too long. She wraps her arms around his neck, and his hands slide up her back to the nape of hers, in her hair, as their mouths find the other. The kiss is easy, remembered, born many years ago. But it's not the kiss of before; it's a kiss of certainty and love, of absolution and acceptance, the breaking of chains and the snapping of threads. In it, everything comes storming back: their afternoons in his trailer, the white sweater with the hole in the seam, the way her body quivered under his. The kiss drags her deeper and deeper into the memory of before and into the threshold of something entirely new. Ellis feels the same, tastes the same. Because he is the same and completely different, better, all at once.

Ellis pulls back, breaking the kiss, the disconnection an electric charge. The lust in his eyes evaporates into a pained expression as he rests his forehead on hers. "It's been a long night. A very emotional one," he says, his breath half-gone. "Let's slow down."

CeCe feels the loss of his lips and the removal of his hands immediately. His touch still burns her skin. The air is laced with hunger. She can't speak. She is barely breathing and she closes her eyes. She knows he's right. Even if she doesn't want him to be, even if it doesn't feel like the end, the comma between them not yet a period. But she stays close to him, in his space, absorbing his warmth and goodness, feeling years of compressed desire release like a dam.

She opens her eyes to see his gaze still holding hers. His hands return. They aren't done. They. Aren't. Done. They will never be done. What started all those years ago in his trailer was love. It was honest and real. It can't be faked.

Or denied.

CeCe doesn't have the chance to answer. She looks up at him, her face soft and wanting. Ellis sees it and breaks.

"Fuck it."

He hooks his arm against the back of her legs and sweeps her up in one motion, water from the tub splashing the floor. His mouth returns to hers, his kisses desperate and wild as he carries her to his camper. CeCe's chest tightens a little with every step, and heat snakes through her despite her nakedness, setting a fire between her legs. After months of numbness, it's invigorating to feel something, a welcomed ache. She can almost cry.

CeCe knows she'll never be able to erase the memory of Mark, of those times in his office. But this, right now, isn't just what she wants. It's what she needs, to be reminded that pleasure doesn't always come at a cost, a necessity of circumstance. Loving Ellis, then and now, doesn't cost anything. It has always been free.

They stumble into his camper and Ellis eases her feet to the ground. They thrust upon each other, a tangle of limbs as Ellis guides them to the bed. An urgency overtakes them as they fight to get close enough, but also an acceptance that slows their movement, her fingers tugging and pulling at the hem of his shirt and his hands slowly fumbling at his jeans. They were out of time and had all the time in the world.

Now, Ellis makes it no secret that it will be him in charge. He lifts and wraps her legs around him, her breath hitching, as he places her on the bed. He makes no apology for the trails of kisses he leaves from her throat to her breasts, her nipples to her thighs. Or for his mouth finding the space between her legs, her legs on his shoulders, and his tongue pressing deeper into the heat of her. Or for the way her body tightens and coils and her back arches with pleasure as waves and waves crash through her.

Ellis moans against the dark as he lifts her again, her body limp as spasms of pleasure roll through her, and sits on the bed, stretching out his legs. He settles her on top of him and wraps her legs around his waist. His hardness presses against her before he slides her down on top of him, parting her, filling her slowly and fully. They fit, face-to-face, chest-to-chest, breath knotted together, bodies as one. It's only then that CeCe understands what he meant by *one body*.

Ellis sets the pace, hard and steady, his hands on her hips, grinding her hard against him, his face buried in her neck, her breasts. CeCe gives herself to him, feeling alive and well for the first time, as she feels her body, once again, coil tighter and tighter, taut as a rope.

"Cecily," he whispers. "Look at me." When she does, her body ripples around him, and she scatters into dust, millions of particles that will never be recovered and put back together again. Moments later, he follows her. Afterward, they hold on to each other, neither wanting to sever the connection. There is no sound but their residual moans and their unified breath. Tired and happy, she smiles against his shoulder. And the last coherent thought she has is that she is finally home.

The next morning, before the sun has risen, CeCe blinks her eyes open to Ellis sitting in a chair across from the bed. He hasn't slept.

He's worried. She can see it in his face.

"Cecily...listen—"

CeCe's heart aches because she knows, just as he knows, today is a new day. In just a couple of hours, the sun will rise, and the truth will find its way there. CeCe's not ready to leave last night behind and for this dream to end. But under the blackened sky, they can hide from it. For so long she dreamed of this, their time in the trailer, immersing herself in that fleeting memory and now a fresh one. One that will last her while she is facing tomorrow.

"Ellis, please don't. Not now. Please."

He nods his understanding.

She reaches out to him. "Come here." And he does. He slides in next to her and pulls her on top of him.

———

Mance plays the day over and over again. He should have seen this coming. He paces the small cell a few times and then slams his fist against the wall.

And again.

And again.

And again.

Until his knuckles bust open, and blood covers them. Until the pain becomes unbearable. He flexes his hand and winces. It's not broken. He knows what that feels like. But the pain is a reminder. Always. Better *he* hurt than someone else.

He collapses on the tiny bed, and the springs groan and screech with his weight. He slumps forward, resting his arms on his legs, and stretches his hand in and out. Mance sees the cut he sustained the day of King's funeral, a cut he has not allowed to heal, and now new ones. He wonders if they will ever heal.

Then he hears it.

The greatest sound in the world: Henry's laughter.

The sound fills his ears, and the world falls silent to it. Just Henry. It's loud and steady as if Henry is here, next to him. Mance closes his eyes briefly to appreciate the sound, every chuckle, every coo. It is enough to calm the throbbing vein in his temple.

Sound is everything.

After a while, the door creaks open, and Mance sees Ellis. He pulls himself upright and opens his mouth to speak but stops when Ellis's head ticks from side to side, the move slight. Ellis steps aside, and Lisha steps forward. Mance approaches the bars and grips them.

Then and there, Mance's heart lurches. He never wanted her to see him behind bars again. He made himself that promise. And now that promise has been broken. He has let her down again.

But there's no trace of displeasure in her eyes. Her even stoicism is more worrying. She asks Ellis, "Can you get him out?" Her face is still toward Mance.

"If we let him out, he'll go after Shad."

"No, he won't," Lisha says, looking hard at Mance.

"Yes, I will," Mance says quickly.

Lisha snaps to angry, finally. "What happened to bending?"

Her words hang in the air between them until Ellis clears his throat. "I'm going to step out for a minute."

Lisha holds up her hand, stopping him. "You don't have to leave. This won't take long." She breathes, fortifying herself, a woman fed up. "I'm going to take a leave of absence from the library and stay here in Charlotte with my mom for a while," she says. "She lives close to Henry's doctors. I won't have to keep making that drive."

"Lisha…"

"I won't keep you from seeing Henry," Lisha continues, her voice dipping softer. "You can come anytime. I just can't be here. I can't watch you do this again. I won't. I love you too much."

Mance curls his fingers tighter around the bar. "Lisha, please listen. All of this is for Henry, I promise. It's almost over."

"It was over before. It's never going to be over."

"It was for the Kingdom," Mance says, the closest he can get to the truth.

"It's always about the Kingdom. It will never end, and I don't want to watch it destroy you. I have to think about Henry now."

"Please don't go," Mance whispers. And that's all he can say. There is nothing he can do now but hope that as Lisha watches Henry grow and thrive on the Kingdom as he did, she will come to realize that Mance has done the right thing. Just as he hopes for her to understand his decisions, he has to understand hers now.

Lisha leans her forehead against the bars, and Mance does the same. She smells as she always does, of vanilla and baby powder, and the comforting familiarity weakens Mance. He knows better than to try and change her mind. It's her fear talking. So, he doesn't try. He tells her that he's sorry and runs his finger up and down her cheek a few times before cupping it with his hand. She leans into it for a second, closing her eyes, before turning and disappearing behind the door.

The door slams, and Mance kicks at the bars several times, fury rising from deep within him. He growls. "You gotta…"

"You've been free since I walked in here," Ellis says, pushing off the wall in the corner and walking over to him. "It's a bullshit charge that I can get kicked. They will never be able to prove that you stole the ring. But you should know—" He pauses. "My source here says they received an anonymous tip about you. What the hell have you been doing? And why am I just now hearing about it?"

Through gritted teeth, Mance explains the entire story about Cedric, the Prescott House, the ring, and Shad agreeing to sign over his interest in the land in exchange for Mance's help.

"I just wanted the Kingdom to be free of Uncle Shad," Mance continues. "And after all of this was over, maybe the original Solomon pact would continue to ring true. That we do not sell anything. Not a plot of land. Not an acre. Not one inch."

"You're right," Ellis says, after Mance finishes. "I just wish you would have let me in on it. I could have helped."

"You would have talked me out of it."

"Or at least stopped you from getting set up."

Mance's vision bleeds red along the edges, and he pulls on the bars with both hands. His temples throb. "Yeah…it was really convenient that Cedric and Uncle Shad were able to leave but I got stopped."

"He wanted you out."

"Yeah," Mance says. "Because…"

"Yup."

It had all been a game. And he walked right into it. No, invited himself in.

"I'm going to kill him," Mance says, pacing the small cell again. "Can you roll with me?"

Ellis sighs. "You know I would, but I can't."

"It's that bad?" Mance stops pacing, knowing it's about CeCe.

Ellis nods. "And Tokey, too."

"Tokey?" Mance's brows lift. "What about Tokey?"

"She's not good. I think she's sick. I left them both at the Kingdom, but I need to get back."

"Go," Mance says, pacing the cell again.

"The guard will be in soon to let you out," Ellis says, clapping hands with Mance through the bars. "Don't make me regret this."

Ellis turns to leave, but Mance calls after him again.

"You're welcome, and they are going to be fine," Ellis says. "Call your brother."

Several hours later, Mance pulls into Junior's driveway.

"Are you going to tell me what this is all about?" Junior asks, slamming the door and settling into the front seat.

Mance turns onto the highway and presses his foot down on the accelerator. "Uncle Shad," he says through teeth clenched so tight they might crack. Time has not lessened his anger. "I'm going to kill him."

Junior nods at Mance's cigarettes in the console. "Can I have one of those?"

Mance flips his pack to him. "You don't smoke."

"I do now," he says, shaking out a cigarette. "Especially if I'm going to be an accessory to murder. Plus, you're not the only person having a shitty day."

"What's going on with you?"

Junior lights the cigarette and takes a huge drag. He coughs out a plume of smoke, and when he stops, he says, "Genesis is pregnant and I'm gay."

Mance can do nothing but look aghast. Junior stares back, chin tipped up. He coughs a few more times and waits.

It makes sense to Mance. All those years ago when Mance and Ellis talked about the girls they dated and the sexual activities they partook in, Junior never indulged. He rarely dated. Mance knew Junior was shy and assumed that bled into his dating life. But, he remembers now, once, he saw the way Junior looked at a male classmate, his gaze lingering longer than usual. And Mance wondered but convinced himself it was probably nothing.

"I know," Mance says, holding his breath a moment and letting it go. "I've suspected."

Junior doesn't ask Mance how he suspected. It would not have mattered anyway. He knew. "And?" Junior asks, staring at him hard.

"And what? I don't give a fuck. You're my brother."

Junior's shoulders slump, a man letting go of something heavy. "I have a boyfriend. His name is Simon."

Mance's eyebrows raise as he processes this new information. "So…what about Genesis?"

Junior tells him of the pause as Mance listens. When Junior finishes, Mance laughs, a sound completely out of place in that moment. "And I thought I was fucked up."

Mance can tell that his laugh catches Junior off guard for a second, but he knows it relaxes Junior, and he settles further into his seat.

"You have to be fair to Genesis, to Simon too. If he's your…" Mance pauses, the word caught in his throat. He doesn't know if he can say it. It doesn't sound right on the back of his tongue, in his mind. Not because he doesn't approve. It just hasn't ever been something he allowed himself to think about. Men liking other men. There are no gay men in Diggs. Gay men live in the big cities, in Charlotte. Or so he thought. He will have to adjust his thinking, but that will take time.

"Boyfriend?" Junior fills in the blank.

"Look…I'm trying."

"I know, and I appreciate it."

"You can't occupy two worlds. You have to choose," Mance says, realizing he could have been talking about himself.

"I know."

"Remember what King used to say about wood? You can't polish bad wood? Trying to have a marriage with a woman and a boyfriend is polishing bad wood."

Junior sighs, before speaking again. "If you suspected, do you think he did, too?"

"I don't know, but if he did, I don't think it would have mattered to him. I think he wanted you to find your place. I think that's why he let you go, especially if your place wasn't here. He wanted you to see it for yourself."

"Like you?"

Mance lets out a shuddering breath. "Not like me. I don't know what the fuck I'm doing."

"What are you talking about?"

"Henry scares the shit out of me."

"Welcome to fatherhood." Junior laughs now and claps Mance on the shoulder. "That scared shitless feeling. It never goes away."

"Without the Kingdom, I have nothing to offer them." Mance sighs. "I wouldn't marry me either. Lisha told me that I can be the one who bends. Hell...I don't know how to do that. I don't even know what that means."

Junior huffs. "I'm the king of bending. That's all I feel like I've done. Bend for others so much that I'm a fuckin' pretzel. I can't even stand up straight."

"Yeah...but something can only bend so much before it eventually snaps," Mance says.

"I should have ripped up that check right in front of them. Taking it made me weak."

"Nah," Mance says. "You did the right thing."

"You would have ripped it up."

"And that wouldn't have made it the right thing to do. We're not the same. I can stand to be more like you."

"And I should be more like you."

"We just have to learn when to bend and when not to, I guess."

Mance cannot recall the last time he opened up to Junior this way, or if he ever has. Ellis provided the shoulder for Mance to lean on and an ear to hold his secrets. They were the same, finishing each other's thoughts and sentences. But, in this moment, Mance doesn't need the same. That was his problem. He needed to think differently from someone who also thought differently.

Mance stops at a stoplight and looks at both sides of his hands, his bruised knuckles, dried and crusted with blood. "This is all I have."

"Marriage and fatherhood are a different kind of fight. Not with your hands but with your heart." Junior shakes his head. "I need to do more fighting with my hands and not my heart. Like you. Like King."

"I don't want to fail him," Mance says. Junior raises an eyebrow. "Both of them."

"You didn't fail King. We're not going to lose the Kingdom. And you won't fail Henry. He's lucky to have you as a father. Like we were lucky to have King."

Mance nods.

"I just hate that it took me all this time to realize it," Junior continues. "King died before he got a chance to be proud of me."

"He was," Mance says, his voice rising, and Junior knows it's true. "You did something he could never do. Walk away. I think he saw strength in that."

Mance watches the statement coil around his brother like a snake as tears silently flood Junior's eyes. Mance removes a hand from the steering wheel and lays it on Junior's shoulder. Mance feels like crying himself, and can't remember the last time he did. But two loud beeps from Mance's cell phone fill the car. Mance looks at it and accelerates, the car jerking forward.

"What is it?" Junior asks.

"It's a text from Earl telling me to get to Lisha's house right now, but she should be in Charlotte."

"Who is Earl?"

"Lisha's landlord and Paul's father. Do you remember Paul?"

Junior twists his lips. "The one…"

"Yeah…"

Mance doesn't remember the rest of the drive, if Junior spoke another word, or how he manages to reach Lisha's house. When he crashes into her yard, he jumps out of the car, failing to put it in park. The front door is open, lights on when Mance storms in, breathless, heart racing. Earl emerges from the kitchen and meets him in the living room.

"They're not here," Earl says.

Relief washes over Mance but he continues assessing the scene wildly, adrenaline still pumping in his veins. Junior stands next to him.

"What the fuck is going on?" Mance asks.

"You better come take a look," Earl says, walking back into the kitchen.

Shad is on his knees, holding his side, his shirt slashed and covered with blood. He's still alive, Mance knows, because he hears his ragged and labored breath.

"I was here fixing the sink when this one"—Earl points to Cedric unconscious in the corner—"busted through the door looking for you. I hit him over the head with the wrench. He went down without a fight. Then Shad came in after him. And…" Earl stops and tips his chin upward. "He almost killed my son. I ain't neva forgot."

A strained laugh rolls out of Shad, and they turn their attention back to him. Mance stands in front of him.

"Now you come to kill me," Uncle Shad says, coughing and spitting out blood. He winces. Earl's knife is still lodged deep in his chest. Shad's pearl handled knife, clutched in Earl's hand, slides into Mance's view. Mance takes it and pops it open.

Mance crouches over his uncle, just like Uncle Shad did to him all those years ago. "Tell me why I shouldn't slit your throat right now. Or let Earl finish what he started."

Shad looks at Mance, his eyes bloodshot, and gives a weak smile, his breath heavy and labored. "We. Are not. The same. You are not me."

"You're right. I'm not you." There's truth and freedom in those words, and Mance feels both instantly. He starts to stand, but Uncle Shad reaches for him, seizing him by the wrist.

"Bury me at the Kingdom," Shad coughs, his pleading

eyes holding onto Mance. "I want to be with my brother…my daddy…my people."

"Do you think you deserve that? Deserve mercy when you've given none?"

"It ends with me." Uncle Shad takes one final breath in, and the laboring stops. His body falls over.

Junior walks over to Shad and presses two fingers on his neck. He shakes his head and stands.

"Get out of here, Mance. I don't want this to come anywhere near you," Earl says. "I'll take care of this."

Mance doesn't pretend to understand any of this. His heartbeat slows, and he feels a release without relief. It is enough to ease the tightness in his chest, enough to numb it all. He should feel more than he does. And he will. Later, despite everything, he will mourn Uncle Shad, not the criminal, but the man he chose to become. Later, he will come to understand that, like him, Uncle Shad followed an invisible path he never truly understood. Later, Mance will marvel that his uncle's death saved him from following the same path.

For now, Mance does the only thing he can do. The right thing.

Mance stands. "Take him to the Kingdom. There's a road at the far north end. Follow that until it ends. I'll meet you there."

"Are you sure? I did this, not you. I don't…"

"No one will ever find him there. Every Solomon man is buried at the Kingdom. It's where he belongs."

Cedric jerks awake and moans. "What about him?" Earl asks.

Mance squats next to Cedric, and he recoils, whimpering. "Please don't kill me. Please don't kill me."

"Shut the fuck up," Mance says, resisting the urge to punch him, his fist tightening so hard his fingernails dig into his palm. Instead, he asks the question he's long suspected. "Are you our blood?"

Cedric blinks. "No, he…he…just told me to say that I was."

"Why did he set me up?" Mance knows why. He just wants to hear it.

"He wanted to sell more of the land, and he knew you would never let him. He wanted you out of the picture."

"Where's the furniture?"

"In the warehouse. You were right about us getting hustled. The fence never showed. That's why we came here. We thought you ratted us out."

Mance stands, yanking a staggering Cedric to his feet. Cedric cowers and covers his face with his hands. "Get the fuck out of here and go back to wherever you came from."

"Thanks, Mance."

"Don't thank me." Mance grabs a handful of Cedric's shirt and pulls him close, the motion quick. His voice is wound wire-tight. "If I ever see you around here again, I will kill you and bury you next to him." Mance drags him to the door and pushes him out.

After a few seconds, Junior asks, "How will we explain where he is?" He's still standing next to Uncle Shad's lifeless body. Mance joins him, followed by Earl. The house is strangely quiet as the three of them stare.

"We don't," Mance says. "Uncle Shad died a long time ago. We are just burying his body."

———

Tokey opens her eyes, and she remembers everything. Sleep didn't help. She still doesn't understand. It's not her imagination. The letters were real. So were their contents. Suddenly, she begins to cry, wet and messy tears that dampen her pillow. She moves to sit up and feels a body next to hers. CeCe stirs awake, rubbing her eyes and yawning wide.

CeCe touches her face and grimaces. A reddened bruise darkens her cheek.

"What happened to you?" Tokey asks, narrowing her eyes.

CeCe looks away, and for a second Tokey thinks she may not answer but she does. "The lawyer I've been sleeping with to help me cover up the half million dollars I stole slapped and choked me last night because I would not sleep with him and his friend."

Tokey's tears dry on her cheek and she blinks. "Oh…okay."

"Your turn," CeCe asks, waiting.

After all of these years, they have reached a place of sharing. It's the sisterhood Tokey has always wanted and it is now her turn to admit what she has never said out loud.

"In one of Hazel's letters, I read that King and Uncle Shad killed someone and that Mama slept with James to save the Kingdom and got pregnant with me."

"Oh…okay," CeCe repeats.

"It makes so much sense now. Why I never felt like I belonged in this family."

CeCe pulls herself upright in the bed. "What are you talking about? I don't care what those letters say... You are my sister." She places her hands on both sides of Tokey's face, holding it. "You are more of a Solomon than any of us."

"But I'm not."

"I don't give a damn about blood. You are the best of us, and this family would be nothing without you. Do you hear me? You are my sister. And I'm sorry for not being here, for not being the sister I should have been."

"I'm sorry for being so mean to you," Tokey says, through sobs.

"I deserved it," CeCe says, laughing.

Tokey chuckles, too. "Yeah...you did."

CeCe doesn't ask Tokey about the food, but Tokey can almost feel the question hanging in the air between them.

"I need to go speak to Miss Jessie," Tokey says. "There's still so much I don't know or understand."

"Do you want me to come with you?"

Tokey brightens at the offer. "I thought you and Ellis were meeting with Ethan to discuss tomorrow's hearing."

"We are, but I can let Ellis handle it. I want to be here with you."

"If you don't mind, I'd like to speak to Miss Jessie by myself."

CeCe kisses Tokey on her forehead and taps her head to hers. "When you get back, I think it's time to tell Junior and Mance about what you know. I think it's time we all talk."

An hour later, Tokey knocks on Miss Jessie's door. She opens it wide. "I've been expecting you."

Miss Jessie skips the pleasantries this time. No offer of tea. No tray of cookies. She heads to her living room, the same place where she gave Tokey Hazel's letters. They sit, almost in the exact same spots as before, CeCe on the couch and Miss Jessie in her chair.

"You look worse for the wear." Miss Jessie leans back. "Ask your questions."

Tokey has so many questions for Miss Jessie that they bottleneck in her throat. Miss Jessie said these letters would tell her, but Tokey has more questions than she started with. Hazel's words still carry secrets and Tokey wants them revealed.

"If you knew what was in these letters, why did you wait so long to give them to us?"

"It wasn't my place. I thought King would tell you. If I had known he didn't, I would have given them to you ages ago."

"Why are there no more letters?"

"I came home," Miss Jessie says. "Your Mama and I traded letters for years until I decided that I'd seen enough of the world. Diggs is funny. You spend your whole life trying to leave only to discover everything you need is right here." Miss Jessie adjusts in her seat and a corner of her mouth turns up. "I bet CeCe knows a thang or two about that."

"I don't know. Maybe."

"Diggs gets in your blood, and what you run from is often where you are always supposed to be. Hazel knew that." Miss Jessie smiles. "Girls here didn't go to college. There were very few jobs around here for women. They got married and had kids. That includes Hazel. She loved Diggs. I ain't neva understood how she neva wanted to leave and see the world. She could sang…" Miss Jessie shakes her head. "Coulda been just as famous as Aretha Franklin. But here was enough for her. She met King and decided he was enough, too."

Tears form in Tokey's eyes. "They really loved each other, huh?"

"Oh, honey, yes," Miss Jessie says, smiling. "Back then, love was private. You didn't hold hands, kiss, or hug. But you could see it on them. Everybody could. These letters don't do justice to how powerful their love was. It was like a fairy tale. What I chased for all those years. I would have loved a man like King. Uncomplicated and loving. I ain't neva find it but Hazel did, right here."

"We never saw that side of him. It's hard to imagine him in love." The King Tokey knew and loved was not the same as the King who had fallen in love with her mother. In her day, he was a father—hard, serious, heartbroken. But Hazel's King was tender and soft, Mance and Junior rolled into one.

"I wished you would have seen your father back in the day. He was always serious, but he did laugh and smile. He was a bit of a jokester. It's not until Hazel left that he changed."

Tokey swallows but the knot there remains. "If they loved each other so much, then why? How could she do it?"

"You talkin' about the thing with James." Miss Jessie groans and folds her arms. "He ain't never been a good man even when we were kids. James thought he was better than everybody else. He had everything and couldn't stand that he couldn't have the one thing he wanted. Hazel." Miss Jessie inhales and exhales. "He ain't never like that she chose King over him."

"That still doesn't explain why she did it. If he was such a bad person, how could she sleep with him? How could she do that to King?"

"It was a different time back then. It was hard. Money was scarce. When King fell off the roof, he couldn't work. They didn't have any money except the rent from the lots. Do you know how much taxes are on two hundred acres of land? She did what she felt she had to do."

It seems strange to Tokey that she could feel something for a mother she never met. A cry rises in her throat as the tears start to fall. "Does James know about me?"

"What about you?"

"That I'm his daughter."

Miss Jessie rears back. "What? Who? You're not James's daughter."

"But…the last letter said that King couldn't have any more kids."

"Is that why you are so upset? Because you think James is your father?"

Tokey studies Miss Jessie for a long moment and blinks back tears. "He's not?"

"Heavens no, child!"

"I thought…the letter…" Tokey says. Every ache in her body eases.

"Minnie thought King couldn't have any more kids but it turns out she was wrong."

This should satisfy Tokey but an unfilled space in her heart remains. "Then why am I so different from Mance, Junior, and CeCe? I don't look anything like them or King."

Miss Jessie stands and walks over to a desk table. She opens a drawer and pulls out a tiny photograph. "That's because you look just like her." She hands Tokey the picture. "It's old and it's not the best but you can still make out her features. You have her face."

Taking the picture in her hands, Tokey finally sees what she couldn't in her dreams. Her mother's face, the curve of her jawline, her full nose, her high cheekbones. It's like looking in a mirror.

"I didn't know I had that. I only just found it stuck between the pages of a book." Miss Jessie looks at the picture. "This was taken just after their wedding. They were so happy."

"She's dead, isn't she?" Tokey asks, finally saying what she has long suspected, what she has always known.

Miss Jessie returns to her seat, and a sadness veils her face. "She was nine months pregnant and started having contractions. She held on until she heard you cry, and then she slipped away. You were the last thing she did."

It is now that Tokey gives herself over to the tears. They are full, rolling, wetting her face.

"After Hazel died, King refused to let anyone touch her. He picked her up and carried her all the way back to the Kingdom. People say they ain' neva seen anything like it. People in cars stopped and pulled over on the side of the road and let him walk. He didn't stop once. He walked all night. Cars provided him with light." Miss Jessie sniffles, her own eyes now full of tears.

"There was no funeral. But if you read the letters, you know where she is. He built her casket and buried her close to their favorite spot in the Kingdom." Miss Jessie wipes her eyes. "When I came home, I promised her that if anything happened to her, I would look after you kids and King. And I have."

It's only now that Tokey realizes that Miss Jessie has watched the Solomon kids grow up, a gatherer of sorts over their entire lives, of their secrets, their personalities, and their past.

"I see so much of their lives being repeated in you kids. It's scary."

Tokey snaps her head up. "What did you say?"

"I said that there's so much of you all in their story."

Tokey sniffles and wipes her eyes. "I got that same feeling when I was reading the letters, but I don't know what that means or what I'm supposed to do."

"Have you told Junior, Mance, and CeCe about the letters?"

Tokey shakes her head. "They've been busy trying to save the Kingdom."

"And so have you." Miss Jessie holds her eyes on Tokey. "You reading and understanding these letters, understanding

King and Hazel, is just as important as what they've been doing. You now have the responsibility to tell them. Everything."

"Do you believe that the Kingdom is cursed?" Tokey asks.

"I don't know. I do know that our past really isn't all that far past," she says. "History has a way of being repeated. If that's what a curse is, then maybe."

Junior, Mance, and Earl shovel the last of the dirt on Uncle Shad's grave just as the sky reddens. They are tired and hungry and filthy. But the job is done. It has been an emotional day. Yesterday feels like forever ago, and still Junior feels trapped in it.

Junior had never ventured to that side of the Kingdom. And now twice. First, to bury King and now Uncle Shad. He can't help but slide a look across to King's gravestone, and then the rest of the overgrown and vaguely marked graves. Who else is buried out here?

They pile back into Mance's car, one body lighter. When Mance turns the corner to pull into the Kingdom's driveway, Junior sees Simon leaning against his car.

"What's he doing here?" Junior asks aloud.

"Who?" Mance asks.

"Simon."

Mance pulls in behind Simon, and Simon pushes off his car. Junior opens his door as soon as Mance shuts off his engine.

Simon looks different from the last time Junior saw him

in the school parking lot. He's wearing a shirt Junior has never seen before. His face is eager. A man resolved. A man with something to say. Junior stares at him, hoping to see a flicker of emotion, a sign that there is a chance for them. But Simon's face remains still.

"I get it now," Simon says, his eyes sweeping over the Kingdom.

"What are you doing here?"

Simon doesn't have time to respond because Mance walks over to them, his hand extended. Simon squares his shoulders and pulls himself upright. "You must be Junior's Simon," Mance says, taking Simon's hand and shaking it.

Simon's eyes lift, and he smiles. "I am. And you must be Mance. I've heard a lot about you."

Mance looks at Junior before looking back at Simon. "Whatever you've heard is a lie. Unless it's true."

Mance hates small talk, Junior knows. He's a practical man, finding most words pointless. He said he didn't care about Junior being gay and having a boyfriend. Junior wants to believe that. And maybe, one day, he will. Junior knows it's not something a person accepts so easily. But for now, Mance is trying. Until that moment, Junior didn't how much he wanted Mance's approval and acceptance, how much it would mean to him. It turns out it means the world.

They chuckle, and Simon says, "It's beautiful out here."

They scan the landscape. Junior doesn't remember the last time he did so. He has long ago stopped seeing it. Or, at least, stopped allowing himself to see it. As he takes it all in now, his heart flutters. He forgot how soft the mornings can be. Fields of land that stretch for miles. The beginnings of wildflowers reaching up to the sky. The sun rolling in, a reminder to Junior that he has always loved mornings at the Kingdom best, before the sun floods everything.

The three of them stand there until Mance says, "I'm going to take a shower. It was nice to meet you, Simon."

Simon and Junior watch Mance walk into the house and when he closes the door, they turn to each other. It's awkward when it should feel anything but.

"Why *are* you both so dirty?" Simon asks, speaking first. "Early morning chores?"

Junior looks at his clothes. "We were burying something that finally died."

Simon waits for more, and when Junior offers nothing, he says, "Sometimes things you bury tend to come back to haunt you."

"Why does that sound prophetic?" Junior hesitates. "Is it?"

Simon's attention darts to his feet. "You know it is."

Simon pauses for a beat for Junior to respond, and when he doesn't, he says, "He's tall."

"He's always been more like King than me. He's King made over."

"So...he knows? You told him?"

Junior nods and looks at the front door again. "He said he didn't care. He said that King might have known, too."

Simon lifts his brows. "Really?"

Junior looks at the sky. There's no one there but King, staring down at him. "Maybe. He died before he could ever be proud of me."

"Do you believe that?"

"Yeah, I do."

"Is that why you battle in your dreams? Because nothing you did made him proud of you?"

Junior crosses his arms and leans against Simon's car. "It is never him I'm battling. It's his expectations. I didn't want to be him, and I've done everything opposite to what he did to avoid turning into him. I didn't want my life decided for me."

"I understand, Junior. But you can't keep fighting a ghost," Simon says. "At some point it's just you swinging at air."

"Yeah…maybe."

Simon shuffles, his Adam's apple bobs as he swallows, his lips parting on a breath. Junior reaches for him, a hand offered. It's coming, the end, Junior knows, and he wants to stop it. "I need to tell you something first."

Simon steps away, his face tense. "No, not this time. I need to say this."

"I'm not going to stop you from saying what you came to say. But I need to let you know something."

The skin between Simon's eyes pleats. Junior takes a long, exasperated breath and takes a step toward Simon. "That night. At the school. Us in the car." Junior stops and swallows. "We were not alone. My father-in-law hired a private investigator to follow me and…there are pictures."

Simon blanches. "And what are you going to do about it?"

"What do you mean?" Junior asks, shocked at Simon's response.

Simon crosses his arms. "I mean how are you going to stop him from doing whatever he wants with them?"

"I can't. He wants me to convince Mance and my sisters to sell the Kingdom. I can't do that."

"So, what *are* you going to do? Just let him embarrass you?"

"What choice do I have?"

"Does Mance know about the pictures?"

"I didn't tell him because he would try to fix it. He would storm into James's office and set it on fire. But it's not his problem to fix. It's mine and I don't know how."

"Does Genesis know?"

Junior grimaces and Simon notices. "She does, doesn't she?"

"She knows. She's the one who told him about us. And—" Junior pauses. "She's pregnant."

Simon laughs as though it's the funniest thing he's ever heard. "Of course she's pregnant." He throws his hands in the air and releases them hard. "Why not?"

"I don't know what to do."

"How are we here, Junior? How are we still here?"

Junior knows *here* is not a physical place. Still, he asks weakly, "Where?"

"You know where."

"I don't know."

"You do. Stop saying you don't know. You've always known."

Simon's erupting voice surprises Junior. "I don't know. Tell me, please."

"I can't... It's not my journey. It's yours. But I can't be here anymore." Simon turns and walks toward his car.

"Simon, wait. Please don't go." Junior steps in front of him. "I'm sorry. I'm sorry about the pictures. I'm sorry for everything."

"I don't care about the pictures, Junior. I'm out. My family knows about me. I'm happy with who I am. I'm not ashamed. You are. I'm not the one you owe redemption to. It's not me you've been chasing and it's not King either."

"Then, who?"

"You!" Simon yells. "You've been chasing who you really are. The man you are supposed to be."

Junior scoffs.

"If all that's left of you is this, you would be more of a man than anyone I've ever met."

"Then why don't I feel that way?"

"Why did you work with Genesis to save the Kingdom?"

"Because they can't just take it from us."

"And?"

Junior pauses to consider. "Because it's what King would have wanted me to do. What's expected of me."

Simon smiles. "You can't change your DNA, your blood, his blood, the blood of a King. That's why."

"I'm no King," Junior says. But the words don't sound right. They don't feel right.

"Oh, but you are." Simon places his hands on Junior's shoulders, anchoring him. "And it's time for you to step into your name, your role. You. Are. King."

Those words Junior believes, the force of them landing like a punch in the gut. Simon keeps his eyes on Junior, making sure he really understands. Junior does. Right then. In that moment, Junior sees his life, and he grows a few inches. It becomes true. It is all clear to Junior that he, not King, not Genesis, has been his worst enemy. He has always controlled his own fate. The obstacles he has faced, he placed there without any assistance.

Simon grabs Junior by the shirt and kisses him hard, with finality. Junior kisses him back, holding him tight. Simon's body stiffens in Junior's embrace, as though his fingertips are steel. Junior doesn't care; he continues anyway; he can't help it, panting against his neck, kissing him until his want finally burns out.

Junior releases Simon but keeps him close. Simon smiles, his lips tight. Junior could hold Simon forever, but he knows that's not possible. Lord knows he's tried. Simon's expression is soft in the morning light as they stare at each other for a long time, a minute that seems like an eternity.

Finally, Simon pushes Junior away, playfully. "Go shower. You stink."

"Will you come to the court hearing today?" Junior asks. He knows the answer, but he asks anyway. It's his flesh talking when his mind has already accepted the truth.

"You don't need me there."

"I want you there," Junior says with truth and force. He has more to say, it's overdue, but now is not the time. He will carry it with him, always, and make peace with the idea that he and Simon may never have another opportunity. He has been lying to himself.

Simon's caring expression gives Junior comfort: his strong jaw, the curve of his nose, the peace that cloaks it all. He's never looked so good, Junior thinks. Does he know how beautiful he is? Junior thought he'd have the rest of their lives to tell him. But he only has today, the last day. If this is the end, this is how he wants to remember him. Strong—a man pushed to the edge who stands tall against it. The man who touched him and made him see.

Simon's fingertips rest on Junior's chin for a moment before he walks back to his car and drives off without answering.

TWELVE

———

TOKEY HEARS THE FRONT door open and close again. The time has come. That can only be Junior, the only one left. When she goes to greet him, she sees he's as dirt-encrusted as Mance was, but she ignores that to tell him, as she told Mance, CeCe, and Ellis earlier, that she needs to speak to all of them, and before the court hearing. Junior nods and disappears for the shower. Now that she's seen two filthy siblings, she asks Mance about it. With his jaw set tight, Mance tells her that he will tell them all later.

Tokey descends the stairs, Hazel's letters in hand, gripping the railing tight, and decides the living room, not the kitchen, will be the best location to meet. There will be no food this time. Just the truth laid bare and served up on a platter.

Tokey breathes deeply, looking around the room, quiet for not much longer. Like watching dust motes in a sunbeam, she can practically see the thread connecting them to King. No, it stretches longer than them—through centuries. And it's not a thread. It's a chain, not easily broken. Forged by ancestors before King, their decisions and misfortunes now Tokey's and her siblings'.

Minutes later, CeCe joins her, followed by Ellis and Mance, and then Junior. No one speaks, the mood is heavy and dark. Tokey steps forward into it. She has never felt as sure as she does now, and she will go first.

"I've been keeping something from you all." She runs the letters through her fingers. She waits and when no one speaks, she continues. "While I was packing, I found a letter that our mother—her name is Hazel—wrote to King." She holds the letter up. "This letter led me to Miss Jessie, who gave me letters Hazel wrote to her."

Tokey hands the letters to Junior who reads the first one and passes it to Mance, who reads and passes it to Ellis, who passes it to CeCe, an assembly line accounting of their parents' lives. Tokey watches as their faces rise and fall with emotions. She's read the letters so many times she's familiar with every word and knows which one each sibling is reading by the emotion on their face. Mance grimaces at the part about Uncle Shad. Junior's eyes narrow when he reads about James, and CeCe's expression brightens when she reads about Hazel's pregnancy with her.

When Junior finishes the last letter, his hand automatically reaches for the next. Finding nothing more, he looks sharply up at Tokey. "That's it? No more?"

"That's all," Tokey says. "Miss Jessie came home."

Junior jerks upward, hands balled into tight fists. "That James!" he growls and begins to pace the living room.

"This last letter…" Mance says, the next to finish. "Does it mean that you're not our sister? Is James your father?"

Junior stops pacing, and they all turn their attention to Tokey.

"I thought that, too." Tokey turns to CeCe and Ellis. "I had just read the last letter when you found me last night. But Miss Jessie confirmed that James is not my father."

They're all silent a moment.

"So, where is she?" CeCe asks. "Does Miss Jessie know?"

"She's dead, isn't she." Mance says. It's not a question. He knows. Maybe they've all always known. It has been easier to think of her as being forever unreachable, since well before they could have even tried to find her. Somehow, her being dead makes her just as much alive.

Tokey nods. "She died giving birth to me."

The mood shifts, less a heavy darkness, now deeply sad yet somehow also lighter.

"Where is she?" Junior now asks.

They all know how his question is different from CeCe's.

"Here," Tokey says, arm out toward the woods. Tokey tells them the story of King carrying her from the hospital to the Kingdom. She tells them that he built her casket and buried her in it. She tells them she believes Hazel is buried not far from where they buried King.

There are no dry eyes when Tokey finishes. Even Mance's

hold tears. It's what they have been waiting a lifetime to learn, a conclusion not yet certain until now. And now they can mourn and give the tears permission to fall.

Tokey cries too. She has more than enough tears left to cry. Will always have tears for this, for King, for Hazel's bravery, for their love. But now it is time for Tokey to really step up, even more than she just did, and to summon her mother's bravery in its full power. She feels strangely calm as she wipes her eyes and says, "There's something else. We are living their lives. History is repeating itself. I see that now and we can't let it."

"What are you saying?" Junior asks.

"I'm saying that if King had told us what happened with James and Hazel, then you would not have married Genesis." She turns to CeCe and Ellis. "If King had told you about his love for Hazel, maybe you wouldn't have left." Then to Mance, "Maybe if he had told you about Uncle Shad, you never would have worked with him."

"Do you really believe that?" CeCe asks.

Tokey nods. "I do. You read the letters. You know it's true."

"So, what do we do?" Junior asks.

"We have to talk to each other. We can't keep secrets." Tokey holds up the letters. "See what the secrets did? How they hurt? We have to be honest with each other. Say the hard things out loud. We have to come together as a family."

Tokey sighs. "I'm an emotional eater and I've been one for quite a while now." She pauses, testing her feelings. "Last night, I ate two boxes of strawberry and Swiss rolls. I ate till I got sick. I have a hard time standing and walking. It's probably the weight but I think there's fear behind that too. I don't know where I'm going. I'm stuck. Even now, I want a strawberry roll!" She cries and laughs at once.

Mance's deep voice rises. He tells them about Uncle Shad, his work for him and with him, now and in the past. He tells them about Miss Annie and the Prescotts, his arrest, and Uncle Shad's death. Surprisingly, Mance does not stop there. He tells them about Henry and Lisha and that he is afraid for the first time in his life.

CeCe goes next. They all stiffen when she tells them about Mark, the money, and what happened last night. From Junior, they learn about Simon, the pause, and Genesis's pregnancy.

"What now?" CeCe asks when Junior finishes. They all turn to Tokey as if she holds the answers. It surprises her. That they seek the answers from her, the youngest, the sibling without an important role, that they value her opinion and want to hear it first.

Tokey braces herself and says, "The Kingdom. I don't think we should sell."

Mance stiffens. The air thickens around him. She feels CeCe's ache too. Tokey expects someone to object, to push back. No one does. They all know it to be true. Even if they don't want it to be.

"What if we lose?" CeCe asks.

"Then we lose. We still have the appeal and the rest of the two hundred acres," Junior says. He retrieves the check and lays it on the table. An invisible spotlight shines on it. The check means something for all of them, can change their lives for the better.

And for the absolute worse.

"Junior," Ellis says. "Do you realize what not selling means for you? James is going to release those photos."

"I know," he says. "Let him."

Ellis looks at Mance who nods his approval. He then turns to CeCe, his eyes soft and pleading. In answer, CeCe takes his hand and holds it before asking, "So, we've decided?"

A beat passes as they sit in the knowledge of the decision they've reached together, as a family.

Junior rips the check into several pieces. The paper falls back to the table like confetti.

"We should get ready," Ellis says. "Me and Cecily will meet you all at the courthouse."

Junior stomps toward the door. "Me too," he says without looking back. "There's something I gotta do first." At the door, he stops and side-eyes the sledgehammer before grabbing it.

Tokey is the last to leave. A thick silence blankets the house, and it's almost unbearable, the thought that this will be her last time inside it. She cannot imagine it. But she does not fear it. *Let it be*. She consoles herself and decides on one last look. One more look into King's room. One more look into the kitchen. She thinks of Hazel—Tokey growing inside her—standing at the kitchen window, hand on her belly, watching her other three children wait for King to return. Tokey doesn't know if this quiet little family scene ever happened. It doesn't matter. It's real in her mind, and that's enough.

At the front door, Tokey opens it and turns to look back once more. She expects a surge of pain, of panic. But doesn't feel it. This is how she knows she will survive whatever may come today, tomorrow, and in the future.

Tokey breathes and closes the door behind her.

Let it be.

Junior lifts the sledgehammer and smashes it into the office door. He's amazed at the ease with which he can wield it and at the strength that's been inside him, dormant, patient, waiting for him to summon it. Waiting, as it turns out, for his mother's letters, for him to learn that he inherited King's soft and gentle way, that he was more like King than he ever knew, for his mind to understand everything about him. He's been waiting his whole life to reach this place of understanding, and now it's effortless.

The doorjamb crumbles and falls, surrounding him in a cloud of dust. The door swings open and slams the wall on the other side of it. Gladys is right there. She doesn't speak. She can't. And then she shrieks, a squeal that's more air than sound.

"Let me guess," Junior says, slamming the sledgehammer into the opposite wall. "He'll be just a minute."

Saying that, Junior flicks his eyes almost consciously to the clock on the wall behind Gladys's desk. It brings him back to his last visit here. James wields time like a weapon.

No more.

Junior lifts the sledgehammer again, eyeing the clock as he walks. Gladys draws into a tight ball at Junior's proximity, but Junior doesn't see her. He grabs the arm of her chair and moves it, along with her, out of the way in one quick tug. Gladys rides with the chair before bolting out of the door.

Calmly, Junior removes the clock from the wall and places it on Gladys's desk. Steam from her coffee rises up to meet him. "If you'd like to make a call, please hang up," a voice from her phone receiver, which she must have dropped as he entered, says before a series of buzzes vibrates from it. Junior smashes the clock with one swing. Small parts of the clock fly and scatter everywhere. "If you'd like to make a call…" He swings again and the phone bursts into pieces. The voice goes silent only to be replaced by a new one:

"*There's nothing better than pussy, especially the desperate kind. They give it up better. You can get them to do just about anything, anywhere.*"

Junior hears James before he sees him, footsteps crunching over glass and Sheetrock. Junior turns and enjoys watching James's eyes sweep around the space, taking it all in, before landing on the sledgehammer. He stares at Junior and sees something he's never seen in him, something he's seen only once before, in a man of the same name. He looks at him, stunned. And he understands. The man standing in front of him is different.

He drops his briefcase and runs into his office.

Junior laughs, and it's manic. Of course, James would run. Men like him run. They don't stay and face whatever awaits them. Junior knows this because he is a man who knows a thing or two about running. He's been a runner his entire life.

No more.

Junior repositions the sledgehammer, gripping it by its middle just as he saw King do all those years ago. Just before he reaches James's office, he sees Gladys huddled by the front door and he smiles at her. He knows she's going to call the police. If she hasn't already. He will go to jail. He doesn't care. That is much better than the prison he just freed himself from. And he will happily lie on his bed with the knowledge of who he is and the fact that he is finally free.

But first, James.

Junior turns his attention back to James's closed office door. How many times has he stared at that blank barrier? He lifts the sledgehammer and smashes it against the frame, once, twice, three times. The door falls back like a chopped tree. Junior enters James's office, stepping on the groaning door. He pauses to observe. A phone wire stretches from atop James's desk to underneath it, breadcrumbs to James's location. Such a coward, Junior thinks.

"I'm disappointed, James," Junior says, his voice conversational and light. "Calling the police. Come out and face me like a man."

Rumblings and stirrings roll out from underneath the desk, slow clicks as James dials. A whimper, too.

"I'm going to count to three. One." Junior pauses. "Two." Junior rolls his neck. "Three." Junior grabs the phone line and pulls hard, yanking it from the wall, throwing it down.

"There's no one to call now, James. Stand up and face me."

A drawer opens and closes. More rattles and shuffles.

"We both know you don't keep any weapons in here." As Junior takes another step toward the desk, he bumps a chair. The same chair he sat in just a few days ago. He remembers feeling vulnerable in that chair and wonders if Hazel did too. He knows the truth. It's a shock, and in a fraction of a moment, Junior's anger gives way to sadness. But the memory fades, drowned out by the built-up rage that's always lived inside Junior. He's always believed it's better to possess and control it than the opposite. But he sees red. Blood red. It once more blurs his vision, narrowing it to just the chair.

Junior raises the sledgehammer and brings it down on the chair. Between chops, he says, "Why are you so quiet? You had so much to say the last time I was here, and now, nothing." His forearms burn. He stops swinging and wipes his forehead.

James's head peeks up over his desk, slowly.

"Stand up, you coward," Junior says, through his teeth, looking every inch the feral animal James probably considers him to be. The sight of James sets him ablaze again, his dark-skinned face now pale, almost gray. Sweat and fear crashes off him. "All the way up."

"Now, Junior," James says, his voice brittle.

"I didn't give you permission to speak." Junior releases the sledgehammer and in the same movement grabs James with both hands and pulls him over the desk, his body pushing off its contents. As James crumples on the other side of the desk, Junior slaps him as hard as he can.

James staggers and braces one hand flat on the desk. Junior steadies him, studying him, the sweat misting his face. There is no playful smirk. No callous look. Just a man shaking and stumbling. It is then that Junior realizes that James also split himself in two: a monster, disguised in flesh and bone, who would use his daughter's marriage to advance his profits, and the weak man shaking before him.

Junior thinks again of Hazel in James's office and her fear. He thinks of her bravery and her willingness to stand up to such a villain of a man.

"Now, tell me, what did you say about my Mama?"

James's brows knit together. "Junior..."

"What did you say?"

"Jun—"

Junior smashes the cold steel end of the sledgehammer onto James's hand. James screams in glorious agony and drops to his knees, clutching his hand. Junior grabs him by the neck, his hand a claw pressing into James's skin, and lifts him.

"Now...for the last time," Junior whispers. "What did you say about my Mama?"

"Junior...I'm sorry."

Junior yanks James closer. "No, that's not what you said.

You said something about how the desperate give it up better. You can get them to do just about anything, anywhere. Right? Does that sound familiar?"

James shakes his head, the fear visible on his body, rendering him still.

"No, that's what you said. It's okay if you don't remember. I do." Junior squeezes James's neck and moves his mouth close to his father-in-law's ear. "You said I might very well fuck you. Well...I am." James's eyes expand, blinking wildly. "And I'm going to let you decide how." Junior lifts the sledgehammer again.

James stutters, tongue-tied, through sounds that may be words.

"Hurry, James. I have a hearing to get to and then I'm off to jail."

James starts to cry. It is a child's cry—uncontrolled and snotty.

"Oh, James. There's nothing for you to cry about. But you go ahead. There's no shame in it. I'm a crier too."

James paws at Junior's shirt. "Please...I'm sorry."

Junior gives James the barest push, and he falls back against his desk. Junior steps to him, hovering over him.

"Get on your knees," Junior says, pulling him up, and James drops his head into his chest. Junior squats. He puts his forefinger under James's chin and lifts until they are eye to eye, their faces barely an inch from each other.

"Do you know what my last words to my father were? I'll

tell you. I saw him lying in that casket, the casket I built, a casket that he taught me to build and told me to build for him." James continues to cry, harder now, his shoulders heaving. "I will honor you." Junior snorts. "That's what I said to him. I had no idea how I was going to do that. But I know now." Junior rakes his eyes over James's desk, remembering.

James looks up at Junior with wide eyes. "Junior…"

"Why do you keep calling me Junior?" Junior asks, standing.

James sputters his words, his lips quivering, spit flying from his mouth.

Junior takes one step closer. Just before he slams the butt of the sledgehammer into James's mouth and he spits out two of his front teeth and they skid and roll across the floor like dropped coins, Junior smiles, a grim one playing across his lips, and says:

"It's King now."

⊢

The mood is ominous when CeCe and Ellis pull into the courthouse parking lot. Maybe it's because of what they learned about King, Hazel, and James. Or maybe it's because they know they've already lost so much when the judge is about to tell them they may lose some more.

Court, when it comes to real estate matters, is nothing like you see on television. Order and structure, a docket, not theatrics and personalities. There will not be a trying of the case in front of a jury of peers, and there will not be an eager crowd of spectators looking on. A judge will hear them, and that judge will make the ruling. One judge. One bang of the gavel. Today will be quick, Ethan warns them, no time for commercials, let alone multiple cliffhangers. Just a ruling on the letter of trespass, a determination if they can remain in the house while they fight the Torrens appeal. But CeCe knows today will be it, today's decision will decide their fate.

Her fate, too.

By now, Mark has turned her in to her firm and maybe even reported Ellis to the police. She will soon face charges, a fine, and the loss of her law license, the life she worked so hard for wiped out quickly. Selling the Kingdom still provides her with, if not a solution, a balm. Any potential money from the sale would pay her fine, pay restitution, and help her hire a good lawyer.

As Ellis throws his truck into park, she hates herself for thinking this, that her mind goes there, especially after everything, especially after last night. She scoffs at the idea, her body shivering, the wrongness in her clashing against the right thing.

CeCe knows she must let go. There's nothing left to hold on to at this point. But she doesn't know how. She's held her fingers together so tightly she doesn't know if she can open her fist. Ellis should be enough. Her family should be enough. King's wishes, too. But she had a plan. She had a goddamn plan for this. What has she been living for if not the life that she planned? It's an internal battle fought within the recesses of her mind.

"Are you ready?" Ellis asks. At eight in the morning, they have already lived an entire day. Barely sleeping and awakening early to return to the Kingdom before Tokey woke.

CeCe forces herself to smile. Ellis studies her and sighs. He knows. He always knows.

"You are going to have to turn yourself in," he says. "I'll go back to New York with you and be with you every step of the way."

Ellis rubs her leg, and it jolts her to the past and present. CeCe remembers last night and the early hours of the morning, and she melts with satisfaction. She doesn't recall the number of times they reached for each other, but each time made up for all the lost time. Now, she gazes at his beautiful face, one she isn't sure she deserves but one she knows she cannot live without.

"You have to convince Mance to sell the land," CeCe says, the words pushing their way out. Even she can't believe she said them.

"Goddamn it, Cecily! Did you hear anything I just said? It's over."

"This is for us, so we can be together. If we sell, I can use the money in a plea deal. I can possibly get off with a fine and probation."

"This is not for us. This is for you." Ellis says, his voice descending into an unexpected calm. "You are still not ready." He shakes his head.

"Ready for what?"

"What comes after."

"And what's that?"

Ellis turns to her. "Me. Just me. All of me. Here, in Diggs. Your family, who needs you. Is that what you want? Can you handle that?"

"I want to but…"

Ellis growls. "I love you, Cecily, but I can't love you like this. I can help you, but I can't save you from yourself."

"What do you want me to say? I love you, Ellis, but that means nothing if I'm in prison."

"I will love you the way you need to be loved. And it will be hard, but I'll be here—only if you are ready. I can't be in this alone. I can't do this if you're not willing to do the work."

"Tell me how," CeCe says, in barely a whisper.

"You accept what you've done. You sit with it and in it. You live with it, all the pain, all the hurt, all the guilt. Until it's done with you. Until you are done with it. You survive it." Ellis places his whole hand on the side of her cheek. "Let it be. No matter what happens today. Let it be."

CeCe draws back and stares at him. It's something King said to them. It's what he always said, what he believed. Ellis holds her gaze, almost drilling his eyes into her.

Let it be.

CeCe hears those three words when they get out of the car and enter the courtroom. She hears them again when Ethan joins them at their table, and they huddle one final time. She hears them again when she looks at the other table and sees the two lawyers for Malone & Kincaid and two men who CeCe assumes are the actual Malone & Kincaid sitting behind them.

She turns and smiles at Tokey sitting with Miss Jessie and Genesis directly behind her. Mance stands along the wall in the back, pacing back and forth. Junior bursts into the courtroom just as she wonders about him. He is panting, and his shirt is stained with sweat and blood. He stops to speak to Mance. Concern pinches Mance's face, and he pulls Junior close, studying him. Mance's brows lift and recede; he smiles and nods approvingly. Junior nudges his head toward the front and Mance shakes his head and remains along the wall. Junior squeezes into a space next to Tokey. He does not look at Genesis.

"Regardless of what the judge rules today, it's not over. I want you all to know that. We have the appeal and we will keep fighting," Ethan says.

They trade looks. There's fight there, but exhaustion, too. A holding of something heavy. They all smile, believing, hoping, wanting what he says to be true.

After that, everything happens fast, so fast, CeCe wonders if she is imagining it.

The judge enters the courtroom, and everyone stands and sits just as quickly. He bangs the gavel and the courtroom quiets. He slips on his glasses and lifts the papers in front of him, then looks at both tables.

"Mr. Wiley," the judge says, removing his glasses. "You are a long way from Charlotte."

Ethan stands. "Yes, your honor. It's a pleasure to be here in your fine court."

If Judge Matherson appreciates the compliment, it doesn't

show on his face. "I'm afraid you drove all the way here for nothing. I've reviewed the presented documents and see no cause to stop the notice of vacancy."

"Your Honor, if I may, my clients' family has lived on that land for over two hundred years. They were not aware of the sale of five acres to Malone & Kincaid." Ethan gestures to the table at his right. The table is suddenly full of statues.

"Mr. Wiley, I see that you have filed an appeal against the Torrens decision, but we are not here today to argue that. Today, I'm to make a ruling in regard to the notice of trespass, and you have not presented me with any evidence to overturn it."

A commotion behind them yanks everyone. CeCe turns and sees Mance exiting, the door slamming behind him. This riles the small gallery. The Malone & Kincaid table trade looks with each other, but no one moves.

The judge bangs the gavel and it's the loudest sound in the world.

Time seems to have slowed and disjoints itself. The room bends in and out of shape. Around her, CeCe feels and senses movement, hears voices, but cannot focus on anything.

Finally, Ellis grabs CeCe's shoulders, worry flooding his eyes, and says, "We have to get to the Kingdom."

———

Mance stops on the courthouse steps. He reaches into his pocket and pulls out his cigarettes. One left. Shaking it out, he puts it to his mouth and lights it; the sound of the flame hissing against the tobacco echoes in his ears. He takes a long drag and holds the smoke in, his eyes closing, before exhaling, the smoke forming a ribbon of white in the air.

He tips his head back and looks at the sky. He doesn't remember the last time he looked up. Or if he ever has. Traffic hums and buzzes on the street, people coming and going to work. Driving home. Oblivious to the fact that Mance no longer has one. He pinches the cigarette, between his thumb and index finger, and takes another long inhale before flicking the cigarette onto the sidewalk, not watching where it lands.

There's no question now of what he must do. He's known since this all began, the knowledge coming to him early, days after the notice of trespass. The thought has been rooting, and now it's a tree ready to yield its fruit. It's been insistent. It will be done. And he will do it.

He hears the command now, again, once a whisper against the wind, now a shout. He listens for a moment, and the words echo in his head again. He nods, satisfied.

Let it be.

Mance chuckles, a quick snort, the sound breezy and light, strange, considering the circumstances. He is so certain of what he must do and can't explain why. Nothing in his life has been as absolute as this. He thought he would feel differently, the magnitude of his decision settling inside him. Not like this, as certain as a blink.

Now he knows there is not a moment to lose.

THIRTEEN

———

MANCE MAKES HIS WAY to his car just as Junior pushes open the courthouse doors.

He doesn't speed, doesn't want to draw too much attention to himself. The cops and everyone else will be behind him soon enough.

A task to do.

Mance pulls into the Kingdom's driveway and hops out. He feels a familiar flash of anger, but it douses quickly at a sound: Henry's laughter. The wind tricks him into hearing this. But it's enough to bring it to the forefront of his mind. It plays like a skipping track, bending and looping around him.

His eyes are open wide. And now he can see everything.

He is learning.

Sound is everything.

Junior parks his car next to Mance's and runs to him.

"What are you doing?" Junior yells, breathless, at Mance who should be moving to do what he came to do, but is not.

Mance's chest pumps up and down as he sinks to his knees. "Bending."

━

Some decisions happen all at once. Mance doesn't have to say the words, but Junior hears them as if he did. And for the first time, he doesn't fold into himself, and his nose does not bleed. He knows what to do. He is ready.

Junior runs to Lou's forgotten excavator and hops in the seat. The key dangles from the ignition and he turns it. It cranks right up as if it has been waiting for him, for this moment. It has, its presence looming at the Kingdom since before King's death. Junior pops it into gear and the excavator jerks forward. Junior knows right where to steer it.

The front of the Kingdom is sagging, and the second-floor porch now droops, the old columns, last replaced a hundred years ago, no longer able to shoulder the weight of the roof. Junior remembers Mance telling him. The entire facade of the house, not just the second-floor porch, would have collapsed already if not for the twelve white columns circling the house, balancing and distributing the weight. Another hurricane before repairs are finished and the home their ancestors built will fold in on itself.

Or a hit in the right place.

The journey from where the excavator sat over to the house feels like an eternity. The smell of diesel and exhaust fills the air. On the way, Junior sees Mance, still on his knees, not moving but watching. He nods. So comfortable. So certain of himself. Equally certain of Junior.

They never discussed that this is what they would do. There are just some things you can't explain. Or maybe Junior, too, always knew it would come down to this. Junior is not thinking. Thinking was his problem. All he ever did was think, his mind constantly churning. The more he tried not to think, the more he did. Thinking was the last thing Junior wanted to do after knocking James's teeth out, his imminent arrest, and losing the hearing today, so when Mance moved, Junior didn't think—he moved too.

Junior positions the excavator a few feet from the first column and pushes the stick directly into it, the arm bent upward. The column moves, but the force of the stick splits the column in half, and the top buckles and falls, taking part of the roof with it. Junior reverses the stick; it rattles and shrieks, echoing across the land, and moves to another column. He repeats the treatment from the first column, and it collapses faster and in a more dramatic fashion. The column does not split. Instead, it slides and falls in one whole piece. But only a portion of the roof falls this time.

By the time Junior reverses the stick of the excavator for the third time, he barely recognizes that it's him doing it. Here, now, it dawns on Junior that he isn't afraid. He has long run out of fear. He's operating on full adrenaline now, his heart hammering in his chest, beads of sweat cascading down his face. He no longer hears the rattle of the machine nor the shrieks it produces. He doesn't hear the arm split another column in half or the sound it makes when it buckles and falls. This time, more of the roof falls, and the middle of the house buckles in on itself.

It's not enough. He quickly deduces that at least two more columns will need to fall in order to take down the entire roof. He assesses quickly and identifies the two.

Junior doesn't notice the two police officers until they are pulling him out of the excavator. He doesn't resist, but he doesn't help them either. He hits the ground after falling for what feels like forever, and it knocks the wind out of him. The two officers are on top of him now. One is pulling his hands behind him and the other one is kneeing him in the back to restrict his movement. Junior feels the cold steel of the hand-cuffs around his wrists and hears the click of them.

Junior sees Ellis and CeCe are there, too, moving toward the excavator. He turns his head and sees Mance also hand-cuffed just a few feet away from him. Junior feels his heart slowing through his ribs, returning to normal. For an instant, only an instant, King is there. In Mance's face Junior sees a flash of King's—confident and defiant. Junior closes his eyes, and his heart leaps at the possibility of King being proud. It's all he ever wanted.

He blinks and Mance is back. He expects to see sadness and anger in Mance's expression. No one loved the Kingdom more than Mance. No one worked as hard to maintain it. And yet, he sees triumph in his eyes. It's odd, considering, and for a fraction of a moment, he is confused. Then Junior sees what Mance sees—the house, halfway destroyed by their own hands—and he smiles too.

———

CeCe and Ellis arrive a few minutes after Junior. They watch as he rams the excavator arm into the first column.

"What is he doing?" CeCe says to Ellis.

But Ellis is no longer by her side; he's running toward Mance kneeling in the grass. CeCe follows on his heels, reaching Mance seconds after he does. Mance doesn't speak and neither does Ellis, but something passes between them without words.

"We have to stop him! Come on!" CeCe screams. Mance looks up, and she sees King looking at her. Sees the younger version of him from her childhood, hands in his worn overalls, the collar of his dingy white shirt tucked into his chest.

Ellis grabs CeCe by the shoulders. She blinks and sees Mance again, his focus squarely on Junior's progress with the excavator. "CeCe," Ellis says. "Let it be."

Three words that stop time.

Three words that stop her movement.

Three words that represent a beginning and an ending.

CeCe twists and squirms under his grasp, understanding slowly infiltrating her soul. But she's not ready to accept it yet. She doesn't want to let go. She had a plan. She had a goddamn plan.

Ellis reaffirms his grip, holding her tighter, steeling her to him, and says, "Let it be."

There are some truths you cannot accept, not on your own, CeCe understands. It takes a special kind of power or person. Ellis tips her face to his. "You can't change what you did. But you can choose where you go from here. Decide."

Ellis releases her, and she stands alone, the scene around her blending into nothingness. CeCe flushes with sadness as if every pain of her life occurred at once. She gazes up at the cloudless sky, seeing it, its wideness, its beauty for the first time since she came home. Ellis is right. She *has* missed it. She looks back at the scene in front of her and sees King standing in a field of wildflowers, the same wildflowers he let her plant. They are in full bloom, a sea of purple, against the stark blue sky.

"I'm sorry," she whispers, breathing through the ache in her chest and wishing he could hear those words, the ones she whispered at his funeral. She didn't know King to smile, but she swears she sees a corner of his mouth turn up. CeCe wants to hold on to this moment, lock it in her mind, remember it always. She isn't ready to let go.

But it is time. CeCe knows that it is done. That she is done. That this is the end. Right here, right now.

"Cecily!" Ellis yells, snapping the world back into focus.

She hears the police sirens in the distance. She sees two police officers pull Junior out of the excavator and two more officers handcuffing Mance. Ellis is yelling at the officers to release Mance and Junior but more police officers flood the scene and grab Ellis, pulling him to the ground. CeCe's feet refuse to move, her mind still processing until Ellis yells, "Go!"

CeCe runs to the excavator, several officers behind her. She jumps in the cab and slams and locks the door just before they reach her.

She pulls the joint stick on her right, and the boom and bucket lift. She moves the joint stick on her left up and the stick lifts high, then she pushes the stick to the left, and the entire cabin turns in a half circle.

CeCe's heart pounds in her chest as she assesses the columns. Two more to go. The police yell at her to come out. Several officers inch closer, so she turns the left lever to the left and back to the right. The entire cabin whips in both directions and the officers jump and duck out of the way, but do not retreat. Then, she knows what to do. She moves the joint stick on her left up and the boom lifts up. Then she turns the right lever to the left and the cabin turns, slamming into one of the columns. She turns the right lever to the right and the stick hits the column again. CeCe continues moving the stick to the left and right until finally, the column splits and falls. Briefly, CeCe celebrates, and, in that moment, an officer breaks the window to the cabin and opens the door, pulling her out.

A shuddering sob pushes out of CeCe as she too is hand-cuffed. The tears, finally, rolling down her face. She looks at the house not yet fallen and knows that it doesn't matter. She feels relief, not a weight, a life restored. But right now, she's thinking only of her family, and that she has finally made her family proud.

Tokey arrives last with Miss Jessie and Genesis and quickly evaluates the scene. She cannot believe it. It makes no sense. Mance is on the ground in handcuffs, Junior on his stomach being held down by two officers, Ellis yelling at the officers holding Junior. Half of the house has collapsed, and the other half is barely hanging on. At first, she doesn't understand. Then, she does, the realization a slap to the face. It's obvious. Maybe they always knew it would come to this. Or maybe they didn't. Either way, they all understood that this, not selling all of the land, is the best option. For them, for the past, and for the future.

A group of people gather along the driveway, their cars lined along the road, parked in the ditch. More police cars pull onto the scene. Someone screams, and Tokey turns her attention to it. The excavator is moving left and right seemingly out of control. It slams into one of the columns and the next one. Back and forth. Back and forth. For a second, Tokey wonders who can be operating it. Then, she knows. It's the one person she doesn't see: CeCe.

Tokey doesn't remember exactly when she decided to do so, but she takes a step forward. Because this is how it works, to walk, one foot in front of the other. But it's been a long time since Tokey has taken an unassisted step, and her left knee buckles just as it always has, always on the first step. Too much pressure, and it gives, threatening to take her down. It's the mental weight, too, pressing down on her. It's moving and not knowing the outcome.

But now she has a goal. She knows the outcome.

On the next step, her knee protests, lightly. She knew better than to walk. It's in her nature to stand perfectly still. It was too much to ask of her body, herself, to support so much and yet not enough. But the ache in her knee is not enough to stop her. She continues walking, slightly unsteadily, across the yard. She will begin again. She will change everything. And she can do this. All she has to do is walk. Maybe it will not be enough, but it is what she can do. Tokey takes another step and does not fall.

Chaos blooms around her. Genesis runs past her, yelling at the officers to release Junior. One officer chases and catches her, tackling Genesis to the ground. This enrages Junior who yells, "She's pregnant! She's pregnant!" Tokey is aware of officers moving, running. *Keep going*, she tells herself. One foot in front of the other. Now, in the center of the yard, she keeps expecting someone to stop her, realize who she is, and restrict her movement, but everyone's focus remains on CeCe in the excavator and on Genesis.

The excavator is still moving back and forth between the two columns. Now, an officer has jumped on the cab and is forcing his way in. The excavator turns once more and the stick slams into the column and it finally buckles and splits in two before collapsing. Most of the ceiling comes down with it and most of the second-floor porch. Shrieks and screams mixed with the sound of wood collapsing ring out. But the other column does not fall.

Tokey is closer now, still moving, shuffling her feet, her knee aching. Sunlight burns her face, and for an instant, she thinks of stopping. But she wills herself to go on, to not fall. She reaches Junior's car, winded from the effort, and sees the sledgehammer sitting in the front seat. She pauses against it, a chance to catch her breath. She pulls it out and uses it as a crutch to help her walk. She sees Mance on the ground. He looks as if he might speak but doesn't. He can't; two officers are holding his shoulders, anchoring him to the ground. He tilts his head toward the house. She knows what he is telling her and is already on her way.

An officer pulls CeCe out of the excavator and another one stops it. They hold her on the ground and handcuff her. She's not resisting. She is not moving. Her job is done. It's now Tokey's turn.

Tokey finds her stride—it's easier now—and reaches the final column. Sweat pours down her face. She knows she has only one swing before the officers stop her. She lifts the sledge-hammer and its weight lists her. She closes her eyes for a second, the barest fraction of a beat to breathe. In that second, she sees Hazel, the vision from her dream, and it's enough to power her, to give her the courage and the strength to swing. It's been in her all along.

She swings with all her might, screaming the entire time. The butt of the sledgehammer connects with the column and it teeters. She lifts to swing again but an officer pulls her down backward. They fall to the ground just as the column gives way. It tumbles down and the rest of the roof and the second-story porch follows.

It is done.

In the end, it takes twenty minutes for the entire roof of the house to collapse in on itself. Twenty minutes. The length of a rainstorm. To clean away hundreds of years of residency.

Several minutes later, all four siblings, Genesis, and Ellis are handcuffed, sitting on the ground in a row. They stare at what's left of their house. They are silent, realization wrapping around them. Until Mance chuckles. The others stare at him, perplexed, but then Junior joins him. CeCe smiles. Soon, all their laughter rolls around them.

They huddle together, scooting on their butts, hands clasped behind their backs, as close as they can get, and tap their foreheads together.

EPILOGUE

——

JUNIOR PUSHES THE DOOR open to the workshop. Here in the quiet, before the day begins, he thinks of Simon. Just as he always does, every day since the last day he saw him three months ago. It's the only time of day he allows himself to do so. It's all he can handle, the pain still too raw, too real. Junior hurt people, and losing Simon was a steep price to pay for the blood on his hands. No one could cause that much damage and survive unscathed. Junior hopes he'll see Simon again. They never said goodbye. And if he does, Junior will stand tall, armorless, and confident in who he is. A King. A carpenter's son. For better or worse. He was always supposed to be here. He knows that now. He doesn't fold into himself. He is present, steady. The inner and outer man at peace. Finally. He takes pleasure in not having had to fight. Shed armor. Battle. He is exactly where he is supposed to be and no longer trying to escape the inescapable.

Now, Junior sees the possibility of time instead of walls.

Men couldn't love each other in the open. Not in Diggs.

Not as a principal at a school. Junior was fired once word about him and Simon spread through Diggs like kudzu. People avoid what they don't understand. Junior knows that, and he doesn't hold it against them. It feels good to be free from expectation, from pretending. Plus, he has a new job.

"You're out here early," Mance says through an extended yawn.

It has become Junior's habit to be at the workshop just before sunrise. But today, it's even earlier. He had an idea and he wanted to talk to Mance about it.

"I gotta cut out early today, and I wanted to finish that dining room table for Mr. Kane."

He has started building again, taking it up as a hobby. Mance was right. His skills have come back and so he has a deeper appreciation for the artistry and craftsmanship of the work. Watching nothing become something. First, a table for Tokey's new house. That table led to another one, and two nightstands, until he started helping Mance fill orders. He was no longer a guest in the workshop. King built things. And his sons would, too. Both sons. Together.

Mance slips on his apron and grabs the clipboard, flipping through the pages of orders. "What time is the hearing?"

"Noon."

"What did Ellis plea it down to?"

"Probation and community service," Junior says. "He's good."

Mance nods. "No more bending?"

"No more bending," Junior says.

It took Junior's assault on James to finally end his marriage to Genesis. Incredibly, she agreed to split custody with the girls. That was enough for him. Maybe it wasn't so incredible. With the revelation of Junior's hidden sexuality and her growing belly, she could power a city on the attention she received. And that was enough for her.

"Ellis's house is coming along nicely," Junior says.

"Home," Mance corrects.

"What's the difference?"

"Life and love," Mance says. "I once asked King the same question about the Kingdom and that's what he told me. The Kingdom stopped being a home when Mama left. I think that's what he meant."

"It was still there. Or I think King was trying to find it."

"He wanted to believe that it could be great again," Mance agrees.

"It still can. It has us. We'll see to it. For him."

Malone & Kincaid offered to buy the land a second time, for double the first offer, but Junior hung up and refused all other offers. Without the house, they abandoned their project, and the five acres of land sits unused. James's work concluded with Malone & Kincaid after he failed to deliver the two hundred acres of the Kingdom to them. That and his inability to speak after dentists wired his mouth shut. He will be eating his meals out of a straw for another month, Junior heard.

Mance looks at him, an eyebrow raised.

"This land has a purpose. It always has. It's time to bring it back to its former glory."

"How do you suppose we do that?"

"Build another Kingdom," Junior says, crossing his arms.

Mance shakes his head and breathes out an exhausted sigh. "Are you kidding?"

"I could use your help," Junior says, smiling.

Mance remembers and matches Junior's smile with his own. "Starting from scratch? I wouldn't know what to do."

"It'll come back to you."

Every Solomon sibling was handcuffed and arrested the day the Kingdom fell, Ellis too, and one by one, they were all released. They may have lost the land, but they still owned the house, Ethan argued. It's not illegal to destroy your own home. Soon, all charges were dropped. Because of his priors and recent arrest, Mance was held the longest and eventually released, one week after everyone else.

He drove straight to Charlotte, silently thanking Ellis for finding her. There was something he needed to do, and it could not wait a minute longer.

It's amazing to Mance, when you boil life down, how little you actually need. He knows that now. Not two hundred acres. Not a house. But a sound. A sound that he played over and over again, kept in his ears during the long nights in jail. Sound is everything.

Two women greeted him when he approached the front desk.

"I'm here to see Miss Annie Talbott Prescott," he said.

The older woman looked earnestly, and skeptically, at him for a long moment before saying, "Is she expecting you?"

"No, ma'am," he said, realizing his ill-conceived plan. He redirected and reached into his pocket. "I have something that belongs to her." He showed the woman the ring and the two women glanced at each other. Then the older woman shook her head and stood. "I'll take you to her room."

"Or I can just leave this with you," Mance said.

"She would appreciate some company. Miss Annie hasn't had many visitors since she got here."

They reached a room located at the end of the hall. The older woman rapped her knuckles on the door before turning the knob and pushing it open.

Miss Annie sat in a chair by the bed with a book in her lap.

"Miss Annie," the woman said, her voice an octave higher. "This gentleman is here to see you."

Miss Annie furrowed her brow, regarding him for a moment, and then smiled. "Tim," she said. "Did you bring Patches?"

An hour later, Mance knocks on Lisha's mother's door. Lisha opens the door, and a heavy silence greets him. She waited for him while he served his first prison sentence, and then she waited during his second one. She refused to do it again. Now, two arrests in two days. He has taken her for granted and he cannot blame her if he's lost her, this time for good.

But being a good woodworker means knowing how to fix your mistakes. So, he tries.

"Lisha, please. I know you are not happy with me, but I had

to do it." Mance is speaking fast now, his tongue coming loose. "And I hope one day you will understand why. Even if I can never fully explain it to you. I did it for us, for Henry. I'm going to keep coming here and I'm going to earn you. I will bend for you and humble myself and be the man you deserve. The father Henry deserves. And I…"

"Mance," Lisha says, stopping the flow of his words. The context in which she speaks his name is unclear; her face gives nothing away. He waits for what seems like forever. He hesitates, exhales, exhausted at everything he said and everything he didn't. "What you did. What you all did. Destroying the Kingdom." She pauses, searching for the words. "It was so brave. People haven't stopped talking about it."

Mance stares at her. Lisha steps closer, and he meets her halfway, scooping her up in his arms. Jasmine fills his nose, and he presses her body against his. Then he kisses her with all the love in his body.

"I have nothing to offer you," Mance says, releasing her but holding her close. "Just ten acres of nothing. But I will build you a home by myself if I have to."

"I know you will," Lisha says, smiling.

Mance falls to one knee and pulls out the ring. Lisha's eyes grow and a smile lights up her face. She extends her hand; it shakes with nerves. "Lisha, will you marry me?"

Lisha wipes the tears away and nods her head. Mance slips the ring onto her finger and it's just as he expected—a perfect fit, like it was made for her. And, maybe, it was.

Mance tried to give the ring back, but Miss Annie refused. She didn't have a ring like that, she said, he must be mistaken. It must have belonged to his girlfriend. Mance shook his head and looked at the ring again. He said that he would love to give his girlfriend a ring like this but could never afford it. Miss Annie stood abruptly and announced it was teatime in the grand hall. Mance followed her out and watched as she walked down the hall. But just before she turned the corner, she found his eyes once more and winked.

Now, Lisha and Mance move into the house. Mance hears Henry before he sees him. Finally, that sound is really there with him, wrapping around him. His heart fills to the brim with love and fear, both pressing, demanding to be felt.

"How is he today?" Mance asks, approaching his crib.

"A little fussy but he's strong." Lisha looks at Mance. "Like his dad."

"Like his mom."

"He's going to be fine, you know."

"Yeah."

Lisha lifts Henry and settles him in her arms. And then Mance takes Henry from Lisha. He can hold him now, the weight of holding King no longer felt. Mance and Henry stare at each other. Father and son. Mance signs *Daddy* to Henry. It's the one title he wants to focus on. There will be no more Kings in the Solomon family. Second sons either. Just a family as a whole, working together to maintain and keep their legacy alive. Mance smiles, and Henry does, too, his ever-present dimple appearing. Mance is surprised at how big he has gotten and vows never to miss anything else. He makes himself that promise. A new one, the old one fulfilled.

—

What now?

Tokey still doesn't know the answer to that question. And maybe she never will, she decides. For now, she's taking her life, and her addiction, like she takes her steps, one day at a time, one foot at a time. Every day, it seems closer to possible.

Today, she's off to the Grand Canyon. She's always wanted to see it and only yesterday she decided to go. She can do that now, make snap decisions. She's given herself permission. Tokey has forgotten the world and now she wants to see it. All of it. All she ever wanted was to understand her family, to know her mother. Maybe then, she would know herself. And now she's going to try. Loneliness is cruel to the body. People aren't meant to be alone, and she isn't anymore.

Weeks after the destruction of the house, they found Hazel's grave, overgrown with weeds. Once again, they came together, the way Tokey wanted, and created a dedicated path to Hazel's, King's, and even Uncle Shad's grave sites. They were no longer scattered in their grief but in separate homes: Junior living in a used trailer on the outskirts of the Kingdom; Mance staying with Lisha and Henry; and CeCe with Ellis. Miss Jessie offered Tokey her spare bedroom while she waited for her rental house to be ready, and Tokey accepted, using the opportunity to hear stories of Miss Jessie's travels and, of course, King and Hazel. The siblings aren't sleeping under the same roof again, but they did not operate independently of one another either, as they had for most of their adult lives. They attend Junior's hearing, wait at the hospital with Mance for Henry's implant surgery, and even fly to NYC to help CeCe move out of her apartment. Tokey thinks they're still linked to King, and all the ancestors before, but maybe it's by neither thread nor chain, but scar tissue. And it is.

CeCe steps out of Ellis's camper and sees him waiting, leaning against his truck. He knows how to wait, he always has. He's holding a white sweater, and that brings tears to CeCe's eyes. As he watches her watch him, he stays long, his body stretching out against the cab, and it is the way he leans, pumped with confidence and assurance, that CeCe has always loved and loves now. He knows how to wait in that way too. She catches a glint in his dark brown eyes and her body shivers in pleasure, remembering every day of the last three months they've had together. Ellis smiles when he sees her, a smile that lessens the sadness of the day, of the reality she soon faces.

Six months. That's the best plea deal Daniel, Ellis's law school friend, could negotiate. CeCe agreed immediately. Ellis wanted to argue for zero jail time, but CeCe just wanted to get it over with. With good behavior, she would be out in even less time. At Ellis's urging, Daniel did argue, successfully, that she be allowed to serve her time in North Carolina, just a few hours from Diggs.

"It's a beautiful day," Ellis says as he pulls out of the driveway of the Kingdom and onto the highway that will take CeCe to prison. "The fall wildflowers should be out by now."

CeCe casts a glance at the sky. She wants to remember everything about this sky, the last few months, watching Junior and Mance rebuild the Kingdom, and Ellis building their home. She feels his gaze seeping into her before she feels his hand warming her knee, and her breathing slows. "Relax," he says, softly. "You're going to be fine." Slowly, gently, the pads of his fingers rub her knee and leg.

Several hours later, Ellis pulls into the facility's parking lot. He breathes loudly as he slides the truck into park. It's a calming, nerve-busting breath. It's for him as much as for her. They get out of the truck and lean against the front of it.

"I want you to know something," CeCe says. "If I had to do it all over again, I would do it differently. I would have never left Diggs, never left you."

"I know," Ellis says, pulling her into his arms.

It's the first time she gets to say goodbye to him. Once again, she feels the comma between them hooking her closer to him. It's not yet a period, an end. It never will be. They will never be done.

"I'll be waiting right here," Ellis says, his chin lifting, as he releases her.

CeCe knows he will.

She steels herself and walks toward the gate. Over the last few months, in Ellis's arms, back home, permanently, on the Kingdom, CeCe experienced a new awakening and developed a new plan, a new goddamn plan. Serve her time. Rebuild the Kingdom. Be the best sister and auntie. Chief among the items on her list? Marry Ellis.

—

In the middle of Diggs sits a five-acre plot of land surrounded by a broken-down fence. People who don't live there call it the Solomon Plantation. People who do live there call it something else. Most know the story, but many don't. They wonder why it's shaped like that, abandoned, when everything around it thrives. Beds of wildflowers and greenery. Houses with children playing and noise. Many speak of the once-great house that occupied the space. But there's no proof. Not a brick. Not a board. Or an outline. But if you look hard enough, listen to the stories told by locals, you can see it, squint hard enough, and believe. Generations later, when history tells the story of the Kingdom, it will say that the Solomons were crazy to destroy a perfectly good house. But those who were there think otherwise. They know it as the place where intergenerational trauma died. That it saved them, freed them from a life they didn't want to live, freed them from the handcuffs of the past. They chose. It always comes down to choices, and they chose.

They regret nothing.

READING GROUP GUIDE

These questions include spoilers. Do not read until after you've finished the book.

1. What do you think each of the siblings' different reactions to the passing of their father says about them? What do you think it says about grief in general?

2. How did each of the four siblings grow and change throughout the course of the book?

3. The Department of Agriculture calls heir property the leading cause of Black land loss in the U.S. Were you familiar with the concept of heir property before you read this book? What is your take on it?

4. Was there one sibling whose story or struggles particularly resonated with you?

5. Junior's inner man and outer man are constantly battling each other. Do you sometimes feel like a different person on the inside than you are on the outside?

6. Why do you think CeCe was so reluctant to give in to her love for Ellis? What held her back?

7. Why do you think Mance had such trouble accepting that his son, Henry, is deaf?

8. Why do you think Mance was so reticent to hold his son?

9. Tokey feels like an outsider in her own family. Did you ever feel that way in your own family?

10. Why do you think King didn't tell his children the truth about what happened to their mother?

11. How do you see the effects of intergenerational trauma playing out among each of the characters? Do you think they were successful in breaking the "Solomon curse"?

12. Each of the siblings makes some pretty questionable choices. Do you think they all redeem themselves in the end?

A CONVERSATION WITH THE AUTHOR

What inspired this novel?

All of my books are inspired by real and unique circumstances that happen to real people and are not widely discussed. *Long After We Are Gone* is no exception. This book is inspired by the story of Melvin Davis and Licurtis Reels of North Carolina, who went to jail for eight years after refusing to leave the land their great-grandfather purchased more than a century ago. I first read their story years ago and remained frustrated, shocked, and angry, not only at what happened to them but that I had never heard of heir property before. After much research, I was amazed that the Reels brothers were not alone in their fight and that involuntary land loss from heir property is such an important issue that no one really knows about or talks about. It's not recognized as "the worst problem you never heard of" or "the leading cause of Black involuntary land loss" by the U.S. Department of Agriculture without justification. In *Long After We Are Gone*, I hope to shine a light on this issue and how certain laws, policies, and loopholes continue to dispossess families of their land.

Which character was the most difficult for you to write? Which was the most fun to write?

All of them! LOL! It's funny because while writing, I found the hardest character to write was the one I was writing at the time. I should note that I do not see scenes when I write. I hear my characters' voices. It is they who lead me, guide me, and tell me what to write. Looking back now, I think the most difficult character to write about was CeCe. Writing unreliable characters is not easy. Go too far in that direction and readers fail to connect or even relate to them or, worse, dislike them. CeCe made some extremely questionable choices (stealing money from her law firm, ignoring King's letter about the Kingdom, and leaving/denying her love for Ellis), and it was hard to keep a balance between those decisions and not losing the reader completely. The writer must stay true to the character though, and that means sending them down a path that may not line up with the writer's own opinions or beliefs. This is especially true when the characters are whispering to you. Junior was the most frustrating character for me. Only because, like CeCe, he makes some problematic decisions, choices that hurt people he loved. It was difficult to understand Junior's motivations. Mance was the easiest character to write because I know so many men like Mance. For Mance's story, all I had to do was think of what my husband or brother would do or how they would react.

If you could give the four siblings one piece of advice each, what would it be?

First, I would take some soothing deep breaths with Mance and then tell him that life comes at us fast and we are handed roles and responsibilities we never asked for but that it's how we handle them that defines us. Before I tell Junior that nothing good ever comes from hiding who you really are and what's done in the dark always, ALWAYS comes to light, I would hold his face in my hands and ask him what the hell is he doing! Before I talk to CeCe, I would probably shake her a few times! Then I would tell her that there's nothing wrong with having big dreams, but be open to altering them when circumstances change or when you meet the love of your life. Lastly, I would give Tokey the tightest and longest hug before telling her to live her life and that while we are influenced by our parents and the ones who come before us, we are ultimately responsible for the people we become.

Did you find it challenging writing a novel with four points of view?

Yes! And when I turned this book in to my editor, I swore I would NEVER write another book with so many points of view again. As a child, I was taught to never say never, so I will not close the door completely on it, but it's not something I'm going to rush into doing again. That said, this book stretched me in ways I never expected. I'm a better writer because of this book, because I challenged myself to do something I have never accomplished before. *As I Lay Dying* is one of my favorite books of all time and served as my book inspiration for *Long After We Are Gone*. *As I Lay Dying* tells the story of a family who, after the matriarch dies, sets out to fulfill her last wish. To portray this, William Faulkner used fifteen different points of view to tell the story of the Bundrens' plight. Each character, each point of view, moves the story forward while highlighting each of the character's own personal struggles. *Long After We Are Gone* is such an emotional story, so I decided to use Faulkner's method of utilizing multiple points of view to paint the picture fully and accurately. In my opinion, using multiple points of view made all the difference in the story.

Are any of the characters based on people you know?

Yes! Mance Solomon is a composite of my older brother, Ben, and my husband, Jamel. They both love their families very much and are fierce protectors by any means necessary. In the book, CeCe says that she didn't have any boyfriends in high school because all of the boys were afraid of Mance. This was taken from my personal life! Most of the names used in the book were taken from my and my husband's family history. Mance is named after my husband's uncle and grandfather. We both had grandmothers in our family histories named Angeline. Cecily was named after my great-great-grandfather Cecil. The name (not the people) King Solomon was based on my husband's great-grandfather, and Shad was my husband's great-uncle. Junior and Tokey are common Southern nicknames.

What are some of your favorite family dramas or books about siblings?

I'm such a fan of family dramas in movies, on television, and in literature. I mentioned earlier how much I love *As I Lay Dying* but would also add *Everything I Never Told You* by Celeste Ng and *The Vanishing Half* by Brit Bennett as two more of my favorites. I think *This Is Us* was one of the best family dramas ever on television. The emotional heft of that show, from the writing to the performances, is nothing short of extraordinary. I think about that show often. *The Family Stone*, *August: Osage County*, and *Soul Food* are a few of my favorite movies.

How has your job as a collection development librarian influenced your writing?

As a collection development librarian, I'm responsible for the purchase and acquisition of all adult print and digital materials for my library system. Because of this, I read a few hundred books a year for pleasure and work, and I discovered that I am drawn to unique stories, books that I haven't read before and that I could not find many comparable books for. I knew that if I were to ever write a book that I wanted to write a book that readers found to be unlike anything they've ever read before.

ACKNOWLEDGMENTS

A book doesn't write itself. *Long After We Are Gone* exists because of the phenomenal team of family, friends, writers, and acquaintances holding me up. That starts with my brilliant editor and angel, Erin McClary. Thank you for being amazing and kind and caring, and for seeing the beauty in the books I write and for shedding tears while you read. None of this is possible without you.

A huge thank you to the entire team at Sourcebooks. I love you all so much! To Paula Amendolara, Margaret Coffee, Julianne Moore…I mean Valerie Pierce, Emily Luedloff (my sister wife), Teresa DeVanzo (my bodyguard), BrocheAroe Fabian (my everything), Cristina Arreola, Caitlin Lawler, you all made my debut year a dream come true, and I'm honored to be in such amazing company. A special thank you to Jessica Thelander, Heather VenHuizen, Laura Boren, Stephanie Rocha, and everyone else who I have not yet had the pleasure of meeting in person. I'm so grateful for the work you do. And finally, to the trailblazer that is Dominique Raccah, you have my profound respect and admiration. Thank you for leading the way and for making dreams possible.

To all of the Sourcebooks writers who I have the pleasure of knowing: Joshua Moehling, Meagan Church, Sierra Godfrey, Penny Haw, Adele Griffin, Nancy Horan, Ashley Winstead, Ali Kamanda, Shauna Robinson, Derek Baxter, Quinn Connor, and Brooke Beyfuss, thank you for all of your support and for being so freakin' talented! I will always be your loudest cheerleader.

To the best agent in the business, Abby Saul. How you handle it all amazes me. Thank you for everything you do that I see and everything I don't. There's no one else who I'd want to navigate this world with. To Team Lark, there's never a dull day with you guys, and I couldn't ask for better agent siblings. To my brilliant editor, Kristin Thiel, you bring my words to life. I refuse to write a book without you! To Roy and Kathie Bennett of Magic Time Literary Agency, thank you so much for taking a chance on me! Kathie, I will never forget our meeting in my office. You have been such a blessing to me!

Thank you to all of the phenomenal writers I have the pleasure to call my friends: Regina Black, Nikki Payne, Noue Kiwan, and Tee Moore. You guys came right on time. Your support powers me. To my twin and one of my favorite writers, Jason Powell, your guidance has been such a blessing. I'm honored to call you a friend. To Jennifer Bohumueller, thank you for always being there and for your early read. A huge hug to Jocelyn Bates, thank you for always being there.

A special thank you to Catherine Adel West, Julie Carrick Dalton, Kelly Mustian, and Lọlá Ákínmádé Åkerström for your amazing blurbs for *One Summer in Savannah*. And to Kim Michele Richardson and Mateo Askaripour, thank you for not only your blurbs but for your continued guidance and support. And to Rochelle Weinstein, you were the first reader and lover of *One Summer in Savannah*, and I will never forget it. You are truly the best.

Much love to the Bookstagram community who first showed me love. A heartfelt thank you to Catherine Hyzy (thebooked-bakernc), Gabi Gutierrez (whatsgabireading), Kelly Hooker (kellyhook.readsbooks), Maren Channer (marensreads), Linda Lenston (Frecklefacelovesbooks). and Em Rumble (literapy_nyc). Thank you to Gia Mayo for your amazing graphics!

To my early reader and friend, Everlie Bolton, thank you for everything you do. Jennifer Harmonson, you are my loudest cheerleader and I love you so much for that. To my best friends, Kaslina Love Mosley and Sheneka Ezell, thank you for always being a phone call away. A sincere thank you to my Egyptian friends who supported and continue to support me.

I'm blessed to have two amazing families who love and support me. Thank you to the Harris/Griffin family. I truly hit the jackpot with you. To my mother-in-law, Mamie Griffin, thank you for the writing breaks you give me. To Jordan Harris, I'm proud to call you my son. To my brothers, Ben and Adam, thank you for your love. To my niece, Alexis Shelton, thank you for being an early reader and the sister I never had. To the best mother in the world, Leir Williams, there's no me without you. Thank you for your prayers, wisdom, and strength.

To my husband, Jamel Harris, thank you for being you and for loving me unconditionally.

Last but never least, to the one who keeps me from falling down, thank you, God, for everything.

ABOUT THE AUTHOR

Terah Shelton Harris is an author, collection development librarian, and a former freelance writer who now writes upmarket fiction with bittersweet endings. Her work has appeared in *Catapult*, *Women's Health*, *Every Day with Rachael Ray*, *Backpacker*, and more. Originally from Illinois, she now lives in Alabama with her husband, Jamel. Terah is a lover of life and spends most of her time reading or traveling. Her first novel, *One Summer in Savannah*, was a Target Book Club Pick and a LibraryReads Pick.

ONE SUMMER IN SAVANNAH

Can you ever truly forgive if you can't forget?

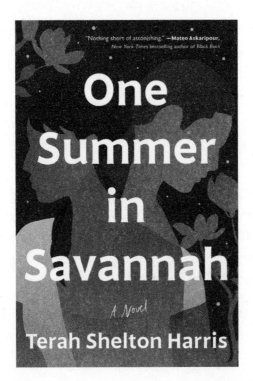

It's been eight years since Sara Lancaster left her home in Savannah, Georgia. Eight years since her daughter, Alana, came into this world, following a terrifying sexual assault that left deep emotional wounds Sara would do anything to forget. But when Sara's father falls ill, she's forced to return home and face the ghosts of her past.

While caring for her father and running his bookstore, Sara is desperate to protect her curious, outgoing, genius daughter from the Wylers, the family of the man who assaulted her. Sara thinks she can succeed—her attacker, who is in prison, his identical twin brother, Jacob, who left town years ago, and their mother are all unaware Alana exists. But she soon learns that Jacob has also just returned to Savannah to piece together the fragments of his once-great family. And when their two worlds collide—with the type of force Sara explores in her poetry and Jacob in his astrophysics—they are drawn together in unexpected ways.

"Terah Shelton Harris's daring debut is nothing short of astonishing. To write a novel that has the capacity to uplift you while it tears your heart to shreds is a balancing act few can achieve, but Harris does with ease and endless empathy."

—Mateo Askaripour, *New York Times* bestselling author of *Black Buck*